P9-DCW-966

ALSO BY STEWART O'NAN

The Speed Queen

The Names of the Dead

Snow Angels

On Writers and Writing, by John Gardner (editor)

In the Walled City

A WORLD AWAY

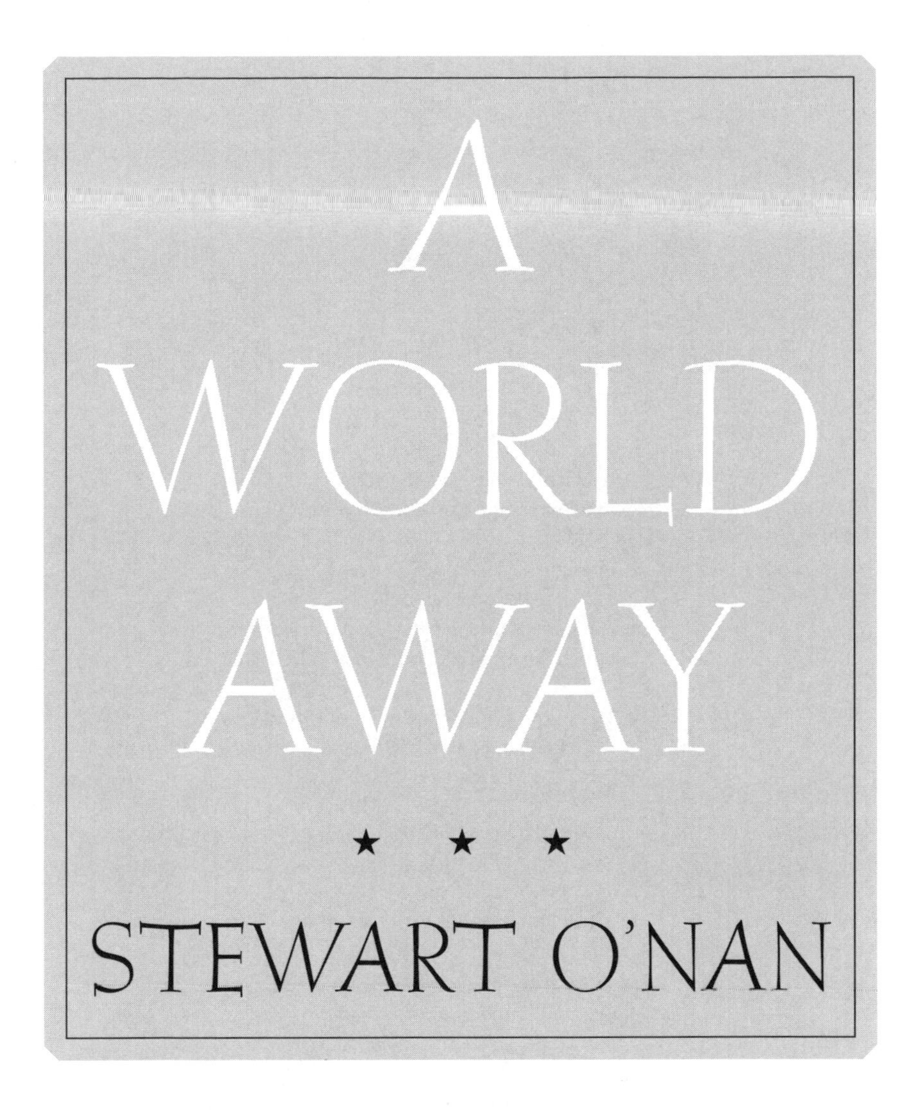

HENRY HOLT AND COMPANY

NEW YORK

Henry Holt and Company, Inc.
Publishers since 1866
115 West 18th Street
New York, New York 10011

Henry Holt® is a registered
trademark of Henry Holt and Company, Inc.

Published in Canada by Fitzhenry & Whiteside Ltd.,
195 Allstate Parkway, Markham, Ontario L3R 4T8.

Library of Congress Cataloging-in-Publication Data
O'Nan, Stewart, 1961–
A world away / Stewart O'Nan.—1st ed.
p. cm.
ISBN 0-8050-5774-9 (alk. paper)
I. Title.
PS3565.N316W67 1998
813'.54—dc21 97-36727

Henry Holt books are available for special
promotions and premiums. For details contact:
Director, Special Markets.

First Edition 1998

Designed by Jessica Shatan

Printed in the United States of America
All first editions are printed on acid-free paper. ∞

1 3 5 7 9 10 8 6 4 2

for Trudy

Oh, I don't know what's right any longer.

Ilsa, *Casablanca*

The only thing we have to fear is fear itself.

FDR

A WORLD AWAY

THEY DROVE THE NIGHT, through the blacked-out city and out along the Island. Fog stole in from the sea, lay heavy over inlets, white wooden bridges. The roads ran empty for miles, starlit, desolate. James had screwed louvers over the Buick's headlights, it was the law. He thought they'd be stopped, Anne roused, Jay shielding his eyes from some air raid warden's flashlight. For hours, whenever they slowed, the boy asked, "Are we there?" and now James couldn't get it out of his head.

They went on, there was no one. The woods, the marshes, the lines slipping under the car. He'd been born here, his father was dying. Coming back to the sea made him doubt the years in between, his life a great work one plans yet never begins. Rennie was still alive, a world away, the name of his ship snipped out of his letters. James thought the South Pacific; Anne said it didn't matter. They hadn't made love in weeks. Their bags whistled atop the car. Are we there? When are we going to be there?

It was the summer of trains. The war needed everything, all the time, like an infant. His son, his students. The filling stations along the shore were closed. He had gas because Anne's father had died, his Plymouth sitting beside the shuttered house, sucked dry, the seats gone brittle in the sun. James's father was beyond driving. His face slid over bone; when he talked he looked off to the sky, as if the enemy were gliding in behind you. At Amagansett four spies had run the night tide in a raft. In May James's sister had called and asked him to come.

"School doesn't end till June," he said.

"Then come in June," Sarah said. She'd been there since the last stroke, tending the peeling beachhouse, the rotting cottages. Their father had been recovering, she said, until this. They'd been on the porch, doing the *Times* crossword. James smelled the wet wicker chairs, their guests' gin breath. She'd just read him a clue. She looked over to find him asleep, nothing unusual.

"When he woke up," she said, "you know what he said? 'Sten. S-T-E-N.' Then he couldn't stand up. The doctor said it's common."

Their father had never liked her, it was a mystery. She lived twenty miles west in Sayville, in another age. The three rarely spoke, their father shocked at the cost of the phone.

"We better hang up," James had said across the night, and went back to his chair, the light on the book he'd put down blinding.

"Another?" Anne said. She'd stopped racing James for the phone after the Kramers got their telegram. The new star bloomed gold in their window, a shrine, an omen. Rennie would have a messenger, like a prince; James and Anne would stand on the stoop and read it together, falling and falling. No, James thought, he wouldn't be home. They'd have to get him in class, a face in the door. He'd stop King Philip's War, the Panic of 1837, the Golden Spike. How far summer was, how soon.

"Sarah wants us to come down."

"What did you tell her?"

He saw no decision, though loading the car this morning he'd burned his hand pulling tight some twine and swore (as Anne had wanted to after his answer but didn't—good Anne, Saint Anne), hopping and holding his raw palm, cursing his luck, his incompetence, his mildness. They'd just come to Galesburg for her father. It was the third time in two years they'd moved.

Their catastrophes had all been expected. Her father died. Rennie resisted—against James's advice, with his hesitant blessing—and was shipped to a work camp, first in New York and then California. After four months, his roommate at Cornell was killed on his way to North Africa, and, shaken, he enlisted as a medic and was assigned to the Pacific, Dorothy following as far as San Diego. Now James's father's stroke, or his latest, for he'd withstood a string of them, none devastating. Since her father died—in front of her, calmly, barely there—Anne had been distant, resigned. She didn't have the energy to fight anymore. Together they were silent, alone spoke to themselves. Jay wandered beyond their orbit, confused, too old to be a boy but unwilling to give it up. It was a time James didn't want to remember from his own life, just as he couldn't imagine himself a few years older, having survived all this, somehow happy. It was like what had happened in Putney, though he couldn't deny that had been his fault. A student. Foolish. He'd been paying for his one slip so long, yet it hadn't lost the power to shame him. He could easily follow the whole chain of events back to that season of intimacy with Diane. His star player, sixteen and already as tall as he was. He'd been insane; it was the only explanation.

"Is it bad?" he'd asked Sarah that night on the phone.

"Yes."

"Can you put Dad on?"

"Not really."

"No?"

"Oh, Jimmy."

They wormed along Montauk Highway, through the strips of beach towns, awnings cranked up for the night, angled parking slots empty. Baskets of geraniums hung from lampposts, sand drifted over the road. People were leaving the late show, the marquee dark. The fog made everything gray and soggy. It was his childhood; he refused to look too closely. They were almost there. Center Moriches, Eastport, Quogue with a view of the bay, a dogleg of banned lights across the water. On shore his old house faced them now, invisible, miles away. He never remembered winter; there were no famous snows. It was cold into mid-July, scorching at noon then chilly under the covers. June had seemed far off once. This would be the last time he'd see the house.

As a child, the sea smashing at night woke him, and he cried. His mother stopped in his doorway in her robe, her candle shaking the walls. When she died, they boxed her clothes and shipped them to her sister in Wisconsin, land of black lakes. Her bureau still stood in his father's room, empty save sheets of newspaper full of wishful prices, going bad at the edges.

The last time he'd been back, three years ago, after his father's first stroke, James had wanted to tell him that he understood, but she never came up (never did, never would), and James didn't want to hurt the old man, suddenly vulnerable, his saint's rage softened to crotchetiness. It was true of himself, James thought, for while he'd been wronged, he couldn't stop loving his mother, his father, the life they'd had there. The boys went to bed, then Anne. The stroke was fresh and they had to sit with his father. In his sleep he whispered bits of scripture. Beside the bed, Sarah held her book at arm's length, squinting in the dim light.

"Sleep," she said.

"I can't."

He went downstairs to the pantry—where as children they'd hidden among the bins and barrels—and sipped his father's scotch in the moonlight by the open window, a connoisseur of night. Hours later when Sarah found him he hadn't finished the glass. He remembered to hide it from her.

"I can still smell," she said. "Don't worry. If I was, there wouldn't have been any left."

"I'm glad."

"And how are you and Anne getting along?"

"Splendid," he said, and thinking back now couldn't remember if he'd actually meant it. There were days, seasons of Anne he kept like treasure, secretly peeked at to make sure they'd been real. Her hands now, clasped even in sleep. Her father's long jaw.

They slipped over the town line into Hampton Bays. It had been his home; he knew it as he knew the boy he'd been, recollected hopefully, forgiven, thanked. Anne slept against the door, turned to him as if to argue. Jay lay across her lap, half under his jacket. In Galesburg, Anne thought they shouldn't tell him about Rennie, when everyone at school knew. James opened his classroom one morning—the door was locked, the key in his hand—and saw on the board a parody of hangman, the word TRAITOR a foot high. There'd been boys from Galesburg on Bataan, men missing at sea. Saturdays Jay came home from the movies and had fiery nightmares. He'd never had his own room before, and woke alone, sobbing in the dark.

Each waited for the other to go comfort him, as if he were a baby, their sleep hard-won. It was her house; he was always smashing his toes. "You're okay," he said, and clicked on the light to find Jay sniffling, ashamed. Spring had been long, breakfast full of silences, the nights partitioned. He was unprepared for class and rambled at the board, punned, the boys in the back grim, impatient. It was a town of stone bridges, mills falling into a cold river. And still he thought of Diane, her long arms, her strong back, though all of that seemed—like their house in Putney—long gone. Galesburg knew only their latest shame. On the sidewalks, women steered around him, spat at his heels. Anne had grown up there; she'd been ready to leave at thirteen. Then in May, on the brink of leaving, she said she didn't mean that, that everyone said that.

"So now you like it here," he asked.

"I have a choice?"

"I don't know," he said, reckless, "do you?"

"We come back. Fall, no matter what."

It was enough, it was all he wanted.

"You tell him," Anne said. "I refuse to."

Jay hadn't left friends, hadn't made new ones. Winter he'd spent in the town library or in his room, Anne's old one, the flocked wallpaper sullied above the baseboards. He read on the floor between his bed and the window, invisible from the hall, the curtains jerking as he kicked his feet. In the fields, crows picked over last year's stubble. Rain in black trees. Anne was always turning a light on for him. The house darkened, the windows glowed. For every book he read, James gave him a nickel. He was going through the Tarzan series—*Tarzan and the Golden Lion*, *Tarzan and the Ant Men*—the library had a whole shelf. With the money he bought comic books, the worst kind of trash. James had a drawerful at school, all muscles, guns and breasts. He was too old to be a father now, had been too old with Rennie. He'd made a pact with himself this year not to talk to Jay in school. Anne said it was hard enough for him as it was.

"I remember the beach," Jay said. It was night, the boy had to have a light on. "There's a lighthouse at the end of the rocks."

"Your grandfather's very sick."

"Will Mom have to take care of him?"

"We're all going to help a little. That's what he needs right now, little things." His sons had never known his mother. She'd gone the summer James turned ten. Her death was lost in his father's grief, the last war, Anne, the wash of odd jobs, rented bungalows and impossible cars. Then Putney, then Diane. It seemed now that he hadn't worried about Rennie at Jay's age, but was that really true?

It was the war, on the radio like a show, London crackling with static. Anne didn't like Jay to hear. James tried to reason with her but she was always right, always questioning his motives when he had none. Nightly he leaned closer to the Pacific, the ozone of warm tubes, listening for the thrum of his son's ship. The Japanese had just given up one of the Aleutians.

"What is it now?" Anne asked.

"More Alaska."

"There's nothing there, don't they know that? Is any of this supposed to make sense to me?"

She read and drank tea, sometimes knitted under the lamp in the corner. She'd only taken it up, and he didn't see what it was supposed to be. At each missed stitch, she swore and threw her head back as if to howl. She hadn't expected Rennie would go, and hadn't forgiven him. Wednesdays after supper James gathered everyone and put down what they wanted to say to him. Jay liked to snip out the comics, the batting averages, the local crimes. He had his own section, like a columnist, half slang. James didn't know what to write, but went on, gossiping. Anne added nothing; at school he typed a section and signed her name to it.

As if to spite him, she wrote Dorothy every week, composing in snatches as she cooked. Anne had never liked her, though, to James, Dorothy seemed the same Galesburg girl his wife had shed over the years. Her family had liked Rennie until he was arrested. Since the marriage, they no longer spoke with the Langers, their younger boy shrinking from James in the hallways. In the lunchroom, James ate, aware of Jay several tables over, like himself, alone. Later, driving home, he passed Jay, and though he had a mile to walk and the other children were nowhere near him, the boy looked down at his boots, or away, across the snowy fields, and James drove on. He'd promised.

Home. His father's study looked out on the ocean. It was half their attic, the sill of the gable window flush with his father's desktop. For years, by candlelight, after the guests had gone to bed and again before they woke, his father fretted over the books and wrote to his mother care of whatever hospital she was in. In the dark, James heard him haul the ladder down and yank it up after him. His father didn't pace, but sat and wrote, then at a quarter to six lowered the ladder, crept downstairs and started the water for baths. Sarah wasn't allowed up there. On the desk a telescope tilted in a turned brass stand. "What do you see?" his father asked James. "Tell me what you see."

The waves. Green, blue, glittering, heavy. His father's hand rested gently on the back of James's neck, steering him. The moon drew up huge, beneath it, sharply drawn, the silhouetted stacks of a great oceangoing liner.

"Do you see it?"

"Yes," James said. His father had taught him wonder and its complement, responsibility; now his father slurred his words, had to ask Sarah to come by and light the pilot.

"I'm not a doctor," Sarah had said that night on the phone.

"I don't want this to hurt Jay. He's been through enough."

"It's never convenient, is it?"

The lower end of Hampton Bays was empty, the bars open but no cars outside, beer signs hooded. In his absence a crop of fried clam and ice-cream stands had sprung up and died. The road curved with the thrust of bay, the berm sandy, telephone poles a-lean. A cinder-block garage stood in one corner of the McCauffeys' field, its whitewash an explosion in the dark. He turned onto the path he'd walked home over, winging buckeyes at the old man's cows. The Buick rocked in the ruts. Scrub pine scoured the fenders, waking Anne.

"See any cows out?" James said.

"What?"

He'd forgotten; the field was overgrown, the McCauffeys gone.

They cleared a rise and the stars dropped, the sea a void. The house stood black against the moon, one downstairs curtain edged with light. Sarah's Hudson jumped in his headlights, the wicker rockers lining the porch.

"Don't tell me we're here," Anne said.

When he stopped the car a wave of dust rolled over them. He turned everything off. Anne waited for him to get out, Jay slumped against her, still asleep.

"It's past somebody's bedtime."

"Just go," she said.

His legs wouldn't straighten all the way. The night was much colder than he'd thought, the sea louder. The moon was new; with the house blacked out, he couldn't see the walk. The front door opened and Sarah appeared; it closed and she disappeared, her flashlight picking out the porch stairs, her feet, the wet grass as she made her way across the lawn.

"James," she said, and kissed him, the flashlight hard on his back. She was always thinner, dwindling. "Dad's asleep. He's been good."

"How about you?"

"Not a drop."

"Honest," he asked, as if it were a joke. He relied on her too much. There was no more younger or older, yet they kept it up.

Everyone kissed in the cold, groggy from the car. Anne had her purse, Jay his cigar box and Rennie's old suitcase. Sarah guided them inside while James unloaded, fighting the twine. Above, a flag flapped, a halyard rang against the invisible pole. One knot was giving him trouble, and he stopped, his arms propped against the car, and looked up at the house. It seemed smaller each time, yet that was little comfort. He liked to sneak up on his mother in the kitchen. She stood at the stove, and when he was halfway across the tiles—beyond the cover of the chopping block, the help's table—without turning from her work, she said, "I see you, James," and he backed out as if he hadn't been caught. The guests were on the lawn playing croquet with their children, dressed for supper.

Behind him, the sea broke and rolled, broke and rolled. Upstairs a light came on, eclipsed by a shade. He found Rennie's old Boy Scout knife in the glove compartment, tore through the knot and took the two heaviest bags down, swearing at Anne for jamming them full, just as she had scourged him for having to pack them all by herself.

The wallpaper stopped him a foot in the door. The blemished mirror, the banister ending in a polished curl. He was always coming back, always stunned at his guilt, the tenderness his mother's lamps filled him with. The light made him realize he was still moving from the car. They were upstairs, he could hear water. He put the bags down, and before the house could claim him, went back out, glad for the dark.

When he came in with the next set, Anne and Sarah were waiting. Sarah's hair was between blond and gray, ashes mixed with dough. Her face looked worse in the light, her lipstick too young.

"Jay's down," Anne said. "I'm going up if you don't mind."

"No, go ahead. I should see Dad."

"He can wait," Sarah said.

"Do what you want," Anne said, "I'm going to sleep. Which bed do you want?"

"I don't care. Whichever."

Sarah helped him bring the rest of the bags in. "Should I ask?" she said in the kitchen.

"Oh, you know how we are."

"It must be awful."

"No," James said, as if he were going to explain, but, tired, let it go. He noticed he still had his coat on and draped it over a chair. "Don't worry," he said. "How are you?"

"Rich. I'm working over at Grumman's where Terry used to, making airplanes. I've got muscles. I'll get you in. They're hiring all the time."

"Sure."

"I've got my bus at six. Did you want to see Dad?"

She led, as if he'd forgotten the way. The back staircase turned, a tunnel of matchboard lit by a single frosted fixture. She'd lost weight while he'd thickened, and he wondered if she had a man again. Terry had been her one love. James had liked him, though ten years ago he could see he wouldn't survive the drinking. He wanted to ask Sarah how she'd come through all that to be here now. He never thought of losing Anne, only leaving her. He never saw beyond his wishes to the truth of his sister's apartment, the weekends of rain, the bait store below open at four in the morning. In his daydreams, he'd designed the bright, airy house he and Diane would live in, the friendly town around them, the constant, perfect weather. Now, without her, he felt dull and incomplete, unable to explain to himself what had happened, let alone to those he was supposed to love. It was as if his heart kept its secrets even from him, and he was terrified he would become resigned to life as a baffled and sad old man. She was a beautiful girl and he had loved her. Was it really that simple? Then when would the merest thought of it not sting him?

Upstairs he was suddenly hot. The doors in the hallway were closed, the window at the end sealed with a blackout curtain. Distant, the sea rained down.

"You have to be quiet," Sarah said, and, like a safecracker, palmed the doorknob, but once in he saw their father was awake, staring off into the dark. His distance was habitual, the strokes only widened his silence. The room smelled like a closet, a hint of moth crystals and belt leather. Their father was propped up with his nightcap half fallen off, his cheek sloping to jowl, gray in the light of the hall. His hands were crossed atop the covers. On the night table stood a glass of water, a splayed Bible, its silk string kinked and hanging off the back, holding no place. James knelt and touched his arm.

"Jimmy came." His voice was thick, as if he'd been chewing a huge mouthful. "I guess I have to die now."

"Dad," Sarah scolded.

"What did you tell him?"

"Nothing," James said. "She said you needed someone to look after you."

"I pee the bed, Jimmy. Imagine that. They never tell you."

"Isn't he great?" Sarah said. "Are you ready for a whole summer of this?"

"Your sister's run out of patience. It's not her fault."

"You're very welcome. You hear this? This is what it's like."

"Your brother's here now. You've done your duty."

"Why do you have to be like this?" she said, suddenly vicious, near tears. "Why can't you just thank me?"

"I'm tired," he said, and closed his eyes. "Go. Both of you."

James took his hand back and stood. Everything seemed smaller this time, oddly wrong, as in a dream. He might brush the door-frame and knock out the wall.

"He's a little better in the morning," Sarah said on the porch, "but not much."

"Why do you let him get to you?"

"I know I shouldn't. God, the bastard. And you just sit there and let it happen. I guess I shouldn't expect anything different."

"Why is it me?" James said.

"Why isn't it you, you mean. It's always me because I'm the girl. It's always been me, and it's always going to be me. I guess I ought to be used to it by now."

"No," he said, but had nothing to follow it with.

She knotted her scarf under her chin and kissed him and got in the Hudson. Her headlights leapt off the cottages, flew over the dunes. He watched her away, then stood in the black, listening to the sea. Across the water came the sweet clank of a buoy; far out, lost in the dark, a troop ship mooed. I see you, James, I see you. At his back, the house creaked in its sleep.

"We're here," he said.

BLUE, OCEAN DAYS. Anne had become accustomed to her father's hours, the restless schedule of the ill. She was up at five, dressing in the white dawn before James's father got out of bed. She bowed her head in the back stairwell, kept a hand on the wall going down.

The steel tables in the kitchen gave back the sky filling with light. The sun came here first; in Galesburg it was still dark, their house a target.

The stove lit with a hushed *whump*. She closed the doors to the pantry, the stairs, the back hall, and waited for the room to warm. The house seemed smaller before dawn, the gray hiding its size. The sun broke over the sea, reached in the high windows, long splinters of light. She squinted at its brilliance, bathed in its favor. She felt entitled to these moments alone, their quenching endlessness. Some days she never had to wake, kept her life inside, quiet as a patient. Flour, powdermilk, oleo.

At the hospital in Putney they made her serve breakfast before going home, and once on the empty bus—finding a blob of egg gone cold on her arm—she'd gotten sick, coughing into the dust under the seat. She was young then, and loved everyone she tended, torn by each bedsore, every child bled white. The confessions of the dying seemed precious, a validation of her father's faith. She didn't have the patience now, the infinite wisdom they needed. She hadn't followed her father's God, remembered flicking the purple hymnal ribbons and playing connect-the-dots while he preached, yet she'd never questioned his certainty. Mondays he drove all over the county, ministering to the sick. "Oh, you missed it," he told them, sitting on the edge of the bed, and when they were well again, they made the trip to town to see him Sunday so they could groan at the new joke and, in the notes before the sermon, wait for him to say their names. After, being received, they held on to his hands. How tiring it must have been for him to bear their desires. The years, the dead. And what of his own? That last morning, she'd gone to her knees beside his bed and meant it, while he lay moaning, telling her why, on his own terms, he was unworthy. His confession was relentless, rending, his self-accusations hateful. "You must never blame your mother." Each morning now she thought she wouldn't recover from it, when she knew it was a matter of days, work, the right light. She didn't want to give up this wistfulness. It was useless, stupid.

The griddle was big enough to do everything at once. James liked his bacon doled out a strip a day, while Jay feasted, willing to wait the week. She ate little, his father nothing, and they had enough. Tuesdays she biked to town to trade her red points for cheap meat. Mothers left their daughters to stand in line. She was the only adult; they called her Mrs. Langer, though she'd never offered her name. They waited for the grocer to open, sullen and dull, fishermen's children, then, when he showed his face at the door, clamored. They all bought horsemeat, lean and gamy, their fathers sick of fish. The eggs were from the great duck farms to the west, reasonable, even cheap. The bacon was strictly illegal. She felt, in the crush, surrounded by bounty, that she didn't need much.

"Thank you," she said, "goodbye," and the girls in line turned to watch her. Pedaling away, Anne laughed at her mystery. She imagined living here alone, a romantic, through the gray, gray days.

But she was, wasn't she? A mystery, a romantic, alone. James was gone all day, Jay off on the marsh crabbing, terrified of his grandfather. On the porch Mr. Langer drifted in and out like fog. Only the gulls kept her company. They stood on the lawn in flocks, shedding feathers and fluff, their droppings caked like spilled paint. His father talked about fried gull, fishhead stew; hers never liked food, came to the table sated with the day, his parishioners, and barely ate. She could see him in Jay, had seen him in James. They had the same dream, to save everyone and owe the world nothing. Her men. Winter she had given too much.

His father came down first, dressed for hard weather, as if the chill might linger into midday. He had tomato juice in the same tumbler, the last of a matched set. She had to walk it out to the porch for him. He sat in a wicker rocker, a blanket over his knees, waiting for the paper. Every morning a thick boy delivered it by bike, shuddering down the sandy drive and across the gravel, then, at the edge of the lot, slamming into a skid and tomahawking it over the porch rail so the paper hopped across the floorboards and slid to rest inches from Mr. Langer's old brogans. To Anne it seemed a miracle—reckless, headlong—yet the old man said nothing, merely reached down, didn't even watch the boy, mortal again, push his bike back up the hill. By then he had the paper open.

She made James's lunch while he ate his breakfast. He'd put on so much weight since Putney that she couldn't watch him eat. Everything went back to that; he was so transparent. He had to bike to town to catch a bus to the plant. He wasn't supposed to say what he made, though they knew it was planes. The night before Rennie had been taken away, James gave him a speech on how he believed in him, in the country, in history, as if he were teaching. Now he came home with grease on his sleeves, bits of metal set in his shoes, and after supper fetched his binoculars and headed out to the lighthouse—extinguished for the duration—and sat until dusk under the dead lens, peering out to sea for waves of invaders. Wednesdays he wrote Rennie letters that opened, *Our dear son.*

It wasn't James who'd changed. She needed to believe; he still did. His optimism was a gamble she'd already lost. It was unfair, the little bitch had ruined not him but her. Anne was supposed to forgive him. The bitch, the bitch. Sixteen years old, her love bloody and pure, girlish. How could she compete? He came to her at night but, rebuffed, tried nothing. They didn't fight: she fought while he fought for compromise, moderation. He no longer asked what was wrong, but went on, tolerant, even gentle, as if she were sick again. She had to cry sometimes, and this he didn't understand, coming to hold her, stroke her. "Don't touch me!" she screamed, "leave me alone!" and he stood back as if she'd caught on fire. She despised him most then, watching her cry, and chased him from whatever room they were in. She didn't care if he was afraid of her or for her. She didn't care about the wasted days.

"Thank you," he said as she gave him his lunch pail, and set off through the gulls, wobbling. The birds stepped aside, then closed over his wake. His attempts at the hill maddened her, and once when he fell she let herself laugh, only to find Jay behind her.

She and Jay ate at the help's table, facing each other over the brushed steel. She couldn't explain her distance to him now, even if he did listen. Though she scolded James for it, she couldn't stop weighing Jay against Rennie. Often she caught herself growing tender when he told her what he planned to do that day.

"I'm going to fish off the bridge," he said, and she wanted to crush him against her. To be that happy, gulping in the thrill of summer.

They ate, then he was off to the salt marsh, biking east along the beach, and the day lay before her like the sea, flat as a table and shimmering, the horizon a line miles out, seemingly reachable. She washed the dishes, dried the dishes, put the dishes away. There were fifteen full sets—water glass, juice cup, salad bowl, soup bowl—yet she stayed with the same four at the top of the stacks. On the porch Mr. Langer grappled with the paper.

She was surprised she liked sitting with him. "Charlatans," he accused the people in the news. "That Churchill is a pisscutter." He could get in and out with little trouble, but sometimes came back from the bathroom downcast. "It's no picnic," he said. "Don't let anyone tell you different." Where James was apologetic, his father was gruff. It was mostly frustration, though sometimes he could be hard on Jay. The sun came all day; they had to move to new chairs just once, after lunch.

"There's the prince," Mr. Langer said, when she could barely pick out Jay coming up the beach. "Two o'clock," he said, pointing to the invisible plane. She peered out over the sea. Blue, blue. In town the noon horn sounded, a distant ship. "On the nose," he said, and tapped his crystal. This other husband, this strange vacation. She knitted for Dorothy and looked up to find him snoring, the sports page drifting across the porch.

"I'm not tired," he said, not arguing. Only one side of his mouth opened. It wasn't that noticeable.

"How do you feel?" she asked, leaning over him. He'd tried to shave that morning, and she could see where he quit.

"I'm tired," he said.

Going up, he clung to the banister but made it all the way. She stayed a step below him, ready to take his weight, and once he was in his room, felt foolish. He wasn't that bad, it was only her. A year ago she'd laughed with her father at the fit of his slacks, though she knew the withering meant the end.

She folded Mr. Langer's blanket, still warm from his lap, and paced the porch. Gull fluff blew and caught in the lawn; they soared offshore, rode the lazy waves. Like Jay, they'd be back at dinner. She didn't know what she'd make. She picked up her knitting, after a few stitches went inside and checked the icebox, but even looking at the food, nothing struck her.

Going in, coming out, the light was blinding. How she'd loved the sea; how she would now without James, his father, his mother's old ghost. It wasn't all her (was, was). Their honeymoon they'd made love in the dunes, guiltless, thrilled by the night sky. Sand worked up into her; she would save it to tell him later. How her body burned with him then. After, she could feel the heat bleed away. He pulled her sweater over her head, and the air shocked her. "What are you doing?" she said, but he had his off and was up, running, and she was after him without pause, across the packed sand and into the surf. The water seemed to freeze all but a warm core. Her skin, alive beneath his fingers, seemed heavy, asleep. He came out shrunken and she thought it funny, and after they found their clothes she took him again.

"James," she said.

"What is it?" he asked, concerned, gone still in her.

"Look up," she said, and for a time they did. When had she last wanted him like that?

She went upstairs and checked on Mr. Langer, went through her suitcase and found her blue suit. She was white from a life upstate, winter lingering into May. She could be pretty, she could still dare the mirror.

She cruised the dunes for a hollow and, not bothering to lay a blanket, spread her body on the hot sand and closed her eyes. The waves, the wind lisping in the saw grass. Gulls, gulls, go away. The day was shadowless, heat seething in her skin. Her father kept the coal stove going through June. She fed him soup. The broth spilled down his jaw onto the pillow. "I don't expect you'll forgive me," he said. It seemed he was pleading. "It's all right," she said, and he hung on her arm, grateful, as if she'd saved him.

The blue drew the heat to it; a slick of sweat grew under her breasts. Should have made lemonade. Jay could tell time by the sun.

Like a hunter, her father said, it's a gift. She sat up. The house burned white, blinds drawn. Not a boat out, not a cloud. This was what she needed to shed her depression—herself, without help.

She lay back and slipped the straps from her shoulders, pulled the suit to her waist and, arching, slid it over her hips. She'd had it as a girl. Silly that it still fit her. Last summer James had made some comment on it. Time for a new one? Now it was loose on her, her middle ribbed from lifting her father in and out of bed, helping him from the tub. She stretched and the sand flared with a new heat. Was it the sun that gave her this sense of strength? Suddenly she felt an overwhelming hope for her father—that his faith, if not restored, was in those last moments not destroyed. That he had the courage to confess, to face her with his insane self-scourging, meant he thought her strong enough. Or was it, as she feared, that she was the only one left? Now, alone as the only child she'd been, she felt him in her, strangely contained, that last part of her, as if she would—under the sun, in her perfect skin—become unlimited. If faith would protect Rennie, who was she to say no? Here, she could almost believe.

"Your mother never knew any of it."

Faintly, a plane was buzzing. She opened her eyes, but, blinded, didn't see it until it was nearly overhead. It was loud and low, close enough to read the stars on its wings. Brazen, she waved, but once its engine died, felt ashamed and gathered her towel around her. *Our dear son.* She didn't hate James, only the little bitch. Above, gulls keened, wheeling.

The front hall was dark, the upstairs twenty degrees hotter. His father was still sleeping, on top of the covers in his shorts, his socks on. Flies fussed against a window. A shade brushed a screen with a zithering sound; she pulled it down farther, then stopped and stood looking at him, oddly long in the mirror of the bureau, the wall beside her alive with explosions of white roses. The blue suit. James's mother had been dead for forty years. She'd never heard Mr. Langer mention her, James only when coaxed. In the same way, her own mother cultivated an invisibility Anne noticed growing in herself. Why? She was no ghost.

Jay came in around dinner with a pail of blues—tough, ugly fish Mr. Langer refused to eat.

"Trash fish," he said in the kitchen, lifting one by the gills. There was no reason. Lunch he had a cheese sandwich, dinner a hamburger cut up so he wouldn't choke.

"Thank you," she told Jay. "I'll make us croquettes for lunch."

He was a child, she could still please him. He muscled the bucket into the sink, then dashed up the back stairs to get ready.

"Where's that hamburger of mine?" Mr. Langer asked, half joking.

"Keep your shirt on," she said, and with her spatula smashed the patty flat.

She waited the spaghetti for James, but after an hour on the porch watching the sun fade, served Jay. Mr. Langer had her turn on the radio. She took Jay outside and tried to play catch with him, using James's old glove. She'd never been any good. Jay played as if he were giving her lessons. One toss skipped off the tip of her mitt and caught her in the breast. "Oh," she said, and held herself, crossing her arms. She kicked the mitt, and Jay said they didn't have to play anymore. The dew was out now, the gulls in for the evening. When James finally appeared at the top of the hill, she didn't feel like eating.

"Seven to seven," he said, chewing. "Seven days a week. Everything over forty hours is time and a half, Sunday's double time."

"You're hardly here as it is."

"It's not like I have a say in the matter."

"I know that," she said, rinsing the dishes. "I'm just lonely, I guess."

"I know."

Outside, Jay was playing commando, scaling the porch railing, leveling a bat like a rifle. In the living room, Nimitz steamed west across the Pacific. James got up and brought his plate to the sink and hugged her from behind while she scrubbed the red sauce off. She broke his hold to get the dish towel.

"I'll dry," he said, hopeful.

"Did you see Jay's fish?"

"Nice." He took the towel from her. "So aren't you going to congratulate me? It's like getting a gigantic raise."

"It's wonderful," she said.

"Don't overwhelm me."

"What do you want me to say?"

"Nothing," he said.

"Did you tell Jay?"

"I've only been home a few minutes."

"It doesn't matter to me," she said. "I'm already doing everything around here. He's the one who's going to miss you."

He stacked a plate, fished another from the sink. "I don't know why you're so unhappy."

"You don't?"

Jay popped up in the window and shot James. He fell, clutching the towel to his chest.

"You're not going to make me feel bad about this," she said, and left him lying there.

He came to her later, in the dark. She heard his bed creak, his feet on the floor. Her covers lifted, exposing her to the cold, and he pressed against her, hard in the hollow of her bottom.

"I can't sleep over there," he said.

She slid out, walked around the foot and got in the other bed.

The next morning she rode to town for a few pounds of sugar. In line behind her stood three or four girls with bandages around their scalps, amateurishly wrapped. Spurts of mercurochrome hinted at extravagant wounds.

"Excuse me," she asked one, "did you do these?"

"Oh, no," a different one answered—red-haired, devilish. "Mrs. Ridley did them."

"Is Mrs. Ridley a nurse?"

They all laughed.

"Mr. Ridley owns Ridley's." A few pointed across the street to a five and dime with RIDLEY in gilt script above the door. "We're having a drill."

"Really," Anne said. "And what are you supposed to do?"

"We get to lie down in the middle of the street."

"And make noises," the shy one said. They made dying noises, ghostly moans.

"Do you know what to do if something real happens?" Anne asked.

"Get Mrs. Ridley?"

"When is this drill?"

"When the horn goes off. Then we have to lie down."

"What happens then?"

"Then the soldiers come on the bus and fix us. Don't you know anything?"

"Where we live we don't have drills."

"Oh," the red-haired girl said, "you have to have drills. Else the Knotsies will get you."

The grocer let one more in and they all moved up a step. As Anne turned to ask where the soldiers came from, the fire horn blew, and everyone around her crumpled to the ground. It was exactly eleven. Mr. Langer needed lunch. She stood for a second holding her purse, the sole survivor, then sat down on the hot sidewalk.

The medics took forever. They had little equipment and spent too much time talking. The one who worked on her was younger than Rennie, a blond boy with big teeth. He was sweating and half distracted by the children's groans, as if afraid they were actually hurt. His name was sewn over his pocket, TEDDER. He started by taking her pulse.

"How do you feel, ma'am?" he asked with a southern lilt.

"I'm in shock," Anne said. "I lost a lot of blood waiting."

He took her blood pressure and wrapped her in an imaginary blanket. "How about a broken leg?"

"Compound, just under the knee."

He seemed defeated. "I can't do them yet."

"It's easy," she said. "You don't. If it's bad, get a compress on it, stabilize the patient and get them to a hospital. Otherwise keep it clean, splint the limb, then move them."

He pressed the heels of his hands against her shin, checked her pulse and pressure again. "You're a nurse."

"Used to be."

"You'll live," he predicted, and, before scooting to his next victim, added, "Thank you."

"Thank *you*," she said.

The all clear blew at noon. It was after one when she put the bag of sugar in her basket and rode for home. Having to hurry ruined the view. Still, she loved the sea peeking through the dunes. She stood on the pedals to take it in, then, late, tried to make up time by racing the last half mile. Coming down the hill, she built up too much momentum and shot across the gravel lot, her back wheel sliding as if on ice. She was ready to jump, one eye on the strip of lawn beside the porch, and then the front wheel dug a rut and she was in control again, her face stinging with the thrill of it.

Mr. Langer had already made lunch. Jay sat at the table, glumly eating his cheese sandwich.

"You two don't need me," she said. "You can take care of yourselves."

"You said you were going to make croquettes."

"Don't whine," Mr. Langer said.

"I'm sorry, Jay. I'll make them for dinner, how's that?"

He looked at her, chewing. In the last year he'd perfected a blank stare balanced between anger and resignation. Whenever she raged or, more often, placated him, he resorted to this passive mask, his silence a judgment, eyes locked somewhere beyond her, as if daring her to strike him. He was so much his father's son.

"Answer your mother," Mr. Langer said.

"Yes," Jay said. "Please."

"Of course," she said, trying (like James!) to smooth things over between the two of them.

With his last bite tucked in his cheek, Jay asked to be excused, and she let him go. Mr. Langer left his crusts. She got him settled on the porch, cleaned up, then went out and lay in the dunes.

Light, heat, the shadows of the grass. Sweat bled and pooled on her stomach, neck and brow. The white line of her suit grew sharper, her hips thinner, as if she were melting. These blue afternoons pleased her, yet even in their deepest reaches, her body burning with the season's fever, an icy trickle of misgiving slid within her like the streams of her childhood, locked long into spring, black, their beds heavy with last year's leaves. Her father would be dead for the rest of her life, the grass high on his grave. She couldn't call up his voice; he spoke to her only words she'd already heard. "People in town knew—some, I'm sure."

She banished him by opening her eyes. The sameness of her days here. Breakfast, lunch, dinner. Shadows angling across the porch. When she thought of Rennie, she saw him face up in the surf, his chest plucked open, each wave floating him up the sand then drawing him back, splashing. It was a picture in *Life*, each week a different beach.

Here there was nothing. The rocks covered with gulls, the squat white lighthouse Jay pretended was a plane. He was up there now, aiming the heavy lens at invisible enemies. She waved on her way in, and he turned to her, all the time firing.

She'd been out less than an hour. The fish had gone bad; later when she told Jay, he went silent.

"Don't you do that to me," she said, pointing, and he stalked out of the house.

At dinner, she tried to be nice. He was polite. Mr. Langer's hamburger was undercooked.

"Then give me it and I'll cook it the way you like it."

"I like it done," he said.

She turned the flame up all the way and grease pricked her wrists.

"You're welcome," she said, dropping his plate in front of him. "I'm sorry," she said. "Excuse me."

Waiting for James was the hardest part, and then when he came she didn't want to talk to him.

"So," he said after detailing his adventures, "what did you do today?"

The medic's breath smelled of chewing gum. Tedder.

"Nothing," she said.

The radio chased her upstairs. She knitted until Jay's bedtime, got him in and went down to say goodnight herself. Only one lamp was on, in a corner, its shade topped with a beer tray. James and his father sat on each side of the big Philco, as if guarding it. They kept the same chairs and spoke—it seemed to Anne—more to the set than each other. They spoke to the war.

She listened for his father coming up first. In the dark she heard James say goodnight to him and then clump downstairs to search the night dial for more reports. New York, of course, and south to Philadelphia. Boston, Portland, and once, before a storm, oddly, Cleveland. The downstairs filled with static, crazy loops of stuck frequencies. She tried to be asleep before he tired of it, but hours later woke to explosions below her and, knocking her knitting to the floor, threw off her covers and from the top of the stairs called him to bed.

"Did James tell you?" his father asked the next morning, accepting his juice. "The Marines are on New Georgia."

He seemed pleased, and she went back to the kitchen to mix James's pancakes, thinking, I cannot stop this, hating her own weakness. She was sitting silently at the help's table when something—a beam giving way, a bureau toppling, someone falling down the stairs—made the whole house jump.

Her fears were for Jay, and she ran to the front stairs.

"Here," Mr. Langer called from the front door. He was standing, holding his juice and his blanket. "It's the news," he said, and pointed off the end of the porch. She didn't understand but ran to the rail.

Below her lay the paper boy, twisted around his bike, his papers scattered around him in the grass. He was bleeding from one ear. She almost ran James down getting to the stairs.

The boy was out. His head was snapped back, showing his throat, and before she had a chance to feel his limbs, she knew—from how many kids diving into the haymow, the summer quarry—that his neck was broken. She got his pulse, much stronger than she'd thought, and started checking his legs. His shorts were seeping blood. Some part of the bike had torn his thigh near the groin. She covered the wound with her hands.

"I need a towel," she said, and Jay, suddenly there and awake, ran.

Under her, the boy stirred.

"James, I need you down here."

He hopped the rail in his pajamas.

She pointed to the boy's head with her chin. "If he comes to and starts thrashing around, you're going to have to hold him up there."

"Here's the towel," Jay said.

"Give it to your father."

The boy was coming out of it. She was wrong about the neck (how rusty she was, how glad to help!). She pressed the towel into the wound, and he shrieked and arched his body against the pain.

"You're all right!" she shouted back. "Calm down!"

"Should I hold him?" James asked.

"He's all right. You're all right!"

The boy lay back on the grass, heaving out long sobs. She peeked under the towel. The gash filled and ran.

"Get the car started," she said. "Jay, get your clothes on, you have to come with me. Where's the nearest hospital?"

"Brookhaven," Mr. Langer said.

"There's an army base around here somewhere," she said.

"I don't know of any."

She asked James when he brought the car around.

"Outside Flanders."

"Where's that?"

He pulled a map from the glove box and patted his pajamas for a pencil.

"Just show me."

James helped her lay him across the backseat. He'd put an old blanket over the upholstery, which she knew was useless. Jay waited, afraid to touch him.

"Get in back," she said. "You're going to have to hold the towel to keep the bleeding down. Okay?"

"Okay."

"I can go," James said.

"You have to work," she said, and (she would remember this later, linger over it like a mystery) before pulling away, kissed him through the window.

She had the map on the seat beside her, and stopped before each turn, wanting to be sure.

"How you doing back there?" she asked Jay. "Don't worry if he yells. It hurts whether you press it or not."

They had enough gas. She sped along the empty highway, so fast they almost missed the entrance, marked like a scout camp with an arch of sticks. The dirt roads of the base were badly marked and choked with soldiers, most just boys, the few men conspicuous. Riding with her window down, Anne followed their directions through the maze of tents to a Quonset marked with the red cross.

Someone had called ahead, because a crew was waiting for her. Before she could turn off the car, two medics had the boy out and on a litter, a clean compress on him. Jay stood aside, holding the soiled towel.

"Thank you," she said. "I know that was very hard. That's what your brother does."

He didn't answer; he was watching the medics carry the boy inside.

"He's going to be okay," she said. "How are you feeling?"

"Okay."

"How about we go inside?"

"Is he going to get stitches?"

"Yes," she said.

"Can I wait here?"

"Are you going to be sick? Do you feel like you're going to faint?"

"A little."

"Why don't you lie down? Here." She helped him into the front and got him situated. The morning was coming on and the blood smelled. "Do you want the door open?"

"Open."

She opened the back doors too. "I'm going to go in. Are you going to be all right?"

"Yes."

Inside, a nurse took her information. She wore cat's-eye glasses on a chain, which made her look younger than she was. Anne was astonished at how much she missed a woman's voice. She hadn't expected any here and was mildly surprised, even pleased, to see three others at their desks. Clipboards hung along the wall. In the back, beyond a cloth screen, the boy was sobbing.

"My guess is it missed the femoral," Anne said.

"I don't know."

"Did you look at him?"

"Not for long," the nurse said. "Those are the kind I hate. And he's only a kid, too."

"I know. Wait till the parents get here. That's when I have the trouble. I'm a nurse too."

"Oh, where do you work?"

Anne told her about Putney and Montour Falls but didn't mention being a shift supervisor. It was nice just to talk shop.

"So where are you working now?"

"I'm not. I'm taking care of my father-in-law—he had a stroke."

"I'm sorry. If he gets better, we could really use you."

"That's very nice of you," Anne said. Her name was Cheryl. In back, the boy stopped. "You did get his parents?"

"The mother's coming," Cheryl said.

"I'd better get back to my patient."

"Think about it."

"I will," Anne said.

The backseat was a disaster. On the drive home, Jay kept his head out the window, just in case. After breakfast he seemed better, then disappeared down the beach. She watched him dwindle from the porch.

"How'd he do?" Mr. Langer asked.

"Good," she said. "He did very well."

"I put the bike around back."

"You shouldn't be doing that."

"The thing rolls," he said.

Midafternoon, the boy's mother called to thank her. Her name was Marion Rodman, the boy's name was Win.

"Edwin," Marion explained. "They say he's going to be fine. In the meantime, I don't suppose your boy is looking for a paper route?"

"I'll check," Anne said, and after dinner, playing catch, asked him.

"Sure," Jay said.

"Starting tomorrow."

"Okay."

James apologized for not calling. He'd begun to fade toward the end of the week, and ate leaning on one elbow, his head bent over the plate. His hands were dirty.

"You should be getting more sleep," she said.

"I keep thinking I'll make it up on the weekend. There isn't any weekend."

"You miss teaching."

"Not after last year."

"Jay has a job."

"So he told me."

She sat down across from him. "I talked to a woman up at the camp. She said they were looking for nurses."

"And."

"Maybe I could work there a few days a week."

"You miss it."

"I do."

"What about Jay?" he asked.

"I think Jay's old enough to take care of himself."

"Can he take care of my father if something goes wrong?"

"You don't understand," she said. "I'm going crazy in this house. You're not here, Rennie's not here, Jay doesn't want to be here. I'm all by myself. I look at your father and I think of my father. I can't keep thinking about him. I need to take care of someone who's going to get better."

"This is going to make you feel better, doing this?"

"I think so."

"Then fine," he said, as if he'd been for it all along.

She told Jay as she tucked him in. He gave her his blank face. "Look," she said, "a lot of things are going to change around here, and you're not going to like some of them. When you don't like something, don't make faces, come right out and tell me you don't like it."

"I don't like it."

"Good," she said.

"What if Grampa Langer dies?"

"Remember I told you when your Grampa Clayborn was going to leave?"

"Yes."

"I'll tell you when Grampa Langer's going to leave. Okay?"

"Okay," Jay said.

James came straight to her bed, cold against her curled back.

"What about sleep?" she asked, but rolled over, opening to him.

Before the sun was up she woke Jay to get ready for his first day of papers. She came down to the kitchen and lit the stove. Outside, gulls stood on the lawn by the hundreds, some with one leg tucked under, still asleep. She made a pot of coffee and was about to sit down to the help's table when she stopped, half fascinated by the light. She set her cup on its saucer, then went to the back door and opened it.

She walked down the steps and onto the wet lawn, her bare feet freezing. The gulls sidled away, eyeing her. She made for them but they scooted off, hopping a few feet ahead of her, jostling to get out of her way yet unconcerned. A few on the edge lazily took flight as she chased them, dropping to the lawn out of reach. "Bastards," she swore, and, as if instructed, a pack of them lifted as one into the air, then another, and shouting "Go!" she sent them all off over the water, their calls like the cries of the dying.

THREE TIMES A DAY JAY HAD TO PASS THE SHOALS, twice on his bike and then again in bed. It stood back from the beach, its porch flush with the line of the woods, a white-shingled elephant of a hotel starting to fall apart. Some of its windows were broken, others covered with illegible, rain-browned bills. Bits of beer bottles glittered on its crossed walks. Win said no one had owned it for a while; there'd been a fire. It was a shortcut between Hickey's Mart, where Mr. Barger dropped off his bundle of papers, and the town road, where most of his customers lived. Laden, Jay crept by the dry fountains and ruined flower beds, then, coming back with his sack empty, blew through the cracked parking lot.

In the dream he was just starting out, his sack so heavy it must have been a Sunday. Win had warned him about the chain strung between the stone posts at the foot of the drive. Each post had had a plaque bolted to it; in the dream they hadn't been taken for scrap. Jay aimed for the rut outside the right post, where Win had worn through to a root. The drive ran under a canopy of trees, tangle on both sides sloping darkly away to marsh. Gravel plinked in his spokes, dinged off the chain guard. Weeds reached for him. The drive split, and, as instructed, Jay followed around to the right and up a slight rise, and there in front of him stood the Shoals, layered like a wedding cake.

By this time, he knew he was dreaming. Though nothing had happened, a faint buzzing had begun, and as he coasted down the drive he began to panic, knowing he wouldn't keep going straight but would curl off and take the circle around to the canopied entrance. In reality only the poles and a few shreds of bleached canvas remained, but here it was, coming into view, a taut bright green, on the end its name in script. The sack's strap bit into his neck, the buzzing became a radio, a lush ripple of static. There was no telling how long it would go on, and knowing it was a dream only made it worse, impossible to stop. Now he would flip down his kickstand. Now he would trip on the curb and his papers would spill out on the green carpet.

Inside the Shoals, far across a wide dining room overlooking the sea, Rennie would be sitting at a table, waiting for him. The weather had turned; a storm light bathed the room. In the dimness, Jay couldn't see his face. He would have a plate in front of him and a napkin tucked into his uniform. Behind him, shadows of water rilled down the wall. Jay would come into the dark dining room, through padded double doors with portholes too high to see through and down the three carpeted steps. A wall-long window gave on a gray view. Far over the sea, explosions lit sinking ships.

The buzzing came high now, on and on, dizzying, like watching wires run above him in the car. Unseen, his mother was shouting the way she did before she hit him, the word and then her hand: "Don't. You. Ever." Down the three steps, down the three steps, and then the arm of lightning would reach, was reaching, reached through the window and shook Rennie.

Jay explained in the dark, his father at his feet, making the mattress tilt.

"I understand," his father said, "but these dreams have to stop. You're too old for this. *I'm* too old for this. Okay, champ?"

"Okay," Jay said, and the bed lifted.

His father filled the door. "Sleep now." The hall went black and the stairs gave. Below, searchlights scoured the clouds, sirens tore across London.

"My light," Jay called, and his father stopped halfway down.

"You want your light."

"Yes. Please."

His father came in, rigid. "What is it with this light now?"

"I just like it on."

"I understand that," his father said, straining as he bent to stick it in the outlet. The light was creamsicle orange and put a gleam in the glass knobs of the dresser. "Better?"

"Thank you."

His father moved to the door, his shadow huge and soft. "We're all worried, Jay," he said, as if this might comfort him, then left him to the whistling fins.

Downstairs the radio stopped and his mother and father talked. Jay lay in the dark, buoyed by his father's soft drawl, waiting for his mother to cut him off or fix him with her wise silence. It was about him but really it wasn't. Outside, the sea rushed; the wind shivered the pane above his head. From the woods, so far in the dark Jay couldn't pick out the clicking of the rails, came the long-drawn call of a train from the base.

Last week when his crabbing pond and the creek feeding it

had turned a stinking black, he'd followed the slick upstream through brush farther than he'd ever gone and found a bridge. It was new, steel painted green, and beneath it in the water sat globs of oil, tarballs—or so he'd thought, for when he was in the shadow of the bridge he saw it was shit, a runny suspension that made him cover his face. Above, the rails began to hum and ring—Grampa Clayborn grinding a knife in the cellar—and nearby a train clattered, echoing over the skinny piles. Slow, a freight hauling potatoes, sea bass packed in ice. He had a nickel and scampered up the bank to set it on the track, then hid under the bridge.

The noise was enormous, drumming the air. The first engine pushed the piling he was leaning against down into the water, and he jumped away. Landing, his feet shot out from under him, and he sprawled, afraid he'd fall in. Above, the train ground across the sky, a string of cattle cars, slat-sided, out of which stuck a hand, a single finger pointing at Jay. Over the throb of the diesels came laughter, hooting. A cigarette butt landed near him, rolling, still lit. The hand turned over, gave him the finger and was gone.

"Soldiers," his father told him, "headed for the war."

"James," his mother scolded.

"What am I going to do, give him nightmares? He already has nightmares."

"This helps?"

"He knows. They show it at the Regal, right after Porky Pig."

"You know it makes me angry," she said.

"Are you going to tell him he can't go?"

"They don't scare me," Jay said. "I like them."

"See," his mother said, "he likes them. This is your brother, for God's sake."

"Anne."

"What, you can say what you want but when I say something I'm damaging him? We're talking about Rennie here."

The mention of his name made Jay angry.

"Rennie's going to be fine," his father said.

"Of course," his mother said, but Jay could see she didn't believe it. Since Grampa Clayborn died she didn't even try to lie about things. That was up to his father now, and he wasn't any good at it.

"Why don't you go on outside," his father said. "I'll be out in a minute."

"It's almost dark."

"Go ahead."

Waiting with his father's binoculars and the spotter cards, Jay swore. He'd forgotten the nickel. It was still back there, probably in the water.

The trains ran all night, their horns warning each other, waking him in the dark warmth of his covers. He had a dream for them. He had a dream for everything, that was the problem. They came on like the newsreels at the Regal except nobody said anything. The *Arizona* blew up to his room, the shouts of the drowning no louder than his Big Ben's ticking.

He heard his mother coming up the stairs, and below, the radio going on again. When she shut the bathroom door, he snuck to the closet and got out his box and brought it to bed. His Indian head pennies jingled in the dark. He kept everything in the box, his little things—a Utica Club church key; half a jawbone of a woodchuck, the seams black between the teeth; a spent shotgun shell; a yellow shard of a clay pigeon; Grampa Clayborn's back door key; the postcard from Rennie and Dorothy's honeymoon in Hawaii.

He kept the box in his closet in case they moved. The time before last, he'd forgotten a miniature syrup jar he'd been waiting for all spring, and when he unpacked he saw the glass cabin standing amid the dim shelves of the pantry, a sliver of light trapped in its chimney. It would be there now, filled with a silt of dust and moth droppings.

That was Montour Falls, where the trains ran up the lake and his father taught shop because they already had someone for history. Leaving, he thought he'd never see the jar again. Now, with the war, he didn't even want it.

That last time, Jay had almost hidden. His father came to find him, clumping through the downstairs, trying to keep his voice nice. The house was empty, swept; it made him sound huge. Jay stood at his bedroom window, trying to memorize the view. Below, under the buckeye tree, their car chugged in a drizzle, his mother's kitchen chairs lashed to the roof, its heavy doors spread like wings. That was at the beginning of the war. Rennie was off at Cornell. His mother was in Galesburg, helping Grampa Clayborn die.

"Let's go, champ," his father called from the foot of the stairs, and clapped his hands twice, as if Jay were at bat. That spring his father came down during his free period and watched them in gym, correcting Jay from the bleachers as he ate his lunch. "Throwing behind the runner," he called. "Missed the cut-off man." His voice echoed in the rafters above the drawn-up backboards. Alone in the stands, he seemed tiny instead of gigantically fat. All year Jay found him drawn in stalls and gouged into desktops, a balloon with a striped tie and glasses, sometimes a pig with a book, curly-tailed, a triangle of handkerchief poking out. Lardass Langer. Lardo. Jay carried an eraser, a brown block that smelled of soap and crumbled like cheese, but after going through a few he understood it was no use and tried, as his father counseled, to ignore it; tried, as he tried to ignore his father's presence, hopelessly, afraid he was betraying him. He would, he was. His father made them the same lunch, and as Jay clung to how many outs there were and which base to throw to, his father called down, "Apple again," as if it were a surprise. The batter tapped the plate, took a few cuts. "Jay, macaroons!"

They'd been in Montour Falls a year. His hiding surprised Jay as much as it did his father, and when they were together in the car, with his father hunched over the wheel, peering through the useless wipers, Jay tried to explain.

"Don't say you're sorry," his father said. "You've put up with a lot this year. I can't promise, but I think we're going to be at this new place a long time."

That was Galesburg, at Grampa Clayborn's. His mother helped him die because he was her father. Winter, those snowy days alone. His mother kept Grampa Clayborn's door closed. A pan of water on the radiator made the air cold and heavy. Once he'd peeked in and seen his grandfather propped up, reading, his mother holding the Bible for him, turning the thin pages. His grandfather said the words—Jay could read his lips—but the voice he heard was his mother's. She knew it by heart, and as she helped Grampa Clayborn say it, she turned her head toward the door where Jay stood, her eyes telling him to go, go.

She never left the house, sent him with a list to town when she needed things. He was happy to be by himself, walking, the black trees crossed against the sky. The library closed at dark; the lights went off in rows. He had class, his father had to teach.

They both got a day off for the funeral. Jay sat between them in the front seat. His mother looked angry and small in black; she said his grandfather had told her to tell him goodbye. In the coatroom, alone, he said it out loud in the mirror of the cigarette machine, but it didn't mean anything. There was a pack of matches in the drop slot he thought of taking. King Edward cigars. It had snowed, the coats dripped on the carpet.

Grampa Langer was going to die, no one knew when. His mother said he was getting better, but all he did was sit on the porch and listen to the radio. In the mornings he wore a winter coat, and again after supper. Half of his face was dead, that eye rheumy, like a blind dog's. His skin was like the Mummy's; if you poked your finger through, out would come a puff of dust. When Jay came back from crabbing, he asked to look in the bucket, then muttered, "A good lot," and Jay wanted to dump them in his lap and run. He was with him all the time now that his mother was working. They were supposed to check up on each other. Jay couldn't wait until Win was allowed out.

Downstairs, his father walked around, locking up. Jay found Rennie's postcard and angled it toward his night-light so he could see the volcano. *Scenic!* the back said. *And real hot!* He imagined Rennie's ship going by the *Arizona*, pushing through the slick, the oil still bubbling up, all those guys inside.

Deep in the woods, a train blew a mournful chord, like a great harmonica. He saw the Shoals, white in a flash of lightning, and stuck the postcard back in the box, stowed the box under his pillow and pulled the covers over his head. "I'll be back," Rennie had said at the station and, surprising Jay, kissed him. It hadn't embarrassed

Jay as much as it frightened him. There was no reason to be afraid, his father always said, as if Jay had to come up with one. If his mother told him not to worry, it would be different. His father said nothing could happen, but he always said that. He'd said that about Grampa Clayborn.

He went to the Regal to see Rennie die. He was the only guy in the balcony not in uniform. They came down from the base on pass and saw the late matinee. All the movies were the war now. The soldiers around him made fun of the story, then got quiet when someone died.

Only one important guy died; the rest of them got maybe one line. The Germans didn't say anything but sometimes they looked surprised. Everyone laughed at that. Everything was in France. Some civilians died first, then some Germans, then some of the underground, more Germans, one of our guys that didn't count too much, then a million Germans, and finally the star—always William Bendix. By then Jay had forgotten Ann Sheridan, the tough nurse, and when her face came down, soft and sharp and flame-lit for a dying kiss, his face got hot and he had to stay still or he might cry. Around him in the dark, the soldiers made slurping sounds—"Oh, baby!"—and Jay saw Dorothy in her swimsuit on the rock below the falls.

April, she had kissed him at the station in Utica, her breasts pressing against him, then her hard belly as she pulled him close. Since winter her face had gone heavy and spread over her cheeks; a pad of fat hung under her chin. With her bags massed at her feet, in her good camel's-hair coat, she seemed almost an adult, and Jay fought to recall those days alone with her—the water flowing over the mossy rock, smooth as the slide at the town pool—when she had no one but him to talk to and everything he said had to be right. It was—he was. She held him sometimes, her chin over his shoulder, her suit hot on his skin, and then, releasing him, laughed at her fear and dove into the chilly water. He thought of her at night when his hands strayed (were they her hands on him or his on her?), then remembered Rennie and stopped, only to succumb the next night. All summer he'd dreamed of this kiss, dreaded it, and now with the meager last snow of the season drifting down outside, Dorothy was more like his mother, not a girl anymore. No one thought she should go, even Rennie, but she'd fought them, and now she was here, leaving. The station was hot, its long benches filled, a few people asleep. Dorothy's neck smelled of talc and sweat and Evening in Paris, like a sour, flowery bread fresh from the oven. "When I come back you'll be an uncle," she said. "Uncle Jay, okay?" She'd been crying since she got out of her parents' Chevy, quietly, dabbing at her eyes with a balled tissue and shaking her head, frowning as if annoyed with her own emotions. She and Mrs. Baines were the only ones crying. Mr. Baines and his father stood back, holding their hats and not talking. His mother had refused to come. At home she called Mr. Baines "that bastard," even after his father asked her not to. "She's just upset," his father explained that night, as if she were sick, her venom temporary.

Ann Sheridan laid a clean sheet over the hero's face. It wasn't a bad death. He'd write the name of the movie on his ticket stub and put it in his box, but he knew he'd forget it. It wouldn't come back the way Grampa Clayborn or Dorothy did, the way the lightning reached in.

For Rennie, he needed something at sea. A beachhead or, better, a torpedoed Liberty ship. He'd seen one in the newsreels, a few crew members floating face up in a swath of broken boards, their heads blackened by burning oil. He hadn't dreamed Rennie into it yet.

Sometimes before the credits finished and the lights came up, Jay made for the bathroom and hid in a locked stall, his sneakers on the seat. The usher, Bart the Drunk, never checked, and when Jay knew his mother was working late at the base, he stayed to see the same sequence of cartoon, newsreel, serial, trailers and, finally, again, the feature, shocked at how often the movie he'd liked earlier that afternoon wasn't any good. For the second show he always took the best seat—in the middle of the last row, under the projector hole. When things got slow, he spied on the guys who invited and then paid for the girls who waited outside every day.

Jay knew some from his route; they came straight from the Waquaumsett Country Day School, still in uniform but with lipstick and their buttons undone to show a stretch of neck. Each wore a ring of plain, polished jet to show they were waiting for someone overseas. Those closer to his age just talked and teased, sisterly; an older one might kiss and cuddle, the big question whether she'd let whoever it was slip his hand into her shirt. Jay watched with the same outrage and admiration, the same concentration he reserved for that slacker Musial. And like Musial standing on second, regal even in his shame, the girls came the next day, the pawing forgotten, to stand outside before showtime, french-inhaling Luckies. He thought of their houses, the long lawns and high hedges, the crushed-clamshell drives he rode over. They knew he'd taken over for Win; he hoped they didn't think they were friends.

There was one blond girl, Sylvia Jensen, that he seemed to be falling in love with. She was only a year and three months older than him, according to Win, and lived on the bay side of the town road—403, a lopsided saltbox with steep stairs and a peeling porch. A cat hunched in one window, sunning. Her father worked with his father. Fridays he gave Jay a nickel extra for putting the paper inside their screen door, while Jay stood looking past him, trying to see Sylvia, terrified that he might. She didn't seem to like him much, though once she'd looked back at him and made a face while her date tried to kiss her.

Sylvia wasn't here today, he always checked coming in. Ann Sheridan was almost enough to make him stay, and Grampa Langer waiting for him, but his mother would be back at six. The credits ended and soldiers pushed through the rows. They seemed older than Rennie in their uniforms. Bart the Drunk waved them along with his flashlight, shaking the gold fringe of his epaulets. His face was red as a steak, and midway through the second show he fell asleep on the stairs. His flashlight didn't have batteries. Jay waited for Bart to notice him and, when he didn't, got up, unsticking his feet from the floor.

Along the lobby walls hung the coming attractions, framed by dead lightbulbs. Each poster drew a crowd, like paintings in a museum. A new picture was opening Friday night. The poster was just like the one in the window of Ridley's that said SOMEONE TALKED, except above the struggling sailor with his mouth half full of water and one arm reaching hopelessly out to the crowd, it said instead, *Action in the North Atlantic*. Humphrey Bogart was the star, Rennie's favorite, and the black-and-white stills thumbtacked at the bottom—all night and fire and water—made Jay think it might do the trick.

He liked coming outside into the brightness, the slope down to the curtained doors and then the blinding light, but today it was raining, drizzly, the boardwalk slick. The lights around the NOW SHOWING poster (Ann Sheridan stacked and angelic in her nurse's whites) glimmered on the wet wood. The crowd was gone. Three soldiers stood hunched under the dark marquee, lighting up. Out on the end of the pier, the seatless Ferris wheel sat black against the sky, the food shacks shuttered for the duration. His bike was out there under an awning, but with the wind the seat would be soaked.

"Hey, kid," one of the soldiers said, "what do people do around here?"

"I don't know," Jay said.

"What do *you* do?" another asked nastily. The three of them faced him now. With their haircuts, Jay couldn't tell which one might be nice.

"Nothing," Jay said.

"Nothing," the mean one said, as if it were an insult. He wanted a different answer. The other two weren't going to step in.

"Sometimes I fish."

"Fish!" They all laughed.

"Hear that—the kid fishes!"

"Who doesn't, right, kid?" The one on the left grabbed his crotch and made an exaggerated cast in the direction of Ann Sheridan. "For some of that red snapper, huh?"

"That's us, the three fishermen."

"Fucking priceless," the mean one said, and they all walked away laughing, knocking each other off the yellow line painted down the center of the boardwalk, oblivious of the rain.

"Haven't you heard?" Jay wanted to say, like Screwy Squirrel, "There's a war on," but they might have thought he was cracking wise and pounded him. He weighed the real chances of that as he walked to his bike, and decided he was right to be ashamed. He'd been afraid for nothing, like his father always said.

A few hundred yards out, a freighter slid, a new Liberty ship backed by a wall of fog. Jay raced down the boardwalk alongside it. Even so far in, it was too slow for him, and by the empty parking field he'd left it in the fog and was leaning back, knees high, riding no-hands. Dumb jerks. He should have just said, Screw you.

In Galesburg, they came up behind him in the halls.

"Hey," Markie Arnold said, Donald Kosskoff said, "how do you spell coward?"

"Coward?" Tim Ray, Sammy Aaron.

"Yeah, you know, chicken, yellow."

"C?"

"C."

"O?"

"CO. You sure?"

"CO. I'd bet my life on it."

"Don't," they both whispered, their breath on his neck, and Jay stopped and the two walked past him to class. His father told him to ignore the ignorant. When Jay repeated his advice to his mother, she laughed, then, feeling sorry for him, apologized, then laughed again.

"Screw you," he said, his voice dead in the moist air. "Army jerks."

He could follow the fading arrows to the exit and take the town road or cross the lot, hop a curb, ride along the surf for a mile and cut through the Shoals. His mother wouldn't be home yet. Grampa Langer would be inside, reading the paper under the one light, but the rain and the thought of Sylvia Jensen seeing him riding by in it overcame his hesitation.

He regretted it as soon as he started down the beach. The woods beyond the dunes were dark, the sea a foamy green. The wind and the loose sand held him back, and though he couldn't see it yet, he knew the Shoals was waiting for him. He could turn back but really he couldn't. It was like a movie, the Marines going into Buna, and he was the first ashore. Point, they called it, as if one man were the sharp tip of the swooped blue arrows the paper showed arcing across the Pacific. He swung down to the hard sand along the water, cutting through the last bubbling traces of the waves. Out on the water, he imagined, bobbed carriers and cruisers, their engines cut, waiting for the signal flashed through the fog, the first barrage lobbed in. In his letters, Rennie didn't say anything. *Scenic! And real hot!* The Army was supposed to be helping the Marines take the Solomons. *Life* said it could happen anytime.

The Shoals hove into view, dingy and huge. Jay stood up on the pedals and built enough momentum to get across the soft middle of the beach and onto the wooden walk through the dunes. At the edge of the sloping, overgrown lawn, he looked back; he couldn't see the boardwalk anymore, only the vaguest outline of the Ferris wheel. He tacked to fight the incline—where the fighting was fiercest, *Life* said. It had been Win's leg but Jay kept seeing his hands on Rennie's neck, blood running in neat streams from his fingertips. In the pictures, the bodies were half swallowed by sand.

The woods closed on both sides, rain shaking the leaves, tricking him. Above, a curtain billowed in a broken window. He'd wanted to pass the place calmly—he'd been so close, almost heroic—but now with the water pouring from its rusted gutters, its windows black, the Shoals seemed equal to his dreams. He kept pedaling, his eyes on the crest of the hill, and once he reached it, sprinted for the drive.

As he crossed beneath the long window of the dining room, a foghorn boomed behind him. He put his head down and dug. He'd just turned the blind corner around the side when something went under his front tire—white, an animal already dead, or a bandage. He didn't get a good look at it, but he didn't want a good look at it, and he didn't slow down until he hit Hickey's, its interior lit against the gloom. Only then did Jay have time to re-create it, to realize that what he'd seen was a brassiere, wet and specked with grit, and though it was not in itself sinister, he knew it would be when it came back to him.

• • •

The letters they sent never made it to Rennie. They wrote care of an APO number in San Francisco, where workers opened the mail and took pictures of it. The Army flew the film wherever Rennie was and reprinted it on crinkly V-mail stationery. Exactly how, Jay couldn't figure out; *Life* never said. The originals the Army kept. He imagined his clippings and the pages and pages of his father's perfect hand filling cabinets, warehouses, whole wharves sticking into the bay. His mother never wrote anything.

Wednesdays, it was a ritual. His father got home just before dark. His mother heated up what he and Grampa Langer had eaten, mostly leftovers from the weekend and frozen food, fish if Jay had been lucky. Today he'd caught some fluke.

"I may be mistaken," his father said, addressing his fillet, "but I think I met your brother on Monday."

"It would be nice," his mother said, "if I could come home and have someone cook for *me* for a change."

"I appreciate that," his father said. "It's very good. Thank you."

"Spare me," she said, and Jay wished he were upstairs. She took off her apron and dropped it on the table and went into the living room.

"Did you thank your mother for making dinner?"

"Yes," Jay said.

His father plucked a bone from his tongue and wiped it on the edge of his plate. "She's worried. We all are. We just show it in different ways. Like the way you are with your light."

"Yeah." He could see his father was building up to Rennie, and asked if he could go listen to Fred Allen.

"Sure," his father said, disappointed, "I'll be in in a little," and Jay left him to eat alone, angry that they'd all conspired to put him in this position.

In the living room they all had positions, his mother in the corner, knitting fitfully, his father to the left of the set, Grampa Langer to the right, still going over today's paper. Jay lay down on the braided rug, took the sports and started cutting out box scores. Fred

Allen was dumb, and it was impossible to listen with Grampa Langer. He waited all day for Jay's father to come home to show him pictures of local guys killed in action. "You knew Ronnie Cobb," he said, leaning across the speaker to show him the column. "John Tolliver who used to have that hardware store outside Quogue? Ronnie's his sister's youngest. Paratroops, it says, outside Tunis. That was what, two months ago?"

"Jay?" his father prompted.

"May seventh."

"Month and a half's a long time. Not that it matters, I suppose."

His mother packed her knitting in her basket and started to leave. She did this every Wednesday, blamelessly, it seemed to Jay, as if provoked and holding her temper.

"Would you like to say anything to him?" his father asked her. Jay wished he would just let her go.

"You can tell him I'm working again," she said, and disappeared upstairs.

"Well," Grampa Langer said.

"Okay," his father said, writing, as if cheering himself on. "Jay, what have you got?"

He laid out the week's box scores, but for some reason they no longer pleased him. It was like the syrup jar or his tickets, suddenly utterly disappointing. He'd wanted his mother to say something, but now that she had, he wished she hadn't. He didn't know why.

"Senators and the Yankees," his father noted. He'd moved to the floor, and Jay could smell the day's work on him. Lardodo the Great. Mister History. "Rennie'll like that. What else, any new movies?"

"Nothing good."

"*Action in the North Atlantic?* Humphrey Bogart."

"It doesn't start till Friday."

"Got a date?" Grampa Langer asked.

"No."

"Why don't you invite Win?" his father said.

"He's not ready yet."

"I guess your old dad's out of the question."

"I can go by myself."

"I know you can," his father said, and patted him on the shoulder. His hand rested there as if he were going to give Jay advice, then slid off, all consolation. "What about *Terry and the Pirates?*"

"Surc."

"Okay!" his father said.

The newsreel showed goats being driven through a minefield in Tunisia to set off charges before the infantry went in. Jay had never seen so many goats. A sergeant stood with a grinning herdsman. When a goat tripped a mine, it popped into the air. Around him, women clucked with disgust.

"Where are the Japs?" a soldier yelled, and everyone seconded him.

"Slap the Jap!" someone shouted.

"Right off the map," another answered, and the audience caught on, clapping.

Above him in the projection booth, a tin lid clattered. The screen went black and everyone cheered.

The newsreel started again, a different number under the Movietone header. NEW GEORGIA A PEACH, the caption said, silencing them.

Soldiers were going over the side of a ship on a rope net.

"New Georgia, the Solomons," the narrator intoned. "D-Day, H-Hour for the men of the Fourth Marine Raiders." A few Army guys booed but were shushed. Cigarette smoke rose in the scissoring light. In the landing craft, a Marine couldn't keep his lit and flicked it over the side. Swells bucked the camera. Along the beach, the palms nodded. The gray sky was blue, the gray waves green.

He'd seen Guadalcanal, but that was completely Marines, and Rennie was in California then. According to Dorothy, he'd left in late April, just long enough to make it to New Georgia. You mustn't trust rumors, his father said, but Jay could tell from the way he listened to the Pacific—then switching off in the middle of the Air Force bombing Sicily—that he believed.

Rennie would be to the rear of the craft, running in behind the first lines like a halfback. When someone got shot, he had to get to them and try to help. Then, Jay figured, was when he'd get hit. He'd be kneeling by his dying friend, trying to save him, when a sniper would get him in the chest. He'd seen it in *So Proudly We Hail* except it had been Veronica Lake, and as he blinked back tears he thought how close she'd come to saving Rennie.

"In the calm before the storm," the narrator said, "thoughts turned to loved ones, home," and they showed a little guy whose helmet was too big holding a picture of some girl in a winter coat. It was covered with lipsticked kisses. The guy smiled. The craft ahead were almost into the surf. Ships' guns swiveled, palms shook. The music boomed. Jay picked a helmet by the side and bet Rennie on it.

The first craft dropped their ramps, and the Marines waded to the beach. Jay waited for one to fall and float. They were going so slow, like people getting off a bus. One stumbled but another helped him up, and now the craft the camera was on stopped, and the ramp splashed, and everyone piled out. The helmet Jay had picked fell in line with his buddies. He had a rifle and looked shorter than Rennie, and suddenly, unaccountably, Jay did not want him to die, though he knew he had to.

The last Marine shuffled off, the ramp drew up, and the craft backed away from the beach. Offshore, a sailor in his Mae West peered through binoculars. A Wildcat buzzed the palms. The music stopped, only a trumpet whispering thin, indecisive.

On the beach, the men stood in line for chow, helmetless.

"Today no mother loses her son. The Japanese have pulled back to Munda, to the airfield there." With the cheering, Jay couldn't tell what else the narrator was saying. The music came up and then the theme, a jaunty march. Around him couples were kissing, and when the national anthem came on he stood and put his hand over his heart like everyone else, but he felt cheated and ashamed, and he promised not to kill Rennie anymore.

Action in the North Atlantic started all fake. It was supposed to be a night convoy, but you could see the shadow of the boat on the bottom of the studio tank. The couple in front of him were more interesting, the guy working at the hooks of the girl's brassiere. He couldn't help but think of Dorothy stretched on the hot rock, Sylvia Jensen's ruffled front, and he was unprepared for the torpedo ripping into the Liberty ship.

He wasn't trying now, or was now trying not to include Rennie, but once the lifeboats were over the side Jay chose a face to follow. The sailor went where Jay wanted him to, in the water. Like the ship, it had caught on fire. Smoke poured from the portholes. Humphrey Bogart reached over the gunwale, holding out an oar. The man looked like he could barely swim, like in SOMEONE TALKED. It wasn't Rennie, Rennie would be fine, his father said so. It wasn't like the Marine, it was only an actor. His fingertips were inches away from safety, violins trying to build tension, and Jay knew—already resenting the two men—that he would be rescued. In front of him, the girl arched forward, twisted her arm up the back of her sweater and undid her bra. The drowning man went under, a hand frantic, and suddenly the movie stopped, the music stopped, and Jay could hear the town horn outside, blaring its air raid warning.

The lights came up and people pushed into the aisles. "Man your battle stations!" Bart was yelling, waving his flashlight. "This is not a drill!" Girls were screaming. In *Life* there were pictures of Sicily, feet sticking out of the rubble, covered with brick dust. Jay walked over the tops of seats to the bottom of the balcony and wedged himself into the crush at the exit.

He was pressed into the back of a soldier. The crowd closed over him, inching ahead, kicking at his ankles. He couldn't move his arms, and kept them bent against his chest so he could breathe. The heat of people. He caught a panicky whiff of shit, sweat, Evening in Paris. Above, the red exit sign passed, and they were going down the stairs, though his feet had lost contact. He felt himself slipping, sliding sideways, and with both hands grabbed hold of the soldier's shirt.

At the bottom of the stairs, the crowd spread across the lobby, headed for the doors. The soldier shook Jay off, giving him a look. The manager had abandoned the candy counter, turned off the popcorn popper. Someone had knocked over an ashtray as big as an umbrella stand; there was sand everywhere. Outside, the horn wouldn't stop. Jay hadn't heard any bombs yet. He knew from his father that the closest shelter was in town (nothing on the boardwalk had a basement), and like the Marine with his picture, Jay thought of his father, his mother, even Grampa Langer and his stinky blanket, Rennie and the postcard, Dorothy's kiss in the station, knowing that if he didn't get home he was going to die.

Outside he didn't hear engines, only the stampede of feet, shouting, and beyond it all, the horn. People were running down the boardwalk toward the parking lot. The marquee was out, but on the beach, down by the water, a crowd had gathered in someone's headlights. Jay found himself drawn along with everyone else, away from his bicycle and down the ramp to the sand. Another car drove onto the beach—the police—its lights flashing across people's backs. Everyone was running for the first car and then with a shout they changed direction, and Jay was caught in the rush. They were cutting through the water now, splashing, the sand sucking at his shoes—and suddenly stopped, pressing against each other. In the seaweed lay a man, black with oil, his eyes wide open.

It was impossible to believe, as if this man were Veronica Lake, except her death had been perfect. This no one knew what to do with. No one would touch him. Some turned and walked back toward the boardwalk; most just stood there, heaving from the run. Jay thought they were brave for staying, for a second forgetting himself. He wanted to leave but couldn't stop looking at the man. He seemed no more dead than Grampa Langer, asleep under his blanket. Jay didn't think he was afraid, but his right eye kept winking, flinching at something invisible.

A policeman he recognized from Hickey's parted the crowd with his flashlight and knelt by the sailor. It wasn't oil that blackened him, but fire. The policeman checked his neck for a pulse, wiped his hand on his own pants and thumbed down the dead man's eyelids, then turned his light off.

"Okay," he said, "let's give him some room. Come on!" Everyone took a step back but no one left. The policeman kept wiping his palm on his thigh. "Let's have some respect," he said.

"There!" someone outside the circle shouted. A few men flashed past, and the crowd headed off down the beach.

"Hold it, hold it!" the policeman shouted, and seeing that only Jay hadn't moved, swore and hauled the body out of the water's reach. "Stay with him," he commanded Jay, and ran off after them.

He wouldn't look at the man, and then he did and looked away. The waves seemed louder now. It was a clear night, the moon perfect for U-boats. He could see the crowd thinning, disappearing down the beach, their shirts floating ghostly. The man's jaw didn't fit right. A sprig of seaweed stuck to his cheek. A fire truck at the edge of the parking lot shone its spotlight over the waves. The horn wouldn't stop. People were running up and down the beach, in and out of the light. He thought it wasn't so bad, that he could stand there if he didn't think about it. His feet were freezing. Jay looked down and the man was still there, as real as his wet Keds. His breath left him, and he felt lighter, as if he might fly away, up among the blimps meant to protect him. This was all a mistake, he was in the wrong place. Galesburg, Montour Falls. How do you spell coward? Sylvia's thin sweaters. His father should have stopped this.

Debris was washing up now, crates, clothes, torn portions of a raft. The horn, the horn. What picture did Rennie have of him? His kiss in the station had shamed Jay more after Dorothy's.

He was going to be sick but didn't have enough breath to retch. His mother had shut the door to Grampa Clayborn's room and told him not to go in. "Do you hear me?" she said, threatening, as if he might do something to the body. Somewhere out there the ship might still be sliding down through the dark water.

An ambulance pulled up beside the fire truck, and Jay waved. It took the attendants forever to get their equipment, and then they went straight to the police car. Some firemen finally came to Jay, hefting a stretcher.

"Someone look at him?"

"The policeman," Jay said, pointing, then couldn't finish.

"It's all right," the fireman said, and took Jay by the shoulders and moved him aside like a chair. He wanted to explain that he wasn't afraid, but stood by silently as one took the sailor under the arms, the other the knees. Water sloshed from the man's nose onto the canvas and over the rubber sleeve of one's coat.

"Son of a bitch," the fireman said, and they lugged him off to the parking lot.

Jay stood there looking at the dent where the man had lain, then made his way through the crowd. People scampered across the sand; others were arriving from town on bicycles. A photographer's flash went off like a bomb, and Jay headed for the boardwalk.

The Regal was closed, its posters black behind glass. Beneath the Ferris wheel, he unlocked his bike and toed down the generator that powered his light. The parking lot was filled with fire trucks from surrounding towns, ambulances, a few olive Army cars. He weaved through the commotion, leaving the scene like a hero, alone—like Humphrey Bogart, not wanting to remember.

On the town road, taking the long way home, Jay wondered what had happened in *Action in the North Atlantic*, whether the man he'd picked made it, then didn't. What it meant about Rennie he didn't know. Nothing. It was a stupid, kid thing to do. A car passed, blinding, not his father. Starting out, he'd thought the Shoals could no longer frighten him, but now the night closed around him, and he wasn't sure anymore. He could admit he was afraid, though it didn't change anything. His light jiggled in the ditch, over the white lines. The horn, he noticed, had stopped. In the woods, the wind riffled. The man was there, hidden in the dark, his jaw cocked, whispering, a trickle of salt water dripping from his chin. “Do you hear me?” his mother said. “Don’t you run from me.” Jay stood up on the pedals, racing the dark, the dead and Rennie, knowing, though he wanted to, that he was not going to suddenly wake up, that even if this were a dream of his, he could not stop it from coming true.

THEY DIDN'T CALL HIM RENNIE, or even his real name, James. When he first reported to Fort Emory, mustered with the others in humiliating civvies on the baked parade ground, a lieutenant read their full names aloud, and for the first few months even people he'd never met called him Junior. Over time, since he was quiet and knew what he was doing with the injured, the guys in his aid station switched, one by one, to Langer, and finally, now that they were shipping out, to the carelessly affectionate Lang.

"The trouble with Lang here," Burger, their surgeon, liked to say when he'd had a few, as he had now, "is that he doesn't know the value of a single human life—his own. That and he talks too much, right, Lang?"

They were on Treasure Island, dockside in a misty drizzle, passing around a canteen full of good whiskey and pretending the gray flank of the waiting ship didn't intimidate them. Two nights ago the colonel had roused their Quonset, banging Stephenson's helmet against the edge of the bunk, and they'd fallen out in their skivvies. Their orders had come through, but sealed. They'd ridden up the coast in a Pullman with tin sheets bolted over its windows. There were no crowds to watch them off, no streamers, no kisses goodbye, only the gray warehouses. The band's instruments stayed in their cases.

His poncho had a hole in the shoulder, a seam left unstitched, and the chill seeped through. It had been made where he had, in Putney, his name later stenciled across the back, last name first, middle initial. One of his friends' mothers had forgotten to finish the seam, had been interrupted by lunch, gossip, a bobbin popping off. One morning, yanking it on before drill, he'd noticed the tag. "Hey," he shouted, "my old hometown!"

"Old," Fecho said, "you know what that means; they won't let him back in," as if he knew about his father.

"Putney," Mowry said, "what the fuck is a Putney?"

Rennie told them about the mill, the river, all the while picturing Diane Emshwiller in anklets, the uncertain turn of her nose. Once he'd retrieved a basketball for her at practice. She was his father's star, a forward with touch, rough under the boards. Swisher. He'd had a crush on her. She hustled over in her blue-and-white striped jersey, her bobbed blond hair bouncing, one front tooth slightly jutting. Her neck was red and slick with sweat. Chicken skin.

"He's working you hard," he said.

"Always," she said, and dribbled back to the group.

As with everything important, he hadn't known what was going on until it was over and evident to all, then realized he'd seen it whole from the inside, knew better than anyone that he was a dupe.

It was no different now. He didn't know how he felt about Putney; he didn't like to think of it, and the poncho filled him with only an ironic homesickness—or had, for now he was leaving for a place he couldn't imagine, and none of the towns they'd lived in since his father had lost his certificate gave him comfort. In memory, he loved only Putney.

"C'mon, Unc," Burger was saying, pushing him in the chest. It was short for unconscious; they used it for stupid.

Rennie had been blissful since the third sip, cushioned in a soft fog. He'd never left the country before, never been to war, yet he was worried more about making it up the rickety gangplank in his condition. He tipped the canteen back and the ship disappeared.

"Lang, Lang," Fecho said, "leave some for us unwed fathers."

Rennie laughed and passed it along. It surprised him that they liked him, when only months before, in this same state, he had as a matter of course been spit on. In Redwood, not a hundred miles from the pier where the Seventh waited in loose formation, he'd asked the camp director if he could ride into town to buy a work shirt but, once there, found no one would serve him. He went back to the camp truck, a windowless Ford that looked like it had fallen off a cliff, and waited in the back, angry and hurt. A clump of children built across the street, sullen, not talking. Behind them ran a siding; as they waited they seemed to be gleaning loose coal, nonchalantly, as if a communal pride stopped them from stuffing their pockets. A boy picked up a chunk and weighed it like a tomato. They were mill kids, in their good coats and cheap shoes, like his father's students. He knew them from Putney, Montour Falls, Galesburg, too young for work yet but in a few years ready to follow their fathers or, better, enter the service. One way out. He gave them a wave.

As if signaled, all at once they began winging rocks at him. For an instant he didn't believe it, registered the scene frozen as a photograph, the gray shapes suspended in the air between them like bullets streaking for Superman that he knew would never reach him. One struck the bridge of his nose, and he hunkered against a fender, flinching as stones clunked against the metal. He crouched there bleeding, his imagination insisting first that it was a mistake and then that they were going to kill him—when just as suddenly the barrage stopped. The director had come back. He opened the door and motioned Rennie into the cab, shielding him from the gang. "You've had your fun," he warned the kids (at least three girls among them, all Jay's age), but they didn't scatter, merely glared, watching them pull away, and, once the truck was off, ran after them in the dust, tossing a few last long bombs.

The director didn't comment on it.

"I guess that was me," Rennie said.

"Know how old this truck is?"

"Ten years?"

"Two."

"You should have told me."

"You wouldn't have believed me," the director said, "none of you guys do," and Rennie knew he was right. Like his father, he thought the best of people and was constantly shocked when they betrayed him. Even then his father hadn't disowned him, though in his letters at the time Rennie could read his disappointment. Now it was his mother who shamed him by not writing, or writing Dorothy, leaving his father to apologize, a task at which he was sadly expert. In her letters, he said what he wanted her to (she didn't type, held secretaries in contempt), said what he thought Rennie wanted, which made reading them doubly painful. Even Jay seemed cryptic in his clippings. Superman had been classified 4-F; with his X-ray vision he'd read an eye chart in the next room. What it meant escaped Rennie. That they'd drifted this far apart in so little time troubled him, for it was, even more for going unsaid, his own fault. It seemed he was always in the wrong place, headed in the wrong direction. Through everything, only Dorothy supported him—and Cal, though he hadn't known it.

The canteen came around again. He'd grown so quickly accustomed to loneliness, to being reviled, that this simple camaraderie struck him as a luxury, not to be trusted. Those fucking kids. He didn't need them to accuse him. Then, he'd hated himself for being there, now he hated himself for being here. It wasn't so much a lack of conviction, he thought, as a crippling disbelief in himself. In the world. Again, his father. Always, his father. The whiskey sucked the breath from him, and he gagged. To quench the cough he took another slug.

"Somebody cut him off."

"Lang's all right," Burger said.

"I'm all right," Rennie said, and everyone laughed. He raised his hand but someone had taken the canteen. The ship loomed huge. He fell down trying to look at it.

"Just don't let the CO see him," Fecho said, very near.

For an instant the letters sent him into a panic, but then he remembered these were his buddies, that they stuck up for him, and a sunny flush warmed him. A clamp of hands sat him down on his pack. He thought, uselessly, that it was getting wet. Above, the sky spun.

He hadn't been this drunk since college, when each week, it seemed, he and Cal passed some husbandry practical and on the way back from the hog barn stopped at Minton's Liquors for a reward. It was Cornell, and their success impressed them. The campus clung to a hillside deeply cut by three streams. November to May, the lake called down snow. Shocking water rushed under precipitous bridges from which, occasionally, a student threw himself. He and Cal stayed up late, the door to their dorm room locked, mullioned windows open to the cold Ithaca night, sipping cognac from beakers sneaked from chem lab and smoking nickel cigars. The hours passed in elaborate toasts.

"Caliph," Rennie said, feeling for the moment no guilt, "California, Calvin Coolidge, is this the life?"

"Rensselaer, Renoir, Render-unto-God-what-is-his," Cal intoned, "this is the life."

They were not great drinkers but ambitious, and mumbled on until one and then the other passed out—to wake in their chairs, the stale air frigid and sickening. Cal had to convince him to attempt breakfast. "Food," he pronounced, mocking Professor Ruff's pauses, "is fu-el," and pressured Rennie to get dressed and climb the icy hill and cross the slick bridge to Balch Hall, though most times the eggs and toast and sausage forced themselves out again on the way back, poured spectacularly, dizzyingly, into the gorge below.

"Renwick," Cal said, steadying him then, "is this the life?"

"Yes, Calpurnia," Rennie said, washing his mouth out with snow, "this is the life."

When Rennie said he wasn't sure of his draft status, Cal said it didn't matter, he was ready to go. For days they stayed up late, weighing atrocities. The Quakers downtown gave out forms, and one night Cal trumped him with one.

"Do you believe in a supreme being?" he asked, pencil poised.

"I don't know. I think so. I'd like to."

"Are you opposed to military service of any kind?"

"I don't know. Like what?"

"Jesus, Ren. They're going to throw you in Leavenworth and all you can say is 'I don't know'?"

"Because I don't!"

Cal leaped on him, toppling his chair, and began slapping him. He was smaller than Rennie (who had his father's size, his father's nose, his father's heart) and had never wrestled, and with one leg Rennie had him off, then down, pinned.

"Some pacifist," Cal said.

"That's not the point and you know it."

"That's bullshit. You'll go." Cal reached up and cuffed him, and before he could stop himself, Rennie grabbed him by the throat. He let go as if burned, but Cal was already coughing, holding a hand to his neck. Rennie jumped up and pulled his coat off the back of the door. On the stairs, he heard Cal shouting after him, "What is that? What the fuck is that, Renshaw?"

Like lovers, they made up nightly, their talk softening with time. They didn't agree, and so they joked, sniped at each other's reasoning. "Excalibur," Rennie called him; "The Renegade," he countered.

In May, within a week of each other, they received their papers. "Greetings," the letter said, signed by the President. It was a joke around campus, suddenly unfunny. "Greetings," a fellow inductee said in passing, and you were to return them. Out together, Cal responded while Rennie walked on.

They stopped talking about it. Only once, late at night after their last final, did Cal ask if he was going.

"No," Rennie said, and withstood his silence. "I suppose you are."

"Yes."

"Good luck."

"You too," Cal said, and they drank to it, bitterly. "Ren."

"Yeah?"

"This was the life, wasn't it?"

"Yeah, Cal, this was it," Rennie said, and they drank and kept drinking.

The next day he remembered, ashamed, that late that night he'd tried to explain, offering some slop about God his mother wouldn't have stood for. He'd meant to express his deepest secret, whose power would lay to rest any doubt, but in his condition he couldn't even persuade himself, lost what he was saying, and halfway through had given up. Cal had listened carefully, as if making a decision, but now, by the light of day, Rennie saw his hesitation to say anything as embarrassment, tact. They packed, woefully hung over, and said goodbye at Cal's cab, briskly, as if in business. Rennie took the bus home in a sea of Marines.

He was in Redwood clearing brush when he got the letter. It was winter; snow whispered around the bunkhouse. His mother was still writing then. She'd enclosed the letter from Cal's mother. It was addressed to him in Montour Falls. Even then, Putney was gone. He tipped the envelope and a picture slipped out—Cal in his dress grays, on his collar the now familiar Medical Corps caduceus, his ears and chin weirdly prominent—and Rennie knew that he was dead.

It was a note, written and rewritten, it seemed, from its neatness. He didn't want an explanation, and skimmed through Cal's mother's looping script. Casablanca landing, a mistake, going to help, not wasted. The details weren't moving, and he thought he'd be able to get through it if he read fast enough, but had to stop in the last paragraph and sit down on his bunk.

> *Reynolds, Carlton often thought about you. Often in his letters he said that he had nothing but respect for what you are doing. I know he would have liked you to know this. While I myself do not agree with it, I also remember you were great friends. Please remember him in your prayers, as we do you.*

He put the letter in his jacket and walked outside into the thin, sage-tinged air and the distant vista of the Coast Range—the humps of Black Butte and Leech Lake Mountain and Mount Linn marching darkly away, snow in the folds—and kept walking, out of camp and along the fire road up the mountain. An inch of snow had come down since lunch, and he had the pleasure, necessary now, of leaving the first footprints. He came up here sometimes to rid himself of everything, alone among the still, towering trees. Flakes sifted through their crowns, fell their ridiculous lengths like shed leaves. He walked, half distracted by tracks (a nervous bunkmate had sworn to a puma), until he came to a fallen trunk tall as a house. He waded through weighted ferns until he found a limb he could haul himself up on. On top, he saw that the tree had just fallen, held only today's snow, perhaps last night's. He walked back toward the road, careful where he stepped. The boots they'd given him were cheap and bit at his heels. Halfway to the root, he stopped and, with a glove, cleared himself a place to sit.

He'd thought he'd read the letter again, but for a while only watched the snow, and then when he did slip his gloves off and take it out, he couldn't bring himself to open it. He sat with it in his fingers, the snow disappearing into his skin. In the white quiet, he could hear himself breathe. They had been alive, and now only he was alive.

"What the fuck is this, Cal?" he said, but the forest silenced him; only a puff of steam rose.

"What the fuck is this?" he shouted so he could hear it echo, and then was ashamed of the gesture. Cal. Food is fuel. He climbed down and followed his footprints back to camp. He added the letter to the wad in his duffel and went to the mess. He was reading Hemingway (they'd never let him in vet school), there was work tomorrow, and the next day, and the next. The world did not stop.

And yet in the following days he could trace his new confusion from that moment in the woods, the snow drifting down, the icy soles of his footprints. True revelation or not, he revered the scene and came to view the letter and accept its effect as fate, destiny. He worked without anger, ate without appetite. The camp, in its isolation, its patient wasting of his fellow COs' energies, began to seem unreal. Even the stunning scenery had become insubstantial. Pausing on the job, he felt he could reach out and pull down on the too-scenic view of the mountains and it would fly up and wrap around a dowel like a painted window shade. "They will be lost who do not believe," the Jehovah's Witness he slept above said when the Socialists goaded him, and it seemed to Rennie that that was exactly what had happened to him, except now he could sense the workings of something within him, a source or outpouring of feeling for the world he had intelligently held back so far that now he would find the courage to act upon. He felt, strangely, in this enclave of Quakers, Shakers and Mennonites, that he was getting ready to be born again.

When the next month Dorothy said she was pregnant, it seemed another reason to leave, to come down from the mountain, to become, again, part of the country. She didn't understand, but understood.

"Lang," Fecho said now, shaking him awake, "get the fuck up."

Burger took him under the arms and hauled him to his feet. He was dizzy, and the two of them had to help him into his pack. He couldn't stop thanking them. His helmet felt like a shell his head would never break out of, his brain a frozen yolk.

Waiting, they gave him water, and enough of his wits returned to notice they were laid out in formation. The rain had let up but a fog had settled, kicked along by a stiff wind. Farther down, another company invisibly clumped up the gangplank. He checked his pack; the bottom was sopping, a chilly drip trickling down the crack of his ass.

"Goddamn rain," he said, and spit.

"Lang's back," Fecho said, and Mowry cheered.

"Real funny," Rennie said.

"Love you too," said Burger.

The captain came by and ordered them to attention; then the colonel zoomed past in a jeep, holding a salute. Rennie had never seen him with gloves on, and thought it comical. He would have laughed if he didn't feel so bad. Then they started marching.

A hundred yards before the gangplank, the warehouse opposite stopped, and there was just the bare pier, water, fog—nowhere to go but in the ship. White-helmeted MPs stood by with sidearms. The formation moved in jerks, inching forward, then waiting. With each step, a new row reached the gangplank, faced right and boarded. It seemed to Rennie a strange variation on walking the plank. Somewhere out there was Alcatraz. Fecho lit a cigarette from the one he'd just finished. They stepped up, stepped up.

He was worried the gangplank wouldn't be completely solid, like those slat-and-rope bridges in the Tarzan movies that gave way when the villain used them. In basic they made everyone walk across one even worse, with just a rope for your feet and two more for your hands. It hung over an odorous mud puddle that the sergeant who ran the obstacle course improved with manure. His first time Rennie slipped and in trying to save himself suffered wide, ugly brush burns on the insides of his elbows. Worse, he hadn't been strong enough to pull himself up again and, after a minute of being screamed at, dropped into the muck. On the hike back to camp they made him tag along behind like a child. The next time he didn't even try to catch himself, and soon the sergeant waited for him on the far side of the puddle, unleashing a stream of abuse when Rennie came wading out of the ooze.

"Who's going to die for you, Langer? Who is going to come back and drag your scraggly ass out of this shit and get himself killed?"

"No one, sir," he learned to say.

"You're goddamned right, you sorry bastard." It was what he said to everyone, and in this case Rennie knew it wasn't true, but still his failure ate at him. That in his weakness he might be responsible for a friend's death seemed possible, and he prayed for strength, guts and the luck to never become one of the saved.

Already, he wasn't even off the dock and they were covering for him. He unsnapped his canteen and guzzled from it. Above, ghostly in the fog, the other company jammed the rail, waving.

"Dumbfucks!" Mowry shouted. "We're coming with you!"

Something dinged off Rennie's helmet and, much too late, he ducked. Next to him Fecho was doing the same. Between them, pennies rang on the tarmac, nickels jumped like hail. It seemed so much like a dream that he wondered if the whole world was drunk. An MP stepped between them, gloved hands still gripped behind his back, and the clinking stopped. The men at the rail were laughing. Rennie started to pick up just the quarters but Fecho said they were worthless where they were going. He slipped the one in his hand into his poncho's zip pocket anyway.

"For luck," he said.

It seemed to work, for when they reached the head of the formation, facing the colonel, bundled up in a camel's hair coat in his jeep, the gangplank proved to be a rigid steel chute with rubberized hand rails. Rennie pulled himself up it, trying not to look at the water or the fog or the cluttered superstructure—radar antennas, ladders, flags, life preservers. He meant to focus on the gaunt man with an eye patch tending a clipboard (a pirate; he was being shanghaied), but the gangplank suddenly leveled off, his stride anticipated an incline no longer there, and in trying to keep his feet he instinctively looked down. There was a gap between the end of the gangplank and the beginning of the ship; through it, he could see below no more than fifteen feet of dark water separating the hull and the dock. He thought of falling, being ground between the two, drowning, his pack dragging him down. He stopped, hands locked on the rail, but before he could cause a scene, Fecho pushed him, whispering, "You can puke in the head." He recovered, took a few steps, gave the man his name and was on board.

Theirs was the last company aboard; astern another ship waited for the remainder of the division. The cargo hold was filled with amtracs and artillery, glistening wet under camouflage netting. There was room at the rail, and though there was nothing to see but where they had come from, everyone claimed a space. Rennie emptied his canteen and gobbled a chocolate bar. He hadn't noticed the rails on the pier or that above each corrugated door a stubby streetlight burned a halo in the murk. He watched the company boarding the other ship, the black gap of water beneath their feet drawing his attention. It was funny. All along, that was all he had to cross.

He thought of his father and of where they were going and it sobered him. His dizziness lifted, and by the time the second ship hauled in its gangplank his brain felt heavy as lead. The engines shuddered to life, one stack erupting a chuff of black smoke that drifted through them and back over the pier. Steel plate trembled beneath their feet.

"Ever been on one this big?" Mowry asked.

Before Rennie could say no, a horn shook the air, and everyone laughed at their terror. The ship astern answered. The engines growled louder. Below, water began to slide hesitantly along the side of the ship.

"Here we go, gentlemen," Burger said.

They slid along the docks. Dully rainbowed water sloshed the walls of empty slips; garbage bobbed in the scum—soft boxes, curled shoes, a sailor's hat kissing the surface like an interested fish. And then the slips were filled with gray Navy vessels, needle-nosed, identical other than their numbers.

"Destroyers," Burger said. Rennie looked to Fecho to see if it was true, but Fecho was looking at another, larger ship in drydock. Its bow had been smashed in; a ragged gash stretched along its water-line, the metal on both sides of the rupture curled back, edges bright. It had been stripped of its rigging; nothing hung from its lifeboat stanchions.

"Still got that quarter?" Fecho asked.

They turned for the middle of the bay, the air losing its fishiness, wind picking up. The ship was so large it hardly rolled, and Rennie was surprised when Mowry vomited down into the water.

"Combination," he explained, pale but unfazed, and Burger handed him a canteen.

Rennie himself felt better now, even his headache given up to the thrum of the ship, shaken away. Steadily, since his last step across that gap, his guilt had been dissipating. Those worries about himself, so terrible in camp, were no more. He was free now to worry about Dorothy, about his father and mother, about Jay, about—and this, meaningless, what he and Cal had argued over so long ago, came with a burst of self-love that nearly brought tears—what he conceived of when he said America. Like Superman, he seemed weakened by the very land of his birth (deadly Kryptonite! red, yel-low, green); only at a distance could he safely admit he loved it. Even Alcatraz, topped with fog, brought a smile. At the same time he was escaping, he was returning.

Lunch was due soon, or maybe they'd wait until they were well under way. They passed under the Golden Gate. He'd have to remember it to tell Jay. He'd read accounts of jumpers in the Sacramento papers and always imagined making it. Now, looking up at the dark bar, it seemed he had.

The breakwater stopped, and the ship dipped as if bowing to a greater power. A beacon rose on a bluff above them, strobing. Mowry sat on the deck and groaned. Everyone else was at the starboard rail, taking a last look. Once it was gone, Rennie thought, they would serve lunch. The wind shifted. The ship was turning, starting its long, dotted arc over the globe.

"There it goes," Burger said.

No one spoke. The land dissolved into fog, the light diminished, dimmed, and they were at sea, the country invisible behind them.

We're even, he thought.

DOROTHY DIDN'T HAVE MUCH FAT. For days the level of the jar she kept next to her hot plate stayed constant; then, when she remembered to take it in with her to the Schumans' kitchen, it suddenly doubled. She left her vegetables on in the garage, using them as an excuse.

"Thank you," she said, "but I have to get back before my broccoli gets soft."

"It makes no sense, eating alone," said Mrs. Schuman, half scolding. She meant it now, and every morning Dorothy wanted to accept, to bring her dinner in while the Schumans slowly woke over waffles, prunes, powdered eggs. She wanted to, and so refused; it would be too easy to let them take care of her. The first month, Mr. Schuman didn't understand, but she and Mrs. Schuman had come to some truce. She was not a daughter, or was a strong one, loved but let go.

"Sunday," Mrs. Schuman said, "you must."

"Of course," Dorothy said. She was seven months, clumsy, and balancing the plate with her single pork chop atop the hot grease jar was a feat. She shouldered open the door and, knowing

Mrs. Schuman was watching with a pained, brave face, waddled across the immaculate backyard to the garage.

It was slate-shingled, vined, square as a frontier jail. The inside constantly surprised her. Every time she opened the side door she expected an old Chevy, a huge Studebaker, but there was her new fan, her radio, her picture of Rennie. Mr. Schuman had installed paneling, two light fixtures, an almost new Kelvinator; Mrs. Schuman had donated a worn Oriental rug. Dorothy could overlook that on the rare rainy day it still smelled faintly of motor oil and mold. There were only two windows, built at hip level; they looked out through Mrs. Schuman's roses, over her goldfish pond and a stone cupid drawing a bead on a bird feeder. In one hung Rennie's blue star. Rereading his old letters, Dorothy would hear Mrs. Schuman's shears snipping, the birds chirping, and think, I should be asleep.

She drew the blinds against the light, turned her fan down, lowered the radio. She could sleep only on her right side, with a spongy throw pillow her mother had sent wedged under her belly. The skin ringing her navel itched. Shadows of roses nodded on the blind, the radio kept telling her the temperature, and then, as if she were shaken awake, she opened her eyes to Rennie, below him the alarm clock she'd waited in line to pay five dollars for, still cocked, minutes from going off.

The room was gray, night solidifying in the corners. Her sheets were sweaty, cold. When she swung her legs out and stood, the ache of the baby's weight returned. Jennifer—or Stephen, after her mother's father.

She remembered the mail, but there was only something from Rennie's mother. She hadn't had anything from him in a week, and that had been dated in May. It was the post office, she thought. Her own hadn't come back—that was when you knew. Then the telegram, hand-delivered. The receipt, the girls at work called it.

Dearest Dorothy, his mother had written, *I am working again.*

Now she was dearest; before, she was barely even Dorothy. It had never been Anne, always Mrs. Langer. Was she so suddenly old, at peace, an equal? The work would be good for her, Dorothy thought.

Mr. Langer was fine, Jay was fine, Grampa Langer—whom she'd never met—was fine.

Have you heard anything?

What hadn't she heard? One of the ships his division was on went down in a storm a few miles out of port. They were fighting in the Solomons, they had already fought in the Aleutians, they were in Hawaii, waiting for orders. Every day brought a new rumor at work, as if spreading their wild guesses might make them less likely or, if one proved true, soften the shock.

She dug her thumbs into her back and stretched. She'd never had such breasts, such a stomach, such hunger and disgust. Her mother said the last month was the worst; Dorothy believed her.

I was lucky, her mother wrote. *You and Robert were both winter babies.*

It was almost July and already into the nineties. It was not San Diego weather, Mrs. Schuman said. This was the rainy season, the June Gloom. She apologized like a hostess, taking the blame. In Galesburg it never got over seventy-five until August, and then only in the middle of the day, in town, on the asphalt away from shade. She could always convince Rennie to take the afternoon off and hike into the Glen. They snuck a few Utica Clubs from the case his father kept in the basement, chilling them in the river, and when things got silly, played a game, holding the cold bottle against each other for ten seconds. Rennie always lost.

Now her breasts were tender, the rest of her nerveless, thick. In the shower she cupped her nipples, her hands clenched like tents against the spray. The Schumans had an outdoor enclosure, the metal head wide as a sunflower. When the family was young, they came back from the beach and tracked sand through the house. The children had decorated the stall with bright, giant pictures of fish; they swam back and forth under a bumpy glaze of shellac, striped and smiling. This was love, Dorothy thought, and couldn't leave the stall without thinking of Robert and her father. *It will take time,* her mother wrote. For her part Dorothy had accepted her own losses. She had her mother; for now that would have to be enough. The fish slid through a steamy sea, slippery as the possibility of forgiveness.

These evening mornings, their quiet privacy. She liked being outside, the air on her body somehow exciting, not like the stifling garage. Naked, waking up, she watched the sun set. Everything was going to get better.

She wore a uniform, brown on brown, one for each day of the week. The pants were pleated, which made her seem even bigger. She kept letting them out, and still they bit at her. She'd told Mr. Mallon, her foreman, that she was due in mid-August. He hadn't asked, didn't seem to care. She sat at her station, inserting the same spring in every third shell with pincers, fitting the trigger, getting set for the next. At the end of the day her back and eyes and fingers hurt. Thirty-two fifty, straight time. Next week, she always thought, she'd have enough. Then what?

She tucked her turban in her bag. In the women's room, on the back of the door of the toilet nearest the window, hung a safety poster of a small blonde with her scalp torn off. Even at change of shift, no one used the stall. Her bladder offered Dorothy no choice. Coming out, she always checked her turban in the brushed steel mirror.

On leaving, her apartment seemed more than a garage. It was dark, light from the kitchen frosting the yard. In the half shadows, she could imagine the cottage, the roses her own. Mr. Schuman was in the basement, fiddling with his jigsaw, oblivious. Mrs. Schuman, she imagined, was lying on the couch listening to the Longines Wittnauer hour with her eyes closed, fingering her pearls. Their son Ronald was in London, their daughter Elizabeth in Wichita, getting her pilot's license. On their mantel she leaned against a trainer, arms crossed, smiling, her eyes behind shades. Walking to the trolley stop, Dorothy thought her own family wasn't so different. All the Schumans needed was a black sheep.

Sometimes the trolley didn't come; other times it was full and passed by. Almost to the stop, Dorothy thought she'd forgotten her badge again, then found it—sometimes she was brilliant—pinned to her turban.

A few people had gathered, one a girl on her line named Amelia. She was short and thin and had bad teeth. Dorothy envied her pleats. Sometimes the line at work sang, breaking into hymns midshift, spirituals or *Your Hit Parade*'s latest. Amelia wasn't an instigator, but when a song slowed and broke down to a solo, hers was the one voice exposed. Occasionally they talked, not long. Amelia was supposed to have a boyfriend even though her husband was in the Pacific. She ate alone, at break stayed at her station. In the stalls were crude pictures of her and a uniformed Japanese, doing it. The man had huge lips, buck teeth and blurred spectacles. His thing was a bayonet. Still, she sang, and Dorothy admired her for it.

"Hey," Dorothy said.

"Dot," Amelia said, and peered down the street. There was nothing coming. You heard it first, the rails ringing with the weight of the train. They were both alone, and Dorothy thought it silly not to start a conversation, but she could read Amelia. She found a spot behind her where she wouldn't be seen and stood like the others, silent under the streetlight. When a trolley finally arrived, Amelia chose a seat in back, Dorothy found one in front, and they rode, still alone, into the city.

What would she say to her anyway, that she knew what it was like? Last June when she stepped onstage to take her diploma, the crowd went so quiet she could hear her heels clicking against the floorboards. "Quisling," they whispered. "Goddamn Conshie." Rennie was in a work camp in Big Flats, tending seedlings. Her mother had had to cry to get her father to come. Dorothy could hear her clapping and, nearer, Mr. Langer, who'd already been booed. Mr. Richardson, the principal, handed her the scroll and leaned down to her ear, as if to tender words of encouragement. "Dorothy," he said, trying to be kind, "they're not wrong." Walking up the aisle, she kept her eyes ahead, looking over everyone at the caged clock. She sat next to Donald Bahr, and in a minute Mary Baird came back. No one spoke; there was only the black of her gown, her shoes, the worn floor.

The streets ran down to the bay, all neon. Amelia was looking out the window, one hand up to the glass, as if trying to touch the night rushing by. With her guard down, Amelia struck her as just another working girl. She was from Pennsylvania—Scranton—close enough to remind Dorothy of the tougher girls from Galesburg—the Scipios, who owned the bowling alley; Carol Sayer, who gave the sheriff stitches. That scrappiness was a family thing; she'd been stuck with her mother's even keel, her need to please. After graduation she stayed in the house for three days, and that summer took to the woods. Amelia would have asked Mr. Cawley why he didn't need her behind the counter anymore. Amelia would have stood on the porch and scared off the cars that pelted their house with eggs. Amelia would have slapped Marvin Barnes when he called her a Nazi in the parking lot after church. Amelia had the pride to fight, unlike her, unlike her mother.

No, Dorothy thought, it wasn't the same. She'd been blamed for being faithful. Whether Rennie was wrong or not, she was right. Her mother had taught her that much. Her father and Robert didn't understand; men, they didn't have to.

The city was out now, switching shifts, the streets full of sailors. As they neared the plant, the trolley filled with girls wearing her uniform, none of whom she knew. Alone, she was frightened of the city at night, the onslaught of cars and drunken servicemen, but getting off with a hundred others all headed in the same direction gave her courage. They trooped through Balboa Park, strong as an army, then had to wait at the gate, flashing their badges. Above them, brilliantly lit, a sign in giant letters read, ANYTHING SHORT OF RIGHT IS WRONG. Spotlit, the E for Excellence pennon flew below the Stars and Stripes, and though she knew it was corny—oh, and much worse; the whole country was against Rennie, against her—she couldn't help but feel proud, as if singly she were winning the war.

No one had been injured, the numbers above the punch clock said, in eight workdays.

"They mean two and two-thirds days," Maureen explained. She sat on Dorothy's right. Her husband was a Marine, and she acted like one. He'd trained at Twentynine Palms out in the desert and fought on Guadalcanal. Whenever Maureen got in an argument, she drew out this fact like a dagger. Amelia was across from her and down two. She had on a scarf instead of a turban, a red bandanna knotted atop her forehead. Stray wisps escaped near her ears. The light made her teeth look gray.

"Eight shifts," Dorothy said.

"E for Exactly," Maureen said.

Spring, trigger, get set.

Eileen, who would have been to her left, was out today, and to keep the line moving, Dorothy had to do her spring, Maureen her trigger. Mr. Mallon kept coming by to see if they were all right.

They talked about *Stella Dallas*, the Zoot Suit riots, Maureen's husband's car. Maureen wanted to learn how to drive, but her husband wrote back that she could wait until he got home. The car was under a tarp behind her building. Once a month she started it.

The mail, Dorothy thought, it was only a week. It had happened before, when Rennie was at Big Flats. It was the post office.

Maureen dropped a trigger. It clattered on the table and went over the edge, hit Maureen's shoe and rolled over the rubber mat under the line. She handed another to Velma on her right, who fit it in before adding a contact plate.

"E for Explosion," Maureen said.

"E for Eileen," said Velma. She was older, from North Dakota. She had a little girl.

"This yours?" Amelia said, holding up the trigger.

"You can keep it," Maureen said.

"That's okay," Amelia said, and tossed it across the line.

Maureen dropped a spring to catch it.

Everyone stopped to look.

"Trouble?" Mr. Mallon said, coming into it late.

"No, sir," Maureen said.

When he was out of range, Velma laughed.

Spring, trigger, get set.

"Like I was saying," Maureen said, "he's worried I might go car crazy and start driving it around everywhere so when he comes home it's ruined. Some people do that, just pile anybody and everybody in, put in any kind of gas."

"Black market?" Velma asked.

"Black, brown, anything they can get," Maureen said. "Some people are desperate."

Amelia laughed.

"Slut," Maureen said.

"Cow," Amelia said.

They said some things Dorothy didn't want to hear.

"Look," Maureen said, "my husband risked his life so you could have your little Mex."

"If you love Guadalcanal so much, why don't you go live there?"

Spring, trigger.

"Take your badge off and say that to me."

"Anytime, sister."

"Does anyone know what Eileen has?" Dorothy asked Velma.

"Brain damage," Velma said, "but only on Mondays."

"Name the place," Maureen said.

Both sides of the line were waiting to hear, so that when they did get off shift, a small crowd followed them out the main gate and onto a baseball diamond with a railroad spur cutting off right field. The limed foul line went up the gravel bed and continued on the other side. After eight hours on line, anything seemed reasonable. The clear, dreamy light that had astonished Dorothy her first mornings in California broke again, blue and serene, unreal yet somehow comforting, even now. She took a seat in the bleachers and unbuttoned the front of her pants. Across the street, first shift bunched up at the gate.

"This is ridiculous," Dorothy kept telling Velma, hoping she'd step in. "This is like grade school."

"They won't hurt each other. They can both take care of themselves."

Maureen and Amelia shed their jackets and chose a patch of grass in front of home plate. They both turned to the bleachers, as if waiting for a decision.

"Do you really want to do this?" Velma called.

"She's the one," Maureen said, pointing.

"Are you going to fight or not?" asked a girl with a Brooklyn accent. " 'Cause I got laundry."

"Are you ready?" Velma said.

"*I'm* ready," Amelia said.

Maureen shrugged.

"Okay. Go!"

They stalked around like boxers. Neither of them touched a thing. Maureen swung from her ears, bringing her fists down as if she were hammering an elusive nail. Amelia hid her face in her arms and swayed. She seemed even smaller than Maureen now, and Dorothy wanted to waddle out, throw her bulk between them and declare peace. Everyone was laughing. "If this is a dance," Velma called, "one of you's got to lead." There was a bar up the street, the Sloppy Dog, that stayed open twenty-four hours. Dorothy was adding up how much it would cost to treat everybody when Maureen connected.

The fist hit Amelia behind the ear. It made no sound, but she fell as if bludgeoned. For a second Dorothy thought she was faking. They all went out to check. Maureen stood over her, concerned, rubbing one red, ballooning knuckle. "I barely hit her."

Amelia's legs started to shake. Her body arched and her hands clutched the grass, fingers digging. Her eyes were open and fixed, her lips pulled back. Her teeth chattered.

"Jesus," the girl from Brooklyn said, "she's pitching a fit."

"Hold her down," Velma said, "that way she won't hurt herself," but before anyone could help her, Amelia went slack.

"I didn't hit her that hard," Maureen pleaded.

"It's all right," Dorothy told her automatically. The crowd began breaking up. They had come to see Amelia get hurt, and now that it had happened they trailed away in pairs. Velma was trying to revive Amelia, pinching the skin on the back of her hand. Maureen's knuckle was turning purple.

"She'll be all right," Dorothy asked, but Velma didn't answer.

Amelia was coming out of it. She opened her eyes and, with help, sat up, coughing.

"I'm sorry," Maureen said.

Amelia dismissed her with a wave of her hand. She stood shakily and walked away from them in a little circle behind the mound. She bent over and threw up.

"What did you do to her?" Velma asked.

Maureen shrugged guiltily.

Dorothy went to Amelia and helped her, patting her back, holding her hair aside. Her waist was like a child's. When she was done, Dorothy steered her toward a bubbler behind the backstop. Amelia's feet wandered on the grass.

Maureen and Velma came over. The rest of the crowd had left.

"You okay?" Maureen asked.

"I feel sick," Amelia said.

"You'll be all right," Velma said. To Maureen and Dorothy, she said, "Someone should take her home."

"We take the same train," Dorothy said.

"I can make it myself."

"Go with her," Velma said.

They all walked to the trolley, Amelia between Maureen and Dorothy. She was walking better but didn't say anything. The sidewalk sparkled. It was going to be scorching. At the stop, Velma suggested the two shake hands. To Dorothy's disappointment, Amelia did.

A full train came, not stopping. Maureen and Velma had to catch a bus. Leaving, Maureen patted Amelia on the shoulder.

They waited twenty minutes for the next one. It was crammed with sailors. Getting on, it seemed to Dorothy that their eyes lit on her and flew to Amelia, where they stayed, following her down the aisle. A pair emptied a bench, and Dorothy gave Amelia the window seat. The train jerked forward, skating around a curve. Amelia peered off over the shops, the telephone wires, the chimneys. They were not going to talk. The city slid by, bright and hot and sharp behind the glass. If she looked back, she'd see the ocean, filling as they climbed the hills. It was all right, Dorothy thought. It would be.

"You don't have to walk me home," Amelia said at the stop, but Dorothy could see she had a lump above her ear.

"I promised."

"I'm okay. Really."

"All right," Dorothy said. She turned up her street but at the first corner doubled back.

She made up the short block, holding her stomach with both hands. Grim rowhouses shouldered a brick church. The neighborhood was filled with children, none of whom she recognized. They stopped their stoopball games for her, moved out of her way as if she were a bully. Ahead, in the shimmery heat, Amelia crossed, emerging from between two parked cars. Dorothy waited for her to turn—which she did, left—before following.

Across the street, Amelia had a neat lead of a block on her. She seemed steady now, though Dorothy couldn't shake the notion that Amelia had forgotten where she lived and they would wander like this all day. Dorothy was already starting to tire.

A three-story boardinghouse seemed likely, then a row of stucco bungalows. They crossed a boulevard and the neighborhood changed, larger homes spaced farther apart. Dorothy was beginning to think Amelia had caught on, would lead her for miles and leave her panting in the street, exhausted, lost, when she turned into the drive of a yellow colonial with black shutters and a fanlight above the door. A concrete walk crossed the lawn to the porch stairs, but Amelia passed it and kept on down the side of the house. It wasn't a mistake; as she walked she dug through her bag for her keys. Dorothy thought she must have been feeling better, because she found them, reshouldered her bag and had the key ready by the time she reached the side of the garage. By the door hung a mailbox, painted, like her own, with a fraction, and though the mail didn't come until late afternoon, Dorothy knew that when she got home, like Amelia, she would check hers.

That night Amelia came in late. There were no awkward moments; all the girls were concerned. At break she let them look at her lump, golfball-sized and bruising blue. Maureen fit her into the conversation, recounting the fight for Eileen as if they'd made up. It seemed they had, though Maureen never formally apologized, and Amelia, quietly tending her contact plates, never publicly forgave her. The few comments she offered were enough to give Dorothy the feeling she'd had that morning—of hopelessly following—except now it wasn't just Amelia in the bright distance, but Velma, Maureen, the rest of the line.

As the week went on, the one punch turned comic, unlucky.

"I remember eating in my apartment," Amelia said. "Between that and you hitting me is a blank."

"You were a mess," Velma said.

"What did I do?"

Dorothy didn't know why she felt betrayed.

They rode home together. Amelia thanked her for looking after her.

"I was so angry at them," Dorothy said.

"It was my fault," Amelia said, but wouldn't go on. The sea spread behind them.

Mrs. Schuman looked up from her weeding. "How was work?"

"Good," Dorothy said.

"Good," Mrs. Schuman said.

There was nothing in the mail. Anne, her mother. In her room, Dorothy couldn't wait to go to work, then on line wished she were in bed. The grease jar grew new layers, striped like a pricey cocktail. The scalped blonde looked down at her with a martyr's pity. The doctor said six weeks; he'd said that two weeks ago. She couldn't imagine herself getting any bigger.

June 30th, according to Maureen, the Second Marines went ashore in New Georgia. In days they had confirmation. At break they stopped playing hearts and huddled around the radio. Rumor had it that a woman in Quality Control had been called into Mr. Mallon's office to receive the receipt, and from then on the staticky buzz of the PA coming on sent them into a panic of efficiency.

They were winning the war now, making it, paying for it. The Fourth of July they went outside on break, but there were no explosions illuminating the bay, only the rattle of firecrackers, a stray flare ascending. They weren't allowed to smoke within the fence, and sat on the picnic table first shift ate at, sipping Cokes and joking about Velma's No-Doz, looking over the ocean. New Georgia was taking too long. With the holiday, there'd been no mail. They'd all seen the old newsreels, the scorched sand and shattered stands of bamboo littered with small, charred Japanese. This was different, the papers said. Jungle warfare, snipers and trip wires. Dorothy couldn't help thinking of Rennie and their last summer in the woods, in retreat, fleeing the great army of Galesburg through the leaves. She hadn't told anyone here, and wouldn't. He was where their men were. Here, they were together. None of them had heard, there were only the newspapers, the brief radio dispatches pasted and stitched into rumor. They no longer believed anything, and instead of speculating, waited. Talk kept stopping, as it had now, only the far-off thrum of night drifting up. Below, the bay glimmered, the city lay dimmed out, its grids of streets bathed an aquarium green. Dorothy followed a lone car down Fifth as it crossed the streets along the harbor. Ash, Beech, Cedar, Date. Beside her, Amelia began to hum something Dorothy had never heard, and then she sang, no one accompanying, to the night, the sky, the dark Pacific, in which, somewhere over the curve of the Earth, their men were fighting to stay alive.

Do not let us longer tarry when there's work that must be done
And the Lo-ord of the harvest calls today,
There are sheaves that must be gathered ere the setting of the sun
And our moments, like the shadows, fly away.

For behold, the time is flying and the day will soon be o'er,
Let us labor for the Master while we may.
For the night is fast approaching when our hands can work no more,
Oh, be ready when He calleth us away.
Oh, be ready,
Oh, be ready,
Oh, be ready when He calleth us away.

When she finished, they sat in silence. Finally Mr. Mallon opened the door, the light inside blinding.

"Ladies."

"In a minute," Velma said, and he closed the door.

After lunch the PA came on and Maureen began to sob, never letting the line get ahead of her. Mr. Ray, the night supervisor, lifelessly recited a speech on independence. Spring, trigger, get set. It was officially the Fifth. In the morning the streets stank of gunpowder.

Mrs. Schuman was waiting for her in the kitchen, cheery in her apron, offering coffee. Elizabeth had gotten her wings; she showed Dorothy the certificate. It seemed so far from her, this neat testimony. In the skillet her hamburger crackled.

"That's wonderful," Dorothy said, and handed it back.

"Oh, I know I'm going to worry more, but right now I'm proud."

"It sounds exciting." The coffee tasted strangely metallic. She'd asked for half a cup, knowing she'd have trouble sleeping. A doorway gave on the dining room, curtained and murky, a plush Oriental running under a pearwood hutch. The rug was newly vacuumed, a sleek Electrolux set to go back in the closet, its cord neatly rigged. Like the children's fish, this fastidiousness sometimes struck Dorothy as love, but this morning it was little comfort. She had her jar of fat. In the garage her alarm clock waited.

"Have you heard anything?" Mrs. Schuman asked.

"No."

"I'm sure it's the mails."

Dorothy agreed and got up to turn her hamburger.

"If anything had happened, the War Department would have notified you."

"I know." Grease bubbled, smoke rose from the edges. Everything upset her stomach now, yet all she wanted to do was eat. For no reason, she began to cry.

"Dear." Mrs. Schuman touched her shoulder.

"It's nothing. It's just me."

"Sunday," Mrs. Schuman said. "Come."

"Not right now," Dorothy said. "Thank you."

She thanked her again, leaving with the hot jar, not looking back as she crossed the lawn. In her room she was angry with herself, with Mrs. Schuman, and after a few bites, gave up and wrapped the hamburger in waxed paper.

Amelia wasn't at the stop. Riding in, Dorothy read her mail—two letters from her mother, another two from Anne, as if the post office had been saving them.

Have heard from Robert, her mother wrote. *Says he is O.K. Asked after you. Father thinks it will be Italy. I know he worries about you and Reynolds.* Dorothy fitted it into the envelope. She could see her mother at the dining room table, the lace cloth thrown back, worrying over which words to use, gnawing the metal end of her pencil, then touching the point to her tongue. Had her excuses ever moved her?

Anne said she could see Rennie in her patients. Work was what she'd been missing all along. She seemed happy to Dorothy—quite unlike her—and Dorothy thought, greedily, that that was wrong.

The two of them were somehow outside the war, or in it to a different degree. Rennie, when he wrote, asked, *What did you eat today? Did you get new shoes? Tell me about your room again. Is it Schumann with two n's? Where do the shells go?* She answered now without being asked, bright nights in the garage, over lunch at four in the morning. *Our house,* she wrote, *will have an extra bedroom. At the end of the yard I'll have a garden.*

At work, everyone had mail. Maureen's husband was still on Guadalcanal. The letter was from two weeks ago, but to Maureen that didn't matter. She had it out at break and then again at lunch. People from other departments came by, congratulating her. Across from them, the other side of the line tried to cover the gap left by Amelia.

"Must be that red, white and blue flu," Velma said.

But the next day Amelia wasn't at the stop. Mr. Mallon said she hadn't called in sick.

"You know her," Maureen said.

"Not really," Dorothy said. "Let's wait another day."

The next day at break, Mr. Mallon asked her if she'd look in on her friend for him. Velma said she would go if she wanted. Dorothy told her no.

She got off at her stop. The weather had finally met Mrs. Schuman's predictions. It was overcast, cool, only a hole of blue showing. Wind whipped grit out of the gutters. It was weather she knew from Galesburg. It would rain later, when she was asleep.

The children were out, dressed in sweaters and shorts or skirts and knee socks, legs scuffed with dirt. The girls stopped their game of hopscotch. One of the boys playing ball in the street dropped his broomstick and imitated her walk, leaning back and holding both hands out as if carrying a bass drum. She scolded him playfully. The neighborhood was younger than the Schumans', and shabby, but the same, full of families. People like the Scipios and Sayers lived in these dying buildings, or her parents before they moved to the other side of the canal. This city. For an instant Dorothy felt she was beginning to know it, was no longer a visitor; for an instant she admitted she could live here.

She knew where she was. The rowhouses gave way to boarding-houses, pastel bungalows, and then she crossed the boulevard and was on Amelia's block, passing larger homes set back from the street, separated by driveways, steps and boxy hedges. Here were the real parents. Blue stars hung in windows, some doubles, fringed with gold tassels. That a single telegram could level any of these homes seemed wrong, and yet it was true. Behind the blinds, they were all waiting.

What she would do if she received one, she'd never let herself dream. She expected Amelia would be asleep, exhausted with loss, her room a mess. What would she be able to say to her?

There was no car parked in front of the yellow colonial. The windows were dim, reflecting the low sky. The house on the other side of the drive was dark, and Dorothy thought how easy it would be to break in. The garage sat at the end of the drive, ivied, inscrutable. Like hers, the windows were on the sides. Any minute she expected Amelia to burst from the door. In the yard, bees fussed around a pear tree, a finch flicked its tail on the rim of a birdbath, and suddenly Dorothy didn't know what she was doing here, walking blindly into the drama of some other life. Her own wasn't going the way she'd imagined as a girl in Galesburg. That was the problem, she thought. She was still only a girl from Galesburg, would always be. She didn't know Amelia at all. Her coming like this was an insult.

She would help her clean up her place, make her something to eat.

She stopped beside the mailbox and knocked. The lights were off.

Amelia had put up a ruffle in the window; through it, Dorothy could see a fat chair, a lamp, a nap of dark carpet. She knocked again, half glad, hoping no one was home. She might be out driving with her boyfriend. Dorothy was about to give up when someone behind her called, "Can I help you?"

It was a woman on the back porch of the colonial. She was Mrs. Schuman's age and had dark glasses and a dishrag thrown over her shoulder. Even across the yard, her smile was so bright, so perfect, it reminded Dorothy of her mother's dentures. "Friend of Amelia's?" She clopped down the stairs, wiping her hands. "Come to take a look at the place?"

"Yes," Dorothy said, unsure.

"You're from back east," the woman said, as if it no longer existed. "You're the first. I haven't even got it in the paper yet."

"I'm not really looking."

"Or not seriously?" the woman asked, hauling out a key ring. Close up, she reeked of cigarettes. "Let's wait till you see it before anything."

"I have a place."

"Amelia didn't send you?"

"No."

"Then I'm confused," the woman said. "Anyway, while you've got me here, we might as well take a peek." She opened the door and, once inside, clicked on the lamp.

The cupboards were cleared out, the fridge propped open. Atop the hot plate sat the red puck of an ant trap.

"Place is twenty-two fifty not including the electric. Amelia's never run more than four–five dollars. You're paying what now—forty?" She went on, raising the shades and thumping dust from the furniture. The curtains matched the ruffle, and before she realized what it meant, Dorothy considered how easy it would be to move.

"Where's Amelia?" she asked.

The woman quit dusting.

"I'm from her work. Our foreman asked me to look in on her. She's been absent."

"Oh, she's left." When Dorothy showed her she hadn't known,

she sighed as if tired of telling the story. She sat down in the fat chair, drained, looking around as if deciding what to say.

"What happened?" Dorothy prompted.

"The Army," the woman said, exasperated. "Her fella was missing. It took them the longest time to get her word. This is since February. All that time I'd be inside thinking of her out here by herself. Her family'd call and say they were sending someone to get her. The scraps they had! I stayed out of it. It was sad. She got the new one about a month ago and she didn't have to tell me, I knew what it said. The last few weeks I don't think she knew what she was doing. Her family finally came out and got her." She took out a cigarette and lit it. "You girls, God bless you, I don't know how you do it." They stayed like that, her smoking, Dorothy holding her belly with both hands. The woman stood and flicked her ash into a cupped palm. "So I take it you're not interested."

"No."

"It's a nice place," the woman said sadly, then herded her out. She didn't look in the mailbox.

As they walked toward the front of the house, Dorothy felt she should ask her something—not exactly what had happened or how, or the boyfriend, but something important, something about Amelia the woman could answer without thinking. How she'd lived there with her, how, maybe, some mornings they'd shared coffee.

"If you know anyone," the woman said.

"I don't right now, but if I do."

The woman offered her hand—wiped again on the dishrag—and all Dorothy could do was take it, thank her and walk away without looking back.

What, she wanted to ask, do I tell them at work? Halfway home, it started to sprinkle, then in the next block stopped.

She skipped dinner, telling Mrs. Schuman her stomach felt funny.

"Maybe we'll hear something today," Mrs. Schuman said.

"Yes," Dorothy agreed, but the day, for her, was over. In her room, she ate slice after slice of buttered bread.

In the middle of the day, she woke to thunder, the rain drumming the slate. Rennie smiled down, the clock ticked on. In the window, black against the gray shade, his star hung stilly, the fan riffling the fringe. She thought of the woman, the yellow colonial. She couldn't picture it completely. The porch, the door, the windows facing the street. After a while she stopped trying. If there was a star in her window, or none, or two, one blue, the other gold, it wouldn't matter. Like Dorothy, she'd already lost someone.

They were waiting in the break room—Maureen, Velma, Eileen—all of third shift gathered around the urn, the Coke machine, the makeshift card table. It was poker tonight. New zinc pennies speckled the pot. When she opened the door, they stopped in the middle of bidding. She shut it, cutting off the noise of the floor, and it seemed to Dorothy that even the radio stopped talking. It wouldn't have surprised her if they suddenly rushed her and held her down, took the truth from her by force.

"So," Velma said, "what's the story?"

She's gone, Dorothy had planned to say, with such gravity and compassion that she wouldn't have to explain. Her words now had to be perfect, for what, really, did she know? The woman had said everything without resorting to the painful details. "They're not wrong," Mr. Richardson had said, and her heart needed no proof. Dorothy would do the same. She'd practiced, awake in bed, in her mirror, in the shower. It was only on the trolley that she began to doubt herself.

Around her now, they waited—Maureen, whose two-week-old letter meant less every day; Eileen, engaged to a Seabee; Velma, left with a six-year-old who missed her father and waited every night after prayers for her mother to answer her terrified questions. It was ridiculous. She'd received nothing in the mail again, and, like children, they wanted her to tell them everything was fine, everything was going to be all right. It was something her mother still did.

"So?" Maureen said.

"She's gone," she said, and before their silence hardened around her words, Dorothy laughed. "She took off with her boyfriend. She even stiffed her landlady for the rent."

The room broke up.

"That's great," someone said.

"You knew it!"

"What a slut!" Maureen said, as if proud of her.

"Go on," Velma said, but even she believed it.

"Whose bid is it?" Eileen asked.

"Don't be such a prude."

"Check her hand," Velma said, and they were lost again in the game.

At eleven Mr. Mallon came in, and Dorothy told him Amelia wasn't coming back. He transferred a girl from the form shop, heavy, with a lisp. When Maureen mentioned Amelia, she had to know everything. Listening to them telling her story, Dorothy could see the two garages and wondered if this was a secret she really wanted to keep.

That Sunday she ate with the Schumans.

Jennifer or Stephen. Days of sleep. She forced herself to eat, to wake up, to take a shower. Nothing seemed to happen, yet it was all taking so long. In the mail her mother patronized her while Anne, for some reason, stopped writing altogether. Mrs. Schuman gracefully blamed the authorities. The Gloom, she said, it never fails, and then the next day it was blazing. It was Tuesday and then Wednesday. At work the new girl couldn't keep pace and, without a big scene, Mr. Mallon sent her back to the form shop. The doctor said five weeks, but Dorothy hated him anyway. The scalped blonde absolved her. Someone, she noticed, had penciled in her teeth.

And then, inevitable as the weather, the letter she'd been waiting for came. She'd written it weeks ago, care of the Pacific, and now it had returned to her, over how many thousand miles of sea, through how many hands. RETURN TO SENDER, the purple stamp on both sides said. UNABLE TO DELIVER.

She took the letter inside, sat down and began to read it. *I am fine,* it said. *Work is good.*

She fitted it back in the envelope and got her shower things out. The fish slid. The sun set. The lights came on.

"Everything is going to be all right," she told Jennifer, she told Stephen. "Everything is going to be fine."

At work, Maureen had gotten another letter. Spring, trigger, get set. On the trolley, it pleased her that no one knew.

"Getting up there," Mrs. Schuman said, pointing to the jar.

"Yes," Dorothy said.

After she ate, she took the fat to the butcher, who gave her a nickel instead of two red points. That night she used it for the trolley and the next morning started another jar. Mrs. Schuman invited her in, and for the first time Dorothy felt entitled to decline. Chewing her hamburger in the dim garage, she thought that, like having a child, this was something she would have to do alone.

3

JAMES THOUGHT HE'D SEE ANNE RECOVER GRADUALLY, grateful for each stage. In the past, after hating him so openly, she'd made up slowly. In Putney she ignored him for weeks, sailed through rooms, pale and sleepless, unreachable. Then, he'd thrilled to hear her whistling in the kitchen, and though she quit when he entered, went back to the cutting board or stove, if he stayed at the table long enough she might concede a word, if only "Go." He had no excuses and didn't pretend. Dutiful, equally sleepless, he pursued her through the beginning of spring semester, winning concessions merely by surviving her silence. Nights, she stayed up late, reading the Bible in the living room, often taking walks, and one night when she came in—two, three; he had work but, still in the wrong, couldn't be angry with her—she slipped into bed, jostling him, and in the dark said, "I went by her house. I didn't know which room was hers. You do, don't you?"

"Yes," he said.

"They were all asleep. I came back here and we were all asleep. You see? I was the only one not asleep. Do you think that's fair?"

"I've been awake."

"Waiting for me, no doubt. Concerned."

"Yes."

"How gallant."

Even this, after what had happened, was mercy.

"I saw her," Anne said. "The other day, coming home on the bus. She was walking with her friends. She's not even pretty. But you think so. She's beautiful to you. She probably thinks you're wonderful. It makes me sick."

In bed, he projected Diane on the screen of night. They hadn't talked since he'd told her they had to stop. She'd been hurt and angry with him, which he admitted was her right. She'd threatened him, shrilly, sobbed in his office until he thought she'd be sick. He didn't want to touch her, but, unaccustomed to the end of love, he couldn't stop himself. In his arms she seemed pitifully thin, a victim, newly rescued. He'd forgotten she was just a girl. He'd forgotten, conveniently, that he was a monster.

"Why did you have to tell me?" Anne said.

He didn't have an answer that wouldn't hurt her, and so said, "I don't know." He could have talked with her till dawn and still not said everything, but she lay in the dark across from him, not sobbing (what a relief her tears would be!), as if on another continent, their silence like night over open water.

I love you, he wanted to say—any simple declaration to save them—yet didn't dare. Her hopelessness, her anger, gave her a density she laid on both of them like a weight. He could bear Diane's folded notes, her murderous gaze in the hallways, had long ago reshouldered his conscience (oh, untrue, untrue), but, floating on his back in that dark room, the town outside asleep, river sliding icily by, mountains looking down, James feared this heaviness would go on forever.

Yet it had lifted, drifted off like spring fog or the dust following an explosion. He worried about her, grieved for what he'd done, yet of the two she was the stronger. She'd survived Diane while he was unsure if he'd ever recover. He'd planned to lose only one of them. He would keep his sons. Anne seemed to understand, insisting on his punishment. They would stay married but by right she would hate him for the rest of their life together. As if sentencing the entire family, she demanded they move. Guilty, he gratefully agreed.

Their one year in Montour Falls, he'd thought she was if not happy with him then at least content, patient. Rennie was off to Cornell; Jay treated his new school as an adventure, not to be taken seriously. Anne was devoted to her work, sometimes coming home still in uniform, treating her own family—as he caught himself doing from time to time—with a weary, professional kindness. He did the dishes; she picked up her knitting. The mill, the river, the lingering winter. Upstairs, Jay read under the covers. James waited for this time of day, looked forward to it like a reward. He could speak to her without apology, and found, somewhat to his dismay (his sense of fair play defeated, his guilt or innocence irrelevant), her defenses had an end. He was, these few minutes with her, though not alone, forgiven. They made love—once on the living room rug, giggling, to Toscanini leading the *Pathétique*. His knees burned. He didn't expect her depression to return. He began, cautiously, to throw off his own.

Then in December she left to watch her father. He and Jay stayed to finish the semester.

He talks, she wrote. *All day I can hear him in his room. There's nobody there. When is your last day?*

They moved in January. Anne ran out in the yard to meet them, wearing a blouse he remembered from college. Her hair was long, she'd lost a shocking amount of weight in her face, and he thought—frightened by his own coldness—of Diane, her long waist, her pretty hands. She hugged Jay and came away crying.

"Are you all right?" he asked.

"He's almost gone," she said, and regained herself.

When he finally died, she began her walks again. James lay awake listening for the thud of the storm door.

"You can turn the light on," he said.

"I can see."

She shucked her clothes by the window, pulled on her robe and slipped into her bed. "Goodnight."

"Goodnight," he said, and an hour later heard her get up and prowl about downstairs. Once he followed her—or the sound of her voice, unexpected, strange—and found her sitting in the guest bedroom. She stopped talking the moment she saw him in the doorway, but not before he'd seen her rock back, arms crossed, as if listening, waiting to respond, then lean forward and point at the empty pillow, whispering viciously, "Liar."

It was still winter, Rennie had just enlisted, and James thought it had all become too much for her. One day he came home and noticed the house was cold. The window above the kitchen sink was broken, there was glass all over the counter.

"What happened?" he asked.

"Nothing," she said. "It was probably the boys playing ball." She waved in the direction of the kitchen, and he could see her knuckles were bloody.

She needed a rest, maybe a talk with a doctor. When he tried to discuss it with her, she accused him of turning the children against her. "It's you, you're the one!" she shouted, and stopped, sagged back in her chair as if stricken. "I don't know what's happening to me. Please don't put me in the hospital."

He hadn't. An optimist, he glimpsed, that bitter winter, months distant, a different Anne.

Now that she'd appeared, the Anne he'd wished for, his appreciation struck him with the suddenness of love. With him at work, she planned everything now, brought her competence to bear on the household, where before she'd wandered lost, grieving for her father or, worse, herself. Jay gave her his paper route money to hold. His father was in charge of lunch. It was as if James and not she had been gone a long time, and in his absence great changes had shaken his kingdom.

Now at breakfast she was already in uniform, her hair tinted with sun and just a hint of henna, swept up in a breaking wave of curls at one corner of her forehead. Last night, without prompting, she'd contributed a cheery P.S. to Rennie's letter. While she'd rebuffed him yet again in bed, she had done so gently, and here she was pleasant and quick, stopping to sip her coffee, then flitting to the fridge for the oleo. He found himself watching her as if she were an imposter.

"James White!" she hollered, calling his father, and in a minute the old man peered in at the screen door. "Your juice is here."

"Can't even bring it to me," his father said under his breath.

"Who poured it for you?" she asked, and flipped Jay's eggs.

He'd missed this Anne—his Anne—and refused to question her transformation too closely. His suspicions were foolish, accusations leveled at himself, which even in that ugly time of life never stuck. She was working, she was over her father. Perhaps it was the settling pressure of not knowing what was happening to Rennie. He didn't believe any of these reasons, but hadn't been with her enough this summer to posit another. She was happy, that was all he wanted.

He'd forgotten what it meant to be in love. Desire constantly surprised him, tired him. Mornings before the bus, he leaned his bike against a lamppost on the green. Evenings, getting off in fog or to a muted sunset, he was astonished it was not gone—as amazed as he'd been when his father mentioned he'd kept it and, snaking through the crammed basement with a dimming flashlight, he came upon his old Columbia, dusted and webbed like treasure. That it survived his neglect (he hadn't gotten around to buying a lock, had avoided oiling the chain since hauling it out of the basement) seemed proof of its dedication. When, whole days, he left it out in the rain, he felt, stepping down, a rush of guilty love, and softly set his bottom on the wet seat to warm it, as if in apology. Nights, the bike delivered him home; days, waited faithfully, a promise.

"The war is a race to make things," the President said, heroically going on and on over the radio. It was true now, James thought; even twelve hours seemed reasonable. He wore a clutter of pins on his lapel to show how proud he was of his son, his country: the flag, Rennie's blue star, the 10 percent button, a miniature E pennon. His ID badge with his picture he clipped to his pocket. Coming into Grumman, he stirred to the mile-wide buildings, the runway, the clamor of the hangars. He was surprised to find people at work shirking, sitting around reading magazines, but said nothing, redoubled his efforts. When he felt himself going to sleep over a row of holes, he bolstered himself with coffee from the Inspection office and measured them again—and then a thousand diameters later it was time to punch out. The paycheck was icing. On the bus everyone knew him, and didn't let him miss his stop.

He stepped blearily onto the sidewalk, identifying Ridley's, the green, his bike. For years he'd dreamed of this place. Like his mother's kitchen, it returned to him in Galesburg or Montour Falls, stunning him with its blunt simplicity. The rude bandstand, the duck pond, the Civil War Memorial with its list of names. It was still a mystery to him; it was still home.

His only moments alone came on the town road, riding the two miles he knew from childhood in the day's last light. Before, whole weeks seemed the same, days running one into the other. Work, supper, sleep, shower. Now a sharpness crept into his vision, confusing him. She had coyly avoided him this morning, at breakfast half ignored him, asking him what he wanted with her back to him, then turned for his answer, giving him a stretch of neck, her face freshly made up, her new hairdo. Her brightness reminded James of the women in the heroic posters at work, gazing invincibly into the future. How young she seemed, as if she'd reclaimed the ten years that separated them, used youth's brute strength to keep him at bay. She deftly deflected his leer with a cutting smirk. She hadn't done this—become this—for him. Her beauty wounded him. He was fat, on the wrong side of fifty. He was too exhausted to enjoy this infatuation, too old. Beneath him the Columbia creaked. He wheezed, picturing Anne asleep. Since she'd been working, they hadn't made love. When had he ever been young?

Diane. But he wouldn't think of her, laughing in her slicker, singing on the bus back from the Canandaigua game. Or after school, while he was swabbing the chalkboard, sneaking in behind him so that when he turned, ready to go home, she'd be in her assigned seat among the empty desks. It was only three years ago.

He kept pedaling. Anne would be waiting for him, impatient to explain her day; Jay out in the yard playing catch with himself, circling dizzily under a high fly. His father, Sarah, the house itself. The cottages were practically falling down. He'd look at them tonight, at work tomorrow look in on Sarah. He'd never stopped loving his father, or Jay, Anne only briefly, no more—and that had been madness. Now, almost home, the sea opening below him, all the promises he'd made himself seemed, necessarily, within reach.

Jay wasn't in the yard, his father not on the porch or in the living room listening to the radio. Anne had left a note on the kitchen table: *Gone for a walk.* There was no mail. His dinner was in the warming oven, she'd bought beer.

"Swell," he said, and fixed himself a tray to take out to the porch.

Carrying it through the living room, he stopped. He'd done this for his mother, perhaps with this tray, a japanned view of Notre Dame. He—or was it Sarah?—carried their mother's supper upstairs to her room. Gaslit, the hall shivered. He could hear the guests downstairs, their drinks jingling, laughter. He'd dropped the tray once, silverware clattering down the stairs, and his mother had to leave; now he was careful not to slosh the soup, the coffee. He wasn't supposed to wake her, was to shut the door without a sound and immediately give his father the key.

"Funny," he said, and kept going. The house rarely showed its hand. Or was it, he thought, tucking into his fish, that he'd wanted someone to talk to, and she was the only one home?

He'd had a bad day at work. One of the mechanics asked him to pass a row of holes that were out of round, and James said no. The mechanic's lead man went to the foreman, who came to James. His name was Ernie Koenig. He was older and heavier than James and had a crew cut, as if he'd just enlisted.

"Who are you working for," the man said, "the Japs? This is production work, not a goddamn quilting bee."

"The holes are oval," James said.

"So's my foot if I have to stick it up your ass. Stamp that part and stop wasting my time. Christ."

When he checked back with Inspection, they told him he'd be working regular hours from now on.

Spearing his beans, James remembered not so much his frustration at being overruled but the man's utter disgust, as if, like a disruptive student, he'd been willfully difficult. While he loved his new job, he felt nothing he did was good enough. He missed being admired simply for trying. He missed, strange to say, being wrong all the time. He missed the kids, their arrogance, the soft-eyed optimism he feared from time to time he'd lost, as if it were possible to escape faith.

He believed Rennie would come back, that Anne would come back to him.

The sun winked, dropping into the sea. He took his tray into the kitchen; the house had gone gray. The paper lay atop the radio. He pulled the curtains down, turned on the light by her chair and went outside.

He hadn't had time to inspect the cottages, or hadn't wanted to. From the porch, their first morning, he'd seen they'd retained their identical sunstruck white. Each time he returned, their failure to revert to the colors he'd helped his mother pick out—pink, grape, shades of taffy—cut him deeply. Now, turning the stairs' last landing, he saw that whoever his father hired the last time had painted over the name plates. Fischer, Folger, Coffin, Gardner, Shelburne, Swain. They were all locked. The doors had blistered, the grass was high, full of chips.

Laughter floated up from below. He could see them on the breakwater, Anne carrying her shoes and holding his father's elbow, Jay playing in the lighthouse. James waved and Anne waved back, her hair blowing over her face. She'd changed from her uniform into a skirt and sweater. She seemed taller beside his father, strong, where he, wrapped in his jacket, seemed a husk, as if he'd worsened since this morning. Jay came out of the lighthouse, and another boy—Win, limping. They waited for Anne to help his father down to the sand, then Win, and again, up, at the bottom of the narrow stairs. They climbed the side of the dune in twos, his father resting, it seemed, every step.

At the top, James tested the railing, like all his father's work, solid. Winter mornings, he and Sarah galloped down to meet their father, finishing his walk at eight sharp, then scrambled up again, racing to the top. Often they were early, and stood on the breakwater in the knifing light, peering down the beach—and there he'd be in his greatcoat, plodding along with his head bent, hands clasped behind, as if deep in conversation. The son of a doctor, he'd been a formal man, a failed scholar, writer, artist—claims which, even at his teacher's college, seemed to James romantic. The Inn had been James's mother's idea, funded by her father, his Grandfather Cole. His father never truthfully explained to James why Grandfather Cole withdrew his stake. This happened before James was born, and the question would not have oppressed him, except every second Sunday their mother dressed Sarah and himself and, behind a hired driver, the three bumped across the moors in a four-in-hand to the Cole household for high tea. Grandfather Cole was a tiny man with glossy pomaded hair and the trick of tugging his watch chain so his watch leapt to his other hand and opened like a shucked clam. "Again!" they squealed. He applauded Sarah's five-finger exercises and then spun them, one at a time, on the corkscrewing stool. James and Sarah had cider in their teacups; that it was sometimes slightly hard was a joke, and those days the ride back seemed fantastic, the wind blasting the grass, biting his eyes. The Coles had help, uniformed, gliding quietly to his mother's side to refill her cup or to James to wipe away a spill, where they'd had to let theirs go. Now when Grandfather Cole asked, "And how is the help?" he meant their father, home alone, mending an endless succession of screens, chairs, stair treads. When their mother went away, he had to hire a girl to do the cooking. It was her—Marta—who dressed him those winter mornings, Marta who forced cornmeal mush on them and sent them off to school. Their father had advertised in the city paper. Marta had stepped off a steamer, seen the classified, paid a Danish friend who'd been in the country a year to call, and the next day arrived with her bags. "Yems," she called him. "Mister Lonker."

Below, his father stopped again. The other three waited, then followed his lead. In the dusk, silenced by the overwhelming quiet of the ocean, they seemed to James a family, complete, though he did not fully recognize any of them.

"You're home," Anne said.

"I thought I'd look at the cottages."

"Look away."

"My keys," his father said, as if he'd forgotten them.

"You men like to make a little money scraping paint?"

"Sure," they said, already a team, and James envied them.

"Think they're ready?" his father asked, picking at a windowsill.

"We'll find out Saturday, won't we? I've got the weekend off."

"You didn't tell me that," Anne said, and Jay looked away.

"It's true, I'm back to five days. They don't like me. Too much of a stickler."

She laughed. "They know you already. Well good, because I have to work that day."

"Why?"

"Because they need me. Why aren't *you* ever around here?"

"I'm here now," James said.

"And I'm not going to be here Saturday. Why is it different when it's me working?"

She barely raised her voice, yet his father turned to inspect a piece of shingling in the grass, the boys joining him as if it were a meteor, the wreckage of a downed Zero. James wanted to explain that though his position seemed weak, his appeasement wasn't a coward's but that of a town under siege, his retreat strategic.

"It'll be just us then," he said, "all right, men?" and, bless them, they came to his defense.

She didn't try to explain later why, just as for months she gave no reason for writing Dorothy instead of Rennie. They went to bed early. Getting undressed, she kept the bathroom door closed, finally came out in her robe, her face scrubbed pink, and settled into bed with *Forever Amber*.

"If you're not going to read," she said, "please don't stare at me."

"I didn't realize I was."

"It's annoying," she said, not looking away from the page.

He rolled over and faced the wallpaper, great blown roses the size of plates. This was his mother's room—her sickroom—and he had a vision of her propped against pillows, the tray in front of her untouched. Her eyes were closed; in one hand she clutched a handkerchief. The room faced the sea, the curtains half drawn so the sun didn't fall on her, stopped at the foot of her bed. On her dresser burned a hurricane lamp, giving that side of the room the illusion of night. From the door, he watched her sleep. In his memories, she seemed so old, yet she couldn't have been more than thirty. He was supposed to ask her if she wanted anything more and carry the tray back downstairs. "Don't go too close to her," Sarah warned him, and he didn't know if she was joking. Once when he'd reached to take the tray, careful not to wake her, she gripped his wrists.

"James," she said sleepily, and opened her eyes. Her pupils drew in. Her breath smelled of medicine. "Do you know who I am?"

"Yes," he said, clinging to the tray.

"I'm your mother, isn't that right? If I tell you something, you have no reason to doubt me. Because I'm your mother, yes?"

"Yes."

"I'll always take care of you, James. Wherever you go, I'll watch over you. Nothing will ever happen to you, do you know that? You don't ever have to be afraid, because I'm always watching, all the time, like an angel." She leaned forward and kissed his cheek—why only now could he remember the stale, gamy smell of her hair, the tear in the shoulder of her housecoat?—then let him go and he fell backwards, spilling the tray. She laughed. "Don't run," she called after him. "You're running, James. I see you."

He rolled over and Anne sighed and he rolled over again. Her sudden coldness, her utter control. He knew this distance. It had been his. He remembered those drives home after practice, the mile or two from the high school that tried, ridiculously, to bridge his two lives. He had of course only one, and tiny, room for two, though inside it with Diane he indulged the illusion of loving the whole world. To Anne, though he tried, he was dead, and only by a great waste of energy could he be civil with her. She became, by ministering to the kids and bearing the weight of their shame, by putting up with him, a saint, and he, in his damnation, unworthy of her love. Now it seemed it was his turn.

In the morning she apologized. She was just tired, she said. Her face was sharply made up, fresh and hard as a starlet's. Seen through this exhaustion, the offhandedness of her comment seemed calculated. Was it too early to hate her?

She made French toast, sniped from the cover of kindness. Maybe now with his new hours he could give her more support. Did he think he could help with dinner, or would that be too much to ask? And when did his hours start?

"It's very good," he said.

"If you do get home first, we're having meatloaf."

"Is there a specific recipe?"

With a control he'd seen her use on his father, she snatched a card from her file and planted it beside the stove. "What would you do if I died?"

"Eat out."

"You'd starve," she said, grinning wickedly, and though it was an old joke between them (and not at all true), as he rode to town he imagined what pleasure the image of him dead must have given her.

Was it him or did Sarah seem, like Anne, both thinner and in love? They ate lunch together, watching the noon softball league. The island sky; he hadn't thought he'd missed it. In her black sunglasses and short sleeves, Sarah seemed tough, invulnerable. The skin around her mouth was a rucked, gray crepe. She'd met someone, an engineer; it was too early to tell.

"How long does it take?" he asked.

She decided he wasn't serious, and went on. His name was Waite.

"He hates jokes about it," she said. He'd been divorced; she didn't know how she felt about it. "And I haven't told him."

"About yourself."

"Yes."

"How long have you been seeing this guy?"

"Since April?"

"You *are* going to tell him."

"I've been meaning to," she said. The second baseman, trying to turn a double play, forgot to pivot off the bag and the runner nailed him, the ball sailing high, into the stands; Sarah protected her sandwich. "How about you, how's the happy family?"

"We haven't heard from Rennie."

"God, I'm sorry, I didn't mean it like that."

"Anne's fine. Dad's fine. We're just worried. Everyone says it's the mails."

"Everything else going all right?"

"Oh, yeah. We're even fixing up the cottages—starting tomorrow. You're welcome to come out and scrape some paint."

"Got a date," she said.

"Bring him."

"Dad would *love* that."

"He would," James said, and wondered if anything he'd said to her was true.

His new hours started that day. He took an earlier bus; no one knew him. The week he'd been stuck in for the last month was finally over. He'd thought he'd be more pleased.

His bike wasn't leaning against the post. He stood looking at its absence, then scanned the green, baffled. He expected to find it on the far side of the bandstand, lying in the grass, but after twenty minutes gave up.

"Kids," he said, and started the long walk home.

The phone was ringing when he stepped in the door. Thinking that it might have something to do with Rennie, he tossed his lunch bucket onto a chair to get it.

"Hello?" James said. "Hello?"

The line clicked, taking a second to break the connection, then just the hum. He replaced the receiver and waited to see if it would ring again, and as he was standing there, he thought it couldn't be good news.

His father and Jay had been doing reconnaissance in the basement, digging up scrap metal. In Swain, James helped them sort through the rust-starred tools, laying them out like the finds of some Middle Eastern dig. His own ancient history. A few were true relics, leftovers from revolutionary days, when the basement groaned with unlevied rum and thieves' graves; most he recognized from childhood. Here were the planes and files and blades on which his hands had first learned, clumsily, bloodily, skills for which he was still grateful. Those days how quickly winter fled, crazing the basement windows, the coal stove keeping his feet from freezing. Upstairs, Sarah practiced her scales, Marta prepared their supper. His father hoped their mother could come back for part of the summer, but it was up to the doctors. James was making a tray with handles and a place for her silverware. When the chisel slipped, he opened the stove and gave his failure to the flames.

"What's this?" Jay asked, holding up a sprung rat trap. James watched his father expertly set it, then trip it with a grease pencil. The teeth bit through to the blue lead.

"Whoa!" said Jay.

"There's a bigger one in here somewhere," his father said. "I ever show you what a rat did to me?" He held out his right hand and pointed to his ring finger, which was missing the tip. Even Jay knew he'd cut if off with a table saw. It was a bedtime favorite that James—a teacher, no slave to truth—amended to include how a guest later found the tip in an ice cube.

Now Jay looked to him to be sure and, getting the okay, said, "No, Grampa."

"Sure," his father said, "swallowed whole the guy I was trying to save."

"No," Jay said again, but James could see he was pleased with it.

"Don't listen to him," James said, to keep the joke going.

He'd never seen them together like this. It was better than he'd hoped, and he postponed going back inside so that when Anne got home she came down to find them, peeking in the door. The brightness of her makeup gave her tired face a rigidity, like a clown in a washed-out circus poster. Her look sued him, and though he knew he was innocent, he softened his own.

"Meatloaf," she said, and left.

"I was supposed to put it in," he explained.

"She should have asked me," his father said. "I don't do anything around here all day."

"She's tired."

"Aren't we all," his father said, and turned to a box of locks Jay was digging through. James could see from the boy's feigned, weighty attention that he'd taken their sparring to heart. James wanted to tell him that it wasn't serious, and that his brother wasn't going to die, but lately he felt he'd been too reassuring.

"I'm going to go in," James said.

"I guess dinner's going to be supper tonight," said his father.

Anne was in the kitchen, at the block, hammering the chopmeat into fat patties with a fist. She had her apron on over her uniform, her hat still pinned in her hair.

"I thought we were having meatloaf."

"I don't have time," she said. "Did you even think of it? Oh, here." She wiped a hand on her apron and plucked a gas sticker out of the pocket on her skirt. It was a red C.

"What's this?"

"I'm emergency personnel."

"Which means?"

"Which means," she said, "I can drive to work."

"Are you going to?"

"Why do you always make it sound like I'm ruining the war for everybody? It means I'll be home an hour earlier every day. I'll be able to make dinner, which you obviously can't."

"You want me to put it on the car."

"That would be helpful, thank you. And save the A."

"I was going to," he said. Going out the back door, he heard her muttering something. He waited until he was in the car to respond.

She left after breakfast. They hadn't moved the Buick since Win's accident; climbing the drive, it drooled blue smoke. It was his car, he'd kept it going since they paid a hundred dollars for it in Putney. During the trouble, on weekends he snuck out to the garage, ostensibly to overhaul the motor, and after he'd cleaned the spark plugs, sat bundled up in the front seat, listening to the game from Syracuse, Utica, Rochester, imagining Diane in his office at the gym, the two of them safe in the dark, warm heart of the school. They tried not to be seen together outside, but once, because they'd lingered, he drove her home—or close, to the other side of the park that ran to her backyard. He made her lie across the backseat under a blanket of clean uniforms. When he told her it was okay, she popped up in the rearview mirror. They were in the back part of the park, where people came to throw away their old iceboxes. "This is so romantic," Diane said. "Are you sure you have to go?"

By nine, when Win's mother dropped him off, Jay had already opened Swain and begun gouging at the white, his father supervising from a chair, reading the box scores aloud. His father's work gloves were clownishly huge on the boys, but they'd accepted the job as a challenge and, to prove themselves earnest, attacked the shady side of the cottage as if they could finish all six by lunch. It was cool under the rotten, cobwebbed eave; at their backs, Shelburne blazed white, radiating heat. Chips leapt from his blade, trying for his eyes.

"Etten," his father read, "first base. Two at bats, no runs, no hits, no runs batted in."

"What a bum," Jay said.

"They probably walked him," Win corrected.

"He didn't score," his father said. "Keller—"

"King Kong!" the boys erupted. Jay had never taken a great interest in the game, and again James was pleasantly surprised. He thought, not seriously, of lugging the Philco down so they could listen to the Red Sox game this afternoon. The boys and the day itself—the cliffs, the ocean—almost convinced him.

He fell into the rhythm of the morning, stripping swaths, sometimes coming upon a hint of lime. They breached the National League, and the sun found them. The boys took off their shirts. Jay was tan, Win, like himself, blobby and blinding white. They turned the corner; Jay and his father brought them a bag of sandwiches, which they ate on the breakwater, teasing the seagulls. He'd missed half the summer, yet these hours were enough to fill him.

He didn't think of her until he went up to the house to bring down a jug of iced tea. The car not being there struck him as wrong. He saw Diane above him, the bubble light over her shoulder, except she was Anne now, and it wasn't he beneath her but a doctor, a soldier, someone with a young haircut, his hands running up her front. They would park overlooking water, the windows filled with sky, a sea breeze shivering the fenders. Why did it have to be in the car, why not on the beach, in the grass, bobbing in the water? Why not, as Diane teased him, at half court, with all of Putney in the bleachers cheering?

But it hadn't been all of Putney. Their audience had been small and irregular. Even he, caught up in it, didn't see all of their games; sometimes only Anne was there, and like fighters isolated in the glare of the ring, in their pleasure they didn't acknowledge her presence. That year there was nothing but Diane, every second away from her a torture. The mere thought of her face made him frantic, made him pace the floor after supper.

"Do you think I'm blind?" Anne said one night, so calmly, in the silence of the living room, that he wasn't sure he'd heard her correctly. She'd always thought him defenseless, instantly defeated.

His father had left the jug on the counter where he'd mixed it. James dried its sides and hefted it; it was heavy as a bomb. Lugging it across the lawn, he thought that if he dropped it, that would be it, he'd ask her flat out—like her, without rage.

"You've met someone," he'd say—hopefully, as if quizzing Sarah. She'd be sly, loath to give up the advantage she'd had for so long, but controlled, where she'd expected him to fly apart. At the top of the stairs he saw himself tossing the jug like a shotput, it splitting over the railing with a satisfying splash of glass. She had slapped him—something from the movies. He'd sat down as if it hadn't happened, yet his eye kept twitching.

The boys were flagging, and fell on the iced tea like tribesmen, overflow dripping from their chins, dotting their bare chests. His father had his jacket off and was debating taking a nap.

"Go ahead," James said.

"All right, I will then," his father said, but, as they searched for their gloves, hesitated.

"Need help with the stairs?" Jay asked.

"Nice of you to ask, yes," and the two went up, Jay at his elbow, letting him do the work, as if he was used to it. That James hadn't noticed the old man's reliance or Jay's consideration stung him. Had he been gone so long?

Beside him, Win ripped into a windowsill. His thigh hadn't quite healed, the stitches dotting a puckered white scar. Other than the injury, his paper route and his finicky mother, James knew nothing about his son's best friend. Why, throughout his life, did he have this sensation of suddenly waking up?

"How about them Yanks?" James said.

Jay came down with a single piece of mail. James hadn't even heard Mr. Yarborough's car. The letter was from Albany, from the state Department of Education, about renewing his certificate. It was a formality, a waste of paper, yet as the afternoon cooled and they moved to Shelburne, James found himself toying with the possibility of quitting and staying here, running the inn and taking care of his father. He didn't see why Anne wanted to go back to Galesburg. Would Rennie when he came home? Jay had made a friend (he could see himself stating his case), it seemed a shame to separate them. And what of *her* friend, the lieutenant, those burning afternoons in the Buick, in the dunes? Diane wasn't planning on college; she'd be waiting for him in Putney behind the counter of her dead father's bakery, in the park along the river, on the wrestling mat in back of his desk.

Above, the car pulled into the lot. He'd taken off his watch and was surprised to find it was only three.

It was her—or their car, she'd gone inside. He checked the backseat but saw nothing, just the fading bloodstains; he sniffed the leather, the stale air, examined the ashtray. She'd driven twenty-four miles, which seemed about right if she'd actually gone to work.

He caught her upstairs in her slip, pinching her earrings off. He didn't see her clothes, they were probably in the hamper. She hadn't turned the light on, and with the blinds down it was too dim to gauge her face. Since she'd been working, her arms had gone hard—Diane watching a lofted set shot—and the silk straps of her slip seemed unworthy of her, a manufactured attraction her own outshone naturally. She was right, he thought, he was defenseless. If she confessed now, it would be he who begged her forgiveness.

"How was the car?" he asked.

"Good."

"Work?"

"Same."

"Good," he said. "Why are you getting changed?"

"I thought you might want some help."

"Sure."

"Okay," she said, "what are we waiting for?"

"Anne," he said, "is everything all right?"

She stopped in the doorway, turned, looking at him as if he'd said something so strange, so unexpected that, by right, she didn't have to respond. She sighed and said, "I'm fine."

Later, he would think of this moment, the two of them alone in the room, the made bed between them, the shade leaking a blazing frame of light, and wonder if he'd held off because he didn't really believe in his suspicions, or, having discovered he was truly in love with her—impossibly, again—he didn't want to ruin it by admitting she was lying. Because she was.

ON THE GREEN the town had hammered together a Roll of Honor like the one Jay had seen in *Life*. A whitewashed assortment of boards (donated, it said, by Ridley's), it listed the killed in gold and beside them—which seemed wrong to Jay—in silver, the injured. The neat lettering reminded him of the take-out menu painted on the wall of the Newport Creamery. On both sides, the town had left room, a double row of slats blank, as if waiting for new flavors to be invented. Beside the chiseled granite of the Civil War Memorial, it seemed temporary, awkwardly jolly, a booth from a fair passing through or, in a gym, the painted-over names of ex-record holders. New, bright as the cottages they were scraping, it lacked the brooding solidity Jay had come to associate with fear, and so, defenseless against it, he began to see it in his dreams, Rennie's name flashing as if on a marquee. The number surprised him, from this, a town not half the size of Putney. He knew a few of the last names from his route cards and, some nights, collecting with Win, stood paralyzed by the Vogels' porch light coming on, the star in the window going opaque, giving him back the reflection of his own face.

In Galesburg, his mother refused to hang Rennie's in the window; his father said she'd change her mind. Jay didn't ask when, and like his C in Geography it was forgotten—yet he knew his mother kept that one bad report card, like all his others, with the letters from his great-grandmother Clayborn in the tin on her bureau; just as his father had Rennie's star in his sock drawer under the box with the pictures of Jay's mother when she was Dorothy's age. All these documents were locked away, not like secrets, Jay thought, but evidence, in case something bad happened and they had to find out exactly who was to blame.

The Roll of Honor wasn't like that. Here, immediately, just by being dead, these men were heroes, instantly forgiven. Their parents came to the door—or more often just one, Mr. Vogel emerging from the dark front hall, the radio not on, a soft light in the kitchen—paid Win (if they tipped, the boys had pledged to spend the extra money on War Stamps), locked the door behind them, and, before he and Win had made the street, turned off the porch light. Of his own parents, which would open the door, count out the change? What, Jay thought, would they do with Rennie's bad report cards?

They weren't telling him everything about Rennie. They hadn't gotten a letter from him since mid-May, before New Georgia. The Marines were still fighting through the jungle toward Munda. At night, the Japanese crept through their positions, slitting throats; in the morning, the guy sleeping next to you might be bled white, ants scrambling on his tongue.

Win said they tortured their prisoners. "Something like this?" he'd say, holding up an old clamp or awl his grandfather had soaking in Coca-Cola, and then demonstrate vaguely how they'd attach it or what they'd puncture. Jay had envisioned all this himself—or the comic books he blew his profits on had imagined it for him. Hidden in the tangle beside the creek, he thrilled to captured nurses' nipples crushed like overripe fruit, Navy pilots' eyes split like grapes. Working himself up, he saw Sylvia Jensen in the torn blouse and bayoneted bra straps, the Japanese commander peering greedily at her heavy, pink-tipped breasts. Cruelly, he had no intention of rescuing her; he just wanted to watch.

While he tried to keep Rennie out of his daydreams, at night he returned, worse than ever, though never a prisoner. He was always walking up a beach (even if he really was in the jungle), then silently flying backwards through the air, finally landing half in the water, his neck a red rug. Another one Jay had, though not as often, showed him getting shot in the jaw, his teeth shattering like glass. This one upset him more, brought his father running in his pajamas, slipperless—because, Jay thought, unlike Sylvia Jensen's, this one hadn't come from *Amazing War Stories*. This one was his.

There was some comfort in imagining the worst. His parents never mentioned the more vivid parts of the war, and their conversation, by omitting him, became like the Roll of Honor, terrifying in its neatness.

"He's probably somewhere where it's difficult to get word to us," his father said.

"On a ship," his mother offered. "On an island."

He'd never heard her agree with his father so quickly. Normally it was the other way around. For the first time since Grampa Clayborn died, he couldn't tell if his mother was lying.

"What do they have, field telephones? He can't very well call us on one of those."

"He'd have to write a letter."

"Which he may not be able to do; he may not have time."

"I can tell you from working in a regular hospital," his mother said, "that things can get busy very quickly."

"Say he did write a letter. There's any number of things that could have happened to it between where he is and here. You remember how long it took the ones from California."

"And there was no war in California."

"If something had happened," his father summed up, "we would have heard from someone official."

"By telegram," Jay said.

"See, you already know this, why am I telling you?"

Because, Jay wanted to say, you don't want me to know.

It was obvious from the way his father attacked the cottages, heartily played catch with him, and then after supper began spotting again, that something had changed, gone wrong. His mother came home exhausted, and was short with them, making dinner, then disappearing upstairs with a romance or barefoot down the beach, to return when Jay was already in bed, as if in his presence she didn't trust herself with the secret. He didn't like the beach after dark, and when she peeked in to give him a kiss, she seemed both reckless and oddly calm—off, like milk left out on the counter or the Cokes his father hawked at half time, boozy with too much syrup. He pretended he was asleep, but still she didn't leave, just sat there in the dark, the bedsprings giving off soft coiling noises beneath his ear. If a bomb hit your house and you were trapped under the rubble, the Civil Defense pamphlet said you should tap and keep tapping until someone tapped back. *Life* said that was how the divers knew the guys on the *Utah* were alive. Jay lay under the covers, the springs insistent, his mother smoothing her lap and sighing. Rennie rolled limply in the surf.

"Why would they keep it a secret?" Win asked.

"I don't know."

"See?"

"What do you mean, 'See'?" Jay said, scraping. Behind them, Grampa Langer droned on with the box scores. If they didn't shout, he couldn't hear them. "Maybe they already know but think it's a mistake. Like in *Heroes Die*." It was a favorite theory of his, the switched dog tags.

"That was so dumb," Win said, then realized he'd been mean and added, "I guess it could happen."

"Or maybe they don't want *him* to know." Jay pointed over his shoulder with the scraper.

"Man," Win said, as if it all made sense now. He was convinced Grampa Langer was going to die anytime—as Jay had been earlier—and often warned Jay that if the old man keeled over, he wasn't hanging around to make sure. Win was terrified of him. Every time they ran out of blades or sandpaper, Jay sent him to get more from his grandfather, who seemed to both know and delight in his friend's torture.

Jay needed a clown now. There was nothing funny about Rennie anymore. When Jay remembered the time his brother stuck a potato in the tailpipe of Mr. Leitner's Plymouth, the picture came back to him a different shade, slightly darker, as if that long-past afternoon had been in truth menaced by twilight. The time he set all the clocks to chime midnight one after the other, first around the first floor and then in a second circle upstairs, now seemed strangely prophetic.

"Do you remember," his father said, at dinner, "that raft you two lashed together?"

They all did. It had sunk a foot from shore, spilling its cargo of chicken sandwiches. That they were eating tuna sandwiches now (except his grandfather, who got to have a hamburger) didn't stop his father. His bringing it up was supposed to be funny, but no one laughed, everyone kept eating.

"God," his father said, "that was a riot."

His mother got up and dropped her plate in the sink.

"Going for a walk?" his father asked, then answered himself, "I guess so," trying, again, to make a joke.

She came in later, a shadow in the door of his bedroom. He'd been listening to the trains, and she startled him. There was no time to hide, to pretend he was sleeping. She sat by his head, crowding him, blocking the hall light. "Jay." She touched his hair, a gesture he hated, then sat without saying anything, a trick supposed to make him take what she was about to say seriously. He waited for her, annoyed, breathing the oily coconut scent of the hand cream she used whenever she came in from outside.

"I'm not angry with your father," she said, as if he'd asked. "It's everything. Things will be better when we get back home. Don't you think?"

"Sure."

"I know you and your grandfather don't always get along."

"He's okay."

"And your father's working all the time."

So are you, he wanted to say.

"I'm sorry," she said.

For what?

She sniffed as if she might cry, and he didn't know what he was supposed to do if she did. "I didn't want things to be like this."

"I don't mind. I kind of like it here."

"Jay." She shifted on the bed, her hand searching for his. It was under the covers, and she gripped his shoulder. "I can't always count on your father, do you understand that? I need to know that I can count on you. I can, can't I?"

"Sure."

"Thank you," she said, as if it was the most important thing in the world, and kissed him. She sat there a long time in the dark, patting him, before leaving.

Two trains later, his father looked in. "Everything all right, champ?"

It wasn't the first time his mother had come to Jay like that, wanting something, and he thought maybe he should tell his father, but, sorry now that he'd scorned him at dinner, his coldness toward his mother shamed him, and he said, "Yes."

"You don't sound too sure."

"I'm just tired, I guess."

His father came in but didn't sit. "I heard your mother come up. The two of you have a talk?"

"Yeah."

"She's not having an easy time of it. She loves you. I just want you to remember that, no matter what."

"I will."

"And I don't want you getting me up in the middle of the night."

"I won't," Jay said, and when his father shut the door, Jay waited for his footsteps and then the rush of water before he retrieved his box from under his pillow.

His dreams didn't stop. Rennie's volcano billowed, his ship slipped past the *Arizona*, the *Oklahoma*, the *Utah*, then the trains, the Shoals, the three steps down, the lightning, the man with the broken jaw. Like the second matinee, he knew how it would turn out, yet he had to watch it all the way through to the end. Rennie soared backwards, black in the flash; splinters of teeth flew from his lips. Jay called and called for his father. His mother, he noticed, had stopped getting up.

Yet he knew that she—not his father—would be the one to tell him about Rennie, just as, when he was acting up, she was the one to punish him. His father was patient and talked to him calmly, explained like the teacher he was, his mother hit, raged like another child. She gave no warning and never apologized. Once when they were living in Vermont she'd taken him by the neck and thrown him to the floor for ignoring her. Jay wasn't afraid of his father, yet because of his steadiness expected less from him. His mother drew an invisible line you weren't allowed to cross, and while it shifted inexplicably (often quickly), it existed. Though he knew fuzzily that his father had lost his job in Putney for hitting someone—a student, another teacher?—he'd never seen even a hint of his father's limits. The few times he'd seen him argue with Rennie, when his father should have gotten mad he became overly composed, completely logical. With his mother, you knew where you stood. She wasn't afraid—as he thought his father was—of you hating her, and her fearlessness let her say things to Jay that his father couldn't.

He didn't see much of her now. He and Win were splitting the route, and to get to Hickey's on time he ate breakfast early with Grampa Langer. At the door, he gave her a quick kiss, careful of her lipstick. She laughed, trying to draw out the goodbye.

"Take care of your grandfather," she called across the yard. "And be careful."

Out of the house, riding, he thought that he liked her better when he wasn't with her. In her uniform, with her hair just done, she seemed beautiful to him. In the past he'd taken this for granted; now he was conscious of it, like when Win mentioned his tongue or how many times you blink in a minute. It bothered him. He was afraid the tortured nurses might turn into his mother instead of Sylvia Jensen, Sylvia Jensen and then his mother, his mother and Sylvia Jensen. Beside the creek, he felt watched.

With all his jobs, he rarely got there anymore. The only time he had alone was now, doing his half of the route—really more than half. He and Win had the same number of papers, but Jay had to do the long stretch on the bluffs on the other side of town. The houses were all mansions set dramatically back from the unpaved cliff road, and the names on Jay's route cards were familiar: Folger, Coffin, Gardner, Shelburne, Swain. They were laid out in the same order as the cottages; there was even a Fischer but it had fallen down. Jay did most of his serious thinking here, alone, feeling tiny, crushed between the sea and sky. He hadn't known this part of town existed. While Win had been recovering, Mr. Barger delivered these papers by car; the post office hadn't been good enough for Miss Swain.

Now, by default, Jay grunted up the long hill, his back tire spinning sand, stones clinking in his spokes. He saved these five for last; his sack swung limply. He crested the hill and the horizon leapt away behind a high, spiked fence. The fence ran the length of the road on the ocean side down to the turnaround, and made the long, unbroken lawn within look to Jay like the empty edge of a cemetery. A quarter mile down the first gravel drive stood the remains of the Fischer house, the porch rearing like the stern of a sinking ship, below it the rest of the house strewn down the cliffside. The gate was chained. On the other side, heavy tangle masked a few half-buried carriage houses, wild roses and creeper sneaking through broken windows. He trusted no one was living in them.

He'd never seen anyone up here, had only heard rumors of Miss Swain, though each Thursday, delivering his last paper, he found an envelope sticking out from the mat with a dollar and a lollipop. His other four clients paid by the year. The Coffins had a car locked in a dusty-windowed garage, but he'd never seen tracks. Mr. Folger had groceries delivered from Hickey's on Saturdays. Grampa Langer said they all had live-in servants, or at least they used to, with the war he wasn't sure. He was surprised Miss Swain was still alive, and Mrs. Gardner, she'd been old when he was a boy.

Every time Jay made the loop, the view and the wind thrilled him. The way Win had described it, he'd expected to be afraid. Maybe it was different at night, the mute statues and barbered hedges shadowed and menacing, the ghosts—so Win said—of the shipwrecked dragging their waterlogged bodies over the long lawns, seeking revenge; but in the morning, having escaped the house before his father came down, knowing his mother would be gone when he returned, Jay found he was pleased by the ivied turrets and curtained windows, the deserted gazebos, the absolute calm. He could think. At home he was too busy trying not to get caught in the same room with the two of them. It wasn't just the morning light, golden, throwing cold shadows, or the windswept silence. It wasn't all Rennie, though he knew that was a part of it. He liked the quiet up here, the drained, blue-bottomed pools overlooking the ocean, the perfect, invisibly tended gardens, the giant, many-chimneyed houses in which, he sensed, someone very old and very rich was taking forever to die.

It was mysterious the way the Shoals had been before Win took him inside and showed him the burnt floors and water-damaged walls, the rusting beer cans and fossilized turds. Jay had expected fancy furniture, maybe a portrait above the fireplace of some half-famous ancestor whose eyes followed you around the room. He thought for sure he'd see the underpants to go with the bra. There was nothing, they'd even taken the tubs for scrap. Rocks lay scattered about like Easter eggs; Win picked one up and casually smashed what was left of a window, and Jay wanted to run. Win took him into a room he said the high school kids made out in and from a high shelf inside a closet produced a pack of Spud Menthols he'd lifted from Hickey's. Jay was proud that he hadn't thrown up, but later, looking at the crushed butt in the dark of his bedroom, he was sorry, strangely, that he wasn't afraid of the Shoals anymore. Downstairs, his father had fallen asleep beside the radio again, and a soft static seeped through the house like gas. Every time, Jay wanted to go down and wake him up, but never did, and in the morning the chair was empty. What, Jay thought, did his father think when he first opened his eyes and saw the lamp on, the bookshelves, the carved sloop with its shellacked birch-bark sail—when he realized, the way Jay did, what house he was in.

The Gardners' gate was open. Jay got his speed up and rode no-handed, folding a tomahawk as he bumped along the gravel path. MARINES NEAR MUNDA, the headline said. Throughout the morning he'd absorbed the story, like the rest of the front page. The Japanese were dug in, waiting for them in bunkers. He coasted through the Gardners' porte-cochere and winged a paper, pretending it was a grenade, the leaded glass door a pillbox. It was Wednesday, a lot of news and the Market Basket flyer, and his tomahawk broke open on impact, scattering shrapnel. He rode across the parched lawn overlooking the sea, ducking withering machine-gun fire and the real feeling, no longer terrifying—in fact, somehow comforting, as if it were Rennie in a smoking jacket with quilted lapels peering down from behind the gauzy curtains—that he was being watched.

Back at the cottages, scraping, Jay thought of the bluffs, imagined himself in the Shelburnes' or Miss Swain's, reading *Tarzan and the Ant Men* by a window, beside him a plate of cookies on a silver tray. He could fall asleep in the chair like his father, and no one would wake him up. Sometimes he saw himself in a slick leather uniform driving the Coffins' old car or finding the cobwebbed skeleton of Miss Swain stuck to her bed, but often he appeared as he'd been earlier that morning, simply riding with his five papers, the sun cutting between the houses. It seemed strange that he'd dream about something he'd already done, but the mornings were endless now, the white of the cottages blinding, the sky giant. They were on Gardner now, the largest. Without his father, they did about one long side a day, not including the eaves. The sun seemed to stay with them. After a while he wasn't sure what time it was, whether the plane buzzing above was the ten or the eleven-thirty milk run.

"Eleven-thirty," Win said.

"Getting hungry?" Grampa Langer asked.

On the stairs his arm felt light, as if it were hollow. Even being careful, Jay had time to admire the view down the beach, the top arc of the Ferris wheel. "Sorry," his grandfather said, resting. "I used to be able to do this." The peak of the roof appeared and then the rest of the house, step by step. Empty, it seemed for an instant to belong to the bluffs.

Their car wasn't there. Sometimes his mother came home early, or for lunch. She didn't come down to help, but just knowing she was home made Jay nervous. Eventually he'd come up from the cottages, his father would come home and, by playing catch, avoid her (as she, reading in the kitchen, avoided them) until dinner. Each weekday narrowed to this intersection. The afternoons flew. He'd always loved his father's car. Just this weekend he'd sponged the dust from it and, as if it were rewarding him, scrounged a handful of change from between the backseat cushions. Now he was glad to see it missing.

"I'll ring for you," Grampa Langer said in the kitchen. They'd set up a system.

He and Win were just starting the back of Gardner when he heard the bell. Lunch was egg salad, which was a big deal to Win.

"Oh," Grampa Langer said, closing his eyes and touching his forehead, remembering. His mother had called and said she'd be late and to go ahead and get dinner without her. There'd been an accident; a man had broken both his legs.

"Now," his grandfather said, "if you could help me upstairs, I think I'm going to take a nap."

"Both legs," Win said in the lighthouse, "man!" and Jay was tempted to imagine the pain, the long bones cracking, but held off, thinking of his father riding his mother's bike back from the bus stop. Scraping, he coasted through the Folgers' porte-cochere, the Gardners', Miss Swain's, making perfect throws.

Win's mother had already picked him up when his father got home. Jay let Grampa Langer tell him about the call. He got it right.

"Looks like it's just us menfolk," his father said. "How far'd you get?" he asked Jay.

He told him.

"Let me get changed and throw something in the oven and we'll sling it around a little, okay?"

But she's not here, Jay wanted to say.

They threw on the lawn, his father tossing dizzying pop flies. The wind kept shifting. Jay circled, thinking he was under the ball, but as it neared found he was too far away and lunged, falling, the ball thumping the grass a few inches from his mitt.

"Don't be afraid of the ball," his father said.

I'm not.

"Here's an easy one."

It was too easy, an insult.

"Two hands," his father instructed.

Jay threw it back too hard, and his father short-hopped it neatly, scooped it off his shoetops like Rudy York. He was always surprised by his father's grace; like his being a good cook, it didn't fit.

"Hit me in the head," his father said, and they threw back and forth. Jay was careful to use two hands and not duck when it was coming for him. Hidden behind his mitt, he blinked. His father hit the same spot every time, right between the eyes, while Jay was all over the place. His father pretended he was playing first, stretching with one foot nailed to the bag—the Big Chief. "Pick 'em up. Whoa! Okay, right in the head! We're having pork chops, is that okay?"

"Sure."

"Have anything special for Rennie tonight?"

He couldn't get the ball out of his mitt and double-clutched the throw. His father picked it off the grass backhanded. Jay waited for him to return the ball so he could answer. "Not really. The comics."

"Good. He'll appreciate them."

They threw without speaking for a while. Though his throws were all at eye level now, perfect, his father didn't comment on them.

"Had enough?" his father said. "One last one." He always finished this way, with a high fly Jay couldn't possibly catch.

"Sure," Jay said.

His father reared back and launched the ball straight up. In its flight it changed from white to black, a dot hanging for a second above him, directionless in the wind, and then when Jay thought he knew where it was going, it faded on him, drifted as if made of paper. He tracked it across the lawn, his glove bobbling on the end of his outstretched arm. He wasn't going to catch it—usually didn't even get a glove on it—and he bet the world, God, Rennie himself, that if he really tried and missed it, really tried, then Rennie would live. The ball was going to drop to his right; he veered for it, looking up. The lawn seemed to tilt, the flagpole, the sky, as if both he and the ball were falling. He was closer than he thought and, honoring his bet, couldn't slow down. His glove, the ball and the grass were converging, and then the ground rose—he'd headed back for the porch—and he stumbled, twisted sideways and, with one foot planted, lunged. He'd lost sight of the ball, and was afraid it would hit him in the head. Only as he dove did he see his father, a few feet away, reach out his mitt and spear it, having not moved an inch.

"That wasn't fair," his father said. "How about another? Here, come on."

"No."

"Here, here you go." His father launched another, and, hating him, Jay chased after it. He missed, Rennie lived, but it didn't count now.

After his father had gone inside, Jay stood at the edge of the lawn, looking down at the lighthouse. A minute ago he'd wanted to pick up the ball and fling it over the cliff, over the stairs and the cottages and the beach and the breakwater in a titanic arc so that it dropped into the waves and never came back. He fingered it in his mitt. The ball was new, its silky skin bruised the green of the lawn with each miss. His father had bought it for him, had come home Monday with a box stretching his pocket. Jay tried to be grateful. From here, he could probably not make it much past the end of the first flight of stairs, and though he could picture it hitting the water—as he'd seen himself catch the first fly, implausibly heroic—he pulled off his glove and tucked it under one arm and walked back to the house.

"It's going to rain tomorrow," Grampa Langer said over dinner. They'd waited a half hour for his mother, then given up. The chops were tender but Jay wasn't hungry.

His father nodded, chewing a huge bite.

"Thunderstorms beginning around daybreak." He said it just to say it, Jay thought. He didn't see how he could stand hamburger every day.

"Good," his father said, tilting his head so he didn't lose any of his food. "We need it." He'd started a Victory Garden out back with corn and squash and baby peas. There were a few shoots about an inch high. His mother said he'd planted too late. She called it the Dogpatch, after *Li'l Abner*.

"And what are your plans?" his father asked him. "You can't very well work in the rain."

"I don't know," Jay said.

"How about you and Win dig through the basement for scrap? That all right, Dad?"

"Fine with me."

"Why don't you plan on that," his father said, pointing his fork, and just by being there, Jay agreed.

Because they'd waited for his mother, they didn't have time for spotting. His father had the radio on, and said Jay could take the cards and the binoculars and go down by himself. His grandfather was identifying the wounded. Jay went out on the porch with a *Captain America*. The sun was down, dusk thickening over the lawn. He expected his father's car to come rumbling over the hill any second, but the night came on, and with it the mosquitoes, and he went back in.

His father had pulled the curtains and turned on the light by his mother's chair. Upstairs, on his way to the bathroom, he saw her book sitting on her nightstand. On the dust jacket a woman in a frilly dress stood on a bluff, her long red hair blowing behind her; in the background a mansion loomed, in one half-lit window the shadow of someone looking out. *Forever Amber.* The book had been banned in Massachusetts. The librarian, Mrs. Hobbs, kept the town's one copy behind the checkout in a paper bag. Careful of the bookmark, Jay leafed through it, trying to find a juicy part. It was all dukes and earls and what kind of dresses the ladies were wearing. He thought he heard his father and closed the book and put it back perfectly before going downstairs.

"You know him," Grampa Langer was saying. "His father helped manage the sausage plant in Riverhead."

Nazi spies had captured Captain America and were trying to make him talk, punching him in the gut. Jay had to be in bed in an hour, and they hadn't written Rennie yet. He asked, and his father said, "In a little bit," and disappeared behind the sports section.

The news stopped, the chimes bonged, and Fred Allen came on. Everyone applauded.

"Think she's all right?" Grampa Langer asked.

"She said she'd be late," his father said. "You talked to her yourself." He folded the paper and put it on top of the radio. "Okay, champ, let's see what you got."

They were choosing which comic strips they could get rid of when they heard the car. Jay had imagined it would be the police, but it was her. He knew the Buick's engine, could pick it out like his father's voice in a packed hallway. His father didn't look up from the piles Jay had laid out on the carpet. Outside, the car door clunked shut.

"Does he like *Snuffy Smith?*" his father asked.

"Kind of."

She was on the porch.

"Better than *Popeye?*"

His mother opened the door. "I'm home."

His father put the *Popeye* pile aside.

"Hello? I said I'm home."

"Hello," Grampa Langer said.

"Glad you could make it," his father said, thumbing through the *Snuffy Smith*s.

"I'm sorry, but we were busy." She hung her purse on the doorknob and looked to his father again. "I did call." When he didn't say anything, she said, "I have to change," as if she were in a hurry to go out again, and started up the stairs.

"We're writing to Rennie," his father called after her. He leafed through the *Popeye* pile again, through the *Snuffy Smith*s. Upstairs, water ran. Fred Allen laughed and laughed. By the time they decided on *Popeye*, his mother was coming down with her book. Without makeup, out of uniform, she seemed more like his mother.

"Almost bedtime, champ," his father said.

"What about the letter?" It was on the coffee table, half done.

"Maybe your mother would like to write something this week."

She looked up from her book as if she'd been reading for hours. "You can tell him that I'm working and that I'm happy."

"Here," his father said, and pushed the sheets at her. "You tell him."

"James."

"No," his father said, "I think that would be good. Tell him about your job, tell him how happy you are."

"Why are you acting like this?" she asked.

"I think," his father said to Jay, "it's time you were in bed."

He still had fifteen minutes but didn't argue.

"I'll do his bath," his mother said.

"I've got it," his father said, standing. "You just write."

She started reading again as if she hadn't heard him.

"I think I'm done for the day," Grampa Langer said. "If someone would help me out of this chair."

"I'll get you, Dad. Jay, say goodnight to your mother."

She kept her hands on her book, gave him her cheek. Her hair smelled of cigarettes, like the seats of the Regal, the stale air of the Shoals. For an instant, as they traded goodnights, she looked at him, her eyes skidding off to one side, and he thought that whatever she had to tell him couldn't be worse than this silence.

In bed, he listened for their voices over the radio, waves of Liberators pulverizing Sicily to dust. Footsteps—whose?—retreated into the kitchen and then, after a brief eternity through which he held his breath, returned. In the next room Grampa Langer coughed wetly for a stretch, then stopped, commenting on his effort with a low moan. Jay took out Rennie's postcard. His box smelled from the cigarette butt; he slid it under the bed. The volcano's smoke reminded him of the stricken ships they showed in the newsreels, abandoned and ablaze in the middle of the ocean. The morning after an attack you could see them littered for miles behind the convoy, adrift. He was only beginning to imagine himself on one in the middle of the night, a survivor missed by the rescue crews (with the darkness, the wind, the sea rolling in against the breakwater, the house was almost a ghost ship), when the bombs stopped. His father came upstairs, his tread heavy, and went through his routine. In the dark, Jay squeezed toothpaste on his brush for him, counted how many times he spat, waited for him to gargle. Now it came, a faint burbling like a sick motorboat, followed by a squeaking twist of the spigot, a click of the light switch, bedsprings giving, and finally silence. It soothed Jay like the news of some victory. Below, a door thumped shut, shocking his heart.

Grampa Langer was right. It was raining when Jay woke up, his room gray. The lot was full of puddles. His mother made pancakes; her hair seemed redder, her lipstick richer. She promised she'd be home early.

The Marines were trudging toward Munda. His slicker was from before the war and had a rip in it. He pretended he'd been shot and was bleeding. His tires swished. He took his time delivering, fired high, his tomahawk whacking the Vogels' screen door and dropping onto the dry mat. In the woods, the Japanese crouched under bushes, slithered through ferns. Skirting the town green, he saw that the Roll of Honor hadn't changed.

On the bluffs, Miss Swain had turned the light of her porte-cochere on for him. He lifted the wrought-iron latch and swung one side of her gate open. Far down the double-rutted drive, the house waited, windows dark, only the one bulb on, as if it had burned all night. Rain had stained the stone black. Behind it, a wall of fog hid the cliff, the greenhouse half lost, a mirage. He leaned around puddles reflecting clouds. It was Thursday, but suddenly the thought of the lollipop—cherry, always—sickened him.

He stopped under the shelter and pushed his hood back, leaned his bike on its kickstand and got off. A spiraling stream of water gushed from where the gutter met the downspout, fell apart in the wind. Looking up, Jay saw that the roof above him was peeling, the paint hanging in great white flakes. He took the last paper from his sack, holding it away from him, careful not to get it wet, and trudged up the stairs. The envelope wasn't there.

He looked in through the heavy, leaded glass doors. The entrance hall was dark, the floor a checkerboard, a full-length mirror giving him back his face. He thought of knocking, then left the paper on the mat. The dollar was mostly tip anyway. The lollipop coated his teeth so they squeaked together like chalk on a freshly washed blackboard. Riding home, he tried to convince himself he didn't miss it.

Win didn't like mice. He and Jay didn't see any live ones, only a dried-out victim of a trap. The basement was so full of junk that they kept walking around looking at all of it, not wanting to start. Grampa Langer's old gloves were stiff with grease and cool inside; when Jay put them down they kept their shape as if there were still hands in them.

"How we doing down there?" Grampa Langer called from the kitchen, and Win looked at Jay.

"Okay," Jay shouted up the stairs, and tugged the disgusting gloves on. They filled a crate with old nails and rusted saw blades, tin plates and a moldy skillet, some jarless lids, an iron that was being used as a doorstop, a can full of mismatched nuts and bolts, brads and tacks, a grimy coil of picture wire.

"We'll keep the iron," Grampa Langer said, looking it over. He'd been on the porch all morning even though it was cold. The house was dark, gulls stood on the lawn. They helped him make grilled cheese sandwiches and canned tomato soup. After lunch, he climbed the stairs by himself and closed his door.

"He sleeps a lot," Win said.

"That's 'cause he's up all night," Jay said.

"What do you mean?"

"Nothing. I'm not supposed to tell anyone. Even you."

"Aw, you're goofing."

"Sure, that's it. Forget I even said anything."

"I will," Win said.

They played Camelot and Rook and Flinch on the living room rug, cheating to relieve the boredom. She would be early. The radio had on soap operas, all the ball games had been postponed. Jay told Win about Miss Swain.

"Bet she's dead," Win said, and rolled onto his back, eyes closed, tongue sticking out.

"There's one way to check," Jay said. "Go up there at night and see if the lights are on."

"Not me, brother."

Jay made chicken noises.

"You go if you're so brave."

"I go up there every day."

"Day's not night," Win said. "Day is easy."

They both knew it wasn't true, but Jay let it alone. He hadn't thought he'd miss working on the cottages. "Let's play Camelot again," he said.

Jay had just crossed the drawbridge when the phone rang. There was an extension in his grandfather's room; he waited until the third ring to get up and run into the front hall.

It was his mother—or no, another woman.

"Is this the residence of a Mr. J. Langer?" she asked politely, like in speech class. It sounded like it might be a joke. Is your refrigerator running?

"Yes," Jay said, deeply.

"This is Sally Wickes, with Western Union? I was wondering if there would be anyone home to receive a telegram later this afternoon."

His first thought was that his father wasn't home, or his mother. He should wake Grampa Langer and have him talk to her.

"Sir?"

"Yes," he said, "someone will be here."

He put down the phone and stood next to it for a second, as if it might ring again. That they had actually not known had never occurred to him. Now it was official. The curtains glowed. It was raining outside; he'd known all along, so why was it a surprise? He went back in to Win. He'd been winning, but exactly where their pieces had been was a mystery.

"What did you move?" he asked, and Win showed him. He slipped through the castle unchallenged, wary of a trap. There was none; Win had given up.

"Let's play something else."

"Rook," Jay said.

Win shrugged, and they swept Camelot into its box. While Win shuffled the cards, Jay went into the kitchen to get them some grape juice. He was shocked at how simple it was to keep a secret and how hard. A telegram could mean anything. He poured the two glasses and, as he put the pitcher back in the fridge, he remembered the Roll of Honor in *Life,* pages and pages of names bordered by gray stars. He'd immediately flipped to P and found Putney. There was only one name—Wilfred Bush—someone he'd never heard of, but he knew that at some time in his life he'd stood next to him at the magazine rack in the drugstore or passed him in the street, maybe ridden by his house every day. A telegram could mean everything, anything, nothing. He thought of Mr. Vogel turning on the porch light and Miss Swain and the star in his father's drawer and last night and Rennie, Rennie, Rennie, and he didn't know how he would tell his mother, or even what, now, he was telling himself.

MONTAUK SEEMED A FITTING PLACE TO END IT, the thin edge of the continent. Anne wanted to think that the news of Rennie hadn't changed her mind. What did missing mean, that they should trade their worry for hope? Their uncertainty was official now, their fear.

But this had to stop—the lying, the cheap treachery of it. Each day she meant to tell Martin at lunch but, sharing their sandwiches, it seemed so unceremonious, so wrong. She would be cheating them. For weeks they'd planned this one Saturday together, going over the details as if it were their honeymoon. It was, it was going to be. They had reservations at the Grand Hotel. Martin had already paid for his ferry tickets. She imagined them eating on the long porch, dwarfed by the high white pillars, watching the boats come and go. Here she would tell him. The waiter would pour more coffee, pretending to ignore her tears. The end of their affair, so slowly begun, still unfulfilled, deserved this final, perfect setting.

She hadn't been to Montauk since before the children. James had taken her to some cheap beach hotel—the Hollow Hills Inn, something like that. Twin beds and sand in the carpet. She'd have to pass it on the way out; there was only one way. On the map the road wriggled east, the land dwindling, shrinking around the red line; at the lighthouse, both stopped and the huge blue begun. The way they showed it—was it her?—there was no place to turn around.

It was true, Anne thought, driving out. For miles no one had passed the other way. She wore her uniform in case they stopped her. She had her new bathing suit and a change of clothes in the trunk. She had gas. At work she was signed out to support landing maneuvers; it would explain her miles. What an expert she'd become, like a spy icily disposing of an old friend.

Past Amagansett there was suddenly nothing—no houses, no trees, no grass. The land opened up, sand hills dipping, giving on the right a glimpse of the ocean, on the left, bay. The sky fit like a lid. An abandoned, ramshackle snack bar passed; its single bubble-headed gas pump and swinging, rust-eaten sign reminded her of the café in *The Petrified Forest*, Leslie Howard's beautiful chin. This, she imagined, was what the West must be like, empty, the distance thrilling, murderous. She knew it was untrue. Miles on, the road dead-ended in a parking lot; past that, the land narrowed, turned first to rock, then sand. Eventually even the sea stopped. Why did she need everything to be endless?

In minutes the weather turned. A convoy of dark-bottomed clouds streamed across the water, trapping the wan sun underneath. Her arms, burning before, shivered, hair prickling. Years back, the hurricane had come through here. It wasn't the season yet. She'd become accustomed to these quick shifts. It rained whenever they met, as if in judgment. Last Saturday at the clam shack overlooking the bay, Martin laughed and said he hadn't noticed, but here was irrefutable proof.

She'd almost let him last time, she couldn't remember now why she hadn't. He grew steely in her hand, adamant, reassuring. The roof drummed, the windows ran. On the back of the front seat, above the built-in ashtray, curved a browning swoop of blood from the accident. How many times she had imagined James here that winter, the bitch urging him into her. It had only been three years. She wasn't so old, was she?

Martin had let her see the picture of Evelyn he kept in his wallet. A dark blonde, she seemed hard but pretty, a bit vicious around the mouth. The plane of her cheeks seemed uneven, as if she'd been scarred as a child but healed well, learned to cover with makeup. The flash was merciless. Sadly, Anne realized she'd expected her to be better looking.

"She doesn't bother anymore," Martin said. "Neither do I. It's just wasted effort."

"You're lucky," Anne said. "James won't stop."

"At least he's trying."

"I'd much rather he didn't. Mr. Understanding."

"You're so lucky and you don't even know it."

"God," she said, "you wouldn't last ten minutes with him. It's like eating sugar right out of the bowl. He makes me feel like a mental patient."

"And you're not."

"No," she said, "although everyone seems to want to turn me into one."

She'd had him in her hands, and surprisingly it was all right. There was a line she hadn't crossed yet. It reminded her of college, the immense, unbreachable region between kissing and making love filled with detours, diversions, skirmishes. She could have had him then, was unsure why she stopped.

It had been the car probably, fat and sad and broken down as James himself, the chrome smile of its grille still hopeful though missing a row of teeth. That he'd kept her from taking Martin seemed stupid now. It seemed equally foolish that she was here now, going to meet him. He'd have to understand, it was the war, it was her son. And Martin would. They would both be reasonable.

James and his little bitch. Her father holding her arm, wanting her to hear all of it. The smell of his pillowcases. The telegram—missing in action.

She woke at the wheel, surprised to be driving, her eyes dutifully following the white lines. Clouds ground across the sky, the dunes dipped like telephone wires. There was no other traffic; if there were, she thought, it wouldn't matter. The choices she might have made once—the exits and turnarounds—were no longer available. There was one way out, one way back. The car followed the road.

Dark pines grew on both sides, thickened into forest, then just as suddenly thinned and disappeared in the mirror. Tan snakes of sand sifted across the asphalt, lulling, narcotic. She was tired of this second life, as if ungrateful for her own resurrection. If she dozed off, she would deserve the telephone pole, the stone mile marker. She wasn't good at this. Her mother had taught her everything she knew, equipped her with wisdom that, Anne later found out, had already failed her. She'd shown her how to dust and clean an oven, how to fold underwear and beat a rug, jobs that now seemed to Anne like her mother's life, wearisome and hopeless, obsolete. Her mother never drove and was afraid of the phone, shrank from answering it. She liked to be inside, alone. She'd been pretty—a bit of a local beauty—but long before Anne was born had gone to fat (mysteriously, monstrously) and by the time Anne was in grade school had such difficulty climbing stairs that she slept in the guest bedroom. Sundays were a torture for her. After the smiles and frantic hands of the receiving line, she served cake and coffee in the rectory, nodding to the conversation, then came home and slept deep into the gray afternoons. With her knitting and her plate of cookies, what did she know of lust? It was her father she should have asked, a master of the quick disappearance, the missed dinner. When James started coming home late, she'd thought nothing of it. Now she understood how difficult it was, this precious espionage. It seemed that no one had ever bothered to teach her anything; she'd had to learn everything herself.

In her reverie, the speedometer needle had crept to seventy. She took her foot off the gas and the car floated. Peeling billboards riffled by, a gull flattened to a rag. She was still waiting to see the place James had taken her when she hit the city limits.

She had a postcard of Montauk she kept in her desk at work. She pulled it out when no one was around and dreamed of walking the hot streets. Now its accuracy shocked her. She knew every roof. Below on her left, white shops and houses curled around the harbor; above them the Grand Hotel sat like a great ship at anchor, flags whipping atop its oversized cupola. She'd thought she'd remember it differently, but here it was, the same, as if these twenty years it had been waiting for her. Their one time here, she'd asked James if they could eat on the porch, and, flush from a spring of teaching, he decided to humor her. What a girl she'd been then, barely in her twenties. What an idiot.

In town, she was flustered by the number of people. Where had they come from? The sidewalks teemed with boys in shorts and girls showing off their shoulders, children zigzagging through fat families and tanned old men. The first few blocks she didn't see a parking spot. Except for two shore patrolmen sitting stiffly in a jeep in front of a fish market, there was no sign of the war.

It was a holiday of some kind. Bunting hung from lampposts, flags jutted from telephone poles. The Elks had set up a grill on the sidewalk and were selling beer (she checked her watch—ten o'clock). Ahead, the police had blocked off the street; one waved her to the left. She waited for the crowd to cross and eased into a narrow side street, took a right into an alley and shadowed Main. Back here people were parked illegally, fathers hauling out lunch baskets, mothers tucking babies into buggies. She rolled her window down and asked a woman what was going on.

"Independence Day," she said, and when Anne didn't respond, added, "Polish."

"Oh," Anne said, "I'm sorry." Later, waiting for the ferry, she knew she'd been rude. She should have said, "Congratulations."

She'd been afraid that she'd be late, now she was afraid he wasn't coming. She touched up her lipstick in the mirror, fixed her hair. She had on her one perfect pair of nylons. She debated dabbing a hint of Evening in Paris behind one ear and L'Air de Mystère the other, then compromised and used just the one she hadn't worn for him before. Subtly, she hoped, it would signal that things were different.

The car grew too hot, and she got out and walked along the

crumbling seawall. Water weighted the air, the heavy incense of fish; high up, clouds collided and bloomed, backlit, apocalyptic. At the ramp a crowd of natives strained toward their holiday on Shelter Island. With their children and dogs, their bicycles and binoculars, sweaters tied loosely around their necks, they seemed pitifully earnest, alive, blessed—everything she was not. They couldn't see through her uniform; the only one who suspected her was God, and she'd already fought him (what were all these years but a trial?). She thought she'd been reconciled to this sin—then Rennie. She was good at waiting, it was all her life had taught her.

Beyond the black arms of the breakwater, on the horizon, the ferry appeared, a gray dot slowly revealing its size and whiteness. He'd said the ten-twenty and it was ten-twenty, yet she was disappointed, as if suddenly exhausted by their preparations. She shouldn't have come at all.

They'd talked to Dorothy the night of the telegram. It was still day in San Diego, and the call woke her. She'd received hers a few hours ago.

"They do them that way," she said, and Anne thought it was shock.

"What are you going to do?" asked James, on the other line. "You know you're welcome here." He made it sound like he'd overridden her.

"I'm going to stay here and have our baby," she said, as if there were no question. "Rennie's going to come back."

"We all believe that," James said.

"Yes," Anne seconded, but she didn't and hated James for it. There was something smug and sickening in his belief. That he could hold it after all that had happened—all that he'd done—seemed proof of its worthlessness. He thought that witnessing the pain he'd inflicted somehow earned him her forgiveness. She'd never accept his.

The ferry slid across the harbor, a white brick growing windows, stairs, a name. It seemed small to be called the *North Star*. On the top deck, a few people leaned at the rail, tossing popcorn to the hovering gulls. She'd expected him up there, in the open, but didn't see him. She wondered what he was wearing—a simple linen shirt, she hoped, pressed, unbuttoned at the neck. Again, she thought of Leslie Howard, his thin nose. Martin didn't need much to be elegant. That one lunch in the dunes, she'd had to prompt him to unbutton her. "May I?" he asked, and waited, as if serving her at a banquet. He could be such a boy.

The crowd gathered their bags, mounted their bikes. She still didn't see him. The ferry churned past the slip, then backed in, the hull shuddering, and to her embarrassment, Anne found that she was responding to the ship—to him, of course, but, not having glimpsed him yet, it seemed her body was getting ready for the entire boatload of day-trippers, bikes and all. She tugged her skirt straight and folded her arms, scanning the jammed stairwells. The pilings shrieked.

And there he was, waving to her, in uniform, which made her laugh. He was just as bad at this as she was, a pair of absolute beginners. She was ready for him now, here, in the lot, in the car. Panicked, she looked around as if James or, just as plausible, her mother had followed her. The engines stopped, a ramp clanged against the dock, and passengers began to flow past her. When she saw him coming off, she had to stop herself from running to him, and then, surprising herself, did.

He stumbled under the force of her kiss, but recovered, lifting her. His mouth was hot and sweetened with mint, his hair smoky. How long she'd waited to do this in front of other people! She would not be cheated.

"Hel-lo," he said, overwhelmed.

She took his hand in hers and faced the crowd, this time defiantly, feeling beautiful and rude, daring anyone to refute her claim. "I didn't think you were coming," she confessed.

"It's going to rain, isn't it?"

"Yes. God, I had the wildest drive out here. I was thinking about my mother and almost flew off the road."

"Why your mother?"

"Oh, just how terrible her life was, how terrible she'd think this was."

"It *is* terrible," Martin said, as if setting up a joke, but didn't explain. He'd spotted the car.

"Do you really think it's terrible?"

"You do," he said. "And I don't think we should disagree about something so important."

"You said that like you mean it."

"I'm kidding. Is everything all right?"

"Yes." She pushed the telegram back down into the murk, but it stung.

Martin partly understood. "Shall we check in and have a swim?"

"Anything to get out of these awful clothes."

"Swell," he said, and they got in the car. Crossing the lot, she passed a chubby boy accompanying his mother, and for a crazy second imagined it was Win Rodman. She didn't look back to check.

The lot of the Grand Hotel was full; on the porch most of the people were in uniform. The lobby was cold and bustling; the leaves of potted palms shivered overhead. When she and James had eaten here, she'd excused herself and come inside just to see what it looked like. Now she couldn't remember if the carpeting had been this deep plum, the pillars gilded, the windows so high. She recognized only the treacherous polished marble floor, but the scheme of the room, the way they'd laid out the leather couches and wing chairs and glass coffee tables, seemed so complete that she was willing to believe nothing had changed. In the bathroom she'd been impressed by the soap dispenser, squirting the pink cream first onto the porcelain and then into her hand, sniffing it like a spice from the Indies. What a rube she was, even now, terrified of the desk clerk, the lurking bellboy. She held on to Martin's arm, sure everyone could tell how light her bag was.

She had money with her, and though Martin would insist on paying, just having the cash in her purse was a comfort. There was some power in knowing she could afford this. She'd been working all her life, yet never felt entitled to spend money on herself. There was always rent or food or clothes or shoes or the car had broken down again, and then for a time she hadn't been able to work. Her first Army paycheck seemed to seal her return to the world of the living.

With James working at Grumman, they were suddenly comfortable. These last few weeks she'd dreamed—seriously, she thought—of opening her own account. Now it wasn't going to happen, and with no reason to save, she wanted to splurge. It didn't bother her. It was only James who made her feel undeserving; with Martin she knew what she was worth.

She'd practiced signing her name for today, filling pages like a schoolgirl with a crush. Mrs. Anne Creighton. When Martin tilted the register toward her, she couldn't get the nib to lay a steady line and, flustered, rushed and bunched her own name. His came out perfectly. The clerk was busy with the key and didn't even check them; he was used to this. She resented his casual attitude. By tomorrow, Anne thought, she and Martin would rest together under hundreds of other lovers, and while she would never bear his name again, this officially made him hers.

"That was easy," he said in the elevator, and took her hand again. They watched the ornate pointer.

The room was colder than the lobby and smelled of camphor. Martin opened the drapes and light fell across the bed and into the dark bathroom. She put her bag on the low commode and sat on the bed, waiting for him to come away from the window. Now that they were here, she suddenly wanted to sleep.

"How do people do this?" she asked.

"I don't know," he said, and lay beside her, eyes closed, hands folded on his chest. The ends of his eyebrows rose in blond wings. She kissed him and ran her hand down his front and between his legs. She kissed him again, harder, massaging. He pulled her hand away and kissed it.

"We have all day."

"I know," she said, hurt. "I'm impatient."

"Do you want to change first?" he asked.

She took her bag into the bathroom and put on her new suit, checking herself in the mirror. The aqua set off her eyes and hid her waist. She leaned toward the glass and, making an O of her mouth, examined the whites of her eyes, then smiled and touched up her lipstick. In the picture, Evelyn was trying too hard to smile. How old was it, was she? When Anne had turned forty, she noticed a gray beginning to creep beneath her skin, as if she were going bad. Martin had never asked. She found her L'Air de Mystère and, flipping down her cups, touched the dropper under each breast.

When she came out he was already in his trunks, trying unsuccessfully to hide an erection. She pressed against him.

"Are you hungry at all?" he asked.

"Don't tease me like this," she said, then saw he was serious.

"I'm nervous."

"So am I," she said, giving up. She put on her terrycloth robe and stepped into her sandals.

"Swim first, then eat?"

"Whatever you want," she said.

He tried to make up, ridiculing the other tourists as they hiked out to the lighthouse, a pillar of chalk that seemed, in the heat, to be receding. She'd wanted to drive, but Martin, ever conscientious, said it wouldn't be proper. The sky was undecided; Anne was rooting for rain. As if to rebuke her, the clouds dissipated for the first time all day and the sun blazed through. He stubbed his toe on the road, and the malicious glee she felt when she heard a tool drop in the workroom and James curse filled her. Wasn't she supposed to be evil?

She'd hoped he'd take her to some cove where they could be alone, but the beach was covered with day-trippers and fishermen. She let him lead, and after a half mile he settled on a spot between a pair of teenagers and a large, red-haired family. In just his trunks, Martin seemed much longer, all bones. She was so used to James and his thickness. He'd remembered tanning lotion, and, lying with her eyes closed, the heat of the sand soaking through the towel, his fingertips smoothing the oil into her skin, she decided to forgive him.

"What about my front?" she asked.

"Later," he whispered, as if everyone could hear them—as if it weren't obvious.

This time of July the water was still brutally cold, but Martin convinced her to go in. She hid her watch under his shirt, pinned her hair and followed him through the drying wrack and smashed sand castles. She put a foot in and her nipples went hard; his puckered, dark as pennies. She waded in waist deep, then sank to her knees, groaning. A few children splashed in the shallows, laughing when the water knocked them down. She and Martin were the only adults.

They swam farther out, where the waves gathered to attack the shore. She floated, treading water, not wanting to get her hair wet, then gave up and lay back, looking at the sky. Martin's hand nibbled at her suit.

"I hope that's you," she said.

"Who else?" he said, and it was true; a hundred feet from the choked beach, they were alone. She slid a hand under his waistband and cupped him.

"Nervous?"

"Freezing."

"How late do they serve lunch?" she asked.

It was too cold to stay in more than a few minutes. She peed, secretly. Numb, they trudged back to their towels. Lying down, there was hardly any wind. In minutes he was asleep. She covered his hand with hers and gave herself up to the sun. It filled her, the way James had once, the way a look from Jay still could. The sand at her ankles itched. Behind her, two of the red-haired boys were playing catch, the steady rhythm of ball hitting mitt half obscured by the crash and whisper of the surf. She could almost imagine that they were alone, that she wouldn't have to go back—and yet, she thought, she'd never planned to leave James. If she convinced Martin to stay the night, in the morning she wouldn't know where to go.

"Are you willing to marry her?" she'd asked James—one of those insane nights he came home reeking of her. How could she compete with a girl? A wife, she'd learned not to adore him, to fight him over everything, to keep her dignity.

James walked past her into the kitchen. She didn't know why now, but even then she'd kept his dinner warm.

"Are you?" she called after him, and when he sat down to eat, sat across from him. "You think you would but you wouldn't. You're too responsible for that. It makes me sick. You think I couldn't take care of the children, you think I'd fall apart. Then go ahead, go to your little bitch, I don't care. You couldn't take care of them, you wouldn't know how. I've always done everything, you've never helped me with anything."

It was the same every night that winter. He didn't speak, but looked up from his plate, watching her with the patience of the condemned. In the morning she was hoarse. Her anger was like a disease, foaming, full-blown. She didn't stop until he was finished eating, and then (again, why?) she took his plate to the sink and washed it while he waited at the table, where, after blasting him with her back turned, she served him dessert.

"I don't want to leave you," he said one night after coffee, surprising Anne, "I want to leave *her*," and she could see he was helpless, that she could never again consider him hers.

"We were in love," her father said, as if this bland admission absolved him. He didn't name the woman, pointedly avoided any mention of her, as if he'd had the affair himself, without help. It was I or we, never she, but his description of their trysts, his guilt at sneaking down the alley behind the church, gave her away. When you come from a small town, you keep its geography. Only one house that backed the alley had a fire escape. Anne knew who lived there.

She'd never had cause to remember Mrs. Steurmer before. Her first image was of her reading the Lesson in her best dress, white, printed with lilies. As a child, Anne had admired her height. Peter Steurmer was two grades below her, invisible. Her husband worked in the mill and had a hunting cabin. In his den, Anne's father had a picture of the two of them kneeling beside a bear strung upside down in back of the courthouse. They each held a paw and a rifle. The men around them looked off to one side, pointing, as if there were another, larger bear just out of frame.

The Steurmers would have been at her mother's funeral—half of Galesburg was there to hear her father speak—but she couldn't see Mrs. Steurmer in crepe, hiding behind her veil. Frances, her father called her once, a slip which, in his pain, he didn't notice. Anne didn't know her first name—though this didn't seem to be it—and thought desperately that it might be the organist he'd hired after Mrs. Johns died. She'd boarded with the Steurmers, a tiny woman from Boston who wore a pitch pipe on a silver chain and made each row of the choir line up by height. She would have been easier to bear. Mrs. Steurmer was still living in the octagonal house on Breedlow Street, a widow going on twenty years. *F. L. Steurmer,* the phone book confirmed.

His funeral was smaller than her mother's. Unfairly, he'd outlived most of his parish. The ground was frozen, they wouldn't be able to inter him until April, but for ceremony's sake the pallbearers carried the coffin through the new snow and placed it on a pair of paint-stained horses on his plot. In his hard shoes, Jay kept slipping, and she angrily took his hand. It wasn't his fault, James's look said, and she softened. It wasn't hers, she wanted to say. The new minister, whose love of Roosevelt her father blamed for the dwindling congregation, gave the eulogy. Her mother's stone cast a shadow that reached Anne's feet. The trees were full of meaning.

Peter Steurmer accompanied his mother, his hair slicked down like a child's. He'd turned out slow; all day he stalked the shops downtown, talked to himself on the benches in front of the courthouse. It seemed, after her father's admission, a judgment. They stood in back, next to the reporter from the *Record*, breathing steam. Anne had expected her to cry, to give some sign, but after, when she came to pay her respects—Anne was now the family—Mrs. Steurmer lifted her veil, took her hands, and said, "Your father and my Frank were always so close."

Had her mother known and not told her? Or was not knowing worse? She was tired of thinking of it, picturing it, reliving it. She was tempted—as she'd been with her own betrayal—to see everything as an extension of her mother's torment, to retreat into the same crippling, familiar self-pity she hated in James. She thought she wouldn't then, yet it seemed that with time she had. She wasn't strong enough to lose Rennie yet.

The boys' ball landed, spraying her with sand. She let the

two argue over who would retrieve it, then sat up and threw it from her knees, her arm startling them. They waved their mitts in thanks.

Martin was still asleep, his back pink. She rocked him awake.

"What time is it?" he asked.

She reached under his shirt. His ferry left in an hour and a half. "We better get back."

"You shouldn't have let me sleep."

"We should have driven."

"You're right," he admitted.

It was hot in the parking lot, the lines for the restrooms long. The beach was beginning to empty. A scraggly column plodded toward town, families dragging their umbrellas and beach chairs like refugees. They marched down the yellow line, the rare car forcing them onto the spiny scrub of the berm, its wake peppering them with sand. There were no trees, yet cicadas screamed all around them. They stopped to buy lemonade from two girls sitting in a wagon. It was warm and, coupled with the sun, gave Anne a headache. Her suit stuck to her. She looked back to see if she'd heard a car, and the lighthouse towered.

"Lot's wife," she said.

"What about her?"

"What happened to her after she turned to salt?"

"I give up," Martin said, "what?"

"That's what I'm asking."

"Are you all right?"

"I'm hungry, I'm thirsty, I'm hot, I'm tired, and I have a headache."

"I agree," he said. "At least it didn't rain."

"Hasn't, you mean."

Over the town rose a giant thunderhead, white and corrugated like a brain.

"Salt pills," Martin said. "They made her into salt pills."

The hotel was freezing. They stopped at the pharmacy in the lobby for a packet of aspirin. No one seemed to notice them, and she was disappointed. In the elevator she could smell their lotion; gone cold, it fit like a waxy skin. Though they were alone, they didn't say anything. Martin had the key out. He'd gotten some sun. Disheveled, his shirt unbuttoned, he seemed half asleep. She wasn't much better, and she thought that if the doors rolled open and she saw the two of them like this, she'd think they'd been married for years.

The room seemed as new as when she'd first seen it. While they were out, the maid had straightened the bed.

"Are you going to take a shower?" Anne asked.

"Come look at the view," Martin said.

They were perched over the harbor. Below, the jetties reached for each other. It looked like it was raining out at sea, the clouds dramatically breaking the sun into rays.

"Are you going to take one?"

"You go ahead," he said.

Anne's bag sat hidden under the sink. She let the hot run into the tub while she laid out her things. She'd gotten some sun too, the ghost of her suit dazzling. She didn't want to look too closely; she trusted her luck to hold. She trusted Martin would be a gentleman.

The shower was stronger than the one at their place, wonderfully scalding. She opened a soap and washed off the lotion. Sand tanned the water. While she was doing her hair, the door opened and a cold breeze stirred the steam. Martin stepped in with her, one hand on the wall for balance.

He was already long, nudging her hip. He knew she liked to look at him, but hid himself against her as if embarrassed—and somehow he was. She'd thought this was easier for him, had perhaps relied on his expertise too much. Was he thinking of Evelyn or, like her, of his long-buried parents? She didn't want to think now, and kissed him, closing her eyes, one hand soapily cupping him. He murmured her name; he was with her now, the smooth, hard bar of him pressed against her. She tried to guide him into her, but he was too tall, she was too short, it was too slippery, and taking him in one hand, she threw the shower curtain aside and led him to the bed, her hair still foamy with shampoo.

He slipped into her without help, the first delicious, filling slide making her gasp. She laughed. With James she always shut her eyes, and now she looked up to find Martin's closed.

"Look at me," she said, and he did. She'd worried about the light, about her stretch marks, her imperfections. She'd forgotten so much about love. Martin arched, and they caught each other looking down, admiring the sweet point where they had finally, after all this time, joined. It was a discovery that, suddenly humble, neither could take full credit for.

She was meeting him now, trying to find the speed she needed. She hadn't honestly made love in so long that she felt self-conscious, as if she were learning both it and him, just as he, out of nervousness, seemed preoccupied, trying to pay attention to everything at once. They seemed to be hurrying.

Just as her first soft flutterings struck, he slipped out of her. She moaned, annoyed, and reached down and fit him in again. He roughly thumbed her nipples; she thought, not caring, that they would be sore tomorrow. What was tomorrow? He took one into his mouth, his hair tickling her, his chin gritty. She was beginning to lose herself without willing it, and as she'd promised she wouldn't do, closed her eyes and slowly rolled her head from side to side, concentrating, her lower lip pinched between her teeth.

In the swell, she pictured herself, them, centered on the bed, and couldn't stop herself from seeing James's little bitch, her crooked front teeth, her girl's body expertly taking James—and she thought of him when they were first dating, how he liked to park his Chalmers across from the mill and kiss his way into her shirt, the falls whispering, misting the windows.

Martin's breath seized, and he started to pull out. She pulled him deep into her and kept him there, bucking, her calves wrapped around the backs of his thighs. She hadn't thought herself so close, but with him shaking against her, she tightened about him, then let everything go. She felt herself pouring. He went still, then drove forward, knocking the side of his face against the headboard. They'd crept up the bed. He thrust twice, three times, as if exhausted, giving up, then burned into her. Instead of collapsing to one side like James, he stayed above her, balanced on his arms. She nursed the last of him, now soft and drawing out. He looked at her as if it were wrong.

He didn't have to say he'd brought safeties. He'd remembered lotion; he remembered everything. They were probably in his bag, and not the cheap ones from the PX. Her times were so irregular she couldn't remember her last one. She'd known it was wrong, but he'd known how much she wanted him. Now she'd had him.

He rolled off, gone soft, glazed and babyish in his nest of hair, candied. She dabbed at him with a corner of the sheet, wrapped him around her thumb. Hers.

"Annie," he said fearfully, for it was dramatic now, the light in the room suddenly changed, a cloud drifting in front of the sun.

She answered him, and it was true now; it was no longer a game.

On the phone to San Diego, she'd thought that Dorothy's wails and tears were true, while her own were somehow false—that she herself was false, a false mother, a false wife, a false daughter, and, sobbing, she promised to stop seeing Martin. Now she knew she'd been lying to herself as well. They were lovers, they were real.

He had thirty-five minutes. They showered again, soaping each other, marveling at the endless hot water. Toweling off, they fell on each other. She'd gone beyond sore, and held him hard against her. In the steamed mirror, they seemed to blend into one.

She didn't want to get dressed. She wanted to sleep beside him, let his long body settle against hers. It was impossible, yet she wanted him to acknowledge her wish. He stopped her from putting on her bra, kissed each breast, then held her, half dressed in the chilly room. Over his shoulder, drops dotted the window.

"It's raining," she said, and they broke.

"You knew it would."

She buttoned her shirt. "I owe you lunch."

"Do we have time?"

"No."

They packed, sidestepping each other in the bathroom. Their uniforms seemed comic, sad, asinine. Now that they were leaving, she wanted to remember the room, the walls the color of lime sherbet, the cream baseboards and unused brass gas fittings. She resisted taking a pack of matches. They took a last look over the harbor and kissed again. How many times did they have to say goodbye?

"Do you have everything?" Martin asked at the door.

"Yes," she said.

The hall was empty, as it had been all day. Far off, thunder crunched. On the way down, the elevator stopped for two elderly women—sisters, Anne thought, from the way they held each other up—breaking the delicate spell of the afternoon. When the doors opened, the rest of the world flooded in.

The desk clerk accepted the key without looking. The hotel had a taxi that ran to the ferry, a peppermint-striped surrey drawn by a pair of steaming horses. The driver, dressed like a pirate, stood in the parking lot in the rain, ringing a handbell.

"You want to eat," Martin said.

"I want to eat with you."

"Don't be like this," he said. "You'll eat with me on Monday. You've been dreaming of this for weeks. You can see the ferry from here. I'll wave to you."

He kissed her once, dryly, holding her hands. She wanted him to say something (not "I love you"), but he only looked at her, half sadly, as if he were sorry, she would have to be brave. He was the last one on the surrey, squeezing between two Marines. She watched him from the stairs, utterly defeated.

The porch was empty, covered with puddles from the storm. She asked for a table at the far end, ordered coffee and sat watching the thin rain. Her waiter didn't come back until the ferry was in sight, inching toward the gap of the breakwater. With the distance, the ship was too small to see Martin; she didn't wave. It was windy, and the coffee was good. She still had half a cup left when she lost sight of the gray dot. She sat another ten minutes, finishing it before leaving. She figured she was paying for it anyway.

The festival was dwindling, drunks stumbling in the alleys. The police waved her through Main, now open, slick and smeared with horseshit. Children dared her, sprinting curb to curb. She passed, throughout town, a scattered marching band wandering instrumentless, like a routed army. Firecrackers snapped, hot dog wrappers sailed in her wake. Everyone was waving little red-and-white flags, as if, alone, in James's ugly car, she could liberate them.

Outside of town it was foggy, the rain settling into the dunes. She was on time, but kept the Buick above the limit, thinking that if she was early, she wouldn't need an excuse. The road dipped into the pines. She turned on her lights, flicked her wipers to HIGH. Coming over a rise, the car seemed to float off the road a second, her stomach jumping, and she slowed. There were deer out here. She peered into the woods. On the ocean side, where the hill dropped off, stood an inn, lit against the weather. VACANCY blazed in red neon. She glimpsed it for only an instant; in the mirror it was invisible, but Anne could re-create it. The Hither Hills Inn. She remembered when she and James drove out from the Langers' they couldn't find the place, passing the entrance three or four times before they asked at a gas station.

On the porch of the Grand Hotel they'd sat together on one side of the table, watching the harbor, the sun warming her arms. She'd been waiting the whole trip for the moment to tell James she was pregnant, and as they lingered over their coffee, she thought, Not yet; let this be a different kind of perfect.

The pines passed back, the dunes flattened, telephone poles rocketing off to infinity. The sky had gone dark, the bay hidden by a veil of rain. On the ocean side, miles out, lightning cracked, burned in her eye like a dying filament. The sea rolled in, wind beating the car. The Buick smashed through a long puddle, throwing a muddy wave, and she put on the heater. A summer squall, it would pass in minutes. Hurricane season was a month away. In an hour she'd be back at the house, Martin with Evelyn, and time would kick in again. For now, no one knew where she was. The idea pleased her until she remembered, as if she'd forgotten to pick up a quart of milk, that she had meant to leave Martin.

"He's coming back," Dorothy had said, and Anne wanted to believe her, her father, her mother, James.

She thought she should be seeing the abandoned café soon; she couldn't have passed it. In the mirror there was nothing, ahead there was nothing. There was only one road, she knew, yet Anne couldn't rid herself of the feeling of being not missing but monstrously, irretrievably lost.

THREE DAYS OUT OF SAN FRANCISCO it began to snow. Rennie had just come out for the second dog watch, accepting the holstered pistol from Mowry as if it were a diploma. The night was foggy. Lacy, wet flakes swarmed in the light from the hatch. That afternoon Rennie had fallen asleep in the sun and burned his back; now for a second he couldn't process it, stood watching his shadow riding the dark water. To maintain blackout, Mowry had to push him inside and close the hatch.

"Alaska," Rennie said.

"No shit Alaska," Mowry said, stripping off his armband. "It figures, after all that crap about dengue. How's chow?"

"Liver and onions."

"Figures," Mowry said.

The decks were empty, the other ships in the convoy steaming unseen, lost in the dark. Wind sang in the rigging, rimed the twin barrels of the ack-ack battery. Rennie wasn't dressed for the weather, and paced the starboard rail to keep warm, hands in his armpits, leaning with the slow rolling of the ship. The pistol belt and his unsteady gait made him look, he imagined, like a drunken gunslinger. Ridiculously, he had orders to kill anyone who failed to identify himself.

He'd handled an identical .45 once on the range at Fort Emory. A gunnery sergeant with a cleft palate had instructed the company's aid men in releasing the clip and slapping in another, thumbing the safety and lining up the sights. One by one, with the sergeant standing behind them like an umpire, they each emptied a clip at a limbless silhouette no farther than a pitcher's mound. The gun jumped in Rennie's hands. His first two rounds bit into the wooden frame above the target's head.

"You're jerking," the sergeant said. "You want that trigger finger to curl up like a worm. Everybody, watch Langer here show you how it's done."

Holding his breath, Rennie bracketed the center of the torso with the rear sight, tipped the post of the front into the gap and pulled against the stiff trigger. His aim wavered, the post swinging over the target's shoulder. He kept drawing on the trigger, a sweaty knife against the inside of his knuckle. As the sight dipped across the heart, he clenched the grip and fired, exhaling.

"In the kidney," the sergeant announced. "Not a pretty shot, but it'll stop a man. Give 'em again."

He hit the man in the neck, missed to the right of his head, then missed altogether and put his final bullet high in his chest.

"That," the sergeant said to the group, "is why you are medical personnel."

Now Rennie remembered the sound of the gun, the metal and oil and quick spit of smoke overpowering, a raw, foreign liqueur. The sergeant's unfortunate lip. "It is either you," the sergeant said, "or Mr. Nip," and when anyone missed cleanly, poked that man between the eyes, leaving his finger there, and said, "You're dead, Private."

It meant nothing, Rennie thought; he wouldn't be called upon to fire on anyone, just to clean up. They'd attended a lecture in basic, Kill or Be Killed, during which the instructor gouged a dummy's eye out with a thumb, then stomped on his groin with such force that the mess hall floor shook. Rennie couldn't imagine himself doing that to someone, only someone doing it to him. In Alaska, the Japanese waited, dug in, squinting through the falling snow.

Aft, a hatch opened, shedding a buttery light, and a soldier stepped out. Mowry must have told someone, or maybe the man was just sick. Rennie headed toward him, a hand on the icy rail.

It was the colonel, dressed in a flimsy poncho and drab watch cap. He was a small man with a large head, his face withered around his nose and stiff brush of a mustache. In the last war he'd been gassed, and when he formally addressed the company before they left Fort Emory, they could barely hear him. "It is no secret," he'd croaked, "that we are going to the South Pacific." Now he must have come out to check the weather, to see if the rumors were true.

Rennie drew himself to attention and saluted. The colonel returned it and leaned in to read Rennie's name tag. He kept a hand on the rail.

"Langer," he said, "I don't know you," and looked back out to sea, as if dismissing him. Schooled in his father's majestic distance, that teacher's mix of arrogance and absentmindedness, Rennie knew he was supposed to wait for him to speak again. The snow made him blink.

"Langer," the colonel said.

"Yessir."

"Can you ice-skate?"

"Yessir."

"How about the rest of your platoon?"

"Medical battalion, sir."

"A doc that ice-skates," the colonel said.

"Yessir."

"What advice would you give someone who never ice-skated in their life, what one thing?" He looked to Rennie as if, despite his amusement, he really wanted to know.

"To lean forward, sir?"

The colonel laughed and patted Rennie's shoulder. "That's fine, Langer. I'd have said tie a big pillow around your behind, but I like yours better." He glanced out to sea again, then nodded as if satisfied. "You keep this area clear now. That includes colonels."

"Yessir," Rennie said, and saluted him into the hatch.

Later, relieving him, Fecho stopped to marvel at the snow, almost dropping the pistol. "Mowry wasn't lying."

"It's Alaska," Rennie nodded.

At breakfast, everyone knew. Later that morning, Supply verified it by allotting each man a parka and new boots, long underwear. The deck was littered with inspection slips. Rennie checked the seams of the parka before turning in his old poncho.

"It's from Pittsburgh," Mowry said. "You don't have to worry."

"Notice anything different about the pants?" Fecho asked. "No belt."

"So?"

"So this," Fecho said, and, holding a fist level above his head, pretended to hang himself. Only that night did Rennie remember his lucky quarter. In his bunk he swore, and someone told him to pipe down.

He still didn't believe it was Alaska. In training, they'd taken San Clemente Island unopposed. The afternoon had been balmy, the water warm as broth. An amtrac crushed one man's toes; otherwise the assault was bloodless. A crowd of civilians applauded from the roped-off parking lot. Burger waved to the girls, Mowry bowed. The next weekend, on furlough, Rennie took Dorothy to see the beach—covered with umbrellas, as if the Seventh had never been there. Then, sand had erased them, now snow. Fecho figured they had a week.

It hurt Rennie to think of Dorothy now, alone in San Diego. He read her letters in his bunk before lights out, the hardest part of the day. In his worst moments he was sure the baby would be deformed, eyeless, six- or three-fingered, or she would die (that he would die, leaving her the baby). He'd hurt her enough already. His last furlough they'd spent the morning in bed, the clock to the wall. She was enormous and short of breath. She couldn't stop crying, then, temporarily recovered, laughed at herself. They ate lunch on the Crystal Pier, fighting off seagulls. They didn't talk about the war, ignored the stray cruiser headed for the bay, the drunken sailors streaming around them. All day they feigned innocence, asked nothing, brought nothing up, afraid to admit these might be their last minutes together. At the gate, they kissed, wringing the last second from the guard's watch. Here was the opportunity to tell her not to worry, that he would be back, but, stubborn—it was his mother in him, that adamant belief in the truth—he couldn't. "Time," the guard said, and Rennie kissed her and whispered that she would be fine, the baby would be fine. Inside the gate, he waved, walking backwards, then turned and headed for the mess, relieved. Now he saw something unpleasant and cowardly about it, and promised (how?) to make it up to her. Yet in his letters he said nothing, went on about his friends, the chow, the crowding. Though she was stronger than he was, Rennie didn't want his fear to frighten her. He kissed her picture goodnight, and every day sent a letter, but he tried not to think of her, or of his mother and father, or Jay or Cal, and so of course did.

The days grew shorter. Mornings, reveille poured from the caged speaker in their berth, and at night, mournfully, taps. Between the two stretched a soft wall of swing, broken occasionally by the bosun's whistle signaling an announcement. Chow, mail call, the smoking lamp is lit. They were tired of Harry James and *Stars and Stripes* and limp green beans. Making the picture of Rita Hayworth or Marjorie Reynolds speak became a chore. They policed their area, grimly faced KP, and manned the sick bay in pairs, doling out sound advice to the queasy and taping the occasional sprained ankle (every day a few men drunk on pruno or smuggled-in whiskey flew down a ladder), but really there was nothing for them to do. While the infantry stripped their weapons, they lazed about on deck, playing checkers and listening to the band—their stretcher bearers, like themselves, defenseless. They re-created whole games from old box scores, made up new movies. They watched the other ships, the shadows of clouds. Once, a Catalina buzzed them; they cheered the black flash, stood at the rail, hoping it would circle back. It didn't, and they cursed the pilot, spent a minute inventing his death.

They knew where they were going. There were briefings all the time now, the mess rearranged around a sand table from which rose a humped and gullied island—Kiska. Tin models of the convoy stood offshore. They all followed the lieutenant's pointer, imagining the dug-in batteries elevating, their shells whistling, throwing white geysers. The weather officer produced tide tables, presiding winds. The Air Corps had promised the colonel P-38s to keep the Japanese torpedo planes out of their hair. "For what that's worth," he said. Behind him, in the kitchen, Burger waved, stirring a vat of soup with a steel paddle. Staggered waves of landing craft approached the estimated cone of fire. Five tin soldiers established the tiny beachhead and drove inland. There were no questions.

"I am not going to lie to you," the colonel said. "They may not know we're coming, but they're waiting for us. And they've been waiting a long time."

Again, the old man sounded like his father, trying to fire the Putney Millers up before they took the field. It's not the size of the dog in the fight. He'd come to the mound once when Rennie was getting bombed and asked, "Are you giving up? 'Cause that's what it looks like. No? Then this next guy, you hit him."

"Why?" Rennie said.

"So *they* know you're not giving up."

He hit the batter in the back, and the next half inning, when Rennie was up, the other pitcher threw behind his head before striking him out with a roundhouse curve.

"All part of the game," his father had said on the way home (they'd lost, they always lost, it was chronic), just as now the colonel was saying, "Not everyone on this tin can is going to be coming back. That is the nature of war."

"What a heroic bunch of crap," Burger said that night, picking up his hand. They were playing in the head to avoid the watch. Rennie had a pair of eights and junk. "He's the goddamn commander. He knows *he's* coming back."

"Lang can tell who's going to make it just by looking," Fecho said. "Their faces get all green, isn't that right, Lang?"

"Hear that, Mowry? You're not coming back."

"Just ante."

"Want to die?" Fecho asked Burger. "Keep playing the way you're playing."

Rennie discarded one eight.

"Looking to fill the straight," Burger said, and gave him a nice safe six of clubs. Rennie bluffed and lost a dollar, writing it off as an investment.

Now it was cold all the time. The infantry wore fingerless gloves to break down their M-1s. On watch, Rennie had to pace to stay warm. The new boots chafed. To starboard the destroyer escort's bow splash glowed, ghostly. Under the low fog, snow dropped into the sea.

In Putney the river ran black in spring, the thaw piling ice on the banks like smashed china. He stayed out of the house, ran the mile loop between the mills, sprinting down one side and back up the other, walking the bridges, trying not to think. He nearly succeeded. He was in shape for the season, though his father was no longer the coach and, as things turned out, Rennie didn't play. He got a job after school at Wheeler's auto parts, shelving plugs and stacking mufflers in the dusty, windowless gloom. Each week he saved his pay, dreaming of leaving town, and then before graduation his father said he was sending him to college, the money coming from his Grandma Langer, whom Rennie had never met. All his mother would say was that his father's mother had died when his father was a boy. "The mysterious benefactress," Cal toasted, chuckling drunk.

On watch he thought like this, skimming his life, the distant summers and first snows, girls he alone worshiped. Every night he paced, replaying the same dull melodramas until the colonel appeared, lost in his new parka. The colonel liked to take the air after supper. He leaned against the rail, peering off into the fog or snow or, the rare night, up at the stars, seemingly bigger here, bulging from the unsullied black. He knew Rennie now, and didn't straighten up to return his salute, just nodded at the water. Rennie expected they would talk again, cryptically, like mentor and apprentice, and while they never did, his presence was enough to clear Rennie's head.

"Landfall tomorrow," Fecho said, taking the pistol.

"Says who?"

"Mowry heard from Cookie. We're out of flour. We'll take on supplies at Adak, then head for the objective."

"How far is it from there?"

"Less than a day. Get some rest; we'll be busy tomorrow." Fecho seemed disappointed that Rennie didn't ask why. He made a gun of one hand, cocked the thumb and shot himself in the foot.

"Not funny."

"I agree," Fecho said.

On board, the news spread like typhoid. The next morning the deck was overflowing. D-Day-minus-two was brilliant but frigid, windy, the flags cracking. The new parkas were thin, and supply made their old ponchos available. There were three drab haystacks—large, medium and small. Rennie didn't see his, and picked one issued to CARPENTER, L. Everyone looked like a bum, beet-cheeked and badly wrapped. They jammed the rails, sharing borrowed binoculars. Beside them, the destroyer glided low in the water, knifelike, its decks empty, professional.

"Adak," Fecho said. "That what you're going to name the kid?"

Burger laughed. "Adak Putney Lang."

"Kiska if it's a girl."

"Clam up," Rennie said, playing along. Forward, someone shouted and everyone turned toward the noise, pointing off starboard. They began to cheer.

"I don't see squat," Mowry said, and gave Burger the binoculars.

"I got it," Burger said, leaning out and pointing as if he could almost touch it.

Rennie adjusted the ridged wheel, and the blur turned into a dark line riding the water—he would have thought it was another ship if he hadn't expected it. Land. He lowered the binoculars and it disappeared.

"That's it?" Mowry said, disappointed.

Rennie took them back. The island was still there, slowly growing, irresistibly drawing them onward.

Closer, they saw a whole string of islands, mountainous, the land stark, all ice and mud and black rock. There were no trees, not one. They slid through a strait abreast another LST, the companies calling their designations back and forth, the fierce numbers echoing off the sheer walls.

No one left the rail until they made harbor, dropping anchor in sight of a compound of drab tents, Quonsets and whitewashed saltboxes huddled around the docks. A hundred yards to starboard, like a huge new toy, sat a battleship, beside it a heavy cruiser. A few Catalinas dotted the water, lashed to buoys. The wreckage of one floated belly up like a dead fish, still attached. Launches began to ferry supplies aboard. The speakers announced lunch, but no one wanted to go belowdecks. Finally there was something to look at.

Rennie and Burger were in sick bay that afternoon when the first self-inflicted came in. The man was drunk. He was short and heavy, a Swede with a whitish mustache and pink-rimmed eyes; Rennie had seen him on deck, in the mess. He'd broken three fingers of his left hand, badly, a purple dent running across the knuckles. He said his buddy had closed a hatch on him. Burger splinted them and told him to report to his CO.

"Why?" the Swede asked.

"You can't fight with one hand," Burger said.

"Please," the man begged, and Rennie could see he was terrified, that he'd lost even the dignity of being a victim. Before, Rennie had given him the benefit of the doubt, not wanting to know; now, complicit, an immense contempt for the man filled him, though in California he himself had contemplated blowing off a pinky. The act was the decision. It was, he thought, a kind of surrender, one that no longer tempted him.

When the man had left, Burger laughed. "Poor yellow bastard, all he had to do was break one."

Rennie resisted returning his smirk.

There was a form they were supposed to fill out if they considered a wound suspicious. The Ticket to Leavenworth, they called it. Later that day, a man came in who'd shot himself in the foot, and Mowry had to write him up for lack of imagination.

On watch, Rennie expected the colonel to come out to see the land by moonlight, but the aft hatch stayed closed. Rennie found the Cats and other ships distracting. It was his last watch before they went ashore; from here on in they would observe general quarters. He thought he would remember more of Dorothy, or perhaps his father, but he kept seeing the house on Pearl Street, touring the stale, sunlit rooms he'd grown up in, the glass doorknobs faceted like giant diamonds, the wallpaper's endlessly repeated lilies, the rumble of the coal chute. His mother kept the essay he'd written on Ethan Allen in her bookshelf between Charles Lamb and Joseph C. Lincoln. His Green Mountain Boys like Robin Hood's Merry Men, his victory at Ticonderoga. "You can beat these guys," his father always said when they were down a bunch of runs. The smell of his mitt. Fireworks painted their faces after the Fourth of July doubleheader, the finale's curtain of embers dropping into the river, then applause, car doors thunking shut, and finally night. Here, there, the moon pooled on the water, silvered its swirls and currents. He stopped and felt his arm, but it was the wrong poncho, the quarter was gone. Fecho was late relieving him. There had been two more self-inflicteds, one a failed suicide who'd drunk a pint of turpentine.

They left Adak after breakfast, the last launch taking off garbage, a good part of which, Rennie saw, was their old clothes. He thought of the women arriving at the mill those cold mornings. In school, they'd taken the tour, though half of the women were their mothers, their aunts, their older sisters. Rows of sewing machines chittered. Each woman had pictures of her children, her own ashtray and, hanging above the jumping bobbin, a calendar from the bank, the funeral parlor or the hardware, the days religiously crossed off. How many hours and waited-for coffee breaks did this barge represent?

It was foggy. A half hour out, the colonel ordered everyone belowdecks. The infantry stripped their weapons again, dug through their gear, eliminating weight. Toothpaste, underwear, and unloved C rations littered the tables of the mess. Burger asked each medic to inventory his rucksack. They checked off the adrenalin and plasma and caffeine, the morphine Syrettes and sulfa powder, pressure dressings and Vaselined gauze, bandage scissors and hemostats. Except Burger, they were all thirteen-week wonders, untested. They'd supported maneuvers on San Clemente and in the desert, where the shadow of the aid tent, a few salt pills and a dipper of water cured everything. The rest of their training had been films or bloodless exercises, treating each other's imaginary wounds. Now, D-minus-1, they went through the litany again. Administer plasma against shock and loss of blood, douse wound with sulfa, apply battle dressing, administer morphine against pain, remove patient to aid station.

"Gushing blood?" Burger quizzed.

"Sponge off wound," Rennie answered, "locate bleeder, pack with dressing."

"Weak pulse, shallow breathing."

"Adrenalin?" Mowry guessed.

The lieutenant came over and asked if they could do this somewhere else, and Rennie noticed that though the mess was jammed, the tables on either side of them were empty. Burger had never heard of the superstition, but it was true, they moved like ghosts through the living, fearfully ignored. In the gangways, no one said hello.

At the last briefing, only the band acknowledged them. Dinner had been pushed back; the air in the mess was heavy with the smell of roast turkey. The island on the sand table had changed. It was larger, the ships split up, attacking opposite sides. The lieutenant had to blow his whistle to quiet the room.

They had a new objective, Attu. It was supposed to be easier—fewer Japanese, no heavy artillery.

"The Army has decided to follow the path of least resistance," the colonel said. "I know we're all for that."

Rennie's battalion would support the south force beachhead. The first wave of landing craft departed tomorrow at 0730. The weather officer predicted sleet and fog with thirty-mile-an-hour winds from the west.

"Are there any questions?" the lieutenant asked, and when no one spoke, added, "Enjoy your dinner."

It was real turkey, with mashed potatoes and both bread and meat stuffing. The servers, in fresh aprons and preposterous toques, ladled gravy, spooned squash and pearl onions in cream sauce, sliced cranberry jelly still holding the shape of the can. The sectioned mess trays sagged under the weight. For dessert they had pie and ice cream, and afterward sat around their berth, groaning and smoking, supplied by the fifty-tin of Lucky Strikes Mowry's girl had sent him. Burger pulled a pint of rye from his duffel and passed it around.

"Now I know we're going to buy it," Fecho said, and though it wasn't funny, they all laughed.

"How do you want to go?" Burger asked.

"You first," Mowry said.

"I won't. I'll be in my little tent patching your asses. I don't even have artillery to worry about now. Fetch?"

"One shot, right in the head."

After a pause, Mowry softly seconded, "Yeah."

"Lang?"

"The same, I guess," Rennie said.

"Boring," Burger said. "You guys deserve to die."

At the briefing the colonel had suggested they write letters. Lights out would be early tonight, and Burger said they should get started on them. It was important, he said, not to leave anyone out; if there had been hard feelings between you and a loved one, maybe now was the time to put them aside. It was important to be honest. Throughout, Burger rolled his eyes and threw in asides ridiculing the idea of a letter from the dead, as if he was bound officially to give the speech. They enjoyed the act, thin as it was. They knew what he was saying was true. No one wanted to break up the party, but sheepishly they agreed and retreated to their bunks.

Rennie hadn't intended to write anything new, just a short note each to Dorothy, his father and mother, Jay. He began, as Cal had taught him to approach problem sets, with the toughest, but instead of simply saying that he loved him, Rennie found himself telling Jay why he'd enlisted. *I'm here—we're here—to keep people alive. It's a choice the men in my battalion have made not to take lives but not to close our eyes to the war either.* It made sense to him now, but he'd never spelled it out so neatly, and, afraid of appearing self-righteous in his parents' eyes (for surely they'd read it, gauging his sensitivity, this extra blow Jay had taken), he crumpled it up and began another. He was still working on the new version when lights-out sounded.

Mowry was already in the head, working on a letter. He sat on a john, his periscope flashlight sticking out of his shirt pocket. Rennie took the one beside him, clicked his own flashlight on, and hunched over the letter to Jay. Burger and Fecho came in and did the same, the steel floor freezing their feet through their thin issue slippers. On the wall opposite, their hands moved, giant.

"What's another word for miss a lot?" Fecho asked.

"Pine," Rennie said.

"Don't use that," Burger said.

"I got one," Mowry said. "Long."

"Not bad," Fecho admitted.

"Why not just say I miss you a lot?" Burger asked.

Fecho and Mowry looked at each other and shook their heads.

As Rennie went through Jay and his mother, tacking unexpectedly, then crossing the sudden thought off, he found he was writing what he'd first intended. Dissatisfied, resigned, he copied out the stiff, simple sentences. How impossibly elegant the words of Cal's mother seemed now, not only fitting but a kind of gift to him. He thought of reciprocating, surprising her with a letter from the edge of battle—but no, he had his father to argue with now, to thank, to once again petition. Dear Dad. Coach L.

Mowry was done first. He addressed and sealed his envelopes and stood. "I'll see you guys tomorrow," he said, and they all said goodnight back. It was 0200, and Rennie was only starting on Dorothy. Beside him, Burger ran out of paper, and he handed him a few sheets. Fecho yawned darkly above his flashlight, molars glinting.

Dorothy was the easiest. She didn't need a letter. He didn't have to give her instructions on how to feel about him. His insurance wasn't much, he said. He addressed a paragraph to the baby, then deleted it. He didn't know what to call the baby: Jennifer, Stephen, Jennifer-or-Stephen? And if she miscarried, what then? Being a tragedy himself, he saw the potential in everyone else, every endeavor. *I'm writing this in the latrine,* he wrote. *Burger and Fecho and Mowry are here. We're friends, so tonight I'm not lonely. Tomorrow we'll keep an eye out for each other, and that's enough reason to go.* He hadn't known he thought this way until he was done writing it. Even the embellishment was true. Still, he was only convincing himself. He crossed it all out and started again.

Burger finished and reminded them to get some sleep. Again, Rennie copied what he'd settled on, a note quick and predictable as a Christmas card. He left Fecho in a nest of paper.

He thought he'd have trouble getting to sleep, but once in his bunk, lying flattened and still to drum up some heat, he let himself be lulled by the absolute black, the sea, the berth's soft slobber. He woke to darkness, the radium face of his watch barely changed. An hour later he came awake again, and throughout the morning, as if he'd miss an appointment. At five he decided to use the head and found Stephenson dealing a game of seven-card stud. When he finally did drop into a warm dream (their honeymoon in Hawaii, except Dorothy wore a uniform too, and people kept throwing change at them, showered them with hard, silver rice), reveille broke the surface and hauled him into the cold world. It was D-Day.

Everything was the last—the last pillow, the last shower, the last clean fatigues. For breakfast they had steak and eggs, unlimited seconds. The colonel wasn't at his table. Rennie ate quickly and, while they were rechecking their equipment, kept burping. He noticed that he was impatient, half distracted, as if he had a bad headache. It reminded him of the days he was scheduled to pitch, his concentration narrowed by terror. Stanch bleeding with battle dressing, remove to aid station. Burger had them ready ten minutes early.

They fell out in the half-enclosed staging area forward of the cargo bay, by the bow doors. No one would look at them. It was sleeting. The air was heavy, the roll of the ship noticeable. Rennie could smell the rifles. He had his letters tucked under his battle rations, his picture of Dorothy in his vest pocket, cornily over his heart. No longer necessary, bunched camouflage netting hung the length of the bay; two mechanics from the motor pool vaulted the gunwales of the amtracs, turning their motors over. Chuffs of diesel smoke rose into the fog. The colonel addressed them from a stepped platform on which, almost a week ago, the ship's boxing champions had bowed down to accept paper medals. He seemed even smaller to Rennie, like Jay swimming in one of his old coats. The lieutenant signaled for quiet, though there was no need.

"You can relax," the colonel said. "We have an abort due to severe conditions. The weather officer says it's going to be like this all day.

It's my feeling that they'll try to get us in as soon as they see an opening, so don't go anywhere."

The colonel stepped down. The lieutenant raised his clipboard and ordered them back to their berths. A few ranks ahead of Rennie, a man vomited.

"That guy," Burger said later, "I wanted to puke right on top of him."

"A-men," said Mowry.

They tried at 0930, but again the colonel mounted the platform and dismissed them. Those days he was scheduled to pitch, Rennie prayed for rain. In class, he watched the undecided sky, the clouds scouring the mountains. He fought the buttons of his stiff flannel jersey, hands clammy, but with the first pitch his jitters disappeared. His father told him not to try to strike out the leadoff man, to give him nothing but junk.

H-Hour moved to 1100, then 1330. Dressed for battle, they ate lunch—hot turkey sandwiches that set their bowels growling. At 1330 the colonel didn't show; the lieutenant gave them the new time, 1530. Their feet hurt but they were getting better at the stairs. On the way back to their berths, the infantry swore and banged the bulkheads like a team that had blown a three-run lead. They wrestled their packs off, hung up their parkas and lay down on their bunks, their wet boots sticking off the ends.

"This is bullshit," Rennie said.

"That's Lang's idea of a speech," Burger said. "Lang's Attuburg Address."

"Hey," Mowry said, "I'm happy right where I am."

"You would be," Fecho said. "Stuck on a fucking tub in the middle of the war."

"Wake me up when we invade," Burger said.

At 1500 they gathered in the bay. The weather hadn't changed; if anything, it had gotten darker. New orders had come through. The amtracs would follow a radar-equipped destroyer escort toward shore; once visual contact was made, they would proceed in alone, the *Pennsylvania* providing walking fire. With the fog, they hadn't known the battleship had accompanied the fleet, and remembering its calm bulk buoyed them.

"This is it," the colonel said, holding up a communiqué. "We're going in, hell or high water. You all know what you have to do. Remember that you're in the Army. I don't want anyone trying to be a hero, just do your jobs and keep your eyes open. Now God bless every one of you."

A chaplain Rennie had seen eating with the officers climbed the stand and read a blessing over them. They could hear the sea, the wind lipping the opening above.

"Mount up!" the lieutenant hollered, and the formation split into ranks lining each wall. They'd done this only once, at San Clemente, yet everyone knew the routine. Rennie took his position with the platoon of infantry he would ride in with. A mechanic pulled a track forward and relinquished the wheel to its new driver. When the troops were seated, in a burst of diesel the track jerked to its place in the front of the bay—neat rows that reminded Rennie of the Indy 500, which would have been a few days away if it hadn't been canceled again. His father listened all afternoon, the whine of tires driving his mother upstairs.

Their amtrac held an inch of water that soaked through their boots while they were still in the bay. A few men groused about the boots supposedly being waterproof until a sergeant told them to button it. Rennie sat in the corner behind the driver. The guy beside him was a squad leader, a huge PFC with red hair and tiny, wide-set eyes. Like the rest of them, he ignored Rennie. It was forbidden to smoke inside the ship; everyone was chewing gum, working it mindlessly, focused outside themselves, like a dugout watching their last hope step in. The bay was suffocating with exhaust and the dull grumble of engines, and then a second later seemed preternaturally quiet—the burnt stink of oil forgotten—as the *Pennsylvania* opened up.

The explosion onshore reached them, and the man beside him cinched tight the straps of his helmet. Rennie found he could get another inch out of his own. The *Pennsylvania* was banging away now. The men opposite him hunched in anticipation of the next report, trying not to flinch. Rennie was somehow comforted by their terror. None of them wanted to be here. If right now they put it to a vote they would turn for Hawaii.

"This is it!" the driver shouted, twisted in profile.

The bay doors were slowly opening, a gust cutting through the gap, spattering them with sleet.

"Jesus Christ," the driver said, and half the track stood up to look.

The sea was white and pitching, waves slapping at each other, throwing foam. A few feet off the water rose a wall of fog. Within it, a single light reared and dipped, intermittently flashing at them like a beacon—the destroyer.

The doors were open now, water pouring across the floor of the bay. The first row started forward. Their driver followed, throwing them back into their seats. Rennie landed on the redhead and excused himself.

"Don't sweat it," the man said.

The water lifted them off the bay floor and the track swung mushily sideways, like the front of a bumper car. Everyone grabbed for the handgrips welded to the walls. They nudged the track beside them, straightened out, and the door swallowed them.

On the water, the *Pennsylvania* sounded closer. Wind bit through Rennie's parka, sprayed his face. The track rode low among the waves, and everyone stood up, still clinging to the handgrips. His gloves were soaked, his toes numb. He hadn't thought it was this cold. They stayed with their row, followed the one in front of them, led the one behind. The destroyer's light plunged into a trough, then resurfaced in the murk. They rose, cresting the swell, the track to the right lost over the gunwale, and landed hard, knocking a man to the floor.

The man clambered back to his seat, his glasses smashed, his nose spouting blood. It took Rennie a second to remember he was supposed to help him.

With difficulty, Rennie unbuckled his pack. He tipped the man's head back and, holding his jaw, swabbed the blood from his face. The wet gauze warmed Rennie's hand. The others gave them room, after a minute's fascination resumed watching the sea, their friend forgotten.

The man's name was Carlyle; he was from Kentucky. He didn't

seem to understand what had happened and kept checking to see if he was bleeding, staring at his red fingertips. His nose pads had cut into his bridge, and one stem had nicked his temple, but the nose itself wasn't broken.

"You're okay," Rennie said. "You're all right."

"I'm all right," Carlyle repeated.

Rennie dabbed some unguent on the cuts, packed his nostrils with gauze, and gave him a few aspirin.

"Thanks, Doc," the man said, his tone a strange cross of amusement and shame Rennie thought of as exclusively southern. He fiddled with his glasses in his lap.

"Here," Rennie said, and taped the frames.

Carlyle fit them back on his face.

"You all right now?"

"I am," he said, suddenly recovered, and thanked him again.

"Here we go," the driver called back, and Rennie stood up in time to see the destroyer—now towering—slide by to port. Ahead, the first row motored for land—a beach, but black, as if burnt. The driver popped the throttle and they bucked through the chop, spray stinging his cheeks.

"Get down," someone shouted. The redhead grabbed him and spun him into his seat. They waited for the ping of carbines, the clank of slugs flattening against the track. The driver was saying something, but with the wind they couldn't hear him. They slowed, drifted with the motor cut. The hull bumped something.

" 'Bout a minute," the driver shouted. "Looks good so far."

The platoon gathered around their lieutenant, rifles unslung. Rennie sat back, staying out of their way. Behind him, the *Pennsylvania* launched a volley; it landed somewhere ahead of them, an orange blob in the fog. They bunched up at the gate, waiting for it to drop, rifles braced.

"Ten seconds!"

There was no need to be dramatic, Rennie thought. He felt for the crinkle of Dorothy's picture, touched his arm. Gone.

Three, two.

The track bottomed on the sand, crunching, and lurched to a

halt, throwing them forward. They rebounded, the gate splashed, the sergeant shouted, "Go, go, go!" They were through it, high-stepping in the thick, frigid water. Sand sucked at their useless boots. The man ahead of him was fat and slow, his canteen bobbling on his belt. Rennie expected him to stumble into the surf, clutching his gut. Rennie crouched, using him as a shield, just as the fat guy was right up the ass of the man in front of him. They were practically walking, so close together a single mortar would scatter them. On the beach lay bodies spaced in a perfect checkerboard—alive, he saw, and crawling across the black sand on their bellies. The platoon ran through them and advanced another fifteen yards before hitting the dirt. It wasn't beach anymore but muddy, wet grass. The *Pennsylvania* crashed again. Listening for the shell to hit, Rennie realized he hadn't heard any other shots.

They crawled on their elbows, humping the cold mud, waiting for the next wave to overtake them. Sleet ticked against their helmets, melted on their necks. The land ahead of them was empty, a rolling field of the same tufted, half-dead grass with here and there a lump of snow. There were no buildings, no trees, not even brush to hide behind. A Browning clattered somewhere to their right—it was impossible to tell with the fog—followed by a few flat slaps from M-1s. Rennie squinted, trying to pick out a pillbox or gun pit, but saw nothing. Another platoon raced through them and dropped to the turf, and the man to Rennie's right laid his head on the ground, as if, the immediate danger having passed, he could go to sleep. It was the redhead, and automatically Rennie thought the man was with the wrong squad, that he was supposed to be leading them, not back here with the chickens.

Strangely, he wasn't afraid. The danger existed, but outside of him, not something with which he could be concerned. He noted everything about him—the blotch of mud on the redhead's cheek, the cries of unseen gulls, the wind riffling the grass—yet nothing distracted him; he saw it all at once, froze it whole, scanning for the smallest possible change. When he'd first learned to drive, he took his father's car down Route 5 to the flat stretch along the river above Dummerston to see how fast it would go. At eighty-five the wheel began to shake, but he set his jaw and held his foot down. He was aware of the pines rushing by, the fact that if he drifted from the high crown of the road he'd die, yet he was in total control. The sun angled across the dashboard, warming his hands; behind the blurred guardrail, the river calmly sparkled.

The next wave came, and the next and the next—except there were only four. They leapfrogged each other as they had on San Clemente, advancing fifteen yards a clip, unopposed. The *Pennsylvania* had gone silent. The mud was the enemy now, grabbing at their calves. They sank into it, kneed free, their tracks filling with dark water. After ten minutes, the radioman received the hold-fire command. The lieutenant stood up, turned his back on the Japanese Empire and ordered everyone back to the beach.

The beachhead was teeming with supply people. Launches were unloading artillery, oil drums, what seemed to be a field kitchen. A truck spun its wheels in the mud, holding up a halftrack. Rennie found Fecho and Mowry standing on a rock, smoking and watching the stalled harbor traffic. It was starting to get dark.

"This the right island?" Fecho said.

"What's this?" Mowry asked, picking at Rennie's sleeve. It was brown with blood.

"Guy in my track had a nosebleed."

"Our first hero," Fecho said, and whacked him on the back. "We all knew it would be you."

In the harbor the corner of a track poked from the water.

"What happened there?" Rennie asked.

"Gate opened too soon."

"Yeah," Mowry confirmed.

"Everyone get out?"

"None of them."

"How deep is it there," Rennie said, "ten feet?"

"With a full pack it doesn't matter."

"Burger wants us to go over to Graves Point," Mowry said, as if they had a choice. "Says it'll be good for us."

"It probably will," Rennie said.

"You hear that?" Mowry asked.

"What did you expect from Lang," Fecho said. "He loves this shit."

They wandered through the confusion. The truck was still mired, the halftrack butting it, digging a hole of its own. Offshore, the launches were piling up in the fog.

Graves had erected a tent at the edge of the beach and marked off a cemetery behind it with string and white-painted stakes. Burger was waiting for them, skimming stones off the black water. Beyond him the shore was deserted, though Rennie knew they'd established a perimeter.

"Lang's a hero," Mowry said, and held up the bloodied sleeve for Burger to see.

"Lang!" Burger said, and chucked him on the arm. They weren't touching him just for luck, Rennie thought; simply by surviving they'd achieved a measure of intimacy.

"Everybody ready?" Burger asked, and when no one objected, led them to the tent flap.

Inside, a lumpy rubber bag lay on a gurney, zippered lengthwise. A single utility lamp hung from a pole, throwing shadows. A desk rested on the black sand, and in one corner a laundry cart. Against the dank canvas walls leaned a graduated series of white pine boards. Burger introduced them to the duty officer, a gaunt sergeant with steel-rimmed glasses and—rare and beautiful—a steaming cup of coffee.

"Fecho," the man said, shaking their hands (his was warm!), "Langer, Mowry." He kept Mowry's hand and pointed at Rennie. "Langer," he said again, as if he knew his father, had years ago been his student. He spent a moment searching his memory before ushering them to the gurney.

Like the others, Rennie held a surgical mask over his mouth and nose, the limp strings tickling his throat. The sergeant snapped on a pair of rubber gloves and, like a waiter whisking the silver bell from a delicacy, with a single flourish of his arm unzipped the bag, exposing a waxen slice of white. Navel, pubic bush, knee. He began to pull the rubber over the man's feet, and Rennie looked up at the light, their breath gathering in clouds. The sergeant pushed between him and the table, peeling back the edges so they could see everything. Rennie concentrated on the floor—remembering how he did this at church, questioning his shoes—the body hovering at the edge of his vision, a fuzzy white blob.

"This guy's not coming back," Mowry said.

"Now I know what it was," the sergeant said, answering himself. "Langer, come here."

Rennie left the others staring at the man.

The sergeant went to the laundry cart in the corner and rummaged through it. "It's here," he assured himself. "Here we go." He straightened up and pulled out a sopping poncho, holding it so Rennie could see the stencil.

"Yours?" the sergeant asked.

"Yes," was all Rennie could come up with. It occurred to him that he should ask if his quarter was still there. He stopped the thought. Water dripped and disappeared into the sand.

"You don't want it," the sergeant said.

"No."

"I wouldn't think so." He dropped it back in the cart.

"Lang," Burger said, "get your head in here. You need to see this."

And it was true, Rennie did.

DOROTHY DIDN'T REMEMBER EVERYTHING about the birth. At first they'd given her a low dose of morphine, then, when they had trouble and decided they'd have to do a caesarean, applied a general anesthetic. Before each needle, they explained everything to her, as if she weren't at their mercy, her spread legs and stirruped feet hidden beneath sheets, open to the cold air and the doctor's gloved, rummaging hands. The morphine filled her with a listless bliss, as if this were all a cartoon and, like Bugs Bunny riding a log into a buzz saw, she had enough time to crack wise for an audience on the other side of the screen. As the general kicked in, the image on that screen dimmed, then stopped, leaving the still picture of the tiled wall beside her, the shining steel cover of the light switch. ON, it said, ON, ON. She tried to say something back to it.

That had been three days ago, and though everything had gone well (she wished they didn't have to cut but, once under, had no choice), she felt she'd missed the first act of her life that had any significance. Whether it was true or not, the two- or three-hour gap between the chill light of the delivery room table and the gray, reassuring warmth of her covers chafed. Bits of it returned to her—a glass cabinet filled with Red Cross boxes, a masked face lowering—images from some meaningful, forgotten dream, but when she pressed, nothing came. With Jennifer at her breast, she could forget, drift, the heat and insistence of the baby's gums lulling her like a lover's tongue. Dorothy traced her dimpled skull, sifted her fine hair through her fingers. She'd never known such utter satisfaction, and then, when it was time for Jennifer to go back to the nursery, such grief. Only alone did Dorothy feel cheated. In the days following, a sedative depression gripped her between feedings, and the nurses had to prod her to eat. She would be here two weeks.

Daily she was inundated with bouquets, cards and—rarity of rarities—telephone calls. Her mother limited herself to one a day, after the orderly had collected Dorothy's barely touched lunch tray, when, because of the time difference, her mother was beginning to think of what she'd make for her father. Dorothy couldn't picture the two of them alone in the house without inserting Robert or herself, the stored voices of the past.

"Spaghetti, maybe," her mother said, as if fishing for Dorothy's preference, and the smell of onions browning in olive oil crowded the attic rafters. "Dot!" her mother called up the stairs, "Rob-ert! Sup-per!"

"Can he eat that?" Dorothy asked. Though her father didn't admit it, he had the beginnings of an ulcer.

"I was thinking with parmesan and just a little butter."

"How is he?" Dorothy asked, as she did now every time they spoke. The day Jennifer was born, she'd talked to him for the first time since leaving Galesburg. Before he came on the line, her mother told her not to expect too much of him. And vice versa, Dorothy said.

"How are you?" he asked, not even saying her name. "And the baby?"

"Fine."

"Good."

Afraid they'd degenerate into silence, she asked, "How are you doing?"

"Good. Your mother told you we heard from Robert."

"Still in Tunisia."

"Yes," her father said, then surprised her, adding, "We were all sorry to hear what happened."

"No one's sure right now what the story is. I'm trying to be hopeful."

"We are too."

"I don't have any choice."

"I know that," he said.

The line sizzled, a scrap of some other conversation nattering in the background.

"I miss you, Dot." He'd waited an instant for her to respond, then said, "Here's your mother again."

Now she asked after him every day, though she knew her mother had strategically picked this time to call, when there was no chance of the two of them arguing.

"He's worried about you," was her mother's answer.

"There's always chicken à la king," Dorothy suggested.

"Do you want me to talk to him?"

"Over toast points."

"Yes," her mother said, "with the crusts cut off, but what do you want me to do?"

"Nothing," Dorothy said. "I don't want you to do anything."

Besides wiring a dozen white roses, the Langers called every other day, Anne regaling her with nursing stories while Mr. Langer—never James—waited to ask if there was anything she needed. Whenever he mentioned Rennie, Anne went silent. He seemed (if it were possible) even more convinced than Dorothy herself that

Rennie was simply missing, his official status accurate, exact, but rather than cheer her, his surety oddly exposed her own as baseless. Rennie always complained that his father had to outdo everyone, that his optimism swamped and suffocated him. He's just being a teacher, Dorothy said, but now she felt he wasn't leaving any room for her, that rather than supporting her he was taking her place. At least, she thought, he could talk about Rennie. Sometimes they put Jay on, and she teased him, calling him Uncle Jay. Like Anne, he never mentioned Rennie. He had a new friend and, by evading her, admitted he had a crush on some girl. Other than me? Dorothy needled. When she ran out of questions for Jay, Mr. Langer came on again to wrap things up, fumbling for a neat way to say goodbye. Did she have enough money? Because that wasn't a problem. Senior year she'd had him for history; his voice winding down made her think of sleeping in study hall. Though he never said it, like her mother, he wanted her to come back east and wait with them. She thought of what Rennie would want. When she hung up, the bare room accused her. Sleep, so long impossible, was easy.

Mrs. Schuman visited, bringing her mail, and the girls from work—Maureen, Velma and Eileen. Dorothy had received the telegram the week she quit, so only Mrs. Schuman knew, and the few times their visits overlapped she was too polite to mention Dorothy's misfortune. She was concerned and quiet, wondering what Dorothy's plans were, then, when her friends showed up, brightened. She had a picture of Elizabeth flying a B-25; everyone was impressed.

When Mrs. Schuman left, Velma said, "Is she dying for a grandchild or what?"

"She's nice," Dorothy said, and told them how coolly Mrs. Schuman had driven her to the Emergency entrance, searching the dial for a soothing classical station. Beethoven, the Victory symphony, with Toscanini leading.

They stood in the hall looking through the chicken-wire glass at Jennifer in her crib. Though she loved to watch her sleep, Dorothy hated having to wait outside while she had her nap. Her breasts were bursting. She leaked and continually had to change pads. She had more than Jennifer needed, and to relieve herself she leaned over the bathroom sink and, pinching whichever tender nipple's turn it was, squirted the milk down the drain.

"That's nothing," Velma said. "Wait till she gets teeth."

Eileen crossed her arms protectively over her chest, and they laughed.

They kept it light, teasing each other, though they knew it would be months before Dorothy made it back to work—and this only if all of her wishes came true—and that both Rennie and Maureen's husband were officially in combat. They had to laugh, so they did, shouting down the low, echoing halls, daring the nurses to stare. When they left, Dorothy felt deflated.

Her only other visitors were routine—nurses with her pills, orderlies wheeling in meals, occasionally the janitor mopping the john. Between these invasions, the days were warm and formless. She was exhausted all the time, yet had done nothing. She lay in bed, emptied, slack, the skin around her stitches stiff. She'd asked Mrs. Schuman to bring in her picture of Rennie; other than that, nothing in the room was hers. There was a nightstand with two worn drawers, a chair that wobbled so much that Mrs. Schuman refused to sit in it, and in the corner, a clothes tree holding only a wire hanger. The walls were the same bland sea-green of her mother's cream cheese and lime Jell-O mold. The hospital faced the bay below, three piers pricking the water like the tines of a fork. Beyond Coronado and the shriveled tip of Point Loma, the ocean stretched to a blue edge. Propped in bed, Dorothy peeked over the dated *Life* they'd given her, and the horizon filled the window. Gray navy ships inched down the panes. All afternoon the sun projected blazing rectangles across the floor, which, as the day faded, climbed the wall above her headboard, blushed from a weak tea to a hearty sherry, vermilion, cinnabar, and finally a carmine deepening into night. The nurse came in to draw the shade and turn on the reading light—hooded like the one above their bathroom mirror at home, the metal bell of the pull chain slick with her father's clotted shaving soap—and the world shrank to the edges of its bright fall. The curled corners of unread pages, the lumpy mountains of her knees under the covers. It was easier, she thought. She read herself to sleep, fading in and out at the end, scanning the same mysteriously familiar paragraph, then waking to find the heavy magazine toppling toward her face. Recoiling, the pull chain rang against the porcelain hood.

The night nurse came like a burglar, wheeling Jennifer's bassinet into place before she woke Dorothy. Bleary, cold, her mouth sour with sleep, she patted the shoulders of her gown for the safety pin that told her which breast was next. It was her mother's trick, and by now Jennifer knew it. She stopped squalling, waited for her to undo the flap and shift her into position. She was good, she took it. On her rubber soles, the night nurse had left unnoticed. It was one or three or four; her watch lay flat on the night table, keeping track, its ticking lost in Jennifer's breath. The hall was dark. Far off, the purposely deadened bell of a telephone clacked and was picked up before it could finish. The hospital stayed awake. Once, surprised by a rustling, she saw—in a blur, their uniforms wraithlike—a squad of nurses hurrying a man past her door, a bottle of blood sloshing above the gurney. The elevator clanked open and crashed shut, hummed. That was all, the night closed over them like dark water. Now Jennifer relinquished her nipple, eyes shut tight. She was slightly cross-eyed, though the doctor assured Dorothy it was normal. Otherwise, perfect. Then why, when she was alone again, sinking into the black, ticking night, did Dorothy feel she'd failed? Hadn't she earned her rest?

The sea, the sea, the sea. It made her sick to think of it waiting for her behind the shade. In Galesburg when you were tired of going to school, you jumped in someone's jalop and tore up Crow Mountain to the Grayson place. The British had burned it to the ground during the Revolution, but each spring its formal gardens bloomed anew. It commanded a view of fifteen miles; the British had faced their cannon toward New Carthage Pike, their iron wheels ruining that year's crop of Mrs. Grayson's daylilies and creeping phlox. Looking down the valley from the rail of the terrace, you thought of everyone at their desks, the wall clock's torturous progress, and the next day, in class, just knowing there was a possibility of escape sustained you. Here, the sea peeked through every open door, into every stairwell. Even Jennifer lay sleeping beneath a wall of distant blue stippled with miniature ships. The doctor looked at Dorothy's stitches. She still had another week.

She was allowed to bathe herself now, and one afternoon when Jennifer had just gone down, she locked the door and filled a steaming tub. She looked at herself in the mirror, stood in profile, pushing up her slack gut. Jelly, and her breasts were all over the place. Her face fat, her hair dry and dull. She'd stopped bleeding days ago, but her milk still leaked, spotting her tops. She lowered herself into the water, and a gray veil floated from one nipple. Would she ever be herself again?

Her mother had given her a gown for their wedding night. Her friends, like her father, had abandoned her, so there was no shower, no maid of honor, no real wedding, only a license signed by Mr. Stanhope, the same man who had given Rennie his CO hearing. After Rennie joined the Army, they had an actual honeymoon in Hawaii, but their first night together they stayed at the Lor-Ray Cabins out among the fishing camps along the East Branch. Her mother hadn't shown her the gown, and when Dorothy opened the box in the cold bathroom, she laughed, then was ashamed she had. The gown was a gauzy chiffon, tangerine, floor length, with belled, ruffled cuffs. Underneath it sat a pair of matching satin slippers, the dye tinting the white insole. Rennie was waiting for her in bed. Dorothy undressed and tried the gown on, fit her feet into the flimsy slippers. The mirror was unkind. Her mother had meant well, and she didn't want to hurt her, but this was her wedding night. She took the gown off and brushed her hair, checked herself again, and, holding the ugly thing in front of her, walked into the bedroom naked. "Which do you like better? This?" She let it drop. "Or this?"

Now, in the tub, she thought that she'd had no reason to be ashamed (in the morning the scorned chiffon scolded from the floor), that both outfits were from her mother. But how badly worn this one seemed, pouched and stretched, ripped and stitched back together. Her legs heavy, nipples cracked hard knobs. How proud she had been, the perfect virgin, and only a year ago. Now no one would mistake her for a girl again. Would Rennie, when he came back, feel her differently, fingering the silvered stretch marks and scars? And if he didn't come back—but he would, of course he would. For what other man would want this wreck?

Once, two years ago, when she was going out with Rennie, she had let Henry Parini feel her up in the wings of the auditorium. Her breath left her, and a delicious heat seeped through her. She told him to stop, and he did. If she'd told him to keep going, he would have; that he waited for her to tell him one way or the other annoyed her. Nothing had come of it, but for a month or so afterward she felt tremendously powerful. Her body had held such possibility.

That was gone now, the girlishness, the flirting. What was left? Jennifer. She was enough. Of course. But who, Dorothy thought, will take care of me?

She spent the rest of the week like this, wallowing in the bath or in bed, dreamily leafing through *Life* or *Look* or *Collier's*. She expected a flicker of the birth to come to her, another piece of the puzzle, but once she began to think like this it was impossible. She saw the plate of the light switch, the glass cabinet, and that was it, the anesthetic kicked in, sucked her under. The rest was Galesburg, the side streets piled with snow, the fire siren marking noon. She hadn't thought she'd miss it. And their house, the light hitting her mother's plants bunched on the deep sill of the landing. How the dust dulled the ivy's leaves. The teakettle collecting grease on the back burner. This she knew she'd miss—like her father, or Robert, or her mother—but while she was ready, she had no defenses. She tried not to remember Rennie, thinking that there was no need, she'd see him soon. Sometimes she held his picture—idiotically, she knew—to her chest. He was dead, he was alive, he was missing. She had to know, and yet she didn't want to. In case. And what were her choices, in case?

Two days before she was scheduled to leave, her father called her.

"You know," he said, "your mother's been working on me."

"I'm staying here till I hear from Rennie."

"You can do that at home."

"I thought you didn't want me in your house. Isn't that what you said?"

"That doesn't matter now."

"Maybe not to you," she said.

"Would it do any good to apologize?"

"No."

"I didn't think so. But I am. And I'm asking you to come home, if you want to."

"That's very nice of you, but no thank you."

"Are you all right?" he asked, brightening, as if he'd expected everything she'd said. For he had—they had. She was his daughter.

"I'm fine," she said. "You sound good."

"Oh sure," he said, "it's your mother we're putting through hell."

The next morning the doctor removed her stitches and said she could go home tomorrow. Mrs. Schuman would pick her up. The ships crept down the panes; the sun dropped flaming into the sea. Her mother asked if she wanted her to come out, though they both knew it was impossible. Mr. Langer said they were refurbishing a cottage for her—"and Rennie, of course." The nurse drew the curtains. Hours later, the night nurse woke her, then the sun.

They made her sit in a creaking wicker wheelchair and dressed Jennifer in the pink sweater and cap Anne had mailed. She hadn't been in direct sunlight for weeks, and when Mrs. Schuman pulled the car around and the orderly wheeled her to the door, Dorothy shielded Jennifer's eyes. She hadn't noticed the grounds before, the crisscrossed paths and beveled hedges. A tiled fountain burbled blue. The drive curled down the long lawn, giving her a last view of the hospital, now looming above them, stately, calm. She searched the third floor, unsure which window was hers. Mrs. Schuman eased the big LaSalle through the wrought-iron gate and took a cautious left across traffic. Outside the high, spiked fence, Dorothy realized she would never be here again, and an unexpected pang of homesickness for the ugly green room struck her, for the languid minutes and inconvenient feedings, for even, she thought, the empty clothes tree. The fence ended, the hospital passed back. It was foolish, and yet she felt she was losing another home.

The city seemed all concrete, a blinding, sandy tan. It was mid-morning, first shift was on break, graveyard asleep. A few sailors haunted the hot sidewalks, early birds or just now waking up, groggy and parched. Her doctor's office was in another part of town; she'd never seen these streets, the anonymous shops and slowly opening lunch counters. Glassily she watched the storefronts drift by. Jennifer slept in her arms, pouting. Mrs. Schuman was listing all the things waiting for her in the apartment. Mr. Schuman had built a cradle she could rock with one foot; laundry wouldn't be a problem.

"I imagine it will be nice to sleep in your own bed for a change."

"Yes," Dorothy said, barely listening. The city seemed endless, vaguely imaginary in the pure light—like the woman babbling on beside her and the baby she was holding, suddenly unreal and terrifying. How, she thought, did I get here?

Her mind skipped to the Grayson place. There was nothing there; it was just an escape. Like the hospital and its warm corridors, it wasn't a place you could stay. You went and you came back and remembered being there.

But she didn't remember, even now. There was the light switch, and though no one was near it, the air began to thicken and dim, like twilight.

They brought her out of it with oxygen and smelling salts that made her face sweat. The room was cold, though for weeks it had been in the nineties. The skin of her stomach pinched. The nurse leaned over her, her uniform so bright it hurt her eyes. Her lipstick opened. All Dorothy heard was "girl." She accepted the pink-blanketed bundle as if it were flowers.

Jennifer. The night nurse had said it meant white, or fair. How many times had her mother told her as a child that Dorothy meant gift from God. Jennifer shivered, her forehead bluish, fists clenching and unclenching, and Dorothy thought of Rennie and again of her mother and this child she'd prayed for and cursed nearly the past year, and she began to cry, open-eyed, afraid the baby would slip off her chest. Jennifer. Hers. The nurse was there, and suddenly Dorothy loved her, trusted her enough to take her daughter from her. While someone unbuckled her feet, the doctor needlessly explained that she'd had an operation and would have to stay a few more days than planned. He seemed so serious she had to catch her laughter. An orderly covered her with a clean sheet, tucking it under her chin. Dorothy lay back and looked at the perforated ceiling. She could feel herself bleeding somewhere under the sheets, a thin trickle, and then the ceiling swung, the orderly's inverted face bobbed above her. His breath smelled heavily of peppermint with a brown undercurrent of cigarettes. He said something unintelligible yet comforting, his smile funnily upside down, a gold tooth shining like the gilt skin of a boxed chocolate. He had a religious medal that dizzied her. Spanish. San Diego meant Saint James. Their red-tiled settlements. Mr. Langer lectured. The gold of the Incas, the Aztecs. Who first glimpsed the Pacific? Cortez, yes, or Balboa. What had that first man said, standing before the sudden expanse—or had he, like her seeing Jennifer for the first time, stared speechless, wondering why he of all people had been so blessed? The gurney bumped the steel-sheathed doors and the temperature jumped twenty degrees, a sweet warmth wrapping her like a hot bath. She shut her eyes and as they passed through the corridor listened to the sea of voices, the squeaking of the wheels and the thudding of her own heart, amazed at the richness of this new world to which she'd returned.

HIS FATHER SAID THE ARMY DIDN'T KNOW where Rennie was. In Alaska somewhere. Jay knew it from the newspapers and the cracked, tattered map in his father's room at school. Alaska was a pale green head, one tentacle reaching into the Pacific. Rennie was on an island called Attu.

"Never heard of it," Grampa Langer said, even after they showed him.

It was at the end of the tentacle. They found it in an atlas, his father pinning the green chip with a greasy fingernail. His mother didn't want to see. It was so close to Japan. In Jay's history book there was a picture of a baseball game played between two ice-bound clipper ships. Seward's Folly, the Gold Rush, Land of the Midnight Sun.

"Not very big, is it?" his father said.

"There's nothing there," Grampa Langer argued.

Except Rennie, Jay wanted to say.

His father shut the atlas and put it back on the shelf, where, night after night, it lurked over his grandfather's shoulder. The Philco spewed news from both oceans, useless now. In her chair, his mother dug through *Forever Amber*. When NBC's tri-tone chimed nine, his father looked up and said, "Bedtime." Jay's dreams hadn't changed; he'd set everything in the South Pacific, and now the palm trees seemed out of place.

Alaska—but they'd taken that back months ago, with almost no casualties. The newsreels were boring; the only interesting thing was the wind, so strong it blew tents inside out and swatted planes from the sky. Jay remembered a sailor in a furry hood peering through binoculars, one of those stock shots from the Murmansk Run. The rest was rocks and water and snow-shrouded mountain. Attu.

He biked to the town library to look up the front page for the day they invaded. It was off in a sidebar, dwarfed by North Africa and the flooding in Illinois. The article didn't say much, just that they'd met little resistance. Late May. Even he was more interested in reading about the Dambusters, the bombs invented to skip across the reservoir's calm surface, unleashing billions of tons of water on the sleepy villages below. But if the fighting was over and they controlled the island, why was Rennie missing?

He pictured snow, the skull of the woodchuck he'd found sunk in the mud last spring, the moldy, waterlogged balls hidden in the high grass beyond the outfield fence.

In *Life*, Russian archaeologists had dug up a mammoth frozen in a snowbank like a fly in an ice cube; when they chipped it out, the meat was fresh. A spring blizzard cut the party off, and they had to eat it or starve. There were pictures of the native guides cooking it in a pot hung from a tripod. Everyone sat on rocks, eating from tin plates, some holding up bones and smiling. Behind them the mammoth lay on its side like a sick cow. And that was in Siberia, right next to Alaska. The Komandorskie Islands were only a hundred miles from Attu, a hop across the International Date Line.

Or the story about the guy at the Ski Bowl in Norton who got lost in the woods and froze to death. They put him on the toboggan all rolled up in a ball; in the lodge, by the fire, he uncurled like a seedling.

Or Manfred Longo's grandfather's bobhouse dropping through the rotten ice with him in it—the heater meeting the water with a hiss and a puff of steam while the old man, realizing, let go of his jig and lunged for the door. In April, everyone lined the shore, watching the state police drag the bottom with grappling hooks. When they finally snagged something they attached the cable to a tow truck backed up to the boat ramp, and with a chuff of smoke the winch hauled from the black water a weedy DeSoto with a man handcuffed to the wheel—an Irish mobster from Albany, it turned out. Manfred Longo's grandfather was still down there in his bobhouse, was, like Rennie, still officially missing.

His father said it could be anything—a mix-up. His mother agreed, but showily, as if mustering belief. They were cheery for him, their enthusiasm for Flinch or the Yankee game an embarrassment. They tried, yet they couldn't quite hide everything. His father had kept the telegram, stashed it with his star and the pictures of their mother when she was young. Jay considered it an admission. And his mother's silence, her walks at night, her coming home in midafternoon only to leave again. Tuesdays and Thursdays they were together at dinner, the four of them pleasantly discussing nothing over the potato salad, but most of the week Jay spent with Win or alone with Grampa Langer.

"If he's dead, they should tell us that," his grandfather said, out of the blue, as if in the heated middle of some unheard conversation. His voice startled Jay, lost in the paint's intoxicating sheen. He could only talk out of one side of his mouth, so that he always seemed to be muttering, complaining. "I don't understand what good they think is going to come from telling us he's missing. You listening to me?"

"Yes, sir," Jay said.

"They should try and find him before they say they've lost him. Huh?"

Jay wondered if Grampa Langer knew he wasn't supposed to be talking like this to him, but when his father asked if Grampa had had a good day, Jay just said yes.

Saturday his mother worked, and Sunday had begun going to church again. His father stayed home, worked the morning with Jay on the cottages. They were almost done. When Grampa Langer started going off about Rennie, his father stopped painting and, kneeling by his chair, talked to him in whispers, as if Jay hadn't heard it before.

At dawn Mr. Barger dropped off their papers, on Friday collected the taped rolls of change. Miss Swain hadn't forgotten Jay; she'd gone away that weekend and come back with a niece, easily thirteen, with hair like Veronica Lake before the war, a silken lilt hiding one eye. Win had seen her at the Regal with a cousin from Quogue, and the next morning wouldn't stop talking.

"Man," he said, slapping the white on, "man oh man oh man," and then ten minutes later exploded: "Baby!"

"Do you want to do the bluff tomorrow?" Jay asked, knowing his leg wasn't strong enough yet.

"I wish. Honey, come to Daddy!"

Sylvia Jensen, to whom Jay had yet to say a word, was on vacation in New Hampshire with her mother. Strangely, her house lost none of its mystery, and when Jay knocked on the door and waited for her father to answer in his wrinkled shirt, he held himself at attention, chest thrust out as if he were being inspected. Mr. Jensen asked after Jay's father and grandfather. It was a victory of sorts, how easily they got along, as if Mr. Jensen approved of him. Sylvia would be gone another week.

On Monday, when his father was at work, Grampa Langer called Jay over to his chair. "Does your father tell you anything about anything?" he asked, gripping the meaty part of his arm.

"Yes," Jay said.

"You know we all hope your brother's all right?"

"Yeah."

"Most probably he is. But there's a chance he might not be all right, and you should be ready for that. Okay?"

"Okay," Jay said, and Grampa Langer let go of his arm.

"You're betting he's dead, aren't you?" He squinted up at him, his cane across the arms of the chair. The sun polished his face, one eyeball milky, the pores on his nose exploded, his skin rubber. A bubble of spit clung to his upper lip. Mornings when he forgot his teeth, his jaw collapsed, and chinless, stubbly, he seemed already dead. He would be like Grampa Clayborn stretched out on the bed, the back of his arms going dark with his still blood.

"No," Jay said, but his grandfather could see he was lying.

"He might surprise you," Grampa Langer said. "From what I hear, he's liable to. But you know him better than I do."

They were in the stagnant depths of summer now, the endless mornings and labyrinthine afternoons, the gray, fading twilights. He'd seen every movie that had come through the Regal; without Sylvia, only the blue, snow-capped letters touting air conditioning enticed him inside. Soldiers lived, were injured, or died. In the end, they were never missing; it would be a gyp. And yet because he knew now that men did simply disappear—without a flourish of trumpets or swelling tide of violins—the movies with their neat reasoning and just results seemed like lies. He tried to read Edgar Rice Burroughs and found that that too was ruined. Not that he stopped. He kept going to the movies, kept checking out the Tarzan books, even *John Carter of Mars*. There was nothing else to do.

It was the time of year when everything was boring. Even the weather was predictable, every few days a sudden thunderstorm raking the panes, then, minutes later, blue sky again. His father rewired the junction box behind Fischer and splurged on a new table radio so they would have something to listen to. Grampa Langer snoozed in his chair, hands wedged into his pants, as Spud Chandler twirled a three-hitter against the White Sox. Win kept up a steady play-by-play, snakes of paint sneaking along his upraised arm. He'd already told Jay he was sorry, adding that he'd never had a brother. Jay remembered how stupid he'd been about the switched dog tags. They were on Folger, had only Fischer left. The ten o'clock plane buzzed overhead, the eleven-thirty, the four. The light was the same all day.

It had been a week since the telegram. It seemed to Jay that nothing was happening. His mother called the Red Cross from her work; his father sent a letter to their congressman in Galesburg.

"We have to be patient," his father said.

"Yes," his mother seconded, yet he could tell they completely disagreed.

"It'll all straighten out," Grampa Langer said when they were alone, "one way or another."

And so they waited, it seemed to Jay, for the second telegram. Everything was Rennie now. His red-and-blue-striped shirt with the honeycombed holes circling the neckband; the matching Dopp kits they'd gotten a few Christmases ago; his Millers cap, its bill stained white with a tide of sweat. Playing catch before dinner, Jay thought of Rennie pitching—the smack of the catcher's mitt—and his own scrawny arm. Once in Putney his father had coaxed Jay into trying out for Pee Wees; he didn't make the first cut, came away from the list pinned to the corkboard dazed. That night, Rennie talked to him in the dark, whispered from his bed in the far corner as if they were prisoners.

"You didn't want to go out anyway. I don't know why Dad does that."

"It's okay," Jay said.

"No," Rennie said. "He knew, but he made you, and now you feel bad. That's dumb. He should've just let you do what you wanted to."

Jay lay in the dark, silent, unable to say that he'd wanted to make the team, that he'd wanted, despite their father, to be like Rennie.

"Why does he have to be such a jerk?" Rennie said, and all Jay could say, biting his lip so he wouldn't sob, was "I don't know."

Now, his father lobbing him soft tosses, Jay thought that it should have been him instead of Rennie frozen under the crusted snow or bobbing like a block in the dark water. He was small. His grades were average (he knew his father was ashamed of his C in Geography). He wasn't a star at anything. Even here, with the war thousands of miles away, he was afraid. The day, dying in the pines behind his father's garden, seemed to confirm his guilt. The air was cool. Grampa Langer had the living room light on; his mother wasn't home yet.

"Which cottage do you think Dorothy would like?" his father asked.

Jay had been fixing Gardner especially for her, stealing the best screens from the others, lavishing an extra coat on the front, even though they weren't sure she was going to come. Jay assumed she would, if only because he couldn't see her living in someone's garage in San Diego (he couldn't begin to picture the city, saw only her postcards, the bright pastel sky). She belonged to Galesburg, the clear streams and frothing falls. His mother said that if she knew one thing it was that Dorothy wouldn't go back to live with the Baineses. Now that she hated the town—as it had hated Rennie—Dorothy belonged with them.

"I don't know," Jay said, "Gardner? It's in the middle and might be warmer at night."

"I can't argue with that kind of logic," his father said.

"Which one do you think?"

"I'll abide by your decision."

"When do you think she'll come?" Jay asked.

"Maybe never. It depends on how fast they track down your brother. And they will. He's out there somewhere, you can bet on it." His return was wild, biting the grass at Jay's feet. Jay short-hopped it neatly. They looked at each other, amazed yet questioning.

His mother was late again, and after dinner took a walk on the beach. She'd finished *Forever Amber;* from her nightstand the deep-cleavaged heroine tempted him. His father was in his garden, hunting potato bugs by flashlight. Wrapped in an afghan, Grampa Langer dozed next to the Philco, startling at each blast of laughter.

Jay took the atlas from the shelf and traced the necklace of the Aleutians. An island was a mountain under water, like the volcano on his postcard. They'd all thought Hawaii, and the whole time it was Alaska. Land of Midnight. The baseball game between the ice-locked ships had gone on for days. Was it light there now, nightless? Since the telegram his dreams had been placid, but deep in the morning he woke in his dark room. Nothing was where it was supposed to be—the night-light, the dresser, the window. Grampa Langer's, yes. The rest of the house slept. He thought of Putney, Rennie's bed in the far corner, and about how long the war would last, and then he didn't have to be dreaming to see things. He saw the big barrel they pulled the draft numbers from, the Ping-Pong balls jumping like hot popcorn. A hand reached deep, and he was strapping a helmet on; he was going to die.

Behind him, NBC chimed nine. Grampa Langer stirred and came awake. He saw Jay holding the atlas and turned off the radio. "Your grandmother was a worrier. Didn't do her a bit of good. Your father's one too, although you wouldn't know it to talk to him."

Jay put the atlas back.

"Just like your Aunt Sarah. Never say anything but you're always thinking. Isn't that right?"

"I guess."

"That's her, never gives a thing away. Like a spy."

"You don't like her," Jay said.

"That what your father says?"

"My mom too."

"It's not true. I treat her the way she asks to be treated. She plays games, I play games back, except I play fair. Don't I play fair with you?"

"Yes."

"All right then. Your mother and father are worried about your brother, but they're worried about you too. I know what that's like because I worried about your father when your grandmother left us. It's not easy, huh?"

"No."

"It isn't." He stood up, feebly gesturing for Jay to take his arm. When he stayed up too late, he slurred his words. He'd been going to bed earlier and earlier, waking up before his mother and bumping down to the kitchen. She was worried he'd burn the house down.

On the stairs—where Jay couldn't get away—he asked, "Still think he's dead?"

"I don't know."

"All I know," his grandfather said, "is that it's been awhile."

He went out back to tell his father that Grampa Langer had gone up. The yard was dark, and it took Jay a second to spot him sitting in an Adirondack chair with the flashlight in his lap. At first he thought his father was stargazing, but as he came closer he saw he was just sitting there. The moon lit an amber drink on the chair's broad arm, the ice glinting silver.

"Jay," he said, as if glad to see him.

"Grampa went to bed."

"Is your mother back yet?"

"No."

"She's very worried," his father said, but to Jay it sounded wrong, like he was half making fun of himself, or her, and then at the end didn't mean it.

"It's bedtime. Are you coming in?"

"Eventually. You don't need a bath, do you? It's a beautiful night. I might join your mother on the beach. If that's all right with you?"

"Sure," Jay said.

"We'll all go for a walk on the beach, what do you say?" He stood up, the flashlight dropping forgotten into the grass, then bent over to retrieve it.

"I'm going to go in," Jay said.

"I'll be in in a little bit," his father assured him. He stood there, watching him away, and though Jay knew he'd sit down again when he rounded the corner of the house, the creak of the chair frightened him as nothing that summer had.

It was mysterious, Jay reflected in bed, how he'd come to rely on Grampa Langer. He'd been so afraid of him—still was, a little. Grampa Langer was like his mother, able to tell him terrible things, but with his father's calm delivery. Now that they'd retreated from Jay, his grandfather seemed to be standing in for them, substituting, like Superman bridging the damaged rail so the troop train didn't plummet from the trestle. Except Jay didn't really want him to.

His father came in first. He never heard his mother. All he could remember of the dream was Dorothy holding balloons and a pack of boys he didn't know running across blond, wheat-swaying hills into the distance.

The next day Win was having his stitches out, and Jay had to do the whole route. He left early, before his father came down, thanking his mother with his cheeks full of toast. The little time they were alone, she babied him; he couldn't trust her to tell the truth anymore, though he knew she could turn in a minute. Around her, he stayed alert, sifting for clues among the lulling coos and touches, her choice of perfumes.

The bale at Hickey's was fatter than Jay expected, *53,* Mr. Barger's slip said. Win had picked up some new customers. Jay snipped the wire, then folded it and hung it on the doorknob for Mr. Hickey to toss in the scrap bin. *B-24s ROCK AXIS OIL FIELD,* it said, *Stunning Treetop Raid on Rumanian Depot*. Ploesti. They came in low, under the radar. One of the pilots said the farmers waved to them. Jay read a few paragraphs while he folded some tomahawks, then laid the flats in his sack and headed off.

He remembered the route from June, which hedges he could cut through, whose dogs were on chains. He knew their porches' crumbling steps and dusty floorboards, their mailboxes. His sneaks dragged deep green tracks through the dew, his bike at the bottom of the stairs, waiting patiently on its kickstand. In the gray half-light, with the birds gossiping in the woods, the world was intimate, his. Each door seemed a familiar face, a friend, though behind it in the still rooms lay strangers, mystery. Win had given him his cards so he wouldn't miss the new ones. He did Mr. Jensen's, walking a copy to the mat, then at the next house threw wild, hitting a kiddie pool. He didn't have time to go through the cards and, trusting Mr. Barger had given him extra, chucked another.

He hadn't been in town since collecting last Thursday, and kept an eye out for his father's bike. If he saw someone on it, he'd have to fight him, even if he couldn't win. There was nothing, it was too early. The streetlamps were on, their globes bright dots in the fog. The library was dark, and the post office. The silver side of the Roll of Honor had grown by one, D. DUNCAN; Jay didn't know the name, and thought how lucky the guy was.

It was light by the time he climbed the bluff, his sack flapping against his thigh. He was going to be short but, hoping he was wrong (knowing there was nothing he could do, that it was Mr. Barger's fault), didn't count how many he had left. He'd rather short Win's customers, because then Win could just blame him. He couldn't short anyone on the bluff because they were old and alone up here and, like his grandfather, relied on the paper.

Stopped in the Gardners' echoing porte-cochere, Jay saw that he was short two, which made his decision easy. He would do the Shelburnes and Miss Swain, then swing back to town and buy two—three, one more for his grandfather—and drop them off on the way home. It would have worked if he had any money, but he didn't. Then he remembered that Miss Swain owed him for two weeks.

From the Shelburnes he couldn't quite see into her porte-cochere. He wasn't allowed to cut across the lawn, but had to ride back to the road and approach by Miss Swain's drive. Most days he took it slowly, enjoying the view, resting for the long haul home, but today, intent on the envelope, Jay bombed along the grassy hump between the ruts. The sea spread before him, a few sugar-white clouds sailing high. He and Win would finish Fischer tomorrow. Then what would he do? There was a month of summer left.

The envelope wasn't there, and for an instant he debated not giving her her paper. He was whacking the tomahawk in his palm when a figure rippled across the leaded glass and opened the door. It was the niece Win had told him about, in argyle socks and a tomato Sloppy Joe sweater—which, though every girl wore one, he associated with Sylvia. She came out and stood on the top step, brushing her Veronica Lake hair from one eye.

"Throw it," she said, and, with her forearms touching, protecting her front, girlishly put her hands out.

He tossed it underhanded.

She caught it, said, "Thanks," and hurried inside, as if Miss Swain, anxious that the paper was late, had sent her to fetch it.

He replayed it, jostling over the gravel. She had on a locket and a charm bracelet, one of them a four-leaf clover. As the paper twirled toward her, she smiled. He shook his head, trying to catch up to his luck. He hadn't even asked her name—hadn't said anything—and yet he felt, after this past week, unexpectedly lucky, as if he'd won something.

"Man!" he said.

Mr. Hickey said he was sold out, and Jay was forced to short Win's new customers. On the town road Jay tested explanations, knowing his grandfather wouldn't accept any.

When he got home, the car was gone. His grandfather was in the kitchen at the big table with his winter coat on. He had the atlas out, turned not to Alaska but Florida. A drop of sweat hung from his chin, making Jay aware that his own hair was plastered from the ride.

"I don't have your paper," Jay admitted, and when he didn't answer, apologized and offered to run to town and buy one with his own money. His grandfather didn't look up from the pink peninsula.

"Why Florida?" Jay said.

"What?" his grandfather asked muddily.

"What's in Florida?"

"What what zinzinzin Flaaaa," his grandfather said, and toppled—so slowly that Jay made a move to catch him but for some reason stopped in mid-gesture, knees bent, arms out—sliding sideways and then straight backward off the chair, his head striking the floor with a frightening *clop*.

His arms jerked loosely above his chest as if he were trying to clap. His back arched, his old brogans kicked. He tried to cry for help, the good side of his face going (his jaw moving as if he were chewing a tough piece of meat), but it came out a growl, a hungry guttural sound that at first kept Jay from approaching him. When he did kneel and catch his grandfather's hands and press them to his chest, Jay could feel him shaking, as if something were going to burst from within him. He never imagined his withered body could be so strong. He was like Rennie when they wrestled, impossible to pin. Jay looked around the room; no one was coming to help. He held on.

Within minutes the tremors left. Grampa Langer stopped arching, his breath coming less and less in fits, and finally evenly, as if he were asleep. They lay together on the floor. As his mother had taught him, Jay took his pulse. He called her from the phone in the hall, then went back into the kitchen to wait for her. On the table, the atlas gaped. Florida with its pink keys. Jay closed the book, went into the living room and put it back on the shelf where it belonged.

★ ★ ★

ANNE HAD GROWN SO ACCUSTOMED TO EMERGENCIES that at first she didn't recognize the voice on the phone. On base, all her calls were the same, some young noncom panicking over a sprained ankle. "Calm down," she said, and pulled a memo pad to the empty center of her blotter to take down the patient's condition. "Now tell me slowly what the problem is."

"Mom," Jay said, "he just fell over."

He was breathing. It wasn't his heart. Probably nothing, another soft stroke. He could have them indefinitely and never get worse.

"What should I do?" Jay asked.

"Sit tight," she said. "I'll be home."

It was her fault, she thought, though she knew it wasn't true. The way she'd been living, everything could be her fault; nothing really was. She told Jay that he'd be fine, grabbed her purse from the desk drawer and told Cheryl she had to get home.

"My father-in-law," she said, as if she needed an excuse—which, she thought in the car, she did. Cheryl knew of Martin, and disapproved. She never said anything unpleasant, but sometimes when Anne came back late from lunch, Cheryl was short with her, as if she'd cheated her of more than a few minutes' work. "We have to be quieter," Anne told him. Like spies, they spoke in code, watched an invisible clock. Anne was with Cheryl all day, and the Quonset was small. "It's him," Cheryl said, leaving the receiver atop her IN box. Anne didn't expect her to understand, but the little judgments wore on her. She didn't need someone else to tell her she was wrong.

The Buick zipped over the soft-tarred county roads, kicking up dust. She knew each route now, how each lonely four corners fit. It seemed she was happiest here in the car, or padding the beach at night, away from everyone, safe. Lately her time with Martin had been so hard-won that the few minutes in the dunes or the shared basket of clams and fries seemed rushed and unsatisfying. Last Saturday he'd been unable to make love and let it ruin the whole afternoon. It wasn't the first time they'd had trouble, yet they'd been distant since. Their affair, so deliberately pursued, seemed increasingly futile. She kept expecting him to tell her it was over. Because, she thought, she didn't know how to tell him.

Yesterday they'd fought—or she'd been angry with him. They'd driven into Riverhead for lunch at some deli (in her car, always her car), and standing at the display case, she ridiculed the coleslaw James had made the night before.

"He made dinner?" Martin asked.

"I obviously couldn't. I was with you until six, or don't you remember?"

"Poor guy, he's too good for you."

"He feels that way too," Anne said. "I have an idea—why don't you take *him* to Montauk?"

"You know what I mean."

"No, what do you mean?"

"This isn't just us," he said, far too seriously. They glared over their sandwiches, and she thought that this was it. A double agent, she braced for betrayal. For weeks she'd hoped for this moment. Why was she surprised that she was ready for it?

"Annie," he said, "why do we fight?"

"You're not fighting," she said, "you're giving up."

"Am I?"

"We are," she said, then, seeing him flinch, softened. "I don't know."

In the car, she asked if he was worried about Evelyn (because everything with him was Evelyn).

"It's not that," he said sadly, taking it wrong. He could see the end, she thought. On both sides of the road ran potato fields, the flat green broken by farm stands selling bunches of cut flowers.

"Daisies?" he said.

"Time," she said, and reached her watch across the wheel for him to see. Why had she assumed that he knew what he was doing?

They were set for lunch again today. She was supposed to pick him up on the back road out of camp, as if he were hitchhiking. How long would he stand like a fool in the dust? Eager, she'd never stood him up before. Now the timing seemed right. She imagined him tromping across camp in the heat to see what had gone wrong. She hoped he'd see her car was missing; more likely, he'd barge right in and quiz Cheryl. Anne supposed it didn't matter. Driving, everything seemed inconsequential, in another world. It was August; she was just tired.

Mr. Langer was conscious when she got there, fully recovered, sitting with Jay at the table as if nothing had happened.

"False alarm," he apologized, but she could see Jay was shaken. Mr. Langer had fixed him some Ovaltine and, in his winter coat, was patting his arm consolingly. She'd been prepared to see the old man laid out on the linoleum, limp and grayish, and the jump from base to home—disorienting normally—made the scene even more unreal. His color was good. Sweat slicked his neck. She unzipped the front of his coat and asked Jay to run him a glass of water. He drank it as if he'd hiked for miles.

"What exactly happened?" she asked Jay, and he described a simple apoplectic fit.

"I remember coming in the kitchen," Mr. Langer said. "That's about it."

Anne checked his eyes, his heart, his reflexes. She went through a battery of questions meant to confuse him ("How many hands?" she asked, holding up the V for victory), but he knew all of them. It had been a showy but mild stroke. Only Jay had sustained damage.

She called James at work.

"Do you think someone should look at him?" he asked.

"I've looked at him," she said. "He's fine."

"Are you going to stay with him?"

She thought of lunch—she could easily make it back in time—but said, "Yes. Just today."

The three of them sat on the porch. She told Jay she could handle things, but like a candy striper he wouldn't leave his patient's side. The paper hadn't come—he'd run out, Jay explained—and the ball game didn't start until noon. They sat in the shade, making the wicker creak. Another blue day. The wind riffled the grass. She'd been so busy lately, racing between her two worlds. This rest felt necessary, deliciously unearned.

"How do you feel?" she asked Mr. Langer.

"Fine," he said, and ten minutes later, added, "I could use the paper."

She tried to give Jay money but he hopped on his bike and took off.

"I think I frightened him," Mr. Langer said.

"That's normal," she said.

"I was a little frightened myself."

"This is your third?"

"This was the first one like this; the other ones weren't half as bad."

She couldn't tell him it didn't matter, that the damage was done. "Did it give you any warning?"

"A second," he said, and snapped his fingers.

When Jay came back she had lunch waiting. Chicken salad with split grapes, potato chips and fresh lemonade. It was a trick of her mother's, to hold off the world with food. Mr. Langer took the paper up to bed; he seemed slower on the stairs. She eased his shoes off and helped him in. "Thank you," he said, and lost himself in the front page.

Jay wolfed his sandwich, left his chips.

"Are you okay?" she asked him.

"Yeah," he said halfheartedly. "I'm going to go paint."

"He's fine. It looked worse than it was."

He wasn't going to discuss it with her.

"If Win comes, should I send him down?"

"Yeah," he said, "please."

Doing the dishes, she sighed. James would want her to watch his father. Two months ago she'd sat on the porch with Mr. Langer, watching the waves and planes, yet it seemed ages. How miserable she'd been then, still in mourning for her father, Rennie—all her losses.

What, really, had changed since then? She hadn't forgotten the gray, gray days of winter, the stale musk of the sickroom. The night he died, after the younger Benson brother loaded him into the panel truck, she'd burned his sheets in the barrel behind her mother's overgrown garden. Flaming tatters rose into the night sky. She stood in the snow, her face warmed by the fire. James and Jay had come up, the body was gone, but still she was alone with him, with what was left of the family she'd come from; for though she'd taken her first chance to escape, and let her father—so capable, she'd thought then, reverent—tend to her mother in her final illness, Anne had come back to see his last months and days and the last meal (chicken broth, which he wouldn't take; she wetted a napkin and touched it to his cracked lips). In those last moments behind the drawn blinds, she'd gone to her knees beside the bed and meant it, while he strangled above her. How many patients had she seen, yet after the briefest prayer she pulled the covers over him and closed the door. That afternoon she caught Jay peeking at the sheet tented over his nose, and the sickness she thought she'd thrown off in Putney descended upon her. "Stay away from him!" she screamed, and he stiffened, then began to run from her. Later, James said she hadn't hurt him. As if to warn her, he showed her a dent in the hallway wall, the plaster cracked like a tapped egg. "How long have I been like this?" she asked, and he looked at her as if she was asking him to lie. You've always been this way, she answered. This is who you are.

She wanted to think she wasn't that Anne any longer. Neither was she the one heaving under Martin while despising his weakness, his ceaseless mentions of his precious Evelyn. She thought of her father sneaking down the alley in midafternoon, of the quiet privacy of Frank Steurmer's hunting camp. Every December her father packed a bedroll and left them for a week, returned hale and fusty, stuffed with venison. Saturdays she came back from Montauk and complained about the Army. Like her mother, James did nothing. Suffered. After years of weakness, she'd been so proud of her scheming. Now, with the water running over her hands, the lawn outside blazing, she renounced these versions of herself.

Mr. Langer was asleep under the comics. She took a pulse and, satisfied, went to their room for her suit. Fitting herself in, she thought of Montauk, of Martin asleep on the beach, the long hot walk back to the Grand. Every Saturday he reserved the same room, 327. She'd come to think of it as theirs. Beyond the gauzy curtains, the arms of the breakwater reached white through the blue. She slipped her arms through the straps and stood in profile before the mirror, hands pressing her stomach in. She was three weeks late. She'd always been irregular. In her teens she'd skipped months at a time; now she clung to that fact. And it had only been once, the first time. Since then Martin had interrupted their attentions to roll on tough gut safeties that snagged her hair. The last time, he'd wilted as he tried to fit one on. Like Jay tending Mr. Langer, Anne watched helplessly, angry that she could do nothing to prevent this disaster.

Jay was almost done with the last cottage. She was aware that her body embarrassed him, and kept her towel around her. She'd known they were close to finishing, but seeing all six in daylight overwhelmed her. For a week she'd been trying to sell Dorothy on the idea; now she was ready to buy one herself.

"Looks good!" she called from the top of the stairs.

He acknowledged her with his free hand and kept on painting.

She didn't feel like walking, and found a hollow where Jay couldn't see her. A few nights ago a Shore Patrol jeep had surprised her, but today there was no one, the damp sand trackless. She pulled her suit off, the wind thrilling her, and laid her watch on the towel. The sun burned red in her eyelids. When the wind shifted, she could just hear Jay's ball game over the crush of the waves.

James was right to be worried about him. Since the beginning of the summer, his quietness had lapsed into silence, secrecy. Some of it she'd expected. She'd smelled smoke on Rennie's clothes, had scrubbed the same stains from his sheets. The signs had been similar then, but she didn't remember Rennie avoiding her so pointedly, didn't remember any looks of contempt thrown over the dinner table. Was it possible—preposterous thought—that he knew?

James knew. If he still believed her first denial, it was none of her doing. Her excuses had grown slapdash; she'd let the odometer go. After what he'd done, why was she worried that she'd hurt him?

The dunes reminded her of Martin, their rushed lunches. Today was supposed to be Mattituck, a little clam shack on stilts overlooking the bay. They'd gone there once in June. It was raining and they were the only ones in the place. They had to ask for ketchup. The roof leaked, the cook coming out with a bucket. In their slips, rusting trawlers bobbed. She took his hand under the salt-strewn table. Had that been love?

Like a girl, she'd promised not to say "I love you" until she meant it, and then when she did—in the heat of love, meeting him—couldn't stop. Their last time, two weeks ago Saturday, they'd both been tight-lipped, working at it like a long-married pair, intent on the job. Afterward, he thanked her as if she'd cooked a dinner he didn't particularly like.

"No," she'd said, "thank *you*." How proud she was of her hatred, of her love—when there was no reason to be.

She checked her watch, then turned onto her stomach and, using her towel as a pillow, slept.

A plane going over woke her. Her head hurt, and for an instant her nudity confused her. She found her watch—four, Mr. Langer wouldn't be up yet—brushed the sand off with her towel and pulled her suit on. She'd only slept an hour or so, and hadn't dreamed, yet, walking back, she felt as if she'd come to some decision. It was just the sun, she thought. She'd wanted to stop seeing Martin weeks ago.

Win had joined Jay painting the cottage. She fawned over his scar and promised them Pepsis if they finished by five. Mr. Langer was asleep, his pulse unchanged. In their bedroom, a bar of light sneaked under the shade, warming her thighs. She put on a red sundress, but thought it would look wrong and changed into a plain blouse and skirt. In the kitchen, skinning carrots, she had to stop and hold on to the edge of the sink. It had been such a long day.

James was early. She'd been expecting the boys, and when she heard the front door, called, "Done already?"

"How is he?" James asked. Sweating from the ride home, he seemed heavier, and worn. His bike was still missing; he looked ridiculous on hers. His jacket was rumpled from being stuffed in the basket.

"He's fine. Go see him. He should be getting up anyway." She took his lunch bucket, saved the flattened wax paper.

The boys came in, victorious, their hands covered with paint. She gave them their Pepsis and drove them out the back door. She'd forgotten how much she hated this crazy time of day, when everyone else was done with work and running around, and it was her job to fix dinner and make sure they ate. After preparing a meal, she needed a bath; when the food was ready, she wasn't hungry. Tonight was chicken fricassee, and even before she unsheathed the cleaver, she didn't feel like eating.

James helped his father downstairs and onto the porch, then came in to get him some juice. "He seems the same," he said.

"He is."

"He's more worried about Jay."

"I think that's right."

"I'll talk to him," he said, as if it were a burden.

"Are you all right?"

He acted surprised that she'd asked. "Just tired."

"They finished the cottages."

"I'll look at them too," he said, and left. She brought the cleaver down on a leg joint with a thump, and the drumstick skittered off the butcher block to the floor. She rinsed it in the sink and added it to the pan. Its bloody spot of marrow accused. He'd only been home ten minutes and already she was angry with him.

When she had everything going on the stove, she untied her apron and went out to the porch, where it was cool. Win's bike was gone. Mr. Langer sat watching James and Jay play catch, his blanket draped over his legs. She picked the paper off the rocker beside him and sat down.

"How are you feeling?" she asked.

"Never better," he said, and toasted her with his juice.

They watched them throw, Jay flinging the ball with his whole body, James flicking it with his wrist. The two of them were talking, the slap of their gloves punctuating the conversation. With the breeze, she couldn't hear them, but every few tosses a scrap of laughter tumbled across the lawn. In his shirtsleeves, with the sun behind him, James barely resembled the man in the kitchen. They all seemed to have recovered except her.

Saying grace, James added a prayer for Rennie. She thought that there was no need to torture her; she was leaving Martin willingly.

"You cooked," James said, and did the dishes, freeing her to sit in the living room. She needed a book, but the library was out of *The Robe*. She rustled through the front section of the paper, then picked up her knitting. The radio droned on. Jay lay on his stomach in front of the console, scissoring his legs, the toes of his sneakers bouncing off the carpet. James came in and suggested they play chess; she didn't remember James teaching him. He joined Jay on the floor and they set up the pieces. Mr. Langer switched chairs to get a better look at the board. Every move prompted a long discussion. She concentrated on the needle ducking through the loop. Jay kept checking to see if she'd left yet. She was done with one sleeve when James sent him up to run his own bath.

"You were very brave today," she told him, sitting on the edge of his bed. "If it should happen again, you do just what you did today."

"Dad said old people have strokes all the time. It doesn't mean they're going to die."

"That's right."

"But it hurts, doesn't it? It hurts a lot."

"I suppose."

"Dad said he didn't know."

"I really don't either," she said.

"How old is Dad?" Jay asked.

"Your father is not going to have a stroke," she said, ridiculing the idea. "All right?"

"All right," he said.

James helped his father up to bed early, then came down and turned the radio off and put away the chess set. Any second, she thought, he'd ask her to call in sick tomorrow, to quit. The back door was open to cool off the house, and she could hear the ocean foaming in the kitchen. To break the silence, she told him what Jay had said.

He laughed.

"What's so funny?"

"He asked me how old *you* were."

She surprised him by following him up to bed. In the dark, he asked, "He'll be all right tomorrow."

"Which one?"

"Both."

"They'll be fine," she said. "Don't worry."

She had to stop herself from offering to stay home. If he'd asked or even hinted, she would have, but he didn't push it. They said goodnight and after shifting positions once or twice, settled in. He'd given up trying to sleep with her. At first it had been a relief; now it seemed both a confession and an acceptance of their shared failure. How could she have possibly thought he didn't know? In minutes he was sawing away, and she could distinctly hear, as if it were dripping against her forehead, the steady trickling of the icebox. She rolled over and tried to figure out how she would tell Martin. A thunder shower walked in from offshore, dropped its noisy load and drifted on. Hours later, unable to sleep, she thought she should have taken her walk.

At work, first thing, Cheryl said that Martin had been looking for her yesterday. She threw it at Anne before she'd even got her coffee. Why did she have to be so spiteful?

He called at five after nine. She picked up on the first ring, looking over her shoulder; Cheryl was in back, out of earshot.

"What happened?" he asked, and the concern in his voice stirred her. She forgot everything she'd decided. She was telling him about Mr. Langer's winter coat when she heard Cheryl coming. "I've got to go."

"Are we having lunch?"

"I'll pick you up," Anne said. "This time I promise." Off the phone, she was angry at herself for being so pleasant. She didn't mean to lie to him.

The day was murderously hot. Around ten they started getting men with sunstroke. The mess lent them a dust-furred fan, which the victims sat in front of, draped in sopping towels and drinking ice water. The Quonset smelled like a locker room, all sweat and steamy mildew. Her hair was ruined—not that it mattered. At break, she went out and rolled down the Buick's windows.

Five minutes before lunch officially started, she changed her shoes, washed her face and retouched her makeup. Cheryl watched with disdain. Though Anne was dying to lean across her desk and tell her she was leaving him, she wouldn't dignify the girl's reproach, and, picking her purse out of the desk drawer, said she'd be back in an hour.

"Have fun," Cheryl called.

"I will," Anne said.

Even with the windows down, the air in the car was thick and still. It closed around her like a fist. A breeze slipped in as she wove through the tents and clapboard barracks, but with it came the dust, boiling in the backseat. Groups of muscled boys passed, their glances investing her with desire. Her uniform stuck to her, front and back, and her face felt as if it were melting. She blotted the sweat on her brow with the back of her arm. She'd wanted so much to be elegant for this, cool. Oh, but it was typical. Her plans had a way of not falling through but being sabotaged from the start, as if she didn't deserve even the chance to fail on her own.

She wouldn't tell him in the car, that was her only condition. She wanted it to be calm, face-to-face. If it had to be done bluntly, she would do it, but not offhandedly. If he wanted to go to the beach, she'd be careful not to let his attentions distract her—but she wouldn't let it go that far. She had to be able to think.

"Martin," she tested, but her voice was strangled. She cleared her throat and looked meaningfully at the rearview mirror.

Ridiculous. How did she ever get herself into this position?

She cleared the last bivouac and followed the edge of the parade ground. The grass was brittle and golden in the heat. A platoon was marching the perimeter, their sergeant calling cadence, his voice puny in the humidity. In the mirror, her dust rolled over them.

"Sorry," she said.

And there he was, by the side of the road, long and tall, thumb out. Martin loved the old joke: There he is, the farmer, out standing in his field. He knew it was stupid, but laughed and laughed.

She braked and the dust rolled over them. He folded himself into the seat.

"Thanks for stopping, ma'am."

"Glad to give a serviceman a ride," she said, and immediately regretted it. It had become one of their jokes, bawdy and tender, dumb. There was so much she was going to miss. Room 327, the ferry backing into the slip. It had been love, hadn't it? She almost still wanted him.

They reached the county road.

"Which way?" she asked.

They drove a few miles before he dared to lean across the seat and kiss her. His hand slipped into her blouse. She felt sweaty and disgusting.

"Stop," she said, "not while I'm driving," and, chastened, he pulled away.

"I missed you yesterday."

"Martin," she started, then remembered her promise. Not in the car.

"You're leaving me," he said—evenly, with only a breath of a question in it. He didn't want confirmation, though when she looked over at him, her sorrow made his face go hard for a second before he recovered. "I knew weeks ago. It's all right."

"I don't want to talk about this here," she said, thinking, How? Had she been so obvious, such an easy read? She'd only figured it out herself. She hated how sure he was of her. "I don't want to talk about it in the car."

"Over lunch. We're good at lunch. Or we were."

"Please," she said.

"I picked the perfect place today too. You'll love it."

"Can we not talk?"

"I want to talk," he said. "That was our problem, we didn't talk enough. We were always driving around in this goddamn car."

"Please don't be like this."

"I'm not really—being like this. I'm relieved, I guess. I'm tired of sneaking around."

"Can you wait?" she said.

"For you," he said, "anything."

For lunch, he'd chosen the Aquebogue Country Club. The entrance was bunched with sculpted shrubs, the long crushed-shell drive to the clubhouse edged with symmetrical beds of red and white geraniums. Everywhere, hedges blocked the view of the course itself. The clubhouse was low and winged and of white brick, slate-shingled and blanketed in spots with ivy; trumpet vines wound about greening copper downspouts and through the slats of black shutters. Martin said she could leave the keys in the car and someone would come out and park it. Her hesitation amused him, but secretly she was pleased, thinking, Yes, this would do.

Inside, it was surprisingly cool. The halls were deeply carpeted, redolent of wax and grass and cigars. Glass cases built into the walls displayed tarnished trophies, the putters of club champions, balls stuffed with pigeon feathers. Every few feet there were mirrors, paired and facing each other. She peeked to see if she looked how she felt; in her uniform she seemed serious, official, and she thought that that might be the best way—the easiest, at least. At the far end of the hall, a doorway gave on a darkened room filled with wing chairs. On a buffet a fly walked the lip of a dead old-fashioned. Anne was beginning to suspect the place was deserted when Martin opened a side door and ushered her out onto a bright patio dotted with green-and-white umbrella tables, all empty.

Here was the course, its blazing fairways sloping lushly down to the water. Blue and waveless, Peconic Bay shimmered behind a kidney-shaped green on which a threesome was putting. They seemed to be the only ones out, and she thought how, on a day like this, her father would toss his bag in the trunk of the Packard and wind up the hill to the club and not come home until well past dark, smelling of mud and beer and barbecue, full of horseshoe stories and impossible shots. Saturdays, when he barricaded himself in the vestry to drum up a sermon, she swam at the pool while her mother read at a picnic table, tempted by the snack shop but conscious of the other mothers. Anne knew not to ask for a treat until they got home, and then it would be a peach, not an ice cream. She had to eat it at the kitchen table, from a bowl; even as she obeyed, she pictured herself running around the front yard, waving the cone like an airplane for everyone driving by to see, the ice cream running in strings down her arm, her cheeks smudged with chocolate. When she appeared in her father's sermons, she was always wise, reminding him of the elemental, shredding his worldliness with a child's pure logic. Her whole life, hadn't she dreamed of being normal?

After a minute, a bow tied waiter pushed through a screen door and apologetically led them across the damp flagstones to their table. The chairs were white wrought-iron monstrosities; the legs shivered, ringing dully when he pulled them out to wipe the seats down. A dab of mustard clung to the menu he gave Anne, but she wouldn't let it spoil this. They gave him their drink order and sat back to admire the day. The sun hurt. A blue haze floated over the water, and somewhere a lone cicada sawed drowsily. The air carried salt and the smell of freshly mowed grass, underlined by the must of last night's thunder shower. Two great oaks cast a black lace of shadow over a putting green pricked with tiny white flags, upon which an elderly man was practicing, a crop of hoarded balls at his feet.

"A dollar each," Martin said.

"There are hundreds in my father's basement."

"Do you play?"

"No, you?"

"Not this summer," he said. "Too expensive. And it takes too much time."

Yes, she thought, that was exactly it.

"So you knew," she said.

"Today or when?" He paused to let the waiter set their drinks down, asked for a little more time to decide, making a show of opening the menu. "What are you having?"

"I don't care," she said, a bit regally. "Order for me, or isn't that proper now?"

"Club sandwich? They have bacon."

"Is this where you take every idiot who falls in love with you?"

"There's only one idiot, and I want to take her out east tomorrow, but she doesn't want to go. And if she doesn't, I don't. Do you want to go?"

"Yes," she said.

"No you don't, you just don't want to give up. I don't want to either."

"Then why are you?" she said. Without warning, she'd begun to cry. She hadn't meant to, she didn't want to. She folded her arms over her chest and looked away, breathed deep and sighed, but it wouldn't stop. She pushed the chair back with a screech and, picking her purse from the table, got up and went inside to find the ladies' room. Behind her, Martin's chair scraped, but she knew he wouldn't come running after her. He was only standing up; he was only being polite.

She splashed water on her face, and with a tissue swabbed off her ruined mascara. She was still crying, but tearlessly, her ribs hitching every few breaths, sounding huge and forlorn coming off the bright tiles. And there was no reason, that was the awful part. Wasn't this exactly what she wanted?

Martin stood to welcome her back to the table, pushed her chair in for her. He asked if she was all right, and, her tact regained, she dismissed the question.

"We can go tomorrow," he said.

"Why?"

"I've got my ticket. The reservation's made."

"But why?" she said. "What's the point? Last week we didn't even do anything."

"That's not it though, is it?"

"It's everything," she said, and held up her hands to indict the clubhouse, the shedding oaks, the old man putting. "What about you?"

"Everything," he seconded, and smiled to show her it was okay.

"How are we doing?" she said. "Are we at least doing this right?"

"You're doing fine. Me, I'm not so sure about. I *am* going tomorrow, just to torture myself. You're welcome to come."

"For old times' sake," she said. "No." She resisted laying her hand on the table for him to take, instead unfurled a napkin and smoothed it in her lap.

"I ordered you the club."

"That's fine," she said, but when it came, she couldn't eat it. Martin struggled with his, and had to borrow a napkin from another table. He finished and killed his drink, the ice jangling.

"We'd better get back," he said. "Let me visit the gentlemen's first."

Alone, Anne thought what a waste they'd made of such a blue day. Staring off over the tiny threesome, she remembered their lunches after the first time at Montauk. They had no time to eat, no need. By the time she parked the car in a suitably discreet spot, he had her blouse undone. They made love on the sand, thinking it romantic, and when that had grown old (it was hard on the knees, the skin in general), switched to the backseat, leaving the doors open, their heads and feet sticking out, a breeze slipping between them. The car's shocks rocked them like a mushy bed. After, satisfied, they lazed, naked, watching the clock on the dash. Invariably she came in late. Behind her typewriter, Cheryl clucked.

The waiter returned to take their plates. "Shall I save this for you?" he asked.

"No, thank you," she said, and went inside to wait for Martin in the hall. She glimpsed herself in a mirror—her mouth pouchy, gray hennaed away, eyes clownishly rimmed in black. For so long it had been good enough. When had it gone?

He came out smiling, as if he were glad to see her. Out front it was twenty degrees hotter; she could feel her face dripping again. Her car had magically reappeared, but with the windows rolled up. The interior felt sapped of air, like their attic in mid-July. They bumped over the cobblestones, ran the brilliant gauntlet of flowers. Turning out of the drive, she thought, I will never be here again.

On the way back, she asked, "How did you know?"

"How did you?"

They were early, and she thought of stopping for a last kiss. Later she might regret it, but now she regretted everything, and halfway up the back road into camp she let him off. They kissed through the window.

"Tomorrow," he said, "come."

"Martin, don't."

"All right. I love you, Annie."

He was waiting for her to say something, to cry. She couldn't. She turned from him to the road and drove on. In the mirror there was nothing but a storm of dust.

That was it, she thought, heading past the deserted parade ground, and before she could stop herself, she pictured their cramped, reckless history together—the snapshot of Evelyn; James and his rotten vegetables—settling on the misty image of the steamed mirror, the two of them molten and clean in the heat of love. Young. The Grand Hotel was exactly thirty-five and three-tenths miles from James's father's house.

"You're early," Cheryl informed her, feigning surprise.

"Why?" Anne said. "Do you have somewhere you have to be?"

That afternoon, she was dismayed at how quickly her emotions went to work on her. With each dressing and every filled-in carbon, she felt herself slipping into a bitter depression—much the same, she thought, as the one she'd been grappling with the past week. Getting rid of Martin had done nothing. Then why did she miss him, why did she already see today's lunch at the country club in a golden, mote-struck light? At home her responsibilities waited like a dying patient. So this was the end of desire, the giving up. She would never love again.

She called to check on Mr. Langer. Jay answered and said everything was fine, he was taking his nap.

"What are *you* doing?" she asked.

"Nothing," he said, in his dead tone, and for no reason she was furious with him.

"I'll be home early," she said, as if it were a threat.

She beat James home by an hour and had dinner on the table when he walked in the door. His face was sunburnt, raccoonish when he wiped his glasses. He was wearing a seersucker jacket a few sizes too small and had a jar of marinara sauce someone at work had given him. He said hello to his father and Jay and waved to her in the kitchen, exhausted but cheery now that the weekend was here. When had he stopped kissing her?

Again James fitted Rennie into grace. Head bowed, she listened, questioning her knitted fingers. She'd thought stopping the affair would return her, but the same feeling of not really being there lingered. She'd made the potato salad and sliced the cucumbers and fixed the iced tea—why did it all seem foreign to her, the work of some unseen hand?

"Amen," everyone else said. It was too late to casually add hers, and she decided that everything she did until the next grace would be a kind of prayer. This was where she had to live now.

In the living room, with the idiotic radio going on and on, a sad nostalgia for the view from the clubhouse gripped her. That one cicada keeping time with the heat. She kept missing stitches. Jay kicked his feet, Mr. Langer folded and unfolded the paper, James leaned in to hear the bulletin. This time of night, the sand was still warm from the sun, the breeze too much for the bugs. She could be lying under the moon, feeling that odd upward tug of the stars, or strolling with her eyes closed, a frigid hand of surf telling her she'd wandered off-line. She kept the yarn taut across the hardened patch on the side of her thumb, purling as the news poured from the box. There was nothing from Alaska, there never was.

When the phone rang, James looked at her as if she'd been expecting a call. Her instinct was to ridicule the notion by returning his look, but she resisted, instead shrugged. Martin wouldn't call, and it was past five in San Francisco, where the Army was handling Rennie's case. James rose stiffly and trudged to the hallway.

He answered sleepily, then brightened. "Hello, Dorothy," he said exaggeratedly, and with the base of the phone motioned Anne to pick up in the kitchen. As she bumped past him, she heard Mr. Langer turn up the radio.

"That's wonderful," James was shouting. "I know how hard our kids were on Anne, so I can appreciate it. Especially at that age. I think you're making the right decision."

"About what?" Anne cut in.

"Dorothy's coming here," James said. "With Jennifer."

"If that's all right?" Dorothy asked.

"Of course," she said, though with everything that had happened, she couldn't process it. Anne was worried that she didn't know what this would mean to her. She wanted to ask why, and of all times, why now? It wouldn't be polite, and, grabbing at the first thing handy, she added, "That would be wonderful."

After they hung up, James came into the kitchen and hugged her. She noticed with a start that he smelled sweetly of liquor. How big he'd gotten, how thick his features.

"Things are going to work out," he said cautiously, as if he'd just realized it instead of believing all along.

Jay wasn't as excited as she thought he'd be. It was the baby, she supposed, or Rennie. He was getting older. "You know I'm a grandmother," she'd said once, locked in Martin's arms. She hadn't told him she was late, hoping it would go away.

Before bed she drew a scalding bath and lowered herself in, then lay there staring at the ceiling until the water had gone cold. That was what Dorothy's call meant, she thought; now she really would have to leave Martin. She remembered the old man poking putt after putt, chasing his misses across the shaved grass. He hadn't gone out on the course, but gathered his precious balls into a bag and, spikes scratching on the asphalt path, retired into the clubhouse. Now she didn't know whether to admire his patience or despise his timidity. She didn't understand either one.

She thought she'd have trouble sleeping, but she was under before James came up and—rare—slept the night. She woke in the gray hour before dawn. It was Saturday; the sheets needed to be changed. She pulled a cool pillow over her head and waited for the alarm to go off. It was almost funny; James would be suspicious of her staying home. She had fabricated so much of her life out of nothing; now that she wished the imaginary half would disappear, it seemed fixed, rigid. In the other twin, James whistled and smacked his lips. She loved to watch Martin sleep, how his hands lay limply open beside his head. He always seemed sad; she would wake him with a kiss to see his face change.

She silenced the alarm and threw off her sheets. The light had stayed gray, hadn't bloomed on the ceiling like a true dawn. She went to the window at the foot of her bed and pulled back the curtain, then stood looking at the rain painting her car a lustrous black, the lawn a thrilling green. Out at sea, the clouds held a yellow, sulfurous tinge. Steadily, drops etched silver lines on the glass beneath her fingers, and she knew with the same fatal certitude she'd felt in the car with Martin that it was going to rain all day.

She found an old skirt and blouse and hauled them on and, before going downstairs, pushed James's foot.

"Don't you have to go to work?" he asked.

"I'm staying home," she said, though, in truth, for much of the day she would be hard pressed to say exactly where she was.

RENNIE COULDN'T BELIEVE THEY WERE THERE, in Alaska, invading. Tomorrow they would each be assigned their own squad. Already an advance patrol was picking its way inland.

Mowry said the name of the place was Massacre Valley. Around the Civil War a boatload of Russian trappers had butchered a native fishing village. The beach fronted on Massacre Bay and where they were camped now was officially known as Murder Point, but only hours after coming ashore, because of the half-thawed mud and the vegetable stink it gave off, everyone called it Shitville. As they settled in, everything picked up a name. Shit Mountain, Shit Valley, Shit Island. They christened the spot offshore where the one landing craft had sunk Fuck-up Reef, and referred to the wet field behind Graves, which the Army had marked LITTLE FALLS MILITARY CEMETERY with a stenciled sign, as Bagville.

They'd just sat down to dinner when they heard from inland the rattle and crack of machine-gun fire. Everyone waited, sporks poised over their cans. It was nine and dusk—silvery and unreal, like night in a cowboy picture—and still spitting. They hadn't set up the aid station yet; they weren't ready. In the valley another, higher-pitched gun returned fire. Rennie recognized the clatter of the Browning from the range.

"Shit," Burger said.

"Who's out with them?" Mowry asked.

"Stephenson and Tony K," Fecho said.

"Let's get going," Burger said. "They're going to want some of us."

They wolfed their spaghetti-and-meatballs and tossed their cans aside, and, still chewing, began to unfurl canvas and sink posts in the muck. In the distance the valley crackled, a tangle of slaps and echoes rolling to them over the snowfields. A mortar thumped, after a long minute crashed, the glow of the explosion pinking the bottom of the fog. Rennie stopped to watch the snow light up—like, he thought, the fireworks some cloudy Fourth of July. He imagined when he looked down he'd see the train of signs that made up the outfield fence. It was like Ebbets Field; if you hit the Marsden Brothers bull's-eye they made a suit for you. The summer his father lost his job, everyone made jokes about the lighted candle on the Emshwiller Bakery cake. Another burst, and the mountains jumped and blushed before the silver poured in again. Rennie stood and marveled at it the way when he was pitching he'd step off and rub up the ball to check on a steadily advancing thunderhead. He loved the heavy moments before the drops poked holes in the dust, when he knew he wouldn't have to finish the inning. He was surprised that the memory had found him now, to lend its beauty to what he knew he should fear. Yet his vision—the curtain of sleet between the fog and the snow caught for one red instant—was truly moving, or only momentarily, for when he felt for Dorothy, the weird half-light of dusk was back, and with it the rain and the remembrance of the drowned man wearing his poncho, and all he wanted to do was get the hell out of there. The sky lit up again, but this time it didn't work. The heavy air made the fighting seem closer than it was, though Rennie knew the distance didn't matter; they were going there. There was nothing else on the island.

"Lang, get your head out of your ass," Burger warned, almost knocking him over with an armful of tent stakes. He pulled a mallet from a belt loop. "You hold," he said, "I'll hit."

They weren't halfway through when the lieutenant splashed across the compound and told Burger that he needed every medic with their platoons. The ground was too muddy to drive anything big in; they needed every stretcher.

"Listen up!" Burger shouted, calling them together. "These are your guys. Stay with them and stay down. Don't be dumb. Litters, get back here fast and then get back there. Check your packs and make sure and take extra everything. Let's go."

The stretcher bearers assigned to Rennie were trombone players, two skinny guys he'd seen shipboard. Bateman and Hall. They both had big ears and long jaws, and kept a constant sardonic patter of "Man!" and "Crazy" and "Bro-*ther*" going. With their helmets on they were twins. They hovered at his back, trading the heavy litter—Bateman and Hall, Hall and Bateman.

The company mustered in the middle of the compound on the one patch of hard black sand. If you stepped on the grass you sank in up to your knees. Mowry said it was called muskeg. It was like sod laid on top of mud. Even the tractors sent to haul the stuck jeeps and trucks and artillery out had bogged down; the tide had risen and swamped everything, so that, behind them, the invasion appeared to have failed. The rattle and pop of the fighting was steady now, a constant background, distracting, like a radio turned down low. It wasn't getting dark, the silver merely deepened. Out on the water, the ships waited, invisible in the fog. Drizzle collected on Rennie's chin strap and dripped down his neck. His platoon was intact. Carlyle, the guy from Kentucky, remembered him with a nod; the big redhead ignored him. They were placed well back in the pack. Rennie expected the colonel to come out of his tent and address them, but once the last platoon had moved into position, the lieutenant sent them off into the valley toward the noise.

They walked four abreast, following a slippery, narrow trail down the center of the valley. It was the kind of mud that ruined the batter's box even days after a rain, a few inches thick and sticky. Off the path, black water filled the pits of stray footprints. Bateman and

Hall had figured out how to share the litter, each shouldering a pair of handles. Rennie wondered why he'd wanted the colonel to say something. Nothing heroic, just some acknowledgment. He felt somehow cheated. He thought, marching over the spongy muskeg, that the colonel could have at least said goodbye to them.

They dragged along, taking baby steps and cursing the rain, as if the Japanese might not wait for them. Bateman fell with the litter and the column bunched up, laughing at him. The soft Arctic night was coming down—still silver, with shadows—and then, as if they'd crossed the dotted line of some border, snow glowed white on either side, swooped up the lower slopes of the mountains, lighting the sky from beneath, then just as neatly disappeared, topped by rocks and fog.

A mortar thunked going up, whistled coming down, then burst far ahead of them, charging the scene like heat lightning. Everyone ducked, though they were well out of range. Up the valley, to their right, the patrol clung to a slope, under fire from above. Muzzle flashes winked like stars on water, the mill across the river. Shots clicked, close but muffled by the snow—or so Rennie thought; they still had to slog another mile and a half before they neared the fighting, and by then they could barely hear each other cursing their own bad luck for being there. Rennie had had spaghetti-and-meatballs and fruit cocktail, and he could feel the acid and the heavy syrup seeping through his gut—like game day, when everything down there tightened up and he couldn't go, and then when his father cranked the anthem from the top of the stands everything in his stomach dropped to the bottom of his bowels.

A lieutenant Rennie had never seen halted the column. There wasn't room for all of them. The Japanese held a gun pit atop one ridge. Saying this, the lieutenant gestured vaguely toward it; unbelievably, they could see the fighting right in front of them, over his shoulder. There weren't that many of them, but they were dug in.

"I need medics and stretchers only," the lieutenant ordered, walking down the line. He had to repeat it over the crash of a shell—the *Pennsylvania* again, reaching inland. The Pennsy they called her, as if she were an old friend, someone's tough mother, though they still flinched, just beginning to pick up the timing of the *whoosh*, the whistle and the hit itself. "Up front, chop-chop."

"Man," Hall said, "I'm getting homesick for old Shitville."

"Reet petite," Bateman said.

Rennie led them around the stalled column. The snow was ankle deep and lightly crusted. It didn't matter; his boots were already soaking. At the head of the column waited Mowry, Fecho and half the horn section. With the litters slung over their shoulders, they looked like they could be going skiing, and Rennie thought of the Snow Bowl in Putney, the rickety, soap-slicked toboggan run. Every year on opening day someone from Boston broke a leg. He touched Dorothy to ward off any bad luck the thought had caused, and noticed with satisfaction that he'd finally stopped going to his arm.

The lieutenant returned from the rear and ordered first platoon to escort them to the fighting and reinforce the men there. As if this had been the plan all along, the platoon surrounded them, unshouldered their weapons, and, double-time, crouching, cut a new path through the snow.

The fighting was a good four hundred feet above them, but the noise was on top of them now, the lack of trees sinister, calculated. Again Rennie used the man in front of him—Mowry—as a shield, but it no longer bothered him. Mowry was hugging the ass of the guy in front of him, and so on, all the way to the front, where the few truly crazy, brave bastards were. Rennie was more concerned with keeping his spaghetti-and-meatballs down. Food is fuel. His pack weighed on him, and the rain, and the worry—present since his enlistment but only now taking on a real and dangerous weight—of how he would do. He used to wish he were Superman; now the boy he had been seemed stupid, a fool, someone Rennie had no choice but to disown.

At the base of the slope, Stephenson was working on someone. Before they reached him, Rennie spotted a man to their right face down in the snow. In the soft light he looked like a rock. Two infantry went with Rennie to check on him, but Stephenson waved them off and they hustled back to the platoon. He'd been ready to see whatever the man looked like—a single hole, no face, his gut raggedly blasted open—and again (why?) he felt cheated of something. He forgot all of that when they reached Stephenson.

The man had been shot in the chest with something big. He was partly conscious, moaning "Help me, Jesus" again and again, weakly, with the rhythm of breath. Stephenson had covered the entry wound with several pressure dressings, the outlines of which had already begun to run with blood. He needed help to roll him over, and, without thinking, bolstered by a dumb rush of adrenaline, Rennie volunteered. The sopping dressings tore and the man screamed. Rennie could see Stephenson's hand through the hole in the man's back, trying to squish them together. Bits of rib stuck from the man's lungs, which, miraculously, heaved with the moaning, softer now, "Jesus help me, Jesus help me." The view through the hole reminded Rennie of a messy necropsy, a lab in the basement of Stocking Hall with slippery tiles and drains under the tables, except here the tissue was fresh and not culled from some failing Guernsey herd. Fecho knelt and helped the man on his side. Mowry was still standing back with the litters. Rennie thought that he was doing all right; he could look at the man and see the tree of arteries in his medical texts, the overlapping pastel organs packed into the rib cage like trout crowding a wicker creel. Unlike Cal, he'd never had a problem with blood. His father wasn't a hunter, but in early December the whole town got the first day of deer season off, and all week his friends showed him their fathers' trophies, skinned and hanging by the hocks from the garage rafters, the porch roof, the side-yard maple, dripping into the snow beneath like black cherry syrup. With the light, the man's blood seemed darker, tarry. Rennie wondered why he wasn't on a litter, then realized he'd stopped moaning.

"Get him on his belly," Stephenson said.

"He's not going to make it back like that," Mowry said.

"Fuck you," Stephenson said, and started working on the hole.

"Where's Tony K?" Fecho asked.

"Up the hill."

"Where are your litters?"

"Up. Everything's up."

"Keep working," Fecho said, and stood.

"He's not going to make it," Mowry said on the way up.

"I know that," Fecho said, "but fuck you anyway."

Rennie could see, a few hundred feet above them, men spread out and prone in the snow, above them more snow and more men, but the ridge itself—what they were aiming at—was lost in fog. They climbed toward the fighting, their useless boots sinking in the drifts. His legs ached, and his wet skivvies bit at his raw crotch. He remembered San Clemente, the girls waving at them from the parking lot. It was insane to be moving forward, but again that calm awareness that he might be killed gave him enough distance from what he was doing to do it. The lingering light thrilled him, the sleet stinging his cheeks, and though he could take it all in (there was so much, even here in the middle of nowhere), he felt as if he were not really here, as if he were remembering it or seeing it at a theater.

A machine gun opened up, a high-pitched chittering, and everyone dove for the snow. Rennie slid downhill a few feet before punching a grip in the crust. He curled up, protecting his head with his arms, his belly with his knees, willing himself into the side of the hill. He could stay here, he thought, he could wait, and then he heard the gun sputter again and someone cough (as in the broadcast concerts his father listened to Sunday afternoons, the awesome swell of Brahms followed by a polite clearing of some Bostonian's throat). In the sudden silence the cough became a choked retching. Above, someone yelled for a medic, and Rennie thought greedily and with an instantaneous shame (though it was absolutely true) that he was too far away to help him. The man called and called, his voice dwindling. A Browning answered, and a brace of M-1s, and somebody—the platoon sergeant—slapped Rennie on the helmet, telling him to move out. Above, Bateman and Hall were struggling with the litter. As they humped up the hill, the sleet turned to snow. The air filled with the smell of electrified metal, the ozone of burnt-out brakes. Rennie followed in the sergeant's footprints, amazed that his legs complied, that his stomach felt fine, that—most astonishing of all—he was actually there.

Tony K was behind a boulder to the rear of the fighting, working on several men at once, one of them bandaged about the head and still calling weakly for a medic. The wounded were laid out in the snow; one was lazily kicking his legs, and when Rennie looked closer he saw he only had one arm. His face and chest were spotted with small, open wounds.

"Rock shrapnel," Tony K explained. "It's the fucking grenades. They just toss them out and they roll down." He got the man with one arm ready for Hall and Bateman to take down the hill. They covered him with a blanket, trying not to touch the blood, and strapped him in. A shell landed above them in the fog, and, like a willful sled, the litter tried to escape, stopped only when Bateman lunged in front of it.

"Goodbye," Hall said, hefting it.

"And good fucking luck," added Bateman. They made it a few feet before Hall fell, taking Bateman with him, then got up and continued down the mountain.

"Where do you want us?" Fecho asked Tony K.

"Anywhere. It's a fucking nightmare. There are guys all over the place."

It was noisy for a while. They hid behind the rock, pinned down, waiting to dash across the open snow. Streams of red tracers floated up into the fog. The *Pennsylvania* was finding the Japanese position's range; after one staggering burst, a scree of rock and debris tumbled past them down the mountain, in it—clearly—a flat helmet and a pair of leggings. The echo from the blast gave way to silence, only a few sporadic cracks of M-1s and, faint and paralyzing as his mother sobbing in her darkened bedroom, the pleas of the wounded.

First Fecho would go, then Mowry, and finally Rennie. He thought he wouldn't be able to move. The Browning covered them. Fecho looked back at him and Mowry as if to make sure they would follow, then dove into the open, zagging diagonally up the hill. Mowry let him get a ways before he tapped Rennie's chest with the back of his fist and—surprisingly agile for his size—clambered up the hill the other way. The sentimental whale. Rennie would have to remember to make fun of him. He peeked around the rock—snow, fog, darkness. On his right a different Browning had opened up (the new platoon!), and, not wanting to wait any longer, knowing it was a mistake, he retreated a few steps to get a running start, picked the line he wanted to follow and threw himself into the noise.

The Browning disappeared, sucked up along with every other sound into his lungs, his running. He wouldn't hear it if someone was shooting at him now, crouched and scuttling across the snow. He sidestepped a dropped rifle, hopped a crater and fell, and the world returned. A mortar sizzled, went silent, then blew a bright hole in the darkness a few yards above him; in the flash he saw a man fly backwards. He crawled up the mountain toward what he thought was a voice calling for a medic. It was a guess; a piercing, blank frequency interfered. The figure in the snow could have easily been dead (again, he was ready to see it), and then the head rose and fell back.

The man had been hit in the legs. His pants were soaked.

"What's your name?" Rennie asked him.

"It hit me," the man said. "I didn't even feel it at first."

Rennie read his tags—Blaine, Arthur J. "Arthur," he said, trying to get his attention.

"It was like a pinch, then it started feeling hot. I didn't think anything of it at first."

"Arthur, it's not bad," Rennie said, even before he cut away the cloth. There wasn't much to the wounds, just some dark-lipped gouges pulsing blood. It was nothing compared to Stephenson's man, but Rennie thought he should take a good look so he would remember it—his first wounded. He checked to see if either thigh was broken, then sprinkled a packet of sulfa on the exposed tissue and wrapped the worst parts with gauze. All the while, the man kept telling him how it had happened, mumbling as if Rennie had given him morphine.

"It hit me."

"I know, Arthur," Rennie said, "I saw."

"I didn't even feel it," the man said, clutching at his arm and starting to cry. "It hurts. I didn't feel it and now it hurts." Rennie felt his forehead and checked his eyes—swimming—and realized it was shock. For an instant he was outraged at his own incompetence, then just as quickly he relinquished his anger and started a bottle of blood. The man was incoherent now, slurring, his explanation giving way to panic. "I didn't feel it!" he cried, fighting him. Rennie called for a stretcher. He had to hold the man down until it arrived. The bearers were infantry, missing the Red Cross armband.

"Shock," Rennie explained, "it was my fault," but they didn't seem to care. He wondered how Burger was doing. It was past midnight, D-plus-1.

He wiped his hands on the snow and crawled to the next man—half buried in a foot-deep slit trench. There was only room for one, but the man slid over and let him in. The trench was filled with water and had a soft bottom of mud; though his feet were freezing, it made him feel ridiculously, giddily safe. The man was unhurt but said he didn't mind company, and Rennie was tempted to accept and dig in. They traded names—Lang, Burke—and shook hands as if at some fraternity bash. A shell rocked the ridge above them, sending down another avalanche of rubble and pieces of dead Japanese, and off in the dark the screaming started again. A wave of dust billowed over them and settled, the grit making his teeth squeak. Ahead, to the left, someone was down.

"Gotta go," Rennie said.

"So soon?" asked Burke.

This run was just as bad. The man was face down in the snow. Smoke rose from his cracked helmet liner. As a medic, Rennie was obligated to check, though even before he rolled him over, he knew. The man's ear had been blown off, and part of one cheek, all glossy with fresh, red blood. The other side of his face was fine. Dark hair, a day's stubble, a St. Christopher on a silver chain. He didn't recognize the man, and thought of Cal and who had found him like this. A citizen of Bagville. He didn't bother to read his tags. He'd leave the effects to Graves, the smart-ass sergeant with his hot coffee. It was another first, yet he felt as if he'd been doing this forever. He covered the man's face with the smashed helmet and, as if to comfort him, patted his chest once before moving on.

He was still only 0-for-1, the second guy didn't count. The next one would even it up. It was not a game, he knew; things wouldn't get better. His father's logic and optimism didn't apply here, had never applied anywhere—not in Putney or Galesburg or Cornell or Fort Emory—or only in his father's heart, and even there, Rennie suspected, they reigned shakily, yet, 0-for-1, he stole across the snow, looking to better his record.

He headed uphill toward a pair of men sharing a trench, only to find Fecho working on a sergeant shot through the hand. Tracers swooped over them into the fog. With the buzzing in his ears, Rennie couldn't tell how close the guns were.

"What do you know?" Fecho said.

"I missed a guy in shock."

"First guy?"

"Yeah."

"First time'll fool you," Fecho said. He turned the man's hand to snake the tape through the fingers. "First guy *I* had?" He stopped and coughed hard, spraying Rennie's face, and a splash of blood bloomed on his neck. He felt for his throat, missed, and fell face first into the slop at the bottom of the trench. The sergeant gaped, untouched, the roll of tape still hanging from his fingers.

Rennie's immediate reaction was to call for a medic, then he remembered that he was one. His mother had taught him, he'd had classes, he knew what to do. It seemed fortuitous, as if he'd stumbled upon an accident, and he laughed. A startle reaction, it was called; in basic the instructors had warned them of just this sudden distance. He rode it for an instant, and then the cold and the noise seized him, dragging him back into the present.

Rennie could taste Fecho's blood on his lips. The sergeant was whimpering. I am not afraid, he thought, repeating it to himself, trying to believe. Stop bleeding, stabilize patient. He scooted on his knees to Fecho's head and had just taken his pack off when something huge and scalding punched him in the jaw. Falling back, he thought calmly that he wouldn't have to be here any longer, and then a flood of warmth poured over him, drowning him in silence.

"James," the sergeant was saying, far away. "Hold on, James, someone's coming."

James is my father, he wanted to say, but the warmth rose in his throat, filling it, and again he began to slide under the silent water. James is my father, he explained to the mill kids by the side of the road, to Jay, to the baby forcing its way out of Dorothy. My father's name is James.

★ ★ ★

THE SCHUMANS DROVE DOROTHY TO THE STATION, Mrs. Schuman at the wheel, Mr. Schuman in the back of the LaSalle. He'd already said his final goodbye to her once, at the house. It was Saturday, dreamily blue, and he was working on the lathe in the basement. Like her father, he didn't see the point of coming down to watch her off in person, but Mrs. Schuman insisted.

"You know your way around the place," he reasoned.

"And who, may I ask," she'd argued, "is going to help with the bags?"

They were early, and Mrs. Schuman naturally drove slowly. As they poked from light to light through North Park, the momentum Dorothy had gathered packing seemed to dissipate. She thought she couldn't afford to question her decision again; it had been painful to make, and while even now she often caught herself disagreeing, reviling her faithlessness, she thought it best not to backtrack. If it was wrong she would simply have to live with it.

She watched the fat LaSalle slither across the storefronts. Jennifer slept on her lap in her basket; she loved the car's indolent purr. Sometimes after lunch, to put her down for her nap, Dorothy and Mrs. Schuman would take her for a ride around the block. Lately the garage had been so hot that Mrs. Schuman offered them the back bedroom. Dorothy agreed, but only for naps. At night, after the last hand of canasta, she and Jennifer returned to the stuffy cube, the fan squeaking on her nightstand. Mrs. Schuman understood her need for independence; she wasn't an obstacle to conquer, the way in school her mother had been her enemy, but more of a friendly neutral.

The day Dorothy had come back from the hospital, Mrs. Schuman said she knew about the telegram, that she'd known all along.

"You can't hide that," she said. "You can try but—dear, are you all right?"

They ate together now—meatloaf sandwiches and cold chicken—and lounged in the backyard, weeding the garden and tickling Jennifer under the chin with buttercups. Mrs. Schuman thought the Army should be doing more for her.

"I'm sorry," she said, "but you don't *lose* people like that."

She thought, under the circumstances, that Dorothy was making the right choice. It meant so much to Dorothy. At least someone agreed with her.

Her mother wanted her to come home.

"Penn Station?" she said. "We can meet you there."

"Mother, the whole town hates us."

"No. Everyone's been very concerned about Reynolds—very concerned."

"Who, Mother? Who's been very concerned?"

"Your father, for one."

"Who in town?"

"It's not one person, it's everyone. It's a feeling; you feel it. People say hello to me. We haven't had a window broken all summer."

"That's wonderful, Mother."

They stopped talking, and Dorothy wanted to apologize. She wasn't mad at her.

"Your father wants you to come home."

"I know he does," Dorothy had said, and silently damned her for making her feel guilty. "Do you think I want to do this?"

Now, inching through a district of pawnshops and all-night luncheonettes, Dorothy was unsure. As a girl in Galesburg she'd dreamed of living in a city. Every few days a southbound freight came through hauling lumber and ice from the high mountain lakes. There was a horseshoe curve in the river above town, and when you heard the steel wheels shrieking down the valley, wherever you were, you raced headlong for the grain elevator to see the men gaff fat patties of ice into a thundering tin chute. But what Dorothy loved even more were the Sundays in midsummer when the railroad added several maroon, gold-lettered coaches to ferry the rich back to New York City from their lodges in the Adirondacks. The passengers were dressed in winking sequins, dark watered silk and linen; they ate fresh watercress and tipped scandalous cocktails. Dorothy stood apart from the boys tussling in the dust over pennies thrown from the split windows, imagining herself inside the train, peeking out at the hot, ugly town from behind the shade, and then the chuff and tug of the engine taking her away, back to her friends and the splendor of the city. Now that she was finally here, she was leaving.

They cruised by the high iron fence of the hospital. Mrs. Schuman was showing her the sights one last time. Dorothy leaned across to see, but again couldn't pick her window out of the rows and rows. How intimate she'd been with this place, now so strange. She could see the view from her room, the ships slipping down the panes. The night nurse stalked the hall. Dorothy had filled out so many benefit forms that she knew the address by heart. Place of Birth.

"Say goodbye," Mrs. Schuman said.

At Sixth they turned south toward downtown, skirting the bottom of Balboa Park. The tree streets flew—Upas, Thorn, Spruce. Consolidated lay above them, its brick stacks spouting clouds. The company had changed badges since she'd quit, and two days ago when she'd tried to see the girls on third one last time, the guard wouldn't let her back in the factory. Shift was almost over, so she waited outside the gate, swaying with Jennifer. First shift slowly built in the fenced-off pen across the road. The guard unlocked the chain and swung the two halves back. He checked his watch, tapped it, and was just about to put it to his ear when the whistle blew. She could hear them coming. First girls on bicycles whizzed by, followed by a few running with their lunch pails, and then the road filled and a tide of women in the horrible brown uniform poured past her. She recognized faces. Jennifer woke up, grumpy, and Dorothy patted her back. She stood on tiptoes and waved, hoping Maureen or Velma or Eileen might see her. She'd taken too long; Jennifer was hungry, squaulling to be fed. Dorothy thumped and hushed her. She wanted them to see how big she was. The horde thinned, dwindled until the guard thought it safe to bring in first shift. Later she left a message for Mr. Mallon, but yesterday no one had called her back. He always said it was the shop's biggest problem—shifts never talked to one another. Dorothy had thought she'd see them again; now she promised she'd write them, care of the department. The parade of streets dragged on—Ivy, Hawthorn, Grape. A rube, she'd loved them at first, then as a transplant found them dumb, a child's idea of a city; now she knew she'd miss them, in an empty moment tick them off A to Z: Ash, Beech, Cedar, Date.

The station was on Broadway, down by the piers. Mrs. Schuman cruised the blocks for a spot, Mr. Schuman leaning over the front seats between them, calling, "Too small. Hydrant. Driveway. Loading zone." There was a shimmering concrete lot for the piers but it cost a half dollar. A man in a sandwich board paced the entrance, smoking a cigar. They tried the back streets, enclosed on all sides by anonymous office buildings, the stone walls throwing back the guttural chug of the LaSalle's engine. Nothing—it was Saturday, the streets were full of servicemen. They turned in circles, glimpsing the sea, then ducking through the cool gloom between buildings.

"There's one," Mr. Schuman pointed.

"Where?" Mrs. Schuman said as they drifted by an empty stretch of curb. A Chrysler behind them zipped into it.

"There," Mr. Schuman said.

"Do you want to drive?" she asked, and he leaned back.

"I'll pay for the lot," Dorothy said.

"Oh, no dear," Mrs. Schuman said. "We couldn't let you."

After circling for another ten minutes, Mrs. Schuman eased the LaSalle up to the man with the sandwich board and into the lot. "How is this, Norman?"

"Perfect," Mr. Schuman said.

Jennifer sensed the car stopping, and stirred. They were opposite the Broadway Pier; the piping of a calliope reached them, and the greasy smell of hot dogs. Waiting for Mr. Schuman to pop the trunk, she thought of that last day, eating cotton candy and laughing at each other in the wiggly mirrors. Yesterday she'd taken the free bus out to Fort Emory. She didn't know why. His division had been reassigned, his friends were off in the Pacific, like mythical beasts, believed in yet unseen. The Red Cross said it was a good sign that he was still missing, "That theater especially." She got off with the other wives, the girlfriends, the couples coming back happy from a long night of love. She had Jennifer with her for company, and stood outside the fence, watching those going in kiss goodbye, those coming out hello, until she was standing there alone.

"Excuse me, ma'am," the gloved MP asked her. "Are you waiting for someone?"

"No," she said, and went back to the bus.

Mr. Schuman was surprised she had so little, just a suitcase and a garment bag of dresses she'd brought from home but never worn. She'd come with this much and she'd leave with it. The only big thing she'd bought here was the fan, and that she'd left for the Schumans' next guest. There was no room for the cradle he'd made. She had five hundred dollars in her bank account and a fifty pinned to her bra strap. Why did she still feel she wasn't ready yet?

They walked away from the Pacific, up Broadway toward the station. The sidewalk was bright. Sailors filed past, kerchiefs awry, smiling at her holding Jennifer. Near the entrance, a beautifully dressed Mexican man was selling ties out of a suitcase with folding legs. "The best!" he said, fingering the silk for Mr. Schuman, whose hands were full.

Mrs. Schuman stopped to look.

"Helen, I have enough ties," Mr. Schuman said, sweating.

"But your black is getting so ratty."

They chose and then haggled. In those last moments before they turned to go inside, Dorothy looked back to the sea, the sky, the deep even blue. The Pacific had been her enemy, devouring outbound ships, and yet she wouldn't have survived without its sunsets, the brilliant mornings and florid afternoons. Through everything, she could rely on the heat to lull and drug her when she couldn't face being awake, and then, surfacing in the dusty-smelling garage from a long day's sleep, to drive her outside to the children's shower and back into the rhythm of life. And the waves, coming and coming. In the hospital she'd hated it, but before, sometimes at the end of shift, Dorothy would step outside and sit on the picnic table and watch the water swell, still gray under the pall of morning, the white lines running silently in to shore. The sea had made them happy on the pier, slapping the piles and sloshing beneath their feet. And the day trip to the island, the ferry they took, sitting on the top deck and tossing popcorn to the gulls. She didn't hate it. If there hadn't been a war on, she would have loved the sea. But when, she thought, had there not been a war?

In the station, people were sleeping in the ticket lines, passed out on their bags. It was dim. A fog of cigarette smoke hung in the gold rotunda. On each of the four marble walls an oversized clock marked the time. Even with Mrs. Schuman at the wheel, they were still early. They found Dorothy's track on the big board and walked down to the benches under the number. A marine noticed her shouldering Jennifer and gave up his seat.

"Thank you very much," Mrs. Schuman said, then bent over and in a whisper asked Dorothy if she had enough money.

"Yes."

"Why don't you take this anyway?" Mrs. Schuman pushed a folded fifty into her hand. It was more than Dorothy had paid them in rent the whole time she'd been in San Diego.

"Thank you," Dorothy said.

"May I hold Jennifer?"

"Of course."

Dorothy picked at the damp spot on her blouse. Mrs. Schuman hummed, swaying, then, giving Jennifer back, wiped her eyes. It was something her mother did, crying in train stations.

"Don't get me started," Dorothy said.

"Who wants a Coca-Cola?" Mr. Schuman offered.

"I don't think we have time, dear."

"Sure we do."

"Don't you know he has to get one now," Mrs. Schuman said, and he smiled as if given permission and headed off for a machine.

When he returned with an open bottle for each of them, it was five minutes to departure. Dorothy guzzled hers, tipping it back and studying the dirty mural lining the rotunda. Conquistadors in pointy helmets and their armored horses faced a smudged, heroic ocean. The built-up soot couldn't quite hide an idealized sun, its rays bladelike and golden, like the knives of light around the sacred heart in the picture beside her mother's hutch. For years, when Dorothy looked up from her corned beef, Jesus pulled his robe open and made a sign like a Boy Scout, and the nested meat glowed.

No, she didn't wish she were a girl again. It had been hard enough the first time. She wasn't going back to her mother's house, to the town she loved (it was pointless to deny it now) despite its pitilessness. She was leaving one place she'd never been for another, alone and with a responsibility she couldn't fail. As she watched the clock and worked toward the bottom of the Coke, Dorothy felt a part of her life closing. This city. She'd miss the fountains and red-tiled roofs, the whorled stucco package stores and the shattered glass in the gutters, the hot streets and beaches, just as she missed the chilly streams of Galesburg, the heavy smell of wood smoke through rain, the view from the Grayson place. She'd miss working in the dark belly of the night and fighting for a seat on the trolley. She'd miss even this crowded, dirty station. It was the first place she'd seen, and fittingly it would be the last. In between she'd seen so much. She'd gotten a job and made friends and had Jennifer. She'd only been in the city four months, yet she'd lived so much of her life here. Now she was leaving.

A conductor opened the door under the track number, and the benches stirred. The minute hand of the clock pointed toward the ceiling. Mr. Schuman put down his Coke and lifted her bags. Dorothy stood up and checked to see if she had what she needed. She had Jennifer. In her purse she had extra pads and two bottles of formula and makings for more. She had a pacifier, she had diapers and pins. She had her ring, her watch and her little tin alarm clock safely hidden away. In her suitcase she had Rennie's picture and the table radio. Her bankbook, her useless badge, her E for Excellence pin. She had the birth certificate and his insurance and the number of the Red Cross and the Army in San Francisco. She had money. Yes, she thought, I'm ready now. I'll never be this ready again.

She kissed Mrs. Schuman and followed Mr. Schuman into the crowd pushing toward the door, protecting Jennifer with her arm. They were among the last in line, and waited, commenting on the weather, the sleeping accommodations, what she would see.

Mr. Schuman wasn't allowed on the platform because he didn't have a ticket. The conductor called over a redcap to handle Dorothy's bags.

"I guess this is it," Mr. Schuman said. He took her and kissed her cheek, pressing two twenties into her palm. "In case," he said.

Dorothy thanked him, turned and waved to Mrs. Schuman—just as she'd turned (less than an hour ago!) to survey her empty apartment. She could still see the garage it had been, could still park the imaginary Dodge nose in against the fridge, but it had been home to her, hers, dearer than any place she'd ever lived, and while she was grateful, still, to see it stripped and ready for the next girl hurt her. She waved and waved, kissed Mr. Schuman again and followed the redcap through the door.

In the train there was nothing to look at. The paper thoughtfully left on the seat beside her was five days old (and still she searched the headlines for word from Alaska; she'd never seen any, none, only the Greyhound ad showing a muddy road crew gouging the ridiculous new highway through impenetrable forest). With no one on the platform to wave to, she pulled down the shade, closed her eyes and listened to Jennifer's breathing. She thought of Galesburg, the Sunday passengers from the Adirondacks. What kind of lives had she thought they were going back to? Simply being on a train had seemed magical to her; she didn't picture it stopping, the glamorous people getting out and going home. It just went on and on, all cocktails and starched collars and laughter, black cloches with beautiful plumes. She remembered walking home late one Sunday through the empty, shadow-dappled streets, her game of school with her friends erased by the train's arrival, thinking that once again she'd been left behind, that that life, as mellow and golden as the sun slanting under the trees and across the frost-heaved sidewalks, would never be hers.

When she woke up, the train was stopped on the floor of a desert. Jennifer slept across her knees, the bottom of her basket hot against her. Beside them, an older woman slumped, snoring. Dorothy raised the shade. She'd taken a seat on the left in hopes of seeing downtown and the bays on the way out—greedily, as she'd first gazed upon the city—and now felt cheated. There would be more cities, she reasoned, but none that were hers. The windows were closed against the dust. Outside, the desert shimmered, liquid. There was nothing but mesquite and rusted rock to the horizon, a dark hint of mountains in the distance. Above hung a perfect sky worthy of the Pacific.

In the aisle, the conductor stood, facing away from her. The people in the seats across the aisles were standing as well, peering out the window as if the train had hit something here in the middle of nowhere.

"Where are we?" she asked the conductor.

"Twentynine Palms," he whispered, only half turning to her. His hand was over his heart. In the opposite window, the bright stripes of the flag dipped and tilted, a miniature brass eagle gleaming atop the staff. Dorothy sat up to see. It was a Marine honor guard, behind them several men in khaki loading coffins into the back of a truck.

She stood and joined the other passengers—the whole train, she saw—paying homage. They didn't leave until the detail clunked the gate of the truck shut and, with the honor guard marching before it, bumped back toward the base. The train started off, but no one moved; they kept watching the procession across the desert, swaying with the acceleration. The heat made the men's legs disappear, and the tires, so that the whole entourage seemed to be floating, a mirage. They dwindled to dots against the fence, and, as if prompted, like a well-trained congregation, the passengers sat. The sand flashed by, studded with spiky clumps of white-flowered sage.

Dorothy drew her shade—cut by the precise shadow of the split window frame—and realized with a flinch of panic that she'd forgotten his star.

That was the start, Dorothy thought later. She would be alone on the train with Jennifer for four days and five nights, and every minute, with each blinding grade crossing and smoky depot, every stop in the desolate middle of the country to take on water, Dorothy knew that while she thought that all this time she'd been waiting, she had actually been saying goodbye to Rennie. And she had only just begun.

Mr. Langer hadn't changed. He met her train in a rumpled suit she remembered from school and immediately relieved her of Jennifer. Penn Station was ornate and ten times the size of San Diego's. A flurry of announcements, voices, and heels on marble echoed high in the vault above them, on each side of which an arched strip of windows admitted a cleansing light. Mr. Langer ("James, James," he encouraged her) tickled Jennifer's chin and gave her his finger to grip. A torrent of people poured around them. Dorothy was noting the resemblance between the two when he said Jennifer looked just like her. "And where did this hair come from?" It was midmorning but the whole trip seemed to Dorothy like a single neverending day, and she covered one eye with a hand to gauge her headache.

"You must be exhausted," he said, catching on late. She didn't mean to bully him. His look told her it was silly; he'd forgive her anything—and anyway, it was his fault. He gave Jennifer back to her and took her bags from the redcap. "This way," he said, and led her to the Buick, right outside the doors, with a ticket on the window. Fat and black and dented, it was as comforting and familiar as Mr. Langer himself. She hadn't thought she'd missed him.

She sank into the seat and watched New York spool by. Mr. Langer narrated. She'd expected more people on the streets, and better-dressed. The buildings thinned by the river. They swung onto an approach and rose, followed the arc of some famous bridge (he knew the name of it, it would come to him). Behind them, the city toed the lip of the river, a solid wall, the spires and boxy tops of skyscrapers peeking over the front row like the tall kids in a class picture. Mr. Langer pointed out the back window, hardly watching the road. She remembered that when he taught he constantly turned his back to the class and talked to the blackboard; no one could hear a thing he was saying. The Empire State, the Chrysler, the Woolworth Building. Dorothy thought that it would all be more impressive—would all make sense—if she weren't so tired.

They flew through Queens and soon the brick tenements and dark-porched rowhouses gave way to wooded hills and then green squares of farmland. The highway changed with a bump into a tarry county blacktop. The fields spread flat, the sky a wall on all sides. The sun was high now, flashing off passing cars, and a bite of brine seasoned the wind. Mr. Langer asked her about her job at Consolidated; he was working at Grumman and enjoying it. They joked about coffee and parts and quality control. He didn't think he'd like night shift, even with the pay differential.

"Family," he explained, then, as if he'd said the wrong thing, pointed to Jennifer, sleeping. "She's very good."

"She is," she said.

"And how are your spirits?" he asked cheerfully—exactly like a teacher, she thought, abrupt and not at all apologetic, as if given the right answer he could change the way she looked at the subject. He was sincere, and it didn't embarrass her, though she could hear Rennie sneering at his act. She'd always liked his class.

"They're good," Dorothy said, and, seeing that he wanted more, told him what the Red Cross had said. It was easier, though it hurt her to see how eagerly he agreed. She'd defended him from Rennie since they'd met. Now that Rennie was gone, she thought she'd be able to stop. She had so much of him in her.

"How's everyone here doing?"

"Good," he said. "We're all worried, of course. Jay's taking it the hardest, I'm afraid. I think we're all trying to be optimistic."

She could practically hear Rennie laugh.

"I think that's right," she said.

"Yes," he added needlessly, and, relieved that the talk was over, they rode in silence for a while.

"Queensboro," he said, miles later, waking her from a half-glassy sleep. "The Queensboro Bridge."

"Ah," Dorothy said.

They were all waiting for her on the porch of a massive gray-shingled house overlooking the ocean. A parched lawn ran down to the edge of a cliff, and there was the Atlantic, a blue floor, booming softly in the distance. It was noon and the locusts were going. The house was old, the color of ashes. In the shade cast by the single turret, a circle of white wicker furniture waited. It seemed unreal to Dorothy, but, still moving from the train and the car, she was willing to believe in anything that would let her rest.

First Mr. Langer introduced her to his father, a gray man in a white shirt buttoned up to his sagging neck. Jay helped him to his feet. Dorothy had been warned he'd had a stroke, but she wasn't prepared for only one side of his face to open, the other slack as dough. "Pleased to meet you," he said energetically. He could only stand for a moment, then, sloughing off Jay and blindly probing behind him with a hand, lowered himself into his chair again. Mr. Langer rested Jennifer's basket on the old man's lap; Grampa Langer spoke to her, waited for Jennifer's response, then nodded as if he agreed.

"Big kid," he said.

"Like her dad," Mr. Langer said.

Mrs. Langer seemed taller to her, and Jay, oddly, shorter. Anne (Dorothy would never get used to it) had tinted her hair and was wearing not only lipstick but a pancake base that clashed with her deeply tanned neck. She'd lost weight and sported heels, which only bolstered the impression that her head was on the wrong body. She crushed herself to Dorothy, then took Jennifer from Grampa Langer and waltzed with her across the porch, cooing. Her uniform emphasized her shoulders and hips and, watching her twirl, Dorothy realized with a pang that she envied her figure.

Jay seemed wary of her at first, but that was Jay. "Why so glum, chum?" she asked, pinching his arm, and he brightened. He hadn't gotten smaller, in fact had grown, but the change in him seemed minor beside his mother's sudden brilliance. Dorothy couldn't stop looking at her, thinking she was another person completely.

"They cut you, huh?" Jay said.

"Yep."

"It hurt?"

"Nah," she said, "I was O-U-T out," and flopped her head to one side, eyes closed.

"Where?" Jay asked.

Dorothy made a scalpel of her finger and he clutched his stomach.

"I'll show you later," she said. "For a price."

Mr. Langer brought her bags from the car. "This it?" he asked.

"Wait till you see the cottage," Jay said, hauling her up from the chair as if they were going to dance.

"I'm sure Dorothy would like to call her parents first," Anne suggested.

Dorothy thanked her for reminding her. She hadn't meant to, she always forgot, but today it seemed deliberate. On her way east, she'd phoned them from Kansas—Emporia, where second class had a half hour for dinner in the station—to make a joke about the Wizard of Oz and let them know she was halfway. The station house faced three towering grain elevators and, beyond them, the endless wheat fields, and, happy for the first time in months (she knew it was only momentary, for that reason abandoned herself to it), Dorothy had tried to describe to her mother the swallows zipping like dark scissors, the dust and the heat giving way to evening. The bustle of the station made her yell. "From here I can see—I don't know, five miles? You should see it. There's a kind of haze where they're cutting it. With machines, I don't know the name of them. You can see all this dust coming up in a dark cloud over them. And the birds swooping through it, it's fantastic."

"How's your milk?" her mother asked.

"My milk is fine, Mother, I'm not talking about my milk. Did I say anything at all about my milk?"

"I know you're upset, dear, but—"

"I am not upset!" Dorothy said, and another woman on the platform looked at her with fear, as if with Jennifer in her arms Dorothy might drop the receiver and with one punch knock her onto the tracks. "I'll call you when I get there," Dorothy had said, ending their conversation. Had it only been three days ago? Her mother wouldn't leave the house until she called. Already Dorothy felt sorry for making her wait. Their love was an argument, she thought, that she would always lose.

Inside, Grampa Langer's house was musty and cool, crammed with antiques and dark rugs and tarnish-spotted mirrors. Anne led her to the phone, an old candlestick model she needed both hands to use. Dorothy offered to pay.

"Don't be silly," Anne said, and left her.

Dorothy paused before dialing, savoring the moment alone, the quiet. She was still moving, but slower now, as if hours after the fact her nervous system were coasting into Penn Station. She didn't like the idea of calling at such a disadvantage, but thought it would be better to get it over with now when she could plead exhaustion. Her fingers knew the number, had known it her whole life.

Her mother picked up—as she always did, waiting to make sure the caller hadn't changed their mind—on the fourth ring.

"I made it," Dorothy said.

"Good," her mother said. "We were worried."

"Jennifer's fine. I'm fine. The Langers say hi."

"Say hi back," her mother said, and Dorothy could see they weren't going to talk, though her mother was alone in the house, probably just done eating lunch, a sliced-egg-and-lettuce sandwich and tea at the kitchen table (one cup, never two, or sweat sprang from her forehead and she had to lie on the sofa, pressing a wet washrag to her brow). She would dust and vacuum all afternoon, then take the mail out on the porch with a glass of iced tea and wait for her father to come home from work. The streets were empty, the lawns cut with shadows.

"How's Robert?" Dorothy asked.

"Still in Tunisia as of the first."

"Let's hope."

"How long are you planning to stay down there? I'm only asking because that's what your father will want to know."

"I'm not sure. Until school starts."

"It's closer than San Diego, I suppose," her mother said, and, off the phone, Dorothy appreciated how hard it must have been for her to concede that fact.

Her cottage was smaller than she'd envisioned and, once Jay had demonstrated the new light fixture Mr. Langer had installed, intensely bright. The ceiling, walls and built-in shelves were white, the floor a Navy gray. The door framed a view of sea and sky (like the hospital, she thought). A few screens were new, others had patches. Anne had made the curtains. A bed lay against one wall; opposite stood a wicker bassinet with a skirt. On a low table between two wicker chairs sat a radio identical to hers. There was even a fan turning in a corner, a shred of cloth tied to its cage flicking like a windsock. The Langers beamed at her, and Dorothy beamed back. She tried not to make a ceremony of her thanks, but Anne began to cry and hugged her, and, tired, grateful for all the work they'd done for her and touched by her mother's forgiveness, Dorothy honestly returned her embrace. Mr. Langer guessed that she'd like to get settled and maybe have a nap, and, after another formal round of kisses, they left her to unpack.

Rennie had made it unscathed. She leaned him on the shelf above the head of the bed. She took out her alarm clock and wound it and set the time by her good watch. She piled Jennifer's clean diapers on the shelf by the bassinet and lined up her bottles and the tin of formula. Her bankbook, her badge, Jennifer's birth certificate—she made a nest of her papers on the table. She put her clothes away, and Jennifer's outfits, and shoved the suitcase with the radio still in it under the bed. Satisfied, she stripped to her slip and lay down and closed her eyes and let the fan blow over her.

She'd stopped moving, but the sea was loud now, and she couldn't sleep. A spider had begun a web in the rafters above her. She could faintly make out under the new paint a confusion of names and initials gouged into the wood of the ceiling. Lovers, she thought, honeymooners. She twisted her wedding ring around her finger and looked at Rennie. In San Diego, she would have held him to her now, but this wasn't San Diego, this was as far from San

Diego as you could get. The sea outside wasn't the Pacific but its cold sister. The train had taken so long. Missouri, Illinois, Tennessee. She'd had time then to understand that she'd have to live by herself now, that there was no point in waiting, because, unlike her father drifting up from the mill after a Utica Club or two with his buddies, Rennie was never coming home—and if he did, she thought (for even now her mind pursued the miraculous, like water finding a giant dam's weakness), he would discover the garage empty, a monument to her unbelief. And so in retrospect, her decision to take the train—deliberate, a coward's retreat—had killed him.

The Atlantic filled the doorway, a cold blue. She looked around the walls. The white box was sadly familiar. Her new room wasn't that different from the Schumans' garage. All this work for her, all those phone calls. What was it but love? And still it hadn't rescued anyone. She lay in the heat under the ceiling, gazing out at the hazy line between the two blues, thinking of Amelia's empty garage and her landlady with the cigarettes, the mailbox waiting for the second telegram. She thought of his star, and Mrs. Schuman's roses, and found she didn't have the strength to banish them. The sea washed against the shore. Atlantic, Pacific—why did she think it would make a difference? She got up and closed the door, came back and took Rennie off the shelf and held him to her.

The days were the same. She slept as long as Jennifer let her, the clock continually disappointing. The sky wasn't as soft here, but the light was clearer. Each morning she opened the door to the gilded, blinding sea. She dressed Jennifer and climbed the cliff stairs in slippers and a borrowed bathrobe and padded over the dew-drenched lawn and up the porch and inside, where Anne was preparing breakfast.

Anne knew she was coming and made enough for two. In uniform she reminded Dorothy of Rennie—the hollow shoulders and long jaw. They sat across from each other, Jennifer on the table between them. They never talked about him, it was always the weather, or what was for dinner, or what to do with Jay and Win if it rained (it never rained). Anne ran down a list of errands; Dorothy countered with what she was going to do around the house. Like Anne's letters, it was all part of a truce, hastily called for his sake, and one she trusted would be broken.

"He loved poached eggs on toast," Dorothy expected Anne to say (tearfully, insanely, bravely) after some long pause, or, "He wouldn't touch prunes, wouldn't touch them," but day after day they ate alone, talking of nothing until one by one the men came down, and then it was all shoptalk and baseball. Oddly, it was one of the better parts of the day, when everyone was together and the task of getting Jay and Mr. Langer and Anne out of the house distracted her. Once they were gone, Dorothy was left with Jennifer and Grampa Langer, and the day gaped before her, bottomless, impossible to fill.

The radio was a weapon, Jennifer's nap, a walk on the beach. Jay came back from his paper route with Win. They were learning to play chess and kept Grampa Langer entertained. They were bored. The four of them sat on the porch, Jennifer staring up from her basket. It was still morning, not yet hot. In San Diego she would just be getting to sleep, the swallows splashing in the birdbath. Anne had pressed a copy of *Forever Amber* on her, and Dorothy leafed through it, the story eluding her. London in the 1600s, some sort of intrigue. The endpapers were a map of the city that she kept checking, trying to figure out where she was. When she looked up, the sea was still there, the lawn, the paint flaking off the porch floor. The old house creaked in the heat. Jay was down to a pawn and a king making a last stand in a corner. The mail came, nothing to be afraid of. It was almost lunch. This time of day was the worst, when the light seemed so promising. The boys made adventurous plans for bicycle trips; Grampa Langer flagged. She fixed lunch and then it was his nap time. The boys spun off with their poles and tackle box, the pockets of their shorts jingling with change. Anne suspected they spent their afternoons in town or at the movies, looking for girls their age. It was too late, Dorothy wanted to say, the summer was almost over.

The house then, already quiet, gathered its stillness, and for the next several hours Dorothy was left in a brilliant limbo to pore over her life—short, she'd thought, just begun, but now that she was exploring it, it seemed immense, a large part of it hidden within her, friends from childhood startlingly remembered, or the sudden discovery of her hand fishing in her mother's purse on the kitchen doorknob. The obsolete tea-towel calendar, the dark beyond the furnace. She walked the emptied streets of Galesburg, filling in storefronts. She could lie down on the yellow line right in front of the courthouse, could sneak a sticky bun from behind Meeker's counter. She was sitting in class—Mrs. Pinchon's Hygiene, not Mr. Langer's—and she stood up and walked the rows, touching each person on the head, telling the future. The red second hand of the clock rolled, and then she was at the Grayson place, standing at the terrace rail, looking down the blue valley, where years ago (she knew from how many tests and essays, how many crepe paper plays) Leander Gale and his band of rebels had stood watching the British column file along New Carthage Pike before plowing them under with their own guns. The statue in front of the courthouse pointed heroically, directing fire at the Woolworth's across Main Street. Every Fourth of July, the mayor leaned a wreath from Cutler's Nursery against the plinth; the firemen dressed like clowns and threw candy from the truck. So little of it seemed important to Dorothy—how in the Clinton Street Pharmacy the candy bars were arranged by letter, the gum kept separate—and yet she delighted in re-creating the details, fitting Galesburg together shop by shop, house by house, street by street, like a giant puzzle she'd done before yet would never finish.

She remembered Rennie—too easily, she thought. The first time she'd denied herself the grief, reached in mid-reverie for Jennifer and paced the porch with her. It was the summer before the war, before the Langers moved to Galesburg. Dorothy and her friends were lounging around the town pool when Amy Loftis rode up on her bike and reported breathlessly that she was coming back from the reservoir when she saw this boy working on a car in old Reverend Clayborn's yard.

"Is he worth the trip?" Carol Thomas asked.

"Is any guy?" Dorothy joked, but everyone knew they'd go. It was summer, it was Galesburg.

It seemed eerily fitting that her first memory of him now would be her first memory of him ever, the wave he gave all five of them on bikes, fingers black with the blood of his long-lost Mercury. She could bring back the smell of the freshly oiled and cindered road, the high grass waving in the ditches, but at the last minute chose not to continue. (At the reservoir she'd said she didn't think he was that attractive. "She's got it bad," Carol said, and they all hollered, "And that ain't good!" so it echoed over the water. As they passed him on the way back, Carol shouted, "Her name is Dorothy Baines!" and they raced away laughing.) She thought that, as with Galesburg, once she started she would have to remember everything.

She spent the afternoons, then, in Galesburg, but while she resisted the greater temptation, she couldn't stop an occasional frame of Rennie from sneaking in. After a while, she didn't try, but sat happily surprised, as when without announcement "Racing with the Moon" came on, the first song after a ball game. She attended these memories with the low flame she held for Vaughn Monroe's swelling tremolo, a sentiment easily reached and then stored away for the next slow song. She glanced at Jennifer, looked out to sea, and, after the number of pages she'd promised to read before peeking, checked her watch again.

The plane came over at four. She helped Grampa Langer downstairs and into his chair. "How is it today?" he'd ask her, and she'd say she hadn't given up. "Not me," he'd say, "I'm just waiting around now," and though from what she could see it was true, he wanted her to laugh with him, and she did. They were fast friends, thrown together, and owed each other nothing. They would never know each other, and so joked, kept things pleasant and open-ended. Sometimes, getting his juice or his blanket, Dorothy wondered if they believed what they were saying, but while it was a question of the greatest importance to her—maybe the only question left—she understood that with him it didn't matter.

Mr. Langer returned from work, and not long after that, Anne.

Most days Jay rode up alone, but on Fridays when the boys collected, Win ate with them, shy of her and comically polite. It was Dorothy's job to set the table. Jay liked to sit beside her, as did Anne, which Dorothy knew she shouldn't mind. Anne and Mr. Langer traded saying grace, their voices turning grave and heartfelt when they mentioned Rennie. Uncharitably, Dorothy thought it seemed natural to Mr. Langer; with Anne she wasn't sure how much was an act. Dorothy had always been suspicious of her, with a daughter-in-law's eye for flaws. Rennie said his mother was moody and theatrical, but since they'd been going steady, Dorothy had found her frighteningly inconsistent and—even at her best, when she chose one role—overblown and unconvincing. When Anne said grace, Dorothy watched Mr. Langer. There was something wrong between them, Dorothy was sure. Silence filled the gaps between his anecdotes and her list of the day's injuries. Usually quiet, Jay shoveled his food, and when he did say something, spoke only to Grampa Langer or Dorothy herself. She tried—as Rennie would—to side with Anne, but couldn't. Because, Dorothy thought, she wished that, like Mr. Langer, she truly believed. Because she hated being a fraud herself.

Jay was the first one done and, excused, escaped. Dorothy helped clear but Mr. Langer wouldn't let her do the dishes. She and Anne ended up on the porch together, watching the lightning bugs come out. Jay and Grampa Langer hunched over the chessboard. She and Anne talked about Jennifer's day or, if Dorothy's mother had called, what was new in Galesburg, and soon Mr. Langer rescued them with his flashlight, leading an expedition down the beach or behind the house to check on his garden. The bugs were out now. Grampa Langer retreated inside to listen to the radio, Anne to read or knit. With the blackout shades down the yard was dark, the porch steps treacherous. For Dorothy this was the easiest time of day. Jennifer needed her attention, and if she chose she could withdraw to her cottage and listen to the broadcast concerts from the city, a muted trumpet pouring from a starlit rooftop above Central Park. In the background, glasses tinkled, and, rocking Jennifer in her arms, she pictured herself in a strapless, low-backed velvet gown and sequined gloves that stretched to her elbows, swaying to "Stardust" or "Mood Indigo." Silly, she knew, but alone in the cottage, she needed some comfort, and the radio stayed on, a constant friend.

The nights were cold, and Mr. Langer and Jay came down to put up her shutters and ask if she and Jennifer would rather sleep in the house. Though Dorothy worried, she always said no. Waking late at night, she regretted her decision, but by morning summer had returned. Light filtered in; the radio said it was going to be a scorcher. She pointed her toes into her slippers, hauled on Anne's old bathrobe. The sea was still there, the stairs, the house. Every morning, walking across the lawn, she thought it couldn't go on forever, that soon she would have to go home.

One rare rainy afternoon she and Grampa Langer and Jay and Win were sitting on the porch when the phone rang. She waited for Jay to get it, but he was wiggling a rook above the board, and she dog-eared the page she was on. The house was gray, the air weighted and cold.

"Is this the residence of a Mr. J. Langer?" a woman asked prissily.

"This is the Langer residence," Dorothy corrected her.

"This is Sally Wickes, with Western Union? I was wondering if there would be anyone home to receive a telegram later this afternoon."

"When?" Dorothy asked, suddenly dizzy.

"We're not sure when our carrier will get to you, but certainly before five o'clock." It was not quite two; Grampa Langer was overdue for his nap.

"Who is it from?"

"I'm afraid I can't give you that information."

Dorothy thanked her, and, like a librarian, the woman said sweetly, "You're quite welcome."

"Who was it?" Grampa Langer asked, and when Dorothy answered, "Western Union," the boys looked up at her.

"They didn't say who it was from," she said, though no one believed her. She sat down as if the day would simply continue.

"I ought to get home," Win said, and stood.

"Don't be silly," Dorothy said, but he zipped up his jacket and bumped his bike down the stairs. Jay stood talking with him in the parking lot in the rain, and then Win waved ("So long, see you tomorrow!") and Jay came back to the porch with his hands in his pockets.

Dorothy asked him if he knew his parents' work numbers, and he showed her a card on the refrigerator. Mr. Langer said there was no reason to panic, but that he'd head home right away. Anne could make it in half an hour. Dorothy wondered if in San Diego a messenger was speeding for her garage, and thought of Mrs. Schuman watching him coast past her kitchen window and flip down his kickstand.

She asked Grampa Langer if he was ready to go upstairs.

"I think I'll hold off for today," he said. "Jay looks like he needs someone to beat."

"All right," she said, and sat down with her book. She found she couldn't read; the sentences and then words crashed into each other, piled up meaninglessly, the way they did when she'd had wine with dinner. She tried to concentrate, to lose herself in that distant England, the backstabbing and pageantry, but felt shaky, liquid, as if she had the flu, and before she could stand to run for the kitchen, she was sick—on the chair, on her sandals, on the floor.

Her first concern was that Jennifer was all right; she was sleeping, oblivious. Jay and Grampa Langer stared at her from the chessboard, and then Jay jumped up and ran past her into the house.

"I'm sorry," she said.

"It's okay," Grampa Langer said, a prisoner in his chair. "It was time to wash the porch anyway."

Jay came out with a sopping dish towel for her, and a few minutes later a bucket of hot water and a mop. No one wanted her apology. Her sandals were ruined; she kicked them onto the wet lawn. A flock of gulls sat on the grass waiting out the rain; for no reason, she hated them. Her mouth still tasted bitterly of it. She asked Jay to watch Jennifer and went upstairs and took a shower, swishing the hot water and scrubbing her skin till it hurt, then went down to the cottage for some new clothes.

In San Diego when she'd received the first telegram, she'd taken it inside and, leaning against the counter, opened it. She didn't have to read it all, but did, then dropped it into the sink, a corner landing in the one dirty dish, a bowl of soapy water. Angry with herself, she snatched it out and threw it to the floor and, as if it were the enemy, stomped on it with both heels until she'd had enough, then lay down on the warm floor beside it, holding her belly. She'd thought then—wrongly, she now saw—that the second one would be easier.

The rain lingered. Dorothy didn't try to read anymore. Jay and Mr. Langer quit their chess game and listened to the radio—the Yankees from the Stadium. The announcer wasn't allowed to mention the weather, and when play stopped in the middle of the sixth inning, he said, "It's official. Yanks five, Browns one, and we'll see you next time, gang." A crash of static ripped through the Pennzoil jingle. She could see, far out, a cloud dragging a heavy skirt of rain across the water, and in minutes the gray wall swept over the lighthouse and the beach and across the lawn, pushing a chill wind before it. The gulls scattered, screeching. The porch roof crackled, the gutters rushed.

Anne arrived in the middle of the downpour, wearing a sweater over her uniform, her hair and face destroyed. She'd been crying; mascara had crept into her crow's feet. She gave Dorothy a hug, and Jay, and Grampa Langer, still seated. In the gloom, she looked old and frightened. Dorothy thought of Jennifer, if something should ever happen to her (and it would; one thing she could count on was that the world would try to hurt her child), and the smug superiority Dorothy had felt—and that one moment of envy—seemed embarrassing to her now, and shameful.

"Have you called your mother?" Anne asked.

"I'm going to wait," Dorothy said.

Anne only nodded.

A cold fog had settled, but no one left the porch. Only Grampa Langer sat, the rest of them kept getting up and walking to the top of the stairs or pacing the rail. Jay put some music on the radio; with a gentle glance Grampa Langer convinced him to turn it off. The lawn couldn't hold all the water. Rivers formed in the creases, met in a brown delta and poured down the cliff stairs.

"We might listen to the news," Anne offered, and Jay fiddled with the dial.

He was zeroing in on a faint Hartford station when a dark car crested the drive.

"It's Raymond Benjamin," Grampa Langer said.

"I remember him," Anne said. She stood and wiped her palms on her skirt as if it were an apron.

The car was a big Mercury. The driver left the lights and wipers on and ran up the walk, holding the billed hood of his slicker with one hand. In the other he carried a small yellow envelope. Anne waited at the head of the stairs, Dorothy beside her. The man handed it up, half waved to Grampa Langer and headed back to the car.

The envelope was from the War Department in San Francisco. It was addressed to Mr. Langer. Anne turned it over; it was sealed. She handed it to Dorothy, as if it were hers to open. It was light, and Dorothy thought—wildly—that it might be empty.

"We'll wait for him," she said and, unopposed, laid the envelope on the open middle of the chessboard.

"So the Yanks continue to hold the hot hand," the radio said, before Anne shut it off. "Was I supposed to tip him? I was, wasn't I?" She crossed her arms and held herself. "Is anybody hungry?"

"Not I," Grampa Langer said.

"Dorothy? Jay? No? We'll just wait then." She sat down, straightened the edge of *Forever Amber* with the table and got up again. Jay went inside, in a minute came back with the front of his shirt tucked in.

"He said he was leaving at least two hours ago," Dorothy assured them.

"When do the buses run?" Grampa Langer asked, and Jay ran upstairs to look for a schedule, only to return empty-handed.

"Can we all sit still for ten minutes?" Anne said. "Please."

They each took a chair, Jay beside Grampa Langer, Anne by

Dorothy. The rain had died down, and they could hear the sea. Dorothy thought that all of her waiting, all of the late shifts and train stations and days alone in the hot garage, had trained her for this. She remembered standing at the door to the platform with Mr. Schuman; behind her, across the smoky rotunda, Broadway ran down to the bright Pacific. The conductor had called the redcap, and now all she had to do was step across the brass threshold, but suddenly she couldn't remember why she'd decided to leave. A scarf of steam leaked from between the train's driving wheels, and around her the rotunda fell silent. Her doubt was momentary; she'd already decided, never mind how. The murmur of the crowd returned; the redcap hefted her bags and, finding them light, grinned. She waved, kissed, smiled. She stepped across the threshold. But daily on the train, that gap—the unasked and therefore unanswered question—bothered her. Why did she leave? She could list the reasons, beginning with Jennifer (the loneliness really), but it didn't stop her, even now, from wondering why after so long she'd given up so easily.

Jay was the first one to see Mr. Langer walking his bike down the drive. He jumped up, glanced at his mother for permission, and ran across the parking lot. Mr. Langer gave him the bike, and the two came up the front walk. Again, Anne and Dorothy waited at the head of the stairs. Mr. Langer's gray suit was soaked black. The bike's chain had snapped.

"Jay says it came," he said.

Anne pointed to the chessboard.

He climbed the stairs, keeping an arm over Jay's shoulders. He kissed Anne and then Dorothy and, leaving Jay with them, walked over to the chessboard. The floor creaked under his feet. He patted his father's shoulder before picking up the envelope.

"You didn't have to wait," he said, and tried to smile for them. Dorothy, Anne and Jay were still standing at the head of the stairs, watching from a distance, as if he were defusing a bomb.

He turned the envelope over and slid a fingernail under the flap. He opened it and pulled out a thin yellow slip, which he held in front of his face with both hands as if trying to pull it apart. His fingers were black from trying to fix the chain; one of his knuckles was bloody. As he read, he lowered the paper, then, finished, turned to them.

"They found him," he said, and for an instant Dorothy couldn't read his face. Apparently no one else could either, because he looked around at them as if they purposely hadn't heard him, then calmly explained, like a teacher having to remind a slow class of something he'd already taught them, "He's coming home."

MID-AUGUST. Days of heat and stillness, insects. This was the season James waited for, the humid, misplaced heart of summer when the tar on the town road held the imprint of his bike's tires and any water tempted him. He swam before supper, occasionally Jay or Dorothy watching him from shore, and one morning rose before Anne and snuck down the cliff stairs in nothing but a robe and waded completely free into the frigid surf. He floated, let the salt hold him up. He could forget Diane, forget another man touching his wife. All that was gone. Rennie was on a hospital ship out of Honolulu, aboard a troop train crawling for Chicago. Sweating, James took the bus to work, and sweating, rode Anne's bike home, never testing the woods' cool promises. Mornings, fog caught in the trees, a crisp hint of fall coming on, and James thought of Galesburg, his teaching certificate. Even as the heat deepened, summer was beginning to end.

Since Rennie enlisted, James had imagined what he'd say to him the minute he stepped off the train, what his first words would be. He didn't trust himself to come up with something on the spot. He didn't want to make a speech, just something simple that would let his son know how proud he was. Originally he favored "You made it," but as the day grew closer he leaned toward "Welcome home." It seemed less desperate, and if it was on every banner strung across every Main Street in every town in America, it wasn't from lack of imagination or the product of mawkish sentiment but because it was true—and, he thought, after everything that had happened, especially true of their home. He didn't expect any great moment of forgiveness or understanding between them, though he knew that, once there, holding his son in his arms, he would want one. And so now he hedged in the disappointment he knew he would feel, just as he had all these years with Anne. It was his mother, James thought; he had learned too young to accept defeat, to anticipate it, to gauge its slow approach.

"Welcome home," he would say, and hold Rennie a minute before passing him to Anne. He wouldn't press him, as Jay would, on what the war was like. There would be time to talk later, after everyone had gone to bed—maybe on the porch or walking on the beach. He might break out his father's scotch and then just pour and listen. He wouldn't pretend to understand. It wouldn't change what Rennie thought of him (it was too late for that; they were both too old, the past cooled and hardened to rock within), but the image of the two of them talking late into the humid night stayed with him, and on the Saturday Rennie was scheduled to arrive, James placed two chairs at the far end of the porch, not quite facing each other, separated by a knee-high table.

Rennie's train was due into Penn Station at four that afternoon. Sarah had offered to watch their father so everyone could go, but now, well past two, she was late. When James called her apartment, the phone rang and rang. She'd stopped seeing her engineer, and James had to smother his worst suspicions. She'd be here, he thought. She'd been at work all week.

James fumbled with the limp spider of Jay's bow tie. The boy was in his best dress pants and a white shirt; he'd outgrown his jacket these past months. James wore his funeral suit, a loose, cool gray. Anne, still in the bathroom, would choose the same blue scoop-necked affair she'd worn for Rennie's graduation, taken in. Dorothy had come up twice to iron, looking harassed, her hair up in a towel. His father waited for them on the porch, baffled by Jay's Baby Brownie. He was fading, repeating things. Anne had had to dress him. James hadn't seen him in a tie since childhood; the effect was unsettling. He expected guests to drive up in steaming Reos and Maxwells and Lamberts, the lawn set for croquet.

"Ow," Jay said, his chin pointing to the ceiling.

"You've got to learn how to do this yourself," James said.

Anne flashed across the hall in her slip.

"Are you done in there?" James called.

"For now."

He ran water onto a brush and drew it through Jay's hair, finishing just as Anne barreled in, her lips prickling with bobby pins. Since the telegram, things had been better between them. It was just a lull, but James appreciated it anyway, hoped, for now at least, that she was done punishing him. He sent Jay downstairs to show his father how to use the camera again and lingered behind Anne while she made up her face.

"You shaved," she said, and reached a palm over her shoulder to stroke his chin. His arms circled her, and she let him press against her, didn't tense the way she had just a few weeks ago. Was it just Rennie?

The doctor he'd talked to in Hawaii said the damage was superficial, but every time James caught himself in a mirror, he questioned his skin. Gunshot wound, jaw, the doctor said, reading from a chart as if it were a parts list: cracked stabilizer fairing, left hand. At work, when anything failed, James had to inspect the damage and then the repair, stamping and signing everything before they let the plane back on the flight line. Rennie must be all right, he thought; otherwise they wouldn't have released him.

"You're mussing me," Anne said, shrugging him off.

"Tonight," he tried.

"We'll see."

The phone rang in his father's bedroom.

"That's your sister saying she'll be late," Anne said.

"I'm going to be a little late," Sarah told him.

"We guessed that," he said.

"But I will be there."

"Did you ask her where she was?" Anne asked. "How far, how near?"

"She'll be here," James said.

The dining room was festooned with twists of crepe paper, the table already set. In the icebox an illicit leg of lamb marinated beside a legal but very dear bottle of champagne. James joined Jay and his father on the porch. The flag looked tattered; he wished he'd noticed it before. Jay had three rolls of film and was determined to shoot them all today. James stood behind his father, thinking how few pictures he had of him. Dorothy came up carrying Jennifer, Dorothy in a flower print and the baby in a gauzy white gown. Jay clicked away, frowning down into the camera as if it were a bomb-sight. Finally Anne came out, resplendent in blue (what couldn't he forgive her?), and they took a few group shots while they waited for Sarah.

"Go ahead and go," his father said, but no one listened to him.

She showed up twenty minutes later in someone else's car—a beautiful '41 Olds: Hydra-matic, the whole package—and fished from the trunk a white wreath of mums and a collapsible stand. WELCOME HOME, RENNIE, the painted sash read in gilt, and everyone was sorry they were still angry with her.

"That's your sister," his father said.

"Do you want me to take it back?" Sarah said.

"It's very nice," James said, trying to intervene.

"Hold it," Jay said. Peering into the viewfinder, he baby-stepped to one side. His part was crooked.

"One big happy family," Sarah said through her smile, but as they were heading out asked James how he thought their father looked. They agreed he seemed bad.

In the car, Dorothy said it was nice of Sarah to stay with him, and James could feel Anne trying to hold back.

"Yes," she said, "it was very nice of her."

They were late, and he kept expecting cops. Traffic was heavy, people already coming back from the beach. He hadn't driven the

Buick since he picked up Dorothy. He'd lost track of the mileage but was sure it needed an oil change and a new air filter, possibly a tune-up. The floor mats were dusty, the radio on the wrong station. Maybe Rennie could look at it tomorrow, or next week sometime, it didn't matter. They could look at it together, the way they had in Putney, leaning over the engine and consulting like surgeons. Jay could bring them out a beer and the three of them could sit on the front bumper and look back at the house, at his father sitting on the porch. See, he'd say to his father (without words), these are my sons; this is what a family does. And his father would say (without speaking), You don't know how it really was. You don't remember the bad days, you don't remember what she was really like. No, James would say, I remember everything, all the days, the locked door, the tray. Except the day she left. I don't remember her leaving.

Jay leaned over the seat and took a picture of him, and, awakened, James noticed no one was talking. Anne had her window closed to protect her hair and sat fanning herself with an old *Collier's*. She looked at him as if he'd asked a question she didn't quite hear. He shook his head, shrugged. The radio played some kicky swing, fat saxes and tom-toms. "Cherokee." They played it at work, the sound bunched and muffled in the high trusses of the hangar.

"This year," Dorothy said from the back, "I swear I haven't done so much traveling in my life."

"We all have," Anne said, and they watched the green swaths of farms flash past, the fences and clumps of cows, the weathered machinery. Jay rolled down his window and took a few hopeful shots. The hills came. They skirted the railroad at Ronkonkoma and followed the empty tracks all the way to Bethpage, the sun racing in the trees. James imagined Rennie coming from the west, clattering through the slums of Paterson or Passaic with the entire country behind him, and their meeting at Penn Station seemed not routine but destined, their neatly opposed approaches dramatic. By the time they hit Garden City, he felt jittery and lightheaded, as if he hadn't eaten. Sweat trickled down his ribs. "Welcome home" seemed dumb, not enough. He looked over at Anne; she had her headache face on, as if he'd purposely picked the slowest route. He swung north to take Nassau Boulevard in, and the rowhouses began. They passed softball games, catching just the arc of one pitch; theaters with lines of children waiting for the matinee; men selling suits out of the trunks of cars. They shot past heavily guarded factories, windows painted over, and truckyards, all barbed wire and grit, until they could smell the river, and then the road rose and they could make out the tips of the city.

"Dorothy," he said, "what bridge are we on?" Anne shook her head at his incorrigibility.

"The Queensboro Bridge," Dorothy said, and smiled in the mirror.

They were going to be late. He fought the taxis light to light, using the Buick's size. Jay had been asleep when they passed through the city the last time, and opened his window to appreciate the buildings.

"Save some film for your brother," Anne warned. "You're lucky no one's grabbed that out of your hands."

They parked in a lot and walked to the station, Jay hustling to keep up. It was hotter here, humid, the air dirty with exhaust and the smell of baking sidewalks. It reminded James of high summer in Putney, the light heavy, as before a thunderstorm. (The leaves turned around the courthouse, showed their pale undersides; Woolworth's windows seemed rich for a change, warm and luxurious.) The blocks were longer, and Jay complained. Red-fendered cabs streamed past; ahead, traffic stopped and clotted, and the sidewalk was alive with redcaps slinging bags. James pointed, and Dorothy smiled. His suit was a mess. Somewhere a fan blew a rancid gust of fry grease, which lifted only after they passed through the doors and into the cool of the station.

The big clock said they were late, but the signboard above Rennie's track said the train had been delayed. It seemed both a reprieve and an extra measure of torture. A fair crowd had gathered, turned to the closed door. Toddlers perched on their mothers' shoulders; older couples clutched each other's hands. The wall had been done up in bunting, and everyone had a flag. A few stanchions linked by velvet ropes cleared a path from the door.

"Do they know how late it's going to be?" Anne asked no one in particular, and James went off to find out.

The balding, visored man in the ticket booth said twenty minutes tops. "It's the tunnel," he said, as if everyone knew, and James didn't ask him if the twenty included the ten it was already late.

"What tunnel?" Anne asked James.

"I didn't ask what tunnel. I don't think it matters."

"Obviously not," she said, and Dorothy looked off to the ceiling. "I suppose you're right. It's annoying, is all. Thank you for asking him."

They stood there waiting before the door, jostled by the crowd. The benches were filled. There were servicemen sleeping along the walls on their duffels, and near the entrance to a passageway a bum and a ragged woman in heels were grappling over a rolled newspaper, pieces of which tore free and fell around them as they fought. Jay was watching two sailors pitch pennies; James turned to Anne and Dorothy to block his view of the scuffle.

"It's a beautiful building," Dorothy said.

"It is," James seconded. From the door came a wrenching screech, and for a long minute the floor shook. Everyone moved a foot toward the door.

"Is that us?" Anne asked.

The door opened, and a man in a blue uniform came out with a stepladder and changed the sign to ARRIVED, took the DELAYED sign inside and closed the door again. Jay took a picture of the sign. James looked around for the bum and the woman—both disappeared, as were the shreds of newspaper, swept up, James assumed, by a man wheeling a trash can.

From a speaker he didn't see, a mechanical voice announced the train's arrival, and still the door didn't open. The crowd muttered, and a few men shouted, "Let's go!" and "What's the holdup?" Jay looked to James to see if he was enjoying the spectacle as much as he was, then turned back to the door, his camera poised.

The "Marine Corps Hymn" jangled from the speaker and the door opened. Anne took his hand. He'd known the train was all military, but the sight of the young men in their blue tunics, one after another, surprised and heartened him. Each carried a stuffed ditty bag and a rose. A photographer leaned over the velvet rope and let off a flash that sent shadows jumping up the wall. People were cheering (he himself was) and waving their tiny flags as if at a parade. The music crashed and fuzzed and crackled. He noticed a bandage on one man's hand and an eye patch on another, but most were untouched, even those whose Purple Hearts hung beside their campaign ribbons. How quickly they healed, and how brave they were, the young. He cheered and cheered. Even Anne, beside him, clapped politely.

The door closed, the record faded in the middle of a verse, and then it was "Off we go into the wild blue yonder," and the Air Corps in their olive-drab jackets filed out. "It's alphabetical," he told Anne, pointing to the names sewn above their breast pockets. There were only a few, maybe twenty, and a redheaded girl in a peppermint skirt kissed some of them as they passed.

"Why does it have to be such a production?" Anne yelled in his ear. Beside her Dorothy swayed with the baby, who was screaming red-faced and unheard in all the noise.

"Anchors Aweigh" came on, and the Navy marched out, spectacularly clean in white. A few men tossed their caps at the big clock, and one (a New Yorker, James presumed) made a display of kissing the filthy marble floor. Families were beginning to leave with their boys, wives with their men. The Marines, it seemed, were forbidden to smoke in public, but everyone else was lighting up. Mothers had brought food; fathers, beer or cigars. One sailor had a dog waiting for him, a shaggy golden retriever; the two of them danced, and then, like a shepherd hefting a lamb, the man knelt and arranged the dog across his shoulders and walked away between his parents. Jay looked up at James, impressed.

"Rennie's next," James shouted, and pointed to the door, which had closed again.

The pop and hiss of a needle tracking the empty edge of a record droned over the speaker, and then the jaunty, trilling fifes began "The Caissons Go Rolling Along." The door opened. They were wearing their khakis—overseas caps, ties and all. The first was a stubby corporal, comic beside the rock-jawed Marines, but the hand for him was far larger. These were their sons, the enlisted and the draftees who'd gone and fought. In Galesburg, beside the blackboard in every class hung a sheet of oaktag on which students glued snapshots of friends and loved ones in the services. In homeroom, throughout the year, they read letters from them, and occasionally, when called on, a student would stand and say they hadn't heard anything and then sit down, leaving James to move to the next person. He knew they hated him then, and yet it didn't matter. In a way, though they didn't know it, he was teaching them something they needed to learn, because he knew that eventually Rennie would go. Because he knew his son. If he'd lost him in Putney, he had also, in their first years there, earned his love. All those days learning to throw inside and to rely on the curve late in the count had ingrained in Rennie not a love of the game or the urge to win but—what James had lacked—the courage to try to do what he knew might hurt him. And he had, twice, and survived. Like each of these men, Rennie had served (and that in itself deserved love), but James saw now that his son was doubly a hero.

The Army was the largest. The "Caissons" ended and, crackling, began again. As the men and their families drifted off, the cheering died down. They were at the head of the crowd now, pressed against the velvet rope, the soldiers passing at arm's length. The Js filed past, and the few Ks. Jay solemnly framed the door in his Brownie. Anne let go of his hand.

Later James would think it wasn't so strange that none of them recognized him at first. It wasn't only the music and the confusion that disconcerted them. The private who broke from the file toward Dorothy had a thinner build than Rennie. He seemed taller and hollow, a scarecrow with a sharper face and a crew cut. James, having discounted him, had stepped aside to let him through (as had Anne), and was hopefully scanning the next several men. By the time they realized it was him, he had his face hidden in Dorothy's hair.

It had been a year since the wedding, and while it seemed much longer, it was inconceivable to James that he wouldn't know his own son. Anne took his hand again. They closed around the two embracing, eager for a turn, looking to each other to verify that this was him, that this was really happening.

When Rennie pulled away to admire Jennifer, he smiled, and again James didn't know him. There were small white scars along his jaw. He said nothing, but smiled and smiled, as if stunned with happiness. It was Rennie, yes, it was him, but he was so thin, and his teeth were weirdly prominent (James thought of Anne's father on his bier, the waxen skin settling over cartilage). He dandled the baby a moment before stepping over the rope. Anne held him next, her eyes shut tight, and then Jay, first shaking his hand manfully. James thought it was fitting that he should be the last; a father, he was accustomed to it.

Rennie turned toward him, formally—his son, returned as James knew he would. So close, James could see it wasn't the weight he'd lost that made his teeth stand out, but that Rennie was wearing a full set of dentures. Two pairs of silver hooks locked the uppers and lowers together so that he continually seemed to be smiling, as if waiting for a picture to be taken. Along his jaw ran smooth white patches of scar tissue mixed with new, pink skin. It wasn't so noticeable, James thought, embracing him. No, the doctor had done a good job.

They broke, and James held Rennie by the arm, surveying him yet trying not to look at his jaw or the Purple Heart on his chest.

"Welcome home," he said.

Rennie nodded, and through his clenched teeth, only his lips moving, said something—garbled, hard to pick out: "It's got to be bad"? In the second it took James to decode it, he thought that while this wasn't his fault, he also understood that, like his father, when his son came to him much later in life to ask what had happened, he wouldn't be able to explain himself, and would merely sit, an old man, silently acquiring a lifetime of blame.

"Yes," James said, "it's good to have you back."

He took the scenic route, worming through the wide streets of beach towns. In the back, Rennie held Dorothy and Jennifer. As they cruised through Westhampton Beach, he pointed and tried to say something. James, and Anne beside him, leaned back to hear.

"He says he remembers the flower baskets," Dorothy translated. Rennie nodded and put his lips to her ear. "But the house isn't in this town, it's farther on."

They'd come with him once, the summer he'd been eleven. It wasn't so astonishing that Rennie remembered, but, like the little girl trapped in that cave in New Mexico, they needed him to speak now, to hold off the silence. His voice itself—his willingness—was assuring.

Beside him in the mirror, Jay sat watching the hedges and tennis clubs roll past, ignoring Rennie's hands on Dorothy. He was still wearing the Brownie around his neck, but James had had to prompt him to take a shot of all of them before the car. When he suggested a few of just Rennie, Dorothy and Jennifer (the baby between them on the hood, sitting on the bumper under the bridge of her parents kissing), Jay had handed him the camera, and only the day had stopped James from scolding him. It was the shock, he thought, that and a healthy jealousy of Rennie's new family.

Everything was going to take time. Even he himself—for no reason—felt somewhat let down. His son was home, and nothing could be better than that, surely. The jaw could have been much worse. And yet. There was always Diane, haunting him like an unsolved crime, and his mother, and Anne herself, beside him now, trying to figure out how Rennie was going to eat her leg of lamb.

He gave her an encouraging look, received a reserved smile in return. She was being brave; there was no reason to be. She'd always had the power (exclusively female, James thought) of broadcasting and then enforcing her moods so that his joy—sometimes his merest pleasure—was an affront. He didn't want to argue. It was his fault, fine, he was willing to admit it, but, please, couldn't they be happy today?

"Are you allowed to drink champagne?" James asked in the mirror.

Rennie nodded and gave a thumbs-up.

"How about you, champ?"

"I don't know," Jay said, uninterested, and again James wanted to take him by the arm and tell him to fly right. This was an honor. This was his brother.

"Sure you can," he said. Anne gave him a look but he sloughed it off. "Today we can do anything."

Rennie tapped him on the shoulder with something, and James reached back and took it—a straw. He had a whole pocketful.

"He says," Dorothy said, "that it gets you drunk faster. He says he learned that at Cornell."

"You really eat with one?" Jay asked.

Rennie made a slurping noise and smiled wide, showing the hooks.

"It's not funny," Anne said sharply, and they all stopped laughing. The swish and rush of traffic filtered in and quickly grew huge.

Rennie said something to Dorothy.

"He says he's all right."

"I know that," Anne said. "That's not what I'm talking about."

"He's all right," Dorothy said again, as if it were evident, but Anne turned and watched the road, and the rest of the way they said nothing.

The mystery Olds sat alone in the lot. Sarah and their father were waiting for them at the top of the stairs. James had always thought of him as much larger than her, stronger, and it shocked him to see her holding him up. He knew he'd remember this after their father died—the two of them, who'd hated each other so well for so long, standing on the porch with the house rising gray above them—and so he didn't force Jay to catch this uneasy truce on film. Again, it was the day, the state of mind he was in, but for the long moment it took his family to cross the lawn, James had to resist the notion that this would be the last time all of them would be together like this. His father was dying. They would sell the house and, with no place to stay, visit Sarah more and more rarely. Rennie and Dorothy would begin their life elsewhere, leaving only Jay. In six years he would be gone too, the money from their house going for his tuition, and then it would be only himself and Anne—which was all they'd started with, here, only twenty years ago. It seemed an instant, this life, this family of his, and sweet now that it was almost gone. He could see the end here, the rest of his life clear and present as the water and saw grass and sky, and he knew there was no sense in mourning. If, as he feared, he'd failed all those he loved, it was too late to change that now. He wished happiness upon his sons; for Anne, peace; and for himself, nothing but the chance, now, this strange day, to give thanks.

"What happened to you?" their father asked Rennie.

"He says he picked on the wrong guy," Dorothy said.

"His jaw is wired shut," Anne explained.

"God," their father said, plucking Rennie's forearm, "you look awful. You look like me."

"You look fine," Sarah said, and kissed him. Jennifer was asleep, but he wouldn't put her down.

"How about a picture?" James said. "Everybody on the stairs. Jay, get in there with your brother."

Sarah offered to take it; James said she could take a second one.

The house smelled of lamb. They showed Rennie the dining room and took some shots of him by the wreath under the streamers, then he and Dorothy went down to the cottage to change. Jay asked if he could take off his tie and disappeared upstairs.

"Is he all right?" Anne asked James in the kitchen.

"He's fine. He's just upset. Everything's changing for him."

"You make it sound so easy," she said.

"Do you need help with anything?" he asked, to avoid any unpleasantness.

"No," she said. "Jay can pour the water when he comes down. Go do whatever it is you do around here."

There wasn't time to toss the ball around. Rennie proposed a toast through Dorothy, promising not to jaw on too long. They all drank their champagne through a straw, except Sarah, who made do with ginger ale. The lamb was tough and overdone. "Rennie says it all looks wonderful," Dorothy said, but he had tomato soup, which he finished before the potatoes had made it around. He asked for a second cup and another glass of milk, and while Anne tried to sell everyone on more lamb, had a Blatz. James would have to scrounge a blender for him in town. But Rennie was there, that was all that mattered.

Anne had bought a cake. It would be two more weeks before Rennie could eat; there was no point in saving it. They took it out on the porch with coffee, watching the sunset color the west. Anne fixed Rennie a cup of melted ice cream—strawberry, his favorite. They said almost nothing; it was enough to sit with him and admire the calm. Fireflies rose over the lawn, their clumsy silhouettes still visible between blinks. The cicadas settled into a rhythm. James sat by Anne, thinking how close they'd come to ruining everything earlier in the kitchen. He took her hand, and they gazed at Rennie as if infatuated, suddenly in love. In the waning light, his face seemed to heal.

After Jay played their father to a draw, Sarah said she had to leave. A date. Still in the mood, they celebrated her chances, as if they'd gathered to see her off. She kissed Rennie again, and they all thanked her and waved as she rolled the mysterious Olds up the drive and away.

"Beautiful car," James said, walking back to the porch, and Rennie nodded as if impressed. "Not like the old tub. I'm thinking I might tune her tomorrow. I could use a hand."

"Does it have to be tomorrow?" Dorothy said, and, surprising him, looked to Anne.

"I told them I'd watch Jennifer so they could have the day to themselves."

"I guess it can wait a day," James said.

Jay had stayed with his father, and now the two excused themselves, citing the time. They shook hands with Rennie again, Jay a bit stiffly, and James wondered if he would be up again tonight. His dreams hadn't stopped, if anything had become more frequent since the telegram. They all watched him help his father up the stairs, then stood there awkwardly in the glow from the front door.

"Another Blatz?" James asked.

"I'm sure Rennie's tired after the trip," Anne said.

"I think so," Dorothy said, checking with him.

They embraced again, with the same fervor they had at the station, though it was easier to let him go now, knowing he'd be back at breakfast (a damn blender, James thought, nothing was open Sunday). They kissed Dorothy too, and Jennifer asleep in her basket, and called after them as they crossed the lawn by the wiggling flashlight beam, "Welcome home," and "We love you," and "Watch your step," and, after they'd disappeared over the cliff, James stood there with Anne in the light from the doorway. The moon was up; stars spilled across the sky, throwing the ghostly shadow of the porch rail across the floor. Keeping his hand, Anne walked to the far end, where the table and chairs he'd set out for himself and Rennie sat empty. She leaned against the rail, peering out at the black, the invisible sea. He stood beside her, trying to see what she did. He hadn't said anything to Rennie. Tomorrow, he thought. The rest of the summer, what was left of it. No, it wouldn't happen. He'd been foolish to think one day would change things. And he'd known that he'd feel this way now, that was the sad part. Why couldn't he resign himself to this distance between them?

Anne straightened and turned toward him. She chastely kissed him, once, and quietly they moved to the door. She stopped for a last look, though he could see nothing but the starless reach of the sea, and above it, the same island night he'd known as a boy. She took his hands and held them to her chin and then her cheek.

"We're very lucky," she said.

James agreed.

JAY WASN'T AFRAID OF RENNIE'S TEETH. He was still dreaming of the shot hitting and the impact spinning him, tossing a plume of blood that clotted darkly in the sand. That week the Regal was showing *Five Graves to Cairo*, and Rennie dropped not to the frozen snow of Alaska or some palm-lined beach in the Solomons but to the salt-white floor of the Sahara. Beyond a blinding wall of dunes, the German halftrack growled away, and then there was only the wind flicking grains of sand against his cheek. Rennie lay beside the fading stain, the desert shimmering. Franchot Tone and Anne Baxter wouldn't happen upon the body and the still-burning jeep as in the film (even dreaming, he knew who should show up, what they should say). It was up to Jay to find him, on his bike.

He started from the eastern edge of the desert—down a dead end, like the town streets to the beach that stopped at a path through the grassy dunes. Cracked asphalt gave way to sand. His tires sank in, and he had to walk the bike to the top of the first dune. The desert rolled off like the sea. For a second he stood looking at its vastness, then straddled his seat and launched himself downhill. Again, his tires sank in. The bike was useless, yet he dragged it over the endless sand. Soon he was lost and exhausted, but pushed himself onward, farther into the desert. His shirt grew stains; his face blistered. He tossed his empty canteen aside. And then the bike was gone and he was wearing a British uniform. The sun split and rejoined, split and rejoined, and then he was falling down a huge dune, somersaulting out of control, and he wouldn't stop—he didn't stop—until he was lying face-to-face with Rennie.

Though it brought him up from sleep screaming, once awake, Jay knew how foolish he was being. His father charged down the hall, trying hard not to be angry. He swayed above the bed, bleary and rumpled.

"It's just the stupid dream again," Jay apologized.

"Which one this time?"

"The desert."

"Do you think it might help to talk to Rennie?"

"I don't think so," Jay said weakly, to disguise how much he disliked the idea.

"Your night-light's on. I don't know what else I can do."

"Nothing," Jay said.

"Go to sleep," his father said. "They're only dreams. Rennie's with us now."

When he'd left, Jay lay awake listening for the trains and picking through his box. Over the summer he'd added a few shells, some tickets from the Regal and sea-smoothed pieces of glass, the champagne cork, Rudy York's baseball card, the Jensens' stub from Win's collection book, and, most recently, the notice about Rennie in the paper. His father had given the society editor an old picture to print, taken the day Rennie left for Cornell. He grimaced by the porch swing. Jay thought he didn't look that different.

In the few days since he'd been home, Jay had slowly grown used to Rennie's teeth. Not completely. He didn't see him enough. Rennie didn't come up from the cottage that often. He and Dorothy and Jennifer spent their mornings on the beach under an umbrella, in the afternoon, during nap time, he set up a folding chair out on the breakwater and read. At dinner everyone took turns sitting next to him. He didn't say much. The night Jay sat beside him, Rennie clapped him on the back after grace and, passing the fluke Jay had caught that day, said with effort, "I wish I could eat it." His teeth didn't frighten Jay, really; just sometimes it was hard to look at him, like when he laughed. His mouth didn't open all the way. He rocked back like Grampa Langer and barked and, after, groaned and rolled his eyes to show how much it hurt. "Don't make me laugh," he said.

His thinness surprised Jay; it worried his mother more than the jaw. On the beach, Rennie kept his shirt on. For dinner he sipped milk and heavy chowders and chicken à la king run through the blender. His father was always sending Jay out for more beer.

It was dumb of him to worry. Rennie seemed happy with Dorothy and the baby and all. The doctors were just being careful with his jaw because it had been such a bad break. The teeth bothered Jay—and the hole through his tongue—but he wasn't afraid of them the way he was of the man on the beach or of his dreams. Those fears seemed faraway to him, and strange, like the movies or the war, while Rennie was right here, and real, someone he'd always known. So while he was frightened of Rennie's teeth and of what had happened to him, in a way, because he was so close, it was easier for Jay to be brave.

Win said his uncle the machinist had a glass eye. He didn't dare break it; they were all made in Germany, you couldn't get them anymore.

"It's not the same," Jay said. "Everyone has false teeth." They were in the attic, baling old magazines for the latest paper drive. His father wanted to clean out the whole house. Grampa Langer was going to come home with them, though he'd told his father straight out at dinner that he didn't want to. It was hot and dirty under the eaves; sweat glazed their arms. They'd taken a break to leaf through some old *Liberty*s, but had soon grown bored, and sat looking out the dusty gable window, relishing the breeze. Far below on the breakwater Rennie was reading. The sea broke on both sides at the same time, the white lines running evenly past him into shore.

"Does he read like that all the time?"

"He went to college," Jay said, defending him.

"He doesn't say *anything*?"

"He says stuff. He can't say a lot 'cause his jaw's all wired up."

"That's what they said about that guy in Iowa. He didn't say anything, even after they caught him. Shot everybody in the house, the dogs too."

"One guy," Jay said.

"What kind of stuff does he say?"

Jay hadn't asked Rennie what the war was like yet. His father said he'd talk when he was ready, and that then he'd need everyone to listen. They weren't supposed to have the war on the radio when he was around. He didn't read the paper or go to the movies either. Once Jay had overheard Dorothy talking to her father on the phone; if Rennie's stories were anything like that, he didn't want to listen to them.

"Just stuff," he told Win.

"Like?"

"He said the train he came back on . . ."

"Yeah?"

"He said the front half was all guys who'd been discharged. It was like a regular train. You could walk from one car to the other, except halfway back there was this door that was locked. There's these two MPs in front of it, big, big guys. So they stop out in the middle of the desert, and there's nothing around, and all of a sudden out of nowhere come these Marines with swords and the honor guard and everything. No one knows what's going on, but, see, they've got the flag, so the guys stand up, and right in front of them, from the same train they're going to be on all the way across the country, the Marines start taking off coffins."

"You're making this up."

"They load them into a truck and roll them away, and at the next stop they do the same thing, and the next stop and the next, all the way across the country."

"Like they're luggage or something."

"And the worst part?" Jay said. "When they pulled into a station there'd be two crowds waiting. One at the front half of the train and one at the back."

"Man," Win said. He shook his head and looked out the window at the tiny figure of Rennie. "What about when he got shot?"

"He doesn't want to talk about that yet."

"Did you ask him? You gotta ask him. I'll ask him if you won't."

"My dad said we should let him talk when he wants to. We shouldn't force him."

"Yeah," Win said, "I guess."

The afternoon dragged on. The air was so thick with heat it was hard to breathe. The eaves buzzed with hornets and smelled of bat turds. Grampa Langer never threw anything away; in a desk they found stacks of typing paper crumbled to yellow dust. They dug through acrid bins of *Punch* and *Blackwood's* and the *Police Gazette*. When they'd finished hauling the bales downstairs to the porch, Rennie was still reading, his back to them.

On his bike, Win looked hopefully at Jay.

"I promise I'll tell you," Jay said, trying to discourage him. Win's leg was better; he made it up the hill and waved before disappearing over the crest.

On the breakwater, Rennie bent over his book. Jay stood a moment at the porch rail, one hand on a column, and thought of how they used to talk in the dark. Back then he hadn't understood how Rennie could hate their father, but it wasn't a secret between them. Each night after their father closed the door and tromped down the hall, they waited for one or the other to start. Though they both knew the routine, Rennie always asked, "Hey, Jay?" and he always took an extra minute to respond, as if he might really be asleep. His own voice sounded larger in the dark, and truer; Rennie's seemed small and angry, not like at school, where he was polite and everyone said he'd be something big. When the talk dwindled to silence, a few minutes passed, and then Jay asked, "Hey, Rennie?" and on and on into the night. During the day they never mentioned what they'd said, but the next night one might pick up a dropped topic or submit new evidence or even deny they'd ever said such a thing. It had been half the world to Jay then. The day Rennie left for Cornell, Jay lay awake in the empty room in Montour Falls, wondering if across the two blue lakes, in his churchlike dormitory, Rennie would hear him. "Hey, Rennie?" he'd said, huge in the dark room, and his father had come in, concerned—for he was always concerned about him, just as Jay worried about his father, and now, Rennie. Leaning against the column, he thought that this was the only time of day they were alone together. Jay stood there looking down at him a good minute before going inside to wake up Grampa Langer.

Since witnessing the stroke, Jay had watched him closely. He wore slippers now instead of shoes. His pants sagged behind like Rennie's; his cheekbones poked from his face. He rested on every step and some days didn't leave his room, sitting in his chair by the window with a heavy blanket tucked under his chin. The last time they'd tried to play chess, Jay had to show him how to open, and though Grampa Langer shooed his hand, saying he remembered, after a few moves Jay was playing himself. His father said he could stay in the guest bedroom in Galesburg, and Jay pictured winter, frost on the bottom of the panes, his mother reading the Bible to Grampa Clayborn while the humidifier poured out a cold cloud. He wanted her to read him the whole thing, start to finish. When Jay turned off *Superman* or *Hop Harrigan*, he heard her murmuring in the back hall.

Grampa Langer said he wanted to die in his own home. "That's all I ask," he argued calmly across the dinner table, and his father looked around for support. "I appreciate that," his father said, as if they'd already discussed it. Jay thought that it didn't matter. There were three weeks till Labor Day, and any second—Jay was sure—the old man would drop as if shot. He'd spent the last of his strength in Jay's arms on the kitchen floor, and now he seemed to be waiting. Jay was no longer afraid of him. He knew him too well. He'd seen the worst.

Grampa Langer was awake, propped on his pillows. "The prince," he greeted Jay, without raising a hand. His mother had taught Jay how to sit him up and slide his legs off the bed. Sometimes he helped but not today. On Jay's arm he seemed as light and frail as paper.

"Where to?" Jay asked.

"Down."

"Hold tight."

Jay guided him to a shady spot on the porch and found a blanket for his lap. Rennie was gone. It was almost five; any minute his mother would be home to start dinner, and, rocking next to Grampa Langer, Jay thought he'd made it through another day.

His father came home and changed his clothes, and they played catch on the lawn. He'd brought out an extra mitt, and when Rennie came up with Dorothy and Jennifer, convinced him to throw some. Even so skinny, he still had a lot of pop on the ball. Jay bounced one in front of him, and with the same sweep of his arm and snap of the wrist his father used, Rennie scooped it.

"Did you play any out west?" his father asked. "Get some innings in?"

Rennie said something, but was standing too far away for Jay or his father to make it out. He gave up and shook his head.

"Probably didn't have time," his father said, and Rennie nodded. "See how Jay's coming along?" Rennie caught a soft throw, took his hand out of the glove and shook it as if burned.

They threw until dinner, slipping into the easy rhythm of the ball smacking leather. Though they hardly said anything, it was almost like talking. When Dorothy called them in, his father didn't throw Jay the impossible high fly.

The rest of the night would be easy. The porch was crowded, and after dessert his mother let Jay stay inside and listen to *The Man*

Called X. He could hear them carrying on through the screen, his father's hearty chuckle and Rennie's awful bark, and he thought he should go out and at least sit with them. He listened to the end, then went out and sat in the flickering light of the citronella candles, growing sleepy as they discussed the riots in Harlem and Detroit, the traitorous coal strike, the glider that had crashed with the mayor of St. Louis aboard. No one mentioned Italy or the Battle of Vella Gulf. Rennie had his arm around Dorothy and removed it only to go to the bathroom or get another beer. At one point his father made a joke about doing the hula. It stopped everyone. They weren't supposed to bring up Hawaii; Rennie had been in a hospital there. His mother waited to see if Rennie would laugh. He did, looking around to make sure they knew it was all right, he could take it. It was something his father did, checking everyone, and Jay wondered if all of his laughing and palling around was, like his father's, an act.

"Jay," his mother asked, pointing to Grampa Langer in the rocker beside him, "could you look at your friend for me?"

He was asleep, his arms folded in his lap.

"It's past someone's bedtime," his father joked.

Jay said he could take him up himself, but his mother wanted to help. He'd seen Grampa Langer in his skivvies a million times, but once they got him into his room, she sent Jay to wait out in the hall. He sat on the top step, listening to Dorothy's voice, and then his father's, and then the silence that would be Rennie's.

"Is anything wrong?" his mother asked when she saw him sitting there. "You haven't said a word all night."

"I'm sleepy," he said, which was true.

She sat down next to him and smoothed his hair back. "Remember I told you I'd tell you when your grandfather wasn't doing so well?"

"Yes."

"Do I have to tell you that?"

"No."

"When I think it's time I'm going to stop working and stay home to take care of him. Will that be all right?"

"Yes," he said.

"But it's not time yet. We still have a ways to go." She squeezed his shoulder. "All right?"

"Okay," he said, and they both stood up. She said it was fine if he went to bed, she'd say his goodnights for him.

He couldn't hear them in bed, or only an occasional, faint burst of laughter. Wind riffled his curtains, thrashed in the woods beyond the backyard. He thought of the clipping in his box—Bonnie trying to smile by the porch swing—and the tiny island in the atlas downstairs, and in the orange dusk of his night-light, chilly under his covers, Jay held on to his pillow and waited for the blazing Sahara. "The poor blighter," Franchot Tone said, and Anne Baxter had to look away.

Mornings were the easiest. He left before Dorothy came up. The town streets were striped with the shadows of trees. They took turns doing the bluff now. Miss Swain's niece had gone back to Ohio, but Sylvia Jensen had returned from her trip. Jay hadn't given up on her completely. He still talked with Mr. Jensen, but at the Regal she ignored him, and despite Win's advice, he was too timid to confront her directly. Each morning he walked the paper to their porch and slipped it inside the screen door, hoping to find her—like Dorothy the one morning he'd seen her—in a flowing robe with nothing underneath. It didn't happen. At best, Mr. Jensen met him in his boxer shorts and black socks and asked if the Yanks had won again. Jay rode off both disappointed and relieved.

He still loved the bluff, its quiet, cutting light. It seemed possible, bumping slowly over its gravel paths and through its cool, damp porte-cocheres, that he would never have to go back to Galesburg, to the school which, like the one he passed on his way through town, sat dark and empty all summer, only the asphalt ball yard of use. Three weeks, his father reminded them, wasn't a long time. Often Jay stopped halfway to the Gardners' and stood there astride his bike, listening to the sea and thinking how much he would miss it, how, if he could, he'd save this calm, fit it in his box so that late at night he might open it and chase his dreams away.

His sack empty, he cruised through town, one eye out for his father's bike. Rennie had made the Roll of Honor on the green, his name in silver for everyone to see. Technically he wasn't from Hampton Bays, but their father had made a call. J. LANGER, it said, and Jay imagined it was himself. All summer Jay had considered D. Duncan lucky, but not anymore. Rennie hadn't even been to see it.

He met Win at Hickey's and left any extras for Mr. Barger by the front door. If his father had work for them, they headed home then, but if there was nothing to do, they stayed and wasted the morning reading comics and drinking fountain Cokes and playing pinball, trying to decide what to do with the afternoon. He could avoid the house all day. Dorothy would look after Grampa Langer, Rennie would read.

Today there was nothing for them, and they humped and kneed the machine. They had done everything, it seemed, but ticked off the possibilities just the same. Win wanted to go to the Shoals and smoke; Jay said they could do that crabbing from the bridge. They'd already seen *Five Graves to Cairo* twice. They could go down to the flats and dig clams.

"Yeah," Win said, dismissing it. The ball drained and he smacked the glass. Mr. Hickey looked back. "Why don't we go shoot the breeze with your brother?"

"He wouldn't want to," Jay said.

"Why not?"

"Because he wouldn't. He's got a family. He doesn't need a bunch of little kids hanging around him."

They'd had the same argument all week, and were glad when an older kid from town appeared carrying a stack of posters. He showed one to Mr. Hickey, then wedged it into the glass of the door. Jay let the ball drain and they went outside to see what it was. He hoped it was a circus; he'd go even though his father would say he was too old.

On Sunday the American Legion was having a bond rally with a parade for everyone in the services. A red P-38 streaked through a heavy flak of blue letters. CIVIL WAR TO PRESENT, it said. After, there would be a dance at the roller rink. Jay thought of inviting Sylvia Jensen but knew he wouldn't.

"Is your brother gonna march?"

"I don't know. Sure, I guess."

"Why wouldn't he?" Win said.

"I don't know," Jay said. "I'll ask him."

He mentioned it at dinner. Rennie heard him but picked up his cup of potatoes and took a long draw.

"Yes," his mother said, "I saw that. The base is sending a drill team."

"There's gonna be guys from the Civil War."

"Maynard Washington," Grampa Langer said, and paused for breath. "He's it."

Rennie had a sip of beer.

"Aren't we supposed to be doing something Sunday?" his father asked his mother.

"You could all come to church with me," she said, only half joking.

"I'll go," Dorothy said, raising a hand.

"Rennie?"

"No," he said, shaking his head lightly.

"You two go," his father said. "We'll drop you off, come back and do our tune-up, then pick you up after."

"What about the parade?" Jay asked.

No one spoke.

"I don't think Rennie's interested," his father said. "Maybe when his jaw is all better."

Rennie nodded. "Sorry."

"It's all right, dear," his mother said. "Your brother's just proud of you. We all are."

"There'll be time for that sort of thing later," his father said, and looked around the table. After dinner, in the kitchen, he asked Jay if he would please not bring it up again.

On the porch, his mother looked to Jay sweetly, encouraging him to speak. He told the story Win had told him about the lady in Montana who hoarded food in her basement. The river flooded and soaked the labels from the cans so she never knew what she was going to eat. Everyone chuckled, and his mother nodded to him.

Grampa Langer said it was going to rain, then slumped in his chair, whistling. Jay took him up himself.

In bed, he heard his mother come up, and not long after, his father talking in the backyard, under his window. Glass clinked, and Jay went to the sill. His father and Rennie were sitting by the garden, the light above the back door throwing their shadows into the trees. Jay couldn't hear what Rennie was saying, but he was talking, his father hunched forward on his Adirondack chair. A glass sat on the broad arm, and in the grass a bottle tilted. Jay knelt with his face almost touching the dusty-smelling screen, squinting to listen. The cicadas were out, shrilling like an engine; quietly the sea thundered and hushed.

"I understand," his father said. "No one expects you to be happy. But we're happy you're back. You have to give us that."

Rennie got up and walked around his chair.

"Don't think that you're doing this for me," his father said, in the reasonable tone he assumed when he was just starting to argue. "I was perfectly happy to let the matter drop, still am."

Rennie stopped and held on to the back of the chair with both hands.

"Jay can take care of himself," his father countered. "He's matured a good bit this summer, if you haven't noticed. It's been a difficult time for all of us, but we're all here now."

Rennie looked up, and Jay had to duck. He moved to the corner of the window and peeked over. His father had gotten up and stood next to Rennie, sipping and gazing up at the sky.

"That's gone," his father said. "You can't go back there. You have to be here now for Dorothy and Jennifer. They have to be your first concern."

Rennie put his glass down on the arm.

"It's your choice," his father said, then heartily, "All right, I'll see you in the morning," and Rennie walked off.

His father sat back in the chair and held his glass up to see how much was left. He rested the drink on his stomach, looking off into the woods until, suddenly, in one uninterrupted motion, he tipped the drink back, rocked forward out of the chair and headed for the back door.

Jay leapt into bed.

Below, in the kitchen, the screen slapped; water ran in the sink. His father thumped through the living room and into the hall and slowly up the stairs, stopping at the top. Jay curled around his box, his covers up to his ears. His father clicked the switch to turn the downstairs light out. Jay thought his first step was toward the bathroom, but the second told him he was wrong.

His father filled the door, the orange glow turning his plaid shirt black-and-white. He felt his way uncertainly to the foot of the bed, but didn't sit, stood there with one hand touching the wooden egg of the bedpost.

"Jay," he said, "are you awake?" and Jay thought of the dumb joke—no.

"Yes."

"Your brother wants you to know that he *is* going to march on Sunday. All right?"

"Okay."

"I thought that would make you happy."

"It does," Jay said.

Later, alone, he thought that it would have at dinner, but that now it was way too late.

The next morning he left earlier than usual and beat Win to Hickey's. Mr. Barger had already dropped off. Jay cut the loop of wire from the bale and folded it into the scrap bin. He took off the scuffed wrapper of butcher paper and was beginning to count when he saw the front page.

The Marines had landed at Vella Lavella. Everyone knew they would; even Jay had heard the rumors. He was more surprised by a story near the bottom of the page. It wasn't the headline that startled him, but the accompanying map. The tentacle of the Aleutians swooped. There was the chip that was Attu. To the east, another island was boxed and enlarged.

ARMY TAKES BACK KISKA, the headline said, *Clear Jap-held Island—U.S. Northern Route Free.*

Jay sat down on the stack and read the article, trying not to go too fast. The last half of it was back in the food news. The invasion had taken place two days ago. It had been scheduled for months but the fog had been too bad. The fleet lay offshore waiting. It said that when the men went in they found empty barracks lining a barely started airstrip. The field hospital was fully stocked, the dishes in the mess tent clean, but the place was deserted. The Japanese had left weeks ago, under cover of the weather.

"So that's it for them up there," Win said as he readied his sack. "Man, your brother's going to be a hero on Sunday."

It was Win's day to do the bluffs; Jay could take his time in town. Mr. Jensen waved from the breakfast table. The school loomed. On his way back he stopped at Hickey's and bought an extra copy, though he knew that Rennie wouldn't want to see it.

His father had them in the basement again, hauling up cases of dusty bottles and boxes full of scrap wood. Rennie read on the breakwater all day.

When his father came home, Jay showed him the paper.

"Why don't you save it," his father said. "He might like to read it later."

Jay clipped the article and put it in his box.

They threw before dinner. Rennie was getting tan. He'd already had a few beers that afternoon, and waved at Jay's low throws, clowning around when one slipped past him. His father chuckled. They were taking grounders when a bad hop jumped up and caught Rennie in the face. He dropped his mitt, knelt and covered his mouth with a hand. On the porch, his mother stood. Before his father could run to him, Rennie waved him off, found the ball and got up. He reared back and, perfectly imitating Rip Sewell, threw him an Eephus pitch, the ball looping high and dropping sheer past the invisible batter as Rennie finished his motion. Dorothy and his mother—even Grampa Langer—clapped, and Jay imagined the troops storming the beach at Kiska, how they must have felt running crouched across the sand, and then the relief when they heard the Japanese had evacuated. Jay thought that, alone in a land so new and strange, being told you were safe wasn't enough. He pictured them marching inland, rifles drawn, watching for movement in the fog, listening to the wind, convinced that though they couldn't see anything, there was something there.

HIS DRIVER OFFERED RENNIE A SIP OF WHISKEY, and, still fuzzy from the beers he'd had at lunch and throughout the long, oppressive afternoon (not to mention the double shot his father had pushed on him before dropping him off), he accepted. He sat in the back of an open car, a waxed and gleaming Nash with bunting slung from the door handles. They waited with the rest of the motorcade in the cool behind the Presbyterian church, gray-shingled and witch-hatted, just off the docks on Water Street, as if expecting the return of a South Seas whaler lost a full century ago, its promise of salvation faded and antique but still available. But wasn't that him, the prodigal reported lost at sea?

From the wharf came the smell of escape and oblivion—salt and tar and open water—and the ringing of halyards. Out on the bay a breeze was up, and a school of sails bellied and leaned with the wind. Here they felt none of it; the weight of the day, it seemed to him, half drunk and so only half resigned, pressed relentlessly upon him, the air piercingly clear yet heavy as if with fog. Beyond the shadow of the church, spread in disarray across the hot parking lot, the high school band blatted and flammed and trilled. Above Water Street hung the heavy crowns of a row of old elms, shot with light like great green thunderheads, with every puff of air shedding gauzy seeds that floated across the lot and through the band like motes of dust in a blazing room. His driver had the radio tuned to the Providence station, and the music, a languid blues, drifted tinnily up to the perfect sky. "Then carelessly/I told you goodbye." It was the end of a Sunday at the end of summer, and a heat and stillness had settled upon the little town—that glad sense of futility, Rennie thought, when you decided that you'd done enough for the day whether you had or not. "But now at night/I wake up and cry." Over the low row of shops whose backs faced them lay the village green, where the crowd waited. He'd been dreading the parade all week, and now, so close, he didn't see how he was going to make it through it. He wanted to stop now, to protest, to admit that all he wanted was rest, peace, to be left alone. Every few minutes a string of firecrackers snapped in the distance, making him grin at both his own cowardice and his foolishness for letting Dorothy talk him into it. "You can't hide from the world," she'd said, and while that was all he wanted to do, he knew she was right.

There were six cars; his was the fifth, the only man in back of him a deckhand from the Coast Guard lifesaving station on his day off. Riding in the cars ahead were a clerk from Fort Jackson, South Carolina; from the first war, a captain in the balloon corps and a Marine who'd fought at Château-Thierry; and, leading in a gorgeous black Cadillac, the town's last surviving Union soldier. Rennie was the only one who'd seen combat in the last twenty-five years and the only one to be wounded.

His driver was a small, elderly man with crooked, browned teeth who ran a grocery store in town. He'd already given Rennie a twenty-dollar gift certificate and invited him to dinner. He had a fresh pint of Kentucky's Finest stuffed between the maps in his dash. Rennie was wearing his dress uniform for the first time since he'd been back; there were still straws in the breast pocket. He leaned into the front seat and, like a bee siphoning honey, took a good swig.

The marshal, who owned the bank, came by in tails and a purple sash, announcing how long they had until the start.

Rennie's driver held out the bottle.

"Milt," the marshal scolded, then rolled his eyes and took a long swallow before rushing off again. "Five minutes, everybody!"

Rennie took another, larger tug, which further cleared and sharpened his vision. Somewhere in the green heat a xylophone plinked erratically, as if distorted by a sheet of water. His driver tipped the bottle back and exhaled. "Good and good for you," he said, and slapped the glove box shut.

At the first shrill whistle from the jodhpurred drum major, the band fell into ranks, adjusting their heavy, plumed caps and then their music. His driver started the car and turned off the radio. Rennie was supposed to sit atop the back seat so everybody could see him. Sticking from his breast pocket was a small flag; he would wave it while acknowledging the crowd with his other hand. The polished metal of the trunk radiated heat. He struggled to get his shoes off so he wouldn't scuff the upholstery.

"You don't have to do that," his driver said, then, when Rennie had them off, added, "I appreciate it."

"How do I look?" Rennie asked him.

"Huh?"

"How do I look?"

"You look good," the driver said, eyeing his teeth doubtfully. Rennie couldn't close his mouth. There wasn't enough jaw left, the doctor at Aiea explained, not enough skin. He would always look like he was forcing himself to smile, slightly maniacal, as if on the verge of mad laughter or tears. The first time he saw himself in the mirror, the doctor was standing behind him; when Rennie looked to him, he apologized. The jaw was too small for the rest of his head, too narrow, too short, and the dentures they'd fitted him with too large, dominant. In the mirror, the strip of teeth in its perpetual grimace made him look like a fretful cadaver. Only Stephenson, when he passed through on his way stateside, hadn't inspected the damage, gauged it against his old face, and that had been perhaps a result of the news it was his duty to tell Rennie. On the train from San Francisco, he caught people gazing at him pityingly, some missing limbs. There was a face that asked, What happened to you? Dorothy said she could barely tell, but that if after a few months it still bothered him, they'd have a specialist examine him. "Like Dr. Frankenstein," he said. Though it wasn't funny, he'd needed her to laugh, and she had.

"I mean the uniform," Rennie asked.

"It looks great," his driver said, relieved to tell the truth.

"Two minutes!" the marshal called.

"Can we get a last nip in?"

"What?"

"A drink," Rennie said, "a drink."

His driver dug the bottle out and handed it back cheerfully. "You'll have to excuse me, my hearing isn't too good."

Rennie dipped the straw in and pulled deeply. He coughed and remembered the jokes on the ward about throwing up. Everyone there was a Donald Duck; the hateful nickname came from the way they talked with their jaws wired shut, that same spit-spraying quack. ("All you guys?" Stephenson had said, incredulous; in a way it was funny, in another, very strange, and, having seen what happened on Attu, Stephenson seemed to both grasp that and, intent on the dignity of his mission, make nothing of it.) The hospital kept them separate so they didn't have to watch the other patients eat, but the kitchen was directly beneath them. The smell of steak was painful. Once they gave him orange juice and the hole in his tongue burned all day. The doctor had plugged it with skin from his back; like his teeth, the taste buds there were gone forever. Sometimes he thought he could feel the smooth, dead spot, and when he drank something bitter, tried to isolate the neutral circle, the food passing over it unremarked upon. His missing teeth he tried not to think about.

The whiskey made him sweat and he thought that he'd probably had too much already. He handed the bottle back and thanked his driver.

"All set?"

"Let's go get 'em," Rennie said.

The band was high-stepping in place, the drummers pounding out a tattoo. Dorothy had bought him a pair of sunglasses, and he put them on to hold off the glare and the prying eyes of the crowd. He took out his flag and practiced waving it. When the Nash started forward, his socks slipped on the leather of the backseat, and he grabbed a handful of folded canvas roof.

"Careful there," his driver called.

They rolled across the parking lot behind the band, who were searching, like a driver trying to get a car in gear, for the first bars of "Columbia, Gem of the Ocean." When the sections finally did agree on it, the song sounded tired, the brasses sapped by the heat, drums slowing to compensate. His driver turned to Rennie and put a finger in each ear. Rennie waved him off, as if to say they were no worse than any band made up of kids. And they weren't; by the exit onto High Street, they'd reached the correct tempo, and the thunder of the drums echoed off the dark storefronts. The buildings gained a second story as they neared the corner of Green Street. Down the block he could see the green over the waving plumes, and the white confusion of the crowd. Ahead of the band, leading the whole column, surged a flag trimmed with gold fringe. From the sidewalk a loose group of boys playing tag among the parking meters and a few straggling families waved to him, and, remembering his little flag, Rennie waved back.

He'd been here one summer, years ago, and as the noise of the crowd reached down the street, he remembered a bright ice cream parlor with a cracked marble counter and napkins too small and stiff to do any good. There was gum on the sidewalk outside, and one Sunday after church he'd stepped in a clinging red patch with his good shoes, and his mother had hauled him by his collar to the car. "What are you doing?" she shouted, yanking off the shoe. "What do you think you're doing?" His father, all calm, told her it was an accident, and, menacing him with the shoe, she declared, as if citing irrefutable evidence, "He stepped. Right. In it."

The band stopped at the intersection as if for a light and crisply finished the song, to applause. He tried to close his mouth, compressing the brick of his dentures until it bit into his gums, but it didn't miraculously work this time either, and he thought desperately of the pint in the glove box. The band struck up "Stars and Stripes Forever" and, using one line of the crosswalk as a pivot, turned left face and started down Green Street. The Nash inched along, the crowd on High thickening toward the corner. The applause grew and then, when they saw him, dipped—as if the sight of him were enough to physically paralyze them—and returned again, twice as loud. Fingers accused him, pointed to the obvious mark of his courage and guilt, his stupidity. His wound. Rennie waved and waved.

The Nash turned through the intersection, and now he had them on both sides, the slow gauntlet of stares, of pity and admiration, fear, disgust, gratitude. A good part of the crowd was still dressed for church—farm families in bows and bonnets and cheap seersucker suits—and their cheers for him struck Rennie as overly solemn and respectful, not at all hypocritical, and for that reason all the more hurtful. They paid him an attention the other veterans didn't command. Here was the sacrifice, the saint's remains. He was all of their sons, their fears and wishes made terrible flesh. It seemed they were feeding on his face the way on ship he drank in Rita Hayworth or Gene Tierney. He wanted to rise and preach to them like the Jehovah's Witnesses in Redwood or his Grampa Clayborn motoring out the mud roads to the logging camps, but what would he say, and how, muzzled as he was, would he say it? The colonel had said, "Some of you are not going to come back," and Burger called it bullshit. Now Rennie didn't know which it was. Could bullshit be true and still be bullshit?

His wrists were tired from waving, trying to screen people from getting too good a look. He saw one boy younger than Jay touch a finger to his teeth to make sure they were still there. Girls in pigtails lipped snow cones, toddlers dropped popcorn. People waved flags and pinwheels and hats and caps. Ahead, the flag bearer turned the corner and the band rumbled to a halt, the drum major's whistle keeping time. A bottle rocket sang overhead, went silent and then crackled. The brass struck up "The Washington Post March." He tried to find Dorothy and Jennifer in the confusion—Jay, his parents—but the stream of faces dizzied him. The taste of whiskey rose up in his throat and to dispel it he inhaled a cleansing breath, only to smell the unfair, unbearable aroma of chicken roasting over an open flame. Behind the crowd on his right, men in aprons tended a roofed cinder-block barbecue pit from which greasy smoke billowed. Beside it, a bandstand was hung with bunting, and Rennie figured this was where they would hold the ceremonies. All he had to survive were three more sides of the square.

He tried not to look at the crowd, but waved, turning from one side to the other, focused just over their heads. On the green, under the fat oaks and horse chestnuts, families had laid out blankets and sat in the shade, emptying their hampers. He remembered the duck pond with its willows, but the war memorial and the statue of General Gardner in his powdered wig he'd seen only today when his father dropped him off. He thought he recognized some of the stores from that lost summer. Outside stood wire racks of postcards, the same shots at every gift shop: the wharf from above, the church, the oldest house in town; lobster pots piled on a dock or their bright two-tone floats hanging against the wharfmaster's shack; a clumsy nineteenth-century print of men in perilously small boats standing to harpoon the featureless black bulk of a whale; the lighthouse at Montauk, the largest shark on record, the boardwalk at night with its rickety carousel and Ferris wheel brilliantly lit. They were five for a dime, and Rennie wanted one of each. False or not, those were the only images he attached to the town; the rest was guesswork. Ridley's, with its gold key hanging over the sidewalk, he seemed to remember, but, drunk, he wasn't sure. The dark post office, the library, the cavernous bank. Where the postcards were distinct and discrete, neatly self-contained, the town in front of him now had that vague, fluid familiarity he associated with dreams. He was vividly present but he wasn't connected to anything or anybody there, and never would be. Any second, he thought, he would wake up.

He wished he were reading, alone on the breakwater with a tube of tanning lotion and a cold Black Label. It was the only thing that kept his mind from turning in upon itself. What book it was didn't matter; he was going through everything in the house. Now, questioning the black windows of the shops on one side, the cool grass on the other, his thoughts drifted without aim (he knew where they would end up), as they did when his father chaperoned the class trip to hear the symphony in Syracuse. Minutes after the orchestra began to play, Rennie forgot all about the music and floated into the curved space beneath the theater's painted ceiling, thinking of everything he was going to do when he got back home. He vainly waved his little flag, trying to concentrate on the scene at hand—a boy hanging off a telephone pole and eating a candied apple, the heat, the band, his driver laughingly trying to keep the hood ornament centered on the white line—but he didn't know anyone here, he didn't belong here, and as sometimes happened even reading, he thought of Fecho, and like the symphony nattering in the light below, the crowd went silent, there but not there.

When Stephenson had come to see him, Rennie took him up on the roof to see the view. The hospital had set up picnic tables which sank into the hot tar. There was a high fence around the perimeter topped with concertina wire to stop jumpers, but it hadn't stopped enough because day and night an MP patrolled it with a sidearm. Rennie found a table overlooking Pearl, in the distance the planes coming in and out of Hickam. Stephenson sat down with his back to it. He had sunglasses on, and a grim mouth, and Rennie wondered if he was staring at his teeth.

"Look at this view," Rennie said. "You're not even looking at it."

Stephenson half turned and took it in at a glance. "They thought I should come and see you. To tell you everything that happened."

It was foolish, Rennie thought. He'd never liked Stephenson much, and now he felt bad that he'd gone so far out of his way for nothing. He knew what had happened better than Stephenson, and stopped him and told the story himself.

He went over it dully, stringing the facts together as if they couldn't hurt him. He and Fecho had been shot, probably by the same gunner. The same unknown medic had looked at them, and once out of the line of fire, Tony K had treated them both. Bateman and Hall took Fecho downhill first, and when Burger heard Rennie had been hit too, he checked Rennie's wound and put them on the same transport headed back to the ship.

Rennie was conscious but couldn't talk. He'd had three Syrettes of morphine that he knew of, and when Burger leaned over the litter and spoke, his face seemed to glow from inside like a jack-o'-lantern.

"You take care of him," Burger said, and touched Rennie's hand to Fecho's—limp and strapped in.

It was true night now, and a fog lay over the bay. Water sloshed beneath them. Burger had immobilized Rennie's neck, and he could see Fecho only peripherally, but he could hear his breath flutter raggedly through the hole in his throat. It was like a sigh, so soft it was sometimes lost in the transport's engines and the wind, in Rennie's own choked breathing. He patted and squeezed Fecho's hand, the bland and comforting words of encouragement they'd drilled into them in basic going through his mind though he knew them to be untrue, and, besides, he couldn't even say them: It's all right, you're going to be okay, just hang on and we'll be there soon, don't quit on me now.

The transport motored out into the fog, and Rennie thought it wouldn't be long. There were facilities shipboard, and good people. The numbness brought on by the shock and then the drugs was beginning to fade. A salty pool of blood kept filling the back of his throat, and every so often, with great effort and a pain he thought wouldn't stop, he spat it out. He was facing straight up, and the blood ran hotly down his cheeks and into his ears, making it harder to hear Fecho—but, yes, there was the flutter, the shallow soughing. Fog dipped over the walls of the transport, swirled like smoke in the open hold. A man toward the front who'd been moaning stopped, and there was only the dark, the fog, the sloshing water.

With a thump they hit something. There was confusion as the men stirred. The Japanese were rumored to have laid mines. The driver was shouting and swearing, terrified.

A light from far above blinded them and someone yelled down through a bullhorn, "Who the fuck are you?"

The driver explained, shouting through his cupped hands.

"This is the *USS Pennsylvania*," the bullhorn said. "This is not a hospital ship."

"I can't see shit," the driver shouted, his voice skidding up and breaking. Rennie thought he might be crying.

"Right now that is all I'm seeing," the bullhorn said. "Get these wounded clear, pronto—I repeat, pronto."

They followed the light around the bow of the *Pennsylvania* and then headed into the dark again. It began to sleet, the invisible crystals pricking his face, making him blink. The moaner regained consciousness and lost it again. They bumped into a destroyer, and later another transport. One man near him kept threatening to kill the driver, but in a voice so twisted with pain that he seemed to be pleading. By the time they drew alongside the right ship, Rennie's hands and feet had gone numb, and though he held on to him, even when he held his breath he couldn't hear Fecho anymore. When the doctor on board guessed that he'd been dead since they left the beach, Rennie hadn't argued.

"So, see," Rennie told Stephenson across the table, "I already know about Fecho."

Stephenson took off his sunglasses and rubbed his eyes, put them back on and gazed over Pearl, Hickam, the Pacific. He leaned his elbows on the table and held his face in his hands, rubbing his two-day growth. He pinched his lips in one fist, as if mulling over an impossible discard, then dropped both his hands to the table and sat up straight, as if what he had to say required a thoughtful, almost formal presentation. "Yeah," Stephenson had said then, in a voice that seemed to wear the miles of his flight, "I know you know about Fecho."

Now the band was belting out "You're a Grand Old Flag," giving it the cymbals, the xylophone, everything. Rennie waved feebly, like a beauty queen, saving his strength. They circled the square—Federal, India, Union, and back to Green again—and stopped. The band remained in the box of the intersection, marching in place and tootling "Solid Men to the Front!" while the drivers escorted their charges across the walk to the bandstand. The crowd parted and applauded; the more daring boys touched the arms of Rennie's jacket. On the bandstand were a lectern with a microphone and, behind it, two rows of folding chairs. The veterans sat in the front row, their drivers behind them in the same order as the motorcade. It was cooler here, and Rennie thought it wouldn't be long. He'd known it was going to be bad and he was pleased he'd made it this far. Stephenson had stayed only an hour or so, but sometimes, remembering, Rennie was trapped there with him whole afternoons, and he was relieved that that hadn't happened now.

The band stopped, and the marshal in his purple sash stepped to the microphone and asked the crowd to give them a hand, and they did. He made a few general announcements—lost children, the bake sale table, who to see for tickets to tonight's dance—while the band filtered into a perfectly spaced arrangement of chairs to one side of the crowd. Opposite, lining the walk of the Civil War memorial and its spike-fenced garden of graves, sat a group of schoolchildren all dressed in blue shorts and white tops. Each had a flag like Rennie's. They squirmed and wriggled on their chairs, but with an iron glance the teacher overseeing them made sure they stayed seated. With no spectacle to absorb, the crowd itself had grown distracted, chatting and looking around for friends. Women fanned themselves with church programs fished from purses; men had their jackets folded over their arms. By the barbecue pit, teenagers were playing grab-ass and drinking nickel Cokes. The trees above rustled; the shade and the grass and the quiet soothed Rennie. He was thinking it hadn't been so bad when his father called to him through the railing and gave him a thumbs-up.

Everyone was there—Dorothy and Jennifer, Jay, his mother and father, Grampa Langer and Aunt Sarah—and all dressed up. Dorothy had on a dazzling magenta dress he'd never seen. He leaned over the rail and took her hand. He could feel himself smiling, and only hoped they could tell the difference.

"You look so handsome," his mother said.

"I can't believe you're a hero," Jay joked.

Behind him on the bandstand the marshal was introducing someone, to a burst of applause.

"You better get back," his father said. "We'll see you after."

The first speaker was the president of the Hampton Bays Historical Society, a woman in lilac gloves and a huge wicker hat with a gauzy lilac bow. "Hi, everybody," she said, arranging her notes, then, supporting herself with the lectern, bent over and slipped off her shoes. "I won't be too long," she promised, and after a big breath, began, "It is 1848. The Mexican Wars are over."

From where Rennie sat he couldn't see Dorothy, but likewise he was protected from the crowd. The speaker was going on about Hampton Bays' contribution to the Civil War, every so often mentioning the Union vet, Maynard Washington. At the end of the row, the old man curled over his cane; each time the crowd applauded, he smiled and raised a hand to acknowledge them. His dentures,

Rennie saw, were stained the color of sweet corn. Beyond him sat the dark block of the memorial with its names engraved on bronze plaques. Beside it stood a large white sign that he knew from Jay's description must be the town's Roll of Honor.

There, in silver, as if he'd taken second place, was his name—or not—J. LANGER. It was at the bottom of the list. He didn't know any of the other names; they were all from Hampton Bays. He thought of Maynard Washington looking at the bronze plaques, the last in his outfit. He could probably tell you what had happened to each and every one.

"We were there eighteen days," Stephenson had explained. The wind off the sea pushed his inch-long hair about like an uncut field. "The whole time it was nothing but fog. Rain during the day and snow at night. Wind like a motherfucker. It never got any better than the first day. Guys dug in and while they were asleep their holes filled with water. Those new boots they gave us weren't worth a shit. Remember how they chafed? A couple miles and they broke your foot wide open. Guys were coming in with trench foot and we kept telling them to stay dry, take an extra pair of socks, don't just lie there in the hole. But where are you going to get dry socks? Two days later the guy's got gangrene and doesn't even know it. It was wholesale amputation, Burger had trash cans full of 'em. Blue, black, white as fucking ice. I mean fucking trash cans. Our stretcher-ers were coming in with guys with sores on their knees from crawling, they hurt so bad. And no one could get anywhere near the action till it was almost over. It was ridge to ridge, and the Japs were dug in; no way they were giving up. You could see it right in front of you and there was nothing you could do. Right in front of your face—*boom*—and here comes all this shit down the hill."

He lit a cigarette then, fumbling with the wheel of the lighter and inhaling deeply. "Jesus," he said, "I don't know why they sent me to do this." He took off his sunglasses again and wiped his eyes.

"What happened to Burger and Mowry?" Rennie asked.

Stephenson looked at him flatly, and Rennie knew.

He put on his shades again.

"How?" Rennie said.

"Fuck, Lang."

"How?"

He dipped his head and sighed, rubbed the back of his neck, his bristly hair. "Okay.

"The whole thing was nuts. That mud, we couldn't get the big guns in over it, or anything, so the Japs kept dropping mortars on us and there was nothing we could do. They had bunkers up there, all along that ridge. There was too much wind to get planes in, so we were taking every bunker one at a time. What they'd do is move out and leave their wounded with a bunch of grenades.

"You remember how steep it was. We were lowering litters down on ropes. Lots of rock shrapnel, a lot of exposure; it didn't stop.

"And still we couldn't get the little bastards. They were holed up in this last bunker, maybe a hundred of them. I saw some of them later and they hadn't eaten in a while. Some of them just had bayonets, their chambers were empty.

"But we didn't know that then. Every time we went up we'd lose a few people, so we decided to wait them out. Meanwhile we got the field hospital up just below there, so we could take care of people. That's where Burger and Mowry were.

"The weather gets better, and we sic the planes on them. P-38s. *Boom,* and the whole mountain shakes, the bunker's on fire. We wait, thinking there's no way they survived that, and then five minutes later, out comes a grenade on our scouts.

"And still we've got no supplies ourselves because of the mud. No kitchen, no heat. Everything's got to be walked in. We're eating C-rats and burning the boxes to sterilize our instruments.

"Then the weather gets really bad. Freezing, wind, can't see a thing. So we ground the planes and call the patrols in, batten down the hatches.

"Finally at night the weather turns. The next morning we're eating breakfast when all hell breaks loose. Rifle fire everywhere, right on top of us. The Japs are overrunning the camp, some of them coming right through the mess tent. It's a banzai charge. They're grabbing rifles out of our guys' hands and just spraying everything they see. We've got no idea what's hit us. Lot of people killed, just plain craziness.

"Finally a bunch of engineers comes up and saves us. The last

Japs are cornered down in this gully, out of ammo, or so we think, because they bunch up into a group and a few of them whip out grenades. They've had them stashed just for this. 'Shoot,' we're going, 'shoot the bastards,' because we think they're going to throw them, but you know what they do?

"You know what they do? They take them and pull the pin and stick them up against their foreheads. They just hold them there, and *boom*, right in front of us. *Boom*, just like that.

"That's what happened," Stephenson said. "You asked what happened, that's what happened."

"What happened to Burger and Mowry?"

"Yeah. So after that I went back over to the field hospital to see if I could help out. I ran over there just hoping I could do something, you know? The place was a mess, people all over the place. The Japs had gone through and killed the wounded, shot them right in their goddamn beds.

"Right in their goddamn beds," he said. "Guys with casts on, guys missing feet. Burger and Mowry tried to stop them, I guess, 'cause they were there, both of them laid out on the ground right next to each other."

He lit another cigarette and inhaled deeply, looked off over Hickam as if it was time to go. "Yeah, so that's it, the Battle of Attu. What else you want to know about it?"

Though he'd been there, had seen the same fog, the same water, the same snow and fire and blood, Rennie couldn't imagine it.

"Again," he said, "tell me it again," and Stephenson sighed like an old man and flipped the unfinished butt over the fence and lit another.

"Okay," he'd said, slowly, as if Rennie were learning it to tell someone else. "We were there eighteen days. . . ."

Now the crowd applauded the speaker. Startled, Rennie rose politely. She pointed her toes into her shoes and collected her notes and everyone on the bandstand sat down.

The marshall announced Maynard Washington and, while the crowd cheered, helped him to the lectern and bent the mike toward his face. It hadn't been this quiet all day. Leaves swished; miles off, a train thrummed.

"I'd just like to thank," the old man said, turning away from the microphone and sweeping a hand at the men seated behind him, "first God and then all the men and their families who put themselves out for their country. Thank you."

Again, there were cheers, and the band let loose with "When Johnny Comes Marching Home," but all eyes had turned from the bandstand to the group of schoolchildren. Their teacher had opened the spiked gate of the tiny graveyard, and, in a pageant obviously choreographed, five or six children scampered through the stones and planted their flags.

The marshal called for a moment of silence, after which a short girl with red cheeks blew taps. Appropriately, there was no applause.

"I will now ask you to join us at the New Ground for the final part of our ceremony," the marshal said, and pointed across the green. Already a few boys were sprinting in that direction. What more was there? Rennie thought, but, reeling from the day, he didn't have the strength to protest, and let his driver walk him to the car. Again, hands fluttered against him, faces bobbed. He saw at the back of the crowd his father gesture that they'd meet him wherever it was they were going, and waved back, yes, whatever.

In the Nash he sat up front. The crowd, stretched like a forced march, angled across the green. Rennie got the nod from his driver and popped the glove compartment. There was about half left. He let his driver take the first swig.

"What's this New Ground?" Rennie asked.

"New Burying Ground," his driver said. "The cemetery."

After Rennie had his, there was less than a finger. He held it up to show him.

"Go ahead," the driver said, "kill it."

The New Ground was at the edge of town, a sloping derelict meadow hemmed in by falling stone walls. One corner was completely overgrown with the twisted remains of an orchard. Red and brown sandstone markers topped by winged faces with pitted cheeks commemorated names like Hezekiah Goodwin and Elijah Tisdale. Buoyed by the glow of his last sip, Rennie thought the place must have been new a long time ago. The bond people had erected a platform to one side of a large poured-concrete monument to the first war decorated with half pillars and bas-relief eagles. Beside the rows of folding chairs stood a flag, a microphone on a two-piece stand and a table skirted with a banner that read BACK THE ATTACK. Two women manned a cash box. Rennie and the others had beaten all but the fastest boys, and, except Maynard Washington, who had to sit, they paced the grass, not wanting to take the platform yet, like horses balking at a gate. They could hear the band coming up the road, thumping out "It's a Long Way to Tipperary."

The marshal was rushing about with a pen and a sheaf of papers, flitting like a dragonfly from person to person. He caught up to Rennie, dropping a hand on his shoulder. "We might ask you to say a word or two at the very end. Nothing fancy, just a word or two to thank the folks for coming out, okay? You *can* talk?"

"Not much," Rennie began to explain, but before he had a chance to refuse, the marshal patted him on the back and hustled over to the old Marine.

The band stopped playing outside the gate, waited there in formation while the crowd squeezed in. As on the green, the children involved in the ceremony sat to the left of the platform, the band opposite. Dorothy and Jennifer were halfway back in the middle, Jay and his parents and Aunt Sarah off to the side, where they'd set up a folding chair for Grampa Langer. The heat was beginning to lift, the day to fade. The train he'd heard on the green had passed, and again Rennie thought that he'd been through the worst.

The marshal introduced the man from the balloon corps, who told a funny story about a particularly sticky winch on the ground and how each night he and his buddies drew straws to see who would use it. Incredibly, he produced a long straw from his pocket, and the crowd laughed. Then it was the Marine's turn, but like Rennie, he was unprepared, and instead of telling them about Château-Thierry he said that war was hard business and that without money and the right weapons it was outright slaughter; he'd seen it. When he was done the crowd respectfully hesitated a minute before applauding, and then the band played "Over There," and a large number of the children with flags scattered throughout that part of the cemetery. The applause continued until they returned.

"That was the Great War," the marshal said, "but we're in an even greater struggle today." He made the pitch for bonds, ending, "And now here are three of our fighting men that your war bonds support."

The Coast Guard guy was first. He talked about secure borders and the last line of defense. He asked the local air wardens to raise their hands, which they did, garnering applause.

"Very nice," the marshal said, "and very true. We're all in this together."

He introduced the clerk as a soldier in the quartermaster corps.

Rennie didn't hear anything the man said. His stomach had gone sour, his bowel packed and wormy. If, like Stephenson, he told them everything, beginning to end, they'd be here all night. He could tell them about his father and his CO hearing and Big Flats and Redwood and then Cal and San Diego and Dorothy and the voyage out and the landing and seeing Fecho get shot and then getting shot himself. But he hadn't even told Dorothy about Fecho, let alone Burger and Mowry. He'd told her the story of his poncho, that was it, he couldn't go any further than that.

He could tell them how on board that first night after getting shot he'd been so excited to be alive he hadn't even gone to sleep. With his head wrapped in a cast and an IV needle in his hand, he lay awake in the warm damp belowdecks listening to the groans of the other men in the berth and the slopping of the sea, thinking how lucky he was.

So Cal, he thought woozily, sickly, Calpurnia, Caligula, Caliban, what am I going to say to these people? That we were happy once. That we were alive together then. The room. The window and the cold night air. How you would be proud of me now.

The crowd clapped and the clerk sat down.

"Thank you," the marshal said. "And now, our most recent returnee. He's just come back from the Pacific Theater, where he fought against the Japanese on the island of Attu and received the Purple Heart. You may not know him but I know you've seen his name in town. He's the grandson of James Langer, which happens to be his name also. How about a big welcome-home hand for Private James Reynolds Langer."

The crowd had saved their loudest applause for him. Even the other veterans sitting beside him rose. The marshal turned to Rennie, clapping, then extended a hand as if he might need help getting up.

Rennie stood and stepped to the microphone and looked out over the crowd, the band, the graves. Birds chirped. The Nash and the other cars sat gleaming in a line on the drive. He thought he heard bells carried on the wind from town. He saw Dorothy and Jay and his mother and father, waiting on his words like everyone else. What could he say to them? That he was so tired. That it hurt when he yawned. That he dreamed of headless, handless Japanese. That his friends were dead and never coming home, and that no amount of applause or ceremony, no matter how heartfelt and innocent and right, would ever repay him for how much he'd lost.

"Thank you," he said through his teeth. "Thank you all very much for coming," and sat down. For a moment there was silence, and then the crowd cheered, the band played, and, on cue, the children ran through the stones.

DEEP IN THE NIGHT, Jennifer's squalling brought Dorothy up from sleep. She and Rennie had pushed the twin beds together, but when she reached across the drafty gap to wake him, he wasn't there.

Goddammit, she thought, not again.

The radio was on softly in the corner, the dial shedding a weak, tea-colored light. The Armed Forces station out of Newport News broadcast twenty-four hours a day: Jimmy Dorsey, Kay Kyser with Dinah Shore, Fred Waring and His Pennsylvanians. Before Rennie had come home she used to listen long into the morning, floating on the sinfully heartbreaking cushion of make-out music and the DJ's sober yet melancholy intros ("This one goes out to all Americans working for freedom on the late shift, and to all the ships at sea"). Keeping it on now had been her idea. Jennifer could sleep through anything, cried only when she was hungry. The last two nights the music seemed to help Rennie. In the morning Dorothy had rewarded him, both of them lightly riding the springs, careful not to wake the baby.

Dimly conscious, Dorothy weaved around the low table, knocking a wicker chair with a hip. "Mama's coming," she said. Jennifer was on her back, eyes clenched, clawing the air. Dorothy lifted her from the bassinet and checked which side of her nightgown the safety pin was on, shifted arms and got comfortable in the rocker. The night was cool, and Jennifer warmed her. Above, the rafters were boxed with shadows. A soft wall of trumpets and clarinets filled the dim room—"Harbor Lights." His first leave in San Diego they'd gone to some dime-a-dance ballroom downtown and held each other while a mirrored ball covered them and the other couples on the floor with drifting stars. After, they walked out to the end of the Broadway Pier and strolled through the flashing, ringing arcade. Beyond the violent brightness of the prize-lined Skee-ball shed, the sea lapped black and invisible. They stopped before a wall of funhouse mirrors and kissed—too hard for in public, she thought, then let go. His cap fell off, and she leaned back to let him pick it up, but he didn't care about it; he only wanted her. The mirror pulled at them like taffy. Now, with Jennifer tugging warmly at her, she thought of the cap dropping and the crowd breaking around them. How had Rennie smiled at her then? She couldn't honestly remember. His picture was packed away in her suitcase where it couldn't hurt him. As Dorothy reluctantly came awake, her anger cooled to a futile mix of hopelessness and pity. It wasn't his fault, no, but didn't he see she couldn't live like this?

He'd never really explained what had happened in Alaska. He would, she thought, he would have to. One night she woke to find him—still asleep—gripping her arm so hard that she was afraid. Another night she caught him sitting by Jennifer's bassinet, watching her breathe, something Dorothy herself would do, but hours later he was still there. When she talked to him, he said it had to do with the sound of water in the dark. Something had happened to a friend of his. In Hawaii they tried earplugs. Then why, she asked, were they staying here, on the water? Wouldn't it be better to go home to Galesburg? They would, he said, when he was ready. Had he decided yet if he wanted to go back to school? He hadn't, not yet. He seemed to resent her questions, to be ashamed of his evasions, and while she didn't see how he could possibly withdraw further, Dorothy knew better than to press. Tacitly they agreed that he wasn't strong enough.

She knew where he would be now—sleeping in the bed his mother had set up in the maid's room at the back of the house. It had one small octagonal window which his father had stuffed with batting and boarded up so that Rennie wouldn't hear the ocean. Daily the Langers offered Dorothy the guest room next door, but while she was sick of the cottage, she needed to feel that as a family they were independent, whether it was true or not. In the mornings Rennie apologized, though she told him not to. It would take time, she said, because that was what everyone said.

Jennifer had stopped sucking and lay curled in her arms, asleep. Dorothy set her in the bassinet, switched the pin and got back in her cold bed. "For Cape Hatteras, the Outer Banks, and all the boys at Camp Lejeune," the DJ said, "here's Vaughn Monroe, 'Racing With the Moon.' " She listened in the dark with her eyes closed and the covers pulled up to her chin. The music was low and murky and made her want to drink. She knew it was indulgent, that it was bad for her, but the trumpets purred above the soft dark bottom of trombones and bassoons, and when he began to sing, she opened her eyes and, staring up at the rafters as if the roof were the sky, sang with him in a whisper. It seemed then that he'd been with her all this time, through everything, that the song had followed her, that Vaughn Monroe alone understood what she was feeling. She'd heard it here when she knew Rennie wasn't coming back, and on shift in San Diego, straining to pick it out of the noise from the line. Their one week together last fall they'd made love to it on the slippery backseat of his father's car, the moon—like a giant prop—marbling his face with the shadows of overhanging branches. Dorothy couldn't remember the first time she'd heard it, but senior year after Carol Thomas bought a copy of the record, the two of them would sit on her bed with the door closed and play it over and over, taking turns crooning to each other until Mrs. Thomas yelled up the stairs that supper was ready and it was time for Dorothy to go home. Through everything it had served her as a sanctuary, a room she could retreat to; now she found she couldn't give herself to it, could no longer enter that room, and she wondered how she'd become so cold.

She stopped singing. She listened through to the end, then got up and turned the radio off. The cottage went absolutely black. She had to feel her way back to bed, and when she scooted over to her side, banged her ankle on the rail between the two twins. "Dammit," she said, biting the word so she wouldn't wake Jennifer, and soon the throbbing stopped, the bed warmed, and she was left with nothing but the waves.

During the day the sea didn't bother him. In the morning he was thoughtful of her, changing and dressing Jennifer while she went up to the house for her shower. After breakfast, the three of them moved to the backyard, every once in a while Dorothy going upstairs to check on Grampa Langer, who most days now stayed in bed, came down only for supper. Like his father, Rennie liked to putter in the garden. Barefoot, in his mother's unraveling sun hat, he stalked the rows of dwarf corn and ragged lettuces with a trowel, laid out saucers of flat beer for the bugs. Jennifer lay in the shadow of a peeling Adirondack chair, Dorothy beside her in the hot grass, sampling timothy. The rising sun made her sweat; the sea called. The eleven-thirty plane came over, and, standing in the zucchini, he shaded his eyes and watched it out to sea.

"Were there a lot of planes there?" she asked.

"Not many," he said, and peeked under a broad leaf. She'd become so used to his speech that she didn't have to look at him anymore; in a week the doctors would cut the wires. "Actually I didn't see any."

"How about Hawaii?"

"Sure, lots of them. Jay would have loved it." He came up with a heavy zucchini, scissored over the fence and presented it to her.

"Did you sleep?" she asked.

"Yep." He lay down in the grass with his face alongside Jennifer's, imperturbable, as if to say that was all, they wouldn't talk about him anymore. It was almost lunch, and knowing that he would read all afternoon, Dorothy wanted to stop playing the game, but knew that if she pursued it, he'd stop talking altogether. She'd never had his patience, and now his defenses—his indifference, his blank pleasantness—seemed limitless. Daily she chipped away at the mystery, confirming and reconfirming those parts of the story he let slip, and sometimes a new fact emerged—he had a fourth friend, Stephenson—which she later shared with his father, pooling their clues the way her mother's circle traded meat stamps.

"He saw some things," his father explained, "that luckily we'll never have to see." Nights the two of them talked here by the garden. Dorothy was envious. She thought it strange that Rennie should seek him out now, but, glad that he was at least talking to someone, never questioned it. He hadn't come to terms with his father the way she had with her mother. That alone gave her hope. At one time in their lives reconciliation with either had seemed equally impossible. Mr. Langer thought Rennie blamed him for not supporting Rennie's decision to object. While Dorothy knew this to be true, she downplayed it, saying that in San Diego Rennie had been happy. What exactly did Rennie say he'd seen?

"He hasn't actually said. I'd imagine he saw other men hurt or killed. Men he knew."

Only after he said this did she admit she'd taken it as a given. It seemed so obvious that she'd assumed it without thinking it through, investing it with dimension, flesh. These were the friends in his letters, the ones she'd never seen. Though many times this summer she'd felt the weight of loss upon her, Dorothy couldn't fully imagine what Rennie had been through. She needed him to tell her so she could begin to understand.

"I think he's trying to tell us," his father said, but Rennie had taught her not to believe him.

Now, watching Rennie flirt with Jennifer, she could believe that he wasn't unhappy, merely calm, stunned by so many sudden changes, that perhaps after the doctors removed the hooks and wires he'd confess everything and at night instead of fleeing the cottage would turn to her and together they'd make plans to leave for Galesburg, where they could start fresh. Her father said if Rennie wasn't ready to go back to school, the paper mill was hiring. She thought if her mother could take care of Jennifer, both she and Rennie could work and put enough money away in a year for a fixer-upper in town. She would surprise him with a car, maybe buy back his old Mercury from the legendary Mr. Wheeler. They could take a picnic lunch up to the Grayson place and drink beer and fool around while Jennifer took her nap, and, after making love, walk in the garden, holding hands and bending to sniff Mrs. Grayson's ancient roses. There would be haze now in the valley, blue and rippled with the heat. They would stand at the rail and they wouldn't have to talk. The war would be over.

From town came the far-off alarm of the noon horn. Grampa Langer would wonder where his tuna salad was. Anne said it was important to encourage both him and Rennie to eat. Dorothy rolled over close to Rennie and kissed his cheek.

"Cream of Wheat again?" he said.

"There's soup and eggnog, it's your choice. You can have all three if you want. It's just one more week."

"I'll have what the princess is having." He cupped one of her breasts.

"I don't think you can get these through a straw," Dorothy said. "All three?"

"All three," he conceded.

Inside, making tuna salad, she wondered if he'd meant to say that about her breasts. When they were first going out he paid so much attention to them that often she had to pull him up to remind him they were attached to her. Since he'd been back he'd kissed her only a few times, always coldly and never there. He turned his cheek to her lips, and in truth she was halfway grateful. The thought of her tongue reaching between those two solid walls of machined teeth made her close her own mouth. Her nipples were already sore from Jennifer; she didn't want to risk the wires and hooks, especially in the dark, in the fearless rush of love which, despite all their problems, seized them several times a day.

Grampa Langer was waiting for her, propped up in bed. She'd lent him her table radio, and he was listening to the ball game turned up loud. She set the lunch tray across his lap.

"Looks good," he said, and, as if letting her in on some joke, winked.

"You want anything else?" she shouted.

He shook his head and started in on his sandwich, gnawing on it, head bent, as if she'd left the room.

"He looks terrible," she told Rennie. They were at the big table in the kitchen, Jennifer at her breast. Rennie kept eating. "I think your mother should have someone look at him."

Rennie nodded and swallowed. The straw was stuck between his teeth; when only she was in the room he left it in while he spoke. "I'll tell her."

After lunch he'd read. When he finished his melted strawberry ice cream he'd stand and come around the table and give her a hug from behind and tousle Jennifer's fine hair and say, "I'll see you two later," as if he were leaving for work, and the longest part of the day would begin. He seemed to look forward to the time alone, and she tried not to resent it, but every day at lunch she found herself growing angry with him. She knew that he sensed her crossness and thought it unfair, as if they had agreed to this schedule, but later he thanked her for her indulgence, just as he apologized each morning after he'd spent the night in the maid's room.

The straw slurped, and Rennie extracted it from the gap. "One week."

"Seven days," she said.

He picked his book off the table—Hemingway, he'd finished and started it again. She turned to watch him, and Jennifer lost the nipple, the milk tracing a white line over the bridge of her nose. Dorothy pushed and pulled to get her to take it again. Behind her, Rennie touched her shoulder.

"Don't drag it out," Dorothy said, "just go."

"Okay," he said pleasantly, and mussed Jennifer's hair. She purposely didn't watch him, but heard the screen door slap. She would not feel guilty for this, she would not.

She made her own lunch then, and ate it alone at the kitchen table—like her mother and her cup of tea. She'd grown tired of walking the re-created streets of Galesburg, and had started, impossibly, to piece together San Diego. Upas, Thorn, Spruce. She looked in on Grampa Langer before navigating the cliff stairs and putting Jennifer down for her nap. The cottage smelled of the hot tarpaper roof; she stationed the fan beside the bassinet and started it turning, propped open the door with a wooden stop. Below, Rennie sat in his folding chair on the breakwater, reading his idiotic book. She turned away as if slapped and faced the stifling white room, the radio, the made beds. Hadn't she already been through this?

The soap operas made the time go by. They came on at two and went all afternoon. Her mother loved *Stella Dallas*, but Dorothy liked the younger ones—*When a Girl Marries*, *Portia Faces Life*, and her favorite, *Second Husband*. They all had ridiculous plots. Every other week it seemed someone came down with amnesia or turned out to be a spy. Dorothy pulled her chair up next to the radio and half listened while she wrote a letter she owed Mrs. Schuman.

In her last letter, Mrs. Schuman said she couldn't accept the check Dorothy had sent. Dorothy should consider the money a gift. The new girl boarding with them was from Mississippi, very nice but hard to understand. Elizabeth was flying B-25s from Wichita to Birmingham, Alabama, but hadn't met anyone special. Ronald was still in London, something to do with intelligence, they didn't hear from him that often. She hoped everyone was doing well.

How are you? Dorothy wrote. *We are all fine, especially Jennifer, who weighs over sixteen pounds. Rennie is glad to be back and his spirits are good. Before I forget, let me give you my parents' address in Galesburg where we'll be next.*

She'd promised Mrs. Schuman a picture of the three of them and, almost finished with the letter, sure she'd forget, Dorothy pulled her suitcase out from under the bed and searched it for the snapshots Jay had taken outside the station. She found the stack of them and slipped off the rubber bands and thumbed through them, trying to find one she could spare. They stood before his father's car in the parking lot, slightly overexposed, buildings filling the background. Her face was fat, and Jennifer was tiny, but Rennie looked fine in his uniform. You could barely tell.

She lifted his good picture out of the suitcase. She hadn't looked at it since she'd put it away. It was wrapped in corrugated cardboard to protect the glass. As she was peeling the one piece of tape back with her thumbnail to get it open, the cellophane ripped and she thought she should stop, that it was wrong. She checked the door. He was still reading; Jennifer was asleep. On the radio, Portia was trying to decide which engagement ring she should send back. Dorothy cut through the last strip of tape with her nail and sat down on the edge of the bed.

He seemed young in the picture, his skin perfect, touched up in the darkroom. It had been taken late this spring, yet almost none of this face remained. He'd lost so much weight that even the undamaged areas like his brow and eyes and cheeks had changed dramatically. And the damage, the snapshot confirmed, had been complete. It didn't seem possible that she'd wholly forgotten his dimples, the slight cleft in his chin, the fat curl in the middle of his lower lip, and she sat with the picture gripped in both hands, unsure whether she should memorize or forget them. She went to the door and with a hand on the screen looked down at him sitting on the breakwater, knowing she'd never understand what had happened to him.

She wrapped the picture but the tape wouldn't hold. She buried it under several dresses she couldn't wear, chose the shot she'd send to Mrs. Schuman and slid the suitcase back under the bed.

Hope you are doing fine too, she finished, *and thank you again for the money. We will put it to good use.*

Second Husband was almost over, and she had to start thinking about dinner, about getting Jennifer up and checking on Grampa Langer. Jay and Win would be back from their adventures soon. Her mother would call around five, just as Anne rumbled up, and ask her when she could see Jennifer, though she knew it would be two more weeks. It wasn't long, Dorothy thought, if you knew how to waste the days.

Jennifer didn't want to get up, and Grampa Langer was asleep, the radio going full blast. Dorothy peeked into the steaming box of the freezer and picked some frosted spinach to go with the chicken. Jay and Win were still missing—probably at the Regal watching Ann Sheridan in *Edge of Darkness*. The ad in the paper looked good. Dorothy would have asked Rennie to take her if it weren't about the war. She didn't even have to see the movie, all she wanted was an excuse to get out of the house, to be alone with him. By the time he came up for supper, his whole family was home, and he was too busy being cheerful for them to pay her any attention.

"You're with him all day long," Anne said. "We never get to see him."

Dorothy knew her jealousy was selfish but couldn't help how she felt. She was tired of watching him play catch. She was tired of the endless suppers and coffee on the porch and the stories Anne told about Rennie being a difficult baby—as if he were easy now. They never saw his bad times, his silences; he saved them for Dorothy. She knew he was just being polite, but still she wished he wouldn't be so quick to laugh at their unfunny jokes. She wished that tonight after Jay and Anne took Grampa Langer up to bed, rather than going around the house to drink with his father, Rennie would follow her across the yard and down to the cottage. She wished that he would kiss her.

It didn't happen. He was half drunk when he came in, bumping the furniture, and she shushed him.

"Take me out tomorrow," she said when he was under the covers. "I don't care where, I just need to get out of here for one night. Ask your father for the car. Your mother can watch Jennifer."

From the corner came the first chords of "Sentimental Journey."

"Where'll we go?"

"We can drive around in circles for all I care."

"All right," he said, then added, "It's only two more weeks."

"Fourteen days," Dorothy said. "I don't think I'm going to make it."

In the morning it was raining. All day they kicked about the house, but around supper it cleared. There was a dance at the roller rink; Anne thought it was a wonderful idea. They changed after dessert. His whole family gathered on the porch to watch them off, as if she and Rennie were leaving for good. It was Dorothy's first time away from Jennifer, and when they turned onto the town road she wanted to ask Rennie to go back.

"She'll be fine," he assured her—reading her mind—and she believed him.

"We don't have to go to the dance," she offered.

"No, let's go. We're dressed for it."

Behind the wheel he seemed more himself. He'd always loved to drive. She put on the radio, its green glow painting her fingers, and found the all-night station. "Chattanooga Choo-Choo," and then ("For everyone dreaming of home," the hep DJ said) "Somewhere Over the Rainbow." Rennie dropped a hand from the wheel and rested it on her leg. The road curved, the moon flew through the dark trees. She thought, if it could just go on like this.

The roller rink was sweltering, brightly lit and full of kids, some no older than Jay. The man at the door let them in for free, saluting as he stamped their hands. Chaperones lurked, sniffing Cokes for a whiff of bourbon. They found a dim corner, but everyone recognized Rennie from the parade, and while they were swaying to "Blue Moon" or "I'll Be Seeing You," other couples came over to shake his hand. The boys adored him, though she could see some of the girls weren't sure if they'd trade places with her. When Dorothy asked him if he wanted to leave, he said no—for her—and she said she needed some air.

In the parking lot, the cars were busy. Blackout was in effect, which made every giggle and creak of springs and dropped bottle that much louder. Rennie had tried to buy her a root beer, but the woman at the refreshment stand wouldn't accept his money.

"Now everybody loves me," he joked.

They left the car in the lot and walked through town hand in hand. It was their night out, but she couldn't stop thinking of Jennifer. All the shops were closed, the ghostly light of the moon reaching in among the still shelves, the shells and knickknacks and personalized sailor's caps. The hooded stoplight changed and changed. It was humid but cool; the air carried a hint of the sea. The streets were silvered with puddles. She was afraid they'd end up at the green or down by the water, and steered him into the side streets. Behind black-painted windows, men laughed; briefly a door opened and a rainbowed jukebox glowed, the strains of some tune she knew seeping into the night. She was ready for him to suggest a drink, but he didn't. The art galleries were pushing sandpipers and lighthouses, the furniture stores cheap reproductions of the high-priced antiques next door. They walked along window-shopping, their footsteps echoing. The dark facades and empty sidewalks reminded her of the imaginary Galesburg she paced in her daydreams, an idealized, unoccupied model. As if to refute her, a couple whizzed by them on bikes, laughing, their fenders rattling when they hit the cobblestones.

"That's what we need," Rennie said, watching them, then, as if he'd found someone to rent them a pair, exclaimed "Hey!" and started across the street.

Parked with their bumpers even with the sidewalk were a line of cars, a bold price soaped on each window. Above hung a silver fringe that riffled with the breeze. Rennie immediately took to a humpbacked Ford that cost three hundred dollars, walking around it and patting its curves as if it were a horse. One rear wheel rested on a cinder block, but Rennie said it wasn't a problem, which for him was true; he'd built his Mercury practically from scratch. Dorothy was more impressed with a stately Pierce-Arrow, and told him so, just to hear him speak. He hadn't been this lively all night—really, since he'd been back. He went on and on about the two cars, spit occasionally spraying from between his teeth. It was complete gibberish to her, and wonderful, and she kept him going with questions, pretending she wasn't already sold.

"Do you want it?" she asked him.

"What, this?"

"We're going to need a car," she said, and when he saw she was serious, Rennie kissed her so hard he cut his lip.

When they got home, only Mr. Langer was up. Jennifer had been very good, but Grampa Langer had had a bad night. Anne was going to stay home from work tomorrow. Dorothy let Rennie tell him about the car.

"Good," Mr. Langer said, "maybe now I'll get to drive mine once in a while."

The garage charged them a fortune for hauling the car out. They delivered it in midafternoon, and except for a few trips to town for parts and a half-hour break for supper, Rennie was under it until nightfall. There was more wrong with it than he'd thought; he said this not with regret but determination, as if secretly happy to take on the job. He was tired, he said, and they didn't make love. In the middle of the night she woke to hear him snoring, and thought it was safe to turn off the radio.

The days were predictable. As she'd hoped, Rennie stopped reading, but now Dorothy was alone in the mornings as well. He was tearing down the engine. The first few days she sat in the grass beside the lot listening to him tinker, but he didn't want to talk, and now she and Jennifer saw him only when she brought out lunch. Jay and Win fed him wrenches from a toolbox and ran to the house for beers. Anne was upstairs keeping an eye on Grampa Langer. She'd quit her job on base to watch him. It was clear that he was going to die. When Mr. Langer came home he spent time with him, then changed his clothes and lent Rennie a hand. He had an old A sticker they glued to the window. By week's end all they needed was a tire.

She thought that, if not happy, he was at least doing something. He'd stopped drinking at night with his father, which she took as a good sign. Things would be different once the doctor unhooked his jaw. She believed this even more deeply when, the night before his appointment, she woke to find his side of the bed empty.

In the morning she was short with him, tired of apologizing. Later her mother called, and Dorothy closed the door to the living room so no one would hear her.

The doctor was in Southampton; just past him in Water Mill, according to the car dealer, lived a farmer who sold old tires. Mr. Langer's sister came so they could all go. Dorothy and Rennie sat in the back with Jay—for the last time, she thought.

The office was above a drugstore. They had to wait in the hall while he went in, a shadow dwindling to light on the frosted glass door. Some piece of machinery whirred like a dentist's drill, high-pitched at first, then deeply, meeting resistance. Anne took Jay down to look at comic books. Mr. Langer paced the hallway, holding his hat.

"I'm sure it's routine," he assured her.

When the whirring stopped, he clumped downstairs to fetch Anne and Jay. They came up in a bunch just as the door filled with color.

The doctor came out first, ushering Rennie into the hall. They shook hands, and Rennie turned to them. Besides the wires and hooks, his face looked the same to Dorothy, the chin gone, the lips not quite covering the overly white teeth.

"It's me," he said, and, holding him, she thought she should be grateful that his voice was still his own.

On the way to Water Mill he didn't say much. It hurt to talk. His jaw muscles had atrophied; he'd have to stay on a semi-solid diet. He wasn't used to the teeth. The doctor said he had to be careful of his tongue.

The farmer recognized him and gave him the tire for free.

"It's like Halloween," Rennie said. "Show them the scary face and they give you things."

"It's respect," Mr. Langer said.

"They don't even know who I am," Rennie said. "They just see the teeth."

"That's not true," his father said, but unconvincingly.

Later, Dorothy thought Rennie was talking about not just the farmer and the kids at the dance, but his father, herself.

After supper he fit the tire on the wheel and took Jay for a spin. They came back with ice cream. He offered her a ride, but, tired and a bit disgusted with him, she declined. Sarah said she'd like one, and they burned across the lot, flinging gravel.

"It'll get easier," Mr. Langer commiserated. "You have to believe that."

She went to bed early, putting the radio on for him. She heard him come in and set a glass on the shelf above their bed. He took his shoes off, his shirt, belt, pants—easily; he wasn't drunk. The floorboards squeaked, but instead of the springs giving as he got into bed, Dorothy heard the watery clink she knew from helping Grampa Langer clean his dentures, and she was sorry she'd been angry with him.

"How's the car?" she asked.

"Good," he said. "You should have come." His voice was different with his teeth out, his pronunciation mushy. You shud hub come.

"I should have," she admitted. She let a few seconds pass, and when he didn't reply, said, "My mother called."

"What did she say?"

"Nothing. I did most of the talking. She's still dying to see Jennifer."

Again, she gave him room to answer. There was nothing but the swirling strings of the radio. She was tempted to ask him straight out about his friends now, those names in the letters that she'd envied and loved for being so close to him. Did he really think she didn't know? She rolled over to face him. In the dark she could only see his eyes—all boyish innocence, as if nothing was wrong. It was his father in him, she thought. Why did she think he'd confide in her what he needed to deny? And if he was happier that way, why did she want him to?

"I want to go home," she said.

"We will," he said, but he didn't understand.

"Soon, Rennie. I can't stay here."

"Okay," he said.

He had eggs and toast for breakfast, devouring seconds. Anne wouldn't let her near the stove. Since she'd quit her job, she'd taken over all of Dorothy's chores, leaving her to watch Jennifer. The hours dragged, and she felt—as she had in the hospital, in the Schumans' garage—that she was waiting for something, only this time there was nothing coming.

That afternoon she'd joined Jennifer for her nap when Anne knocked on the door of the cottage.

"It's the phone," Anne said. "It's your father."

Her first thought was that he was supposed to be at work. She grabbed her robe off the back of the door. Anne said she'd look after Jennifer. Dorothy ran up the cliff stairs and across the lawn.

Rennie was talking to him, his knuckles covered with grease. When he saw her, he said, "Here she is," and before handing her the receiver, said, "It's about your brother."

"Dot?" her father said.

"Yes."

"We don't want to worry you, but we thought you ought to know that Robert's in Italy right now."

"Where?" she asked, as if she knew the country.

"We don't know," her father said. "We just got the letter from him today. It's three weeks old."

"Is Mom there?"

He put her on, and for the second time in as many days they cried over the phone. Rennie stood by, afraid to touch her until she was done, and then he held her, smelling—as he used to—of sweat and beer and motor oil. She kept forgetting that the fact that she hadn't lost him was a miracle, that he'd returned not merely from a hospital but from the dead.

At supper, Anne wondered if Dorothy wanted to be with her parents. She could call Penn Station and see if they could get her on a train. That way Rennie could stay another week before following with the car. Or he could go with her now, though the doctor who'd visited said it didn't appear that his grandfather was going to improve.

Dorothy didn't like her putting Rennie on the spot, and before Anne could finish said they'd leave at the end of the week, as planned.

"But your mother hasn't even seen Jennifer yet," Anne said.

"I think," Mr. Langer said, stepping in like a referee, "that Dorothy has made her decision."

After supper Rennie took her out in the car. Parked, they talked about leaving. Any time was fine, he said. The car was ready. She thought he should stay for his grandfather's sake, without mentioning the guilt she still felt for leaving San Diego before she'd heard word. Robert was probably fine. Besides, the mail was so far behind that a week one way or the other didn't matter. If he was in combat, they probably wouldn't hear anything from him for a month.

"Since when," he asked, "did you become an expert?"

"This summer," she said.

"So we stay."

"One week," she said. "Seven days."

She would get used to kissing him like this, she thought; all she had to do was keep her eyes closed and concentrate on his tongue.

He took his teeth out before bed, his back to her, shielding the glass. She wanted to tell him it was all right, she didn't mind, but couldn't truthfully.

She woke to Jennifer crying in the middle of the night. Before she even rolled over she knew she was alone. In the corner, the radio mocked her, softly playing "You'd Be So Nice to Come Home To." She cursed him and sleepily made her way to the bassinet, patting her chest for the pin. Jennifer swung at nothing.

Dorothy twisted the radio off. She fed and burped Jennifer and laid her back in her bassinet, then punched her arm into her robe and reshouldered her. Rennie had left the flashlight.

Outside, the sea was loud. The wind whipped her hair. The beam jiggled as she climbed the cliff stairs, throwing shadows between the risers. The lawn wet her feet. She thumped up the porch stairs, not trying to be quiet. The house was dark except for an orange glow above the second-floor railing—Jay's night-light. Dorothy gripped the banister and hauled herself up the creaking stairs. As she padded down the hall she heard one of the Langers stir.

His door was closed but unlocked. He was asleep, under the covers, snoring through his ruined, toothless mouth, and for an instant she faltered. She sat down on the edge of the bed and turned off the flashlight.

"Rennie," she said, nudging him.

It took a minute, but when he saw it was her, he sat up. He hid his mouth behind a hand, as if he were chewing a huge bite. "What is it?"

"I'm leaving," she said. "Tomorrow. You can come if you want, it's up to you."

"I'll come," he said, baffled, half awake.

In his pajamas, Mr. Langer looked in at the door. "What's going on?"

"We're leaving tomorrow," said Dorothy.

"This is news."

"It's news to me too," Rennie said, and they both looked to Dorothy as if she could explain.

"Excuse me," she said, "Jennifer needs her sleep." She kissed Rennie, clicked on the flashlight and made her way past Mr. Langer and down the stairs and outside into the wide black night. In the cottage she was too excited to sleep. The waves seemed incredibly loud, and she had to turn on the radio.

In the morning, first thing, Dorothy called Galesburg. Her mother was flustered, saying she didn't have a thing for them to eat. Dorothy asked her not to tell her father; it would be a surprise. Rennie was going to wear his uniform in case they were stopped; she thought it would be good for her father to see him with his medals. Like her, he had trouble admitting he was wrong.

Anne was civil with her, though Dorothy could see she was hurt that she wasn't in on the decision. Mr. Langer called in sick, and Jay and Win came straight back from their paper route. Anne watched Jennifer while Dorothy packed and Mr. Langer and Rennie went into town to top off both cars.

Dorothy was amazed at how much stuff they had. She'd crossed the country with nothing but a pair of bags, and now they were going to have trouble fitting it all in the car. Most of it was Jennifer's—the new toys and outfits both sets of grandparents showered her with. Mr. Langer said his father had made the good bassinet by hand and wanted them to have it. He offered them the fan in the cottage; he'd only bought it for her and Jennifer anyway. Rennie had a heavy duffel of Army gear he hadn't opened since he'd been back. "Just wait," Anne said. "This is nothing."

She packed her things last—the badges and pins and train tokens, all the useless mementos of San Diego. She packed the clothes she hoped she'd fit into again, and her bankbook and his insurance and discharge and the papers for the Ford. She filled her first suitcase and pulled the other from under the bed and opened it.

He smiled up at her from his good picture, young, unmarked. She wondered how a picture of her taken before the war would look to him now. She'd been seventeen when she met him; she wasn't quite twenty, still officially a girl, yet in the last year she'd aged lifetimes. She'd lived this summer in fear—as he still did, she thought—and now she would have to rid herself of it, drain it from her like blood. It would take Rennie longer, but she had faith he'd get better. Dorothy closed the cardboard flaps and turned the picture over. She no longer needed it. Now that they were finally going home, she could believe they would both survive the war. All they had to do was say goodbye.

★ ★ ★

THE HOUSE WAS EMPTY NOW, AND THE DAYS. James's father had stopped talking. At first Anne had given him a bell to summon her—the kind you might tap at the front desk of a hotel—but now he wasn't strong enough to use it. She had to feed him, guiding the spoon into the good side of his mouth. She had to clean him, dress him, comb his hair. She couldn't leave him for too long. She sat in his room with the window thrown open and read him the headlines. Good days he lay propped on his pillows, covers up to his stomach, wearing nothing but a good shirt, his clean hair brilliantined. He nodded with his eyes if he was interested in hearing the story. The war wasn't as important as the sports or the obituaries.

He'd said his last words after he heard that a woman named Swain had died. He shook his head once and let loose a sigh, as if to say, yes, he knew her, but who could ever have expected it. ELLA GARDNER SWAIN, 82. Anne was halfway through the long list of charities when he'd startled her by rasping, "Fine girl. Crazy family."

She didn't want to hear his confessions. She had enough of her own.

She wasn't pregnant, she'd merely skipped a month, possibly because she wasn't eating enough. She'd returned her uniforms; her old clothes bagged and billowed. James complimented her on her weight, and though she knew she'd lost too much, in the mirror she didn't see herself as thin. Why wasn't she hungry? She no longer wanted to disappear.

She'd never told Martin she was late, hoping it would go away. The last time she'd seen him was an accident. Late Saturday morning she'd driven over to the base to pick up a tank of oxygen for Mr.

Langer, and while she was there decided to stop in at the PX while she still had privileges. James needed to replace a bottle of his father's scotch. Anne was searching for the right brand when she saw Martin walk in the front door. He was alone, his stride purposeful, as if pressed for time. She ducked behind a shelf of Old Overholt rye and watched him cross the fence of bottle necks. He gave the redhead at the register a wave. How he tossed off that killing smile, she thought. He had his ring on, which pleased her. He'd always taken it off for her, the white band of untanned skin a compliment. "Look at me," she'd said, and he had. In room 327, on the Buick's backseat, in the dunes with the sea foaming over black rocks. Now she hid from him as he pondered which mouthwash to choose. She glanced down the aisle to see if anyone else had noticed her, expecting—with her luck—Cheryl sitting in judgment.

Her last day at the field hospital they'd exchanged formalities bitterly. Anne didn't blame Cheryl for her coldness. She was young, and while not uncomplicated, saw too clearly the faults of others, yet was blind to her own self-righteousness. Yes, Anne wanted to tell her, you may be right, but you don't understand anything. There was no ceremony, no cake and presents at coffee break. Anne checked her beds, emptied her desk drawers into a cardboard box and punched out. Cheryl escorted her to the door. Anne thanked her, and, like men, the two shook hands. She shed no tears in the car, felt none of the heartbreak of parting. She'd made no friends here. The summer had passed in waves of fever and torn ligaments and dysentery. Only Martin had saved her from the tedium of days, filled her with crazy expectations. Having dismissed him (had she lost him, him her, or did it just fall apart?), it wasn't hard to leave. The parade ground was crowded; dust boiled in the mirror.

Now, in the PX, no one had seen her, and Anne backed past the ranks of cheap gin and into the next aisle. She followed it into the far corner of the store, where the dregs of seasonal merchandise still lingered—rickety sling chairs and tanning lotion, paper parasols and citronella candles—and stayed there, appearing interested in the clearance specials and peeking over the rows at his back.

It took a minute at most, but, trapped, Anne had time to recall the entire affair, to see both how foolish and rich it had been. The chill of the water off Montauk, the hot sand on her skin. Those long Saturday afternoons she had rid herself of two winters, first her father's, lonely and gray as slate, and then, harder, James and Diane's. Martin would always be summer to her. She remembered her girlish first glimpse of him in the car and the vision of the lighthouse rising out of the shimmering heat. The leaky roof of the clam shack, rain whipping the bay. Sprinklers arcing over the crosscut fairways of the country club. They had stumbled through this perfect scenery, missing entrances, forgetting lines. While their uncertainty and fear had been frustrating at the time, now it made their affair seem even more impossible and romantic. To think she'd believed in this man, who getting in bed with her wound his watch before taking it off; who loved Gene Autry and cackled like Jay at things like "Do you have Prince Albert in a can?" The whole thing was laughable, like this, her hiding from him. She'd never lied to Martin, never had to. Lately she'd been so ashamed—for no reason, she thought now.

She straightened up so that her head was exposed above the shelves and walked down the aisle and back to where she'd been standing. Martin was not ten feet from her, weighing a package of bunion pads. He always said he was too old to march. He'd had his hair cut since she'd last seen him, the line at the base of his neck razor-straight. He used to have to caution her about nipping him. At the end, everything had been Evelyn.

She found a fifth of Johnny Walker Red, and, paying no attention to the man in the next row, took it up to the cashier. She kept her back to the rest of the store, tempting fate. Under the glass counter sat Zippo lighters and Brownie cameras, tie tacks and cuff links and St. Christopher medals, brooches and bracelets and earrings for girlfriends, and, set off to one side, right next to the register, a sprinkling of engagement rings. The week after Montauk, Martin had threatened to get one for her. Though she knew he wasn't serious, she partly wished he was, and wondered what she would do if one lunchtime in the stillness of the hot car he presented her with a small, boxed gift. She must have been crazy. She must have been in love.

"That all?" the cashier asked.

"Yes," Anne said, and casually looked back.

Martin was standing right behind her.

"Hello," he said.

"Hello," she said.

They paid and walked outside together.

"I saw your car," he said.

"Right."

They stood for a while talking in the parking lot. She was supposed to be over him, and yet at that moment she'd felt the same attraction, the same tenderness that had moved her months ago. She thought she'd killed it. Now she was tempted by the mad idea of asking him if he needed a ride and, astonishing herself, did.

"How about lunch?" Martin asked.

"Do you have time?" she said, and it was as if they'd never stopped. She drove to one of their old favorite places, a bluff overlooking the bay. After, they agreed that this was it, no more.

Now, deciphering the line scores for James's father, Anne thought that she would never see Martin again. She had his number somewhere (she knew exactly where, the scrap hidden in the flap of her appointment book), and while she would never call, she often thought of what more they could possibly say to each other. In bed, James's father nodded for her to keep reading. She'd never liked sports, or only for Rennie and Jay's sake. She thought that she needed to talk to someone—not Mr. Langer, and not James—but she didn't have anybody. And so they sat in the stifling room, rooting for teams she'd never heard of and mourning the anonymous, plentiful dead.

She thought she wouldn't forgive Rennie for leaving her now, though just picturing him in Galesburg was enough to soothe her. It wouldn't be long before they returned and the school year started and they could all begin to live again. James had given Rennie a key to open the house and get some clothes, but only after calling ahead. Mrs. Baines said Dorothy's father would go over and take care of any damage so Rennie wouldn't have to see it. James considered it an apology. Anne still considered Mr. Baines a bastard, the town full of gossips and hypocrites, yet how she wished she were there now, past this last test of her strength.

Now she was alone in the house with him. Jay had shied away from Mr. Langer since his last stroke—quiet, in a chair, but devastating. James visited his father every free second, and each day made Jay sit with him in the room for a half hour after supper. Anne sometimes came up to see the three of them. Mr. Langer lay in bed, James's chair pulled up beside him, Jay's back a few feet. James reminisced; the others said nothing.

"Has it occurred to you," Anne asked him in bed, "that Jay's afraid of him?"

"That's why I want him there," James said. "He'd be more afraid if we didn't let him in."

"Like with *my* father."

"All I'm saying is that he's curious. I'd rather have him do it this way than by sneaking around. He's going to see it anyway."

"Fine," she conceded, "you get up with him in the middle of the night."

"I do anyway," he said.

She'd thought—crazily—of telling him everything, just to have someone to talk to. He knew, she was sure, but he couldn't admit that he did. And it was true, she needed her secrets, if only to fight off the constant threat of Diane, the quicksand memories of Putney. Still, every night she could see herself rolling over and whispering it all to him, then letting him rage the way she had. Because, after his mother, he would never leave her. She dreamed of reconciliation, of innocence restored. In Galesburg they would start again, regardless.

The breakwater, the lawn, the rainy days alone. The car had lost its emergency status, and with it the C sticker. It sat abandoned in the far corner of the lot, the tank and trunk filled with a last spree of gasoline.

Tuesday Sarah came so Anne could bike to town and do some light shopping. The Olds she'd been driving the last month or so was gone, as was the new boyfriend, transferred to Louisiana. Just bad luck, she said, but she seemed to lose people constantly. Sober, dried to a wry husk, she was a mystery to Anne. James said she hated their father, yet she tended him patiently, and had for years. Like Anne, she'd never really left home, always found a way back.

Riding the town road, the sea off beyond the dunes, Anne

imagined he would be gone when she got home, Sarah teary. He was that close, she was that tired. She coasted down the slight incline by the boardwalk, joined by boys with their swim trunks rolled into towels and slung from their handlebars. The steel web of the Ferris wheel rose over the gray marquee of the Regal, where Jay and Win were soaking in *Sahara* with Humphrey Bogart. Soldiers lurked outside trying to pick up girls. There was a case in Bridgehampton, a fourteen-year-old found in a potato field; the locals wanted action. After a week in the house, even that seemed like life.

The girls in line outside the butcher's remembered her. They stood in an obedient single file, precious in their white anklets and Mary Janes. Their mothers wanted her to know they were all sorry about what had happened to Rennie.

"He must of been brave to get shot like that," one of them said.

"Yes," Anne said, "he's very brave."

The green was empty, the bandstand stripped of its bunting. The Roll of Honor shone a blinding white. As the whole town stood and applauded him, she'd heard two boys behind her talking.

"Man," one said, "look at that."

"Yeah, you shoot me like that you might as well go ahead and finish the job."

They were teenagers, completely innocent, and she hadn't repeated what they'd said to anyone, but she worried about Rennie. When they talked to him on the phone, he said it was too early to think about school. Dorothy had gotten a job at the paper mill while Rennie stayed home with Jennifer. James thought he seemed happier, that Anne was worrying needlessly. He needed time to get back on his feet; it had only been a month. She'd agreed, but reluctantly. He'd always been the stronger, the child she didn't worry about. He'd never really been hurt.

The butcher had a better selection, which he attributed to Italy. Sicily had fallen, and Patton was massed to invade the mainland. Anne said she hadn't been paying that much attention to the news, but, if she wasn't mistaken, weren't his prices higher now than before?

She rode away, returning the girls' waves, her basket full. She circled the square and passed the New Burying Ground on the town road. The cheap flags had faded from the rains. The boardwalk parking lot came and, after the zigzagging climb, Hickey's, and then the road flattened and she could stand on the pedals and see the sea. She stopped there, mindful of her pork chops, and fought her way to the top of a dune to take in the view.

From here she could see across the woods and the salt marsh with its switchbacked creek and railroad tracks, and all the way down the beach to the lighthouse. Their house stood alone, looking over the water, the parking lot a dark scar. Sarah's Hudson and James's Buick glinted. In the black dot of an upstairs window (she thought), Mr. Langer was clutching air, wondering where she was. "Annie," her father had called as if she were in the next room, though she was squeezing his hand. "Annie, Annie!"

She was careful coming down the drive. The porch was empty, the first floor. She put away the meat and went up to his room. Both he and Sarah were asleep. Slumped sideways with their mouths open, they were unmistakably related, even more than James and Rennie. The stumpy nose was the same, and the heavy jaw. How hard it must have been for her as a girl, Anne thought; and then to have to battle him her whole life, only to end up here, just as pretty, beloved Annie had. Her own mother always said her father would spoil her, that she would turn out demanding and ungrateful. It was just a warning, and funny once, but at times like these, in the presence of such an unbalanced and difficult love, Anne feared it was true. She sat down in Jay's seat and watched the two of them sleep, the blind occasionally lifting with the breeze, filling the dim room with a cold white light.

James came home and relieved them. While she got supper started, Jay rode up with Win, and she watched them through the kitchen window. It would hurt Jay to lose him, but at least he'd made a friend this summer. Being the preacher's daughter and living so far out of town, she'd never had the chance. Saturday afternoons she stood in the front yard and watched the cars full of families going out to picnic at the reservoir. Inside, her father was barricaded in his office, working on his sermon, her mother asleep in the guest bedroom. She waved and the kids in her class waved back. "Why didn't you come?" they asked after church. It had turned her into a good liar.

Sarah stayed for supper again, and Anne wondered if Jay suspected how close his grandfather was. Once he'd asked her why he was dying. She could have said congestive heart failure or pulmonary edema, some combination of the two, but it was easier simply to say old age, and guiltily, she had. If they'd moved him into the hospital a month ago he might have lived until winter, certainly no longer, short of a miracle. He would die here, before the fall. They were his terms, not hers.

Supper was solemn without Mr. Langer and Dorothy and Rennie and Win. Anne didn't recall any of them talking much, but the table was decidedly quiet.

"How was work?" Jay asked, trying to be grown up.

"Good," James said, though she knew he hated it. She wished he would quit; for once, they had enough money. He'd received his teaching certificate in the mail. Surprisingly, no one had complained about Rennie's status as an objector. They had obviously not checked with Putney. He didn't say it, but he was ready to go back. The attic and cellar were clean, the cottages locked up. He'd done everything but call the realtor. It surprised her; she'd thought he'd have trouble admitting his father wouldn't recover.

After supper, they all went up except her. There was no protest from Jay. James said to leave the dishes, he'd get them later. Anne did them anyway; there was nothing else for her to do.

At eight Jay came down to listen to *The Hermit's Cave*, with its weird, eerie laugh and macabre plots. She wondered how much it contributed to his dreams. When she'd told James her theory, he said that the show didn't matter; Jay had an active imagination. She worried about what he'd make of his grandfather now, what he'd already made of her father, Rennie, herself at her worst. When she conjured up her mother, all she saw was a great bulk puffing up the stairs, her flowered housedress trailing like a dragon's tail.

Jay could take his own bath—insisted on it now. Anne laid out his pajamas, resisted taking a look in his box. She knew what was in it already. He'd only made one great addition lately. Before leaving, Rennie had given him his discharge pin, his Ruptured Duck. It was a secret, one she was happy to keep.

She respected his new shyness, and left him to get dressed in private, then took him into his grandfather's room to say goodnight. Mr. Langer was conscious, his eyes unnaturally bright. She'd seen it in cancer patients, the wasted body sending up its last hopeless glow. She was unsure if he could see them. Jay kissed his Aunt Sarah and shook hands manfully with James. "Goodnight," he said loudly to his grandfather, and, as if afraid of burning his fingertips, quickly patted his veined and spotted hand just once before pulling away.

"You can't blame him," James said later, after Sarah had left. He was fixing a whiskey and soda, and Anne could see he needed her to console him but in good conscience couldn't ask for her sympathy.

She went to him at the counter and held him. "He's doing very well," she said. "So are you."

"Was this how it was with you?"

That endless winter. The panes glazed, the river frozen over. There was no comparison. She'd gone through it alone, still sick from Putney, unloved, mad, her son fodder for the war.

"Yes," she said, "exactly like this," and she thought that she couldn't have given him a greater gift.

He took his drink up to his father's room and sat with him in the dark. Downstairs she knitted under the glow of the lamp, listening equally to the radio and the one-sided conversation sifting through the banister. Winter she'd tended that last ember of her family with the same terrible care. They would be discussing his mother. There was so much history at the end. Like James, she'd thought the time alone was a final chance for long-deferred answers, but nothing had suddenly become clear, or only the realization that instead of two people being tortured by these questions, now there would be just one. The problem with her, she thought, was that she'd never stopped talking to her father.

She looked in on him before bed. James was hunched forward in his chair, as if whispering to his father. He'd finished his drink; it sat on the floor between his feet. She leaned in the doorway to get his attention. He looked up and nodded as if to say he'd be along in a minute. She waited for him under the covers, though she knew sleep would reach her first. She was afraid she'd dream of Martin now, the sound of the car rocking.

In the morning it was raining, the sea gray. James had stayed up too late again and wobbled off to work. Jay came back from his paper route with a streak of mud up the back of his slicker. He and Win were going fishing off the boardwalk and maybe to the movies later. She knew he'd already seen *Sahara* but didn't call his bluff. She trusted him enough to let him lie to her once in a while.

It would rain all day. The upstairs hall was dark. She had to turn a light on to read Mr. Langer his paper. The chair smelled like James. His father needed oxygen now, a hose held to his nose with a butterfly clip. His eyes were bright, and fluttered during the obituaries. He seemed better today, a bad sign. The dying sometimes had a brief spell of clarity before the worst, a lull that filled the family with false hope. Cruel as it was, she'd felt cheated when her father hadn't blazed for a day or two, had simply dwindled on the pillow. It wouldn't be long, she thought, then hated herself for wanting him to hurry. She just wanted to leave, to go home.

She was reading him the weather when the phone rang. Mr. Langer blinked. The phone was on the floor to make room on the night table for his medication. She wasn't expecting anyone.

She picked it up and said hello, but the line was silent.

"Hello?" she said again.

"Anne," Martin said.

"No," she said, more saddened than angry, "don't do this."

"Anne, please," he said. He was still talking when she replaced the receiver.

Mr. Langer gazed up at the ceiling. She finished the tide table—high, low, new—thinking it should have been easier for her to hang up on Martin. She wasn't allowed to have doubts now.

At supper, Anne told James to take the next few days off. Jay was at Win's and they could talk freely.

"I guess I might as well quit," he said, "if it's that time."

"I'm pretty sure it is."

"I'll go in tomorrow for my things."

Sarah, eating with them again, said she had a week coming to her. Her last boyfriend had promised to take her to Rehoboth Beach, then ditched her. She made it sound gay, a practical joke.

"You can stay here," James said. "We'll make up your old room."

Saying goodnight, Jay didn't touch his grandfather's hand.

Sarah stayed late. Anne looked in on them before bed. In Putney the orderlies in the terminal ward ran a pool like the one in maternity; for a nickel you picked the date and time of a certain room number's demise. When a patient died, they called it a vacancy. That was the code word they used at the nurses' station—"Do we have a vacancy yet?" Looking at Mr. Langer with a practiced eye, Anne thought three days at the most.

She told James in the dark, talking across the gap between their separate beds. He'd been encouraged by the light in his father's eyes. He didn't want to believe her, but did.

"You know these things," he said helplessly.

"I'm sorry," she said, and thought of everything she hadn't told him.

She went to him then, not out of pity, she thought, but the obligation of sorrow. He was surprised by her. In the last year the few times they'd been intimate had followed some shared triumph or compromise—her returning to work, Rennie's homecoming. That there was nothing to celebrate seemed to confuse him. It wasn't a problem. She knew him. After Martin, his familiarity was comforting. Even after twenty years, she could rely on his desire. She lay beneath him, looking up at his closed eyes. Her own passion may have been feigned (she couldn't stop herself from seeing the steamed mirror, their locked bodies sinking to the cool floor), but she was giving herself gladly, and she knew he appreciated it, that tomorrow he'd hope she'd come to him again. He was such an optimist. He quickened, and she arched, breathing harder. In Montauk, after she and Martin made love, she liked to go to the window with nothing on and look out at the stone arms of the breakwater. On the long porch, people could see just by the way she nursed her coffee that she was a woman in love.

About to come, James pulled out, leaving her empty. It was thoughtful of him, really. Done, he rolled off, panting as if he'd run a mile.

"Thank you," she said.

They both couldn't fit on the bed, so she went back to hers. The covers were cold. Labor Day was approaching.

"If it takes longer," he said, "you and Jay can go ahead and go. I can always take a train."

"We'll stay together. You'd never get a ticket out of New York anyway."

"You're probably right," he said generously, and she thought she was all he needed, that—having survived Diane—she would never lose him again.

Mr. Langer worsened during the night. When she went to check on him before going down to make breakfast, she found he'd soiled the bed messily. A whitish film clouded his eyes. He was still there, but barely. A soapy trickle of water from her sponge made him blink. "Sorry," she said. Changing his sheets, she lifted first his legs and then his torso too easily. Today, tomorrow. She crushed his pills between two spoons, mixed them with water and fed them to him, wiped the excess from his sunken chest. She took a good shirt she'd ironed and buttoned him into it. She ran water over a comb and drew it through his hair. His eyes drifted to her, drifted off again. The silence was a kind of intimacy, one she was comfortable with. Before her father, she'd liked the dying, switched shifts whenever her squeamish colleagues asked. She was such a good student in nursing school, took her duties so seriously that the other girls kidded her about her coldness. It was a tribute to her professionalism, but still it hurt her. She wasn't hardhearted, she thought (trying to recall one person she loved without reserve). When Jay was three he'd had week-long fevers, and she'd felt helpless, but even she was aware that her fear was a mother's, that though he wasn't strong enough to sit up, eventually he'd get better.

She warned James before he left for work.

"I've got to go," he said. "I'll be back as fast as I can."

It was another gray day. Jay came back from his papers with Win to say they were going to town.

She hadn't had a chance to sit down with him and explain everything that was happening, but he seemed to know. He stayed out of the house, and when he did come in, busied himself with a book or a program on the radio, keeping grimly quiet, as if enjoying himself would be a sign of disrespect.

"Be home early for supper," she instructed, then watched the two of them away. On the lawn, clumps of gulls settled in, sensing a storm offshore.

She made him oatmeal, though she knew he wouldn't eat. The untouched bowl sat beside her all morning, hardening around the spoon. Italy was on the radio; after twenty minutes of hopscotching between stations, she was too discouraged to turn, and clicked it off. The Senators had won again, that made seven in a row. She tried to sound excited, something she wasn't good at. Her father had frowned on people who read scripture theatrically. Even this winter when he could no longer form the words, he shook his head at her intonation, how she emphasized questions and slowed for endings. "Evenly," he reminded her in the car on the way to church. Beginning with her confirmation she read every other Sunday, switching off with Mrs. Steurmer. All week she practiced in the mirror in the downstairs bathroom, trying to commit the onion-skinned wisdom to memory. The house built on sand, water from a rock. She pressed the open book to her new breasts and, with her eyes tightly shut, stumbled through the first few lines. Evenly, evenly. The room smelled of dried Bon Ami and her mother's rose-shaped soaps; she liked going there better because of the half-moon rug that hugged the front of the toilet. The first Thanksgiving that Anne took the bus home from nursing school, she found that her mother had bought a new rug a different color. The room was never the same. Each year, coming back, she knew the house less and less. Now it was hers, completely foreign, as were the people who'd lived there. Had she known them so little? Every other Sunday, driving home, her mother complimented her on her reading. "Let the words do the work," her father advised, never satisfied. "We're not trying to sell anything." Anne thanked her mother but thought he was right. Because, unlike her mother, he listened to every word she said.

Mr. Langer's IV was low, so she changed the bottle. She checked his oxygen, read him the fisherman's forecast—rain and eight-foot seas. His chin bristled with tough white stubble. She heard the eleven-thirty plane go over, invisible in the clouds, and soon the noon horn. She was wondering where James was when the phone rang.

It was Sarah. They were leaving from Grumman right now.

"How is he?" she asked.

"Worse," Anne said, trying to be matter-of-fact. "I'd hurry."

His lips were dry. She squirted water on his swollen tongue and down the back of his throat with a needleless syringe. His eyes stayed fixed on one spot before moving to another, as if mildly interested in something she couldn't see.

For her the waiting was over. It was a matter of hours. She wished she'd stopped James from going to work.

In Galesburg, when she'd seen this first ending, she'd left the room and then the house. She stood on the salted stoop in just her sweater, looking out at the snow and the road, the dead cattails lining the ditch, the reaching trees. It was a bright but sunless day, a light wind freezing her cheeks, and she stood there looking at nothing and thinking nothing until she heard the rush of a car approaching. She went inside and, hiding behind the door, watched the car pass, headed out to the reservoir. Then, as if her imagination were hostage to the car, she remembered her father taking her ice fishing there when she was little, dipping the jig into the black water and sitting back as if he'd already caught a fish. He had been—until the end—such a hopeful man. He had been the one person she loved. She opened the door and went outside again, across the yard this time, carefully following her snowed-over tracks to the mailbox. She stepped over the black crust of the berm and walked to the bare, cindered middle of the road and looked both ways. In the gray distance there was nothing. She closed her eyes and felt the wind lift her hair. Trees creaked; the leaves of diseased branches rattled. Her heart seemed to beat in her head, a pulsing at her temples, and again she could think—mercifully—of nothing. She'd been with him so closely the last month. She needed this emptiness. When she opened her eyes, the road returned, the mailbox, the walk. She traced her footprints back to the house. The next time she went outside, a few days later, she thought she must have been mad before.

Now she stayed with James's father, listening to him wheeze. It was raining, fat drops ticking against the panes. The furnace burned on, and the radiator under the window clanged and hissed. Jay would come back soaked and cold. She unfurled the blanket at the foot of the bed and tucked it under Mr. Langer's arms. If he had been merely her patient, she would have been pleased at how well he was doing.

She thought of shaving him, but James was almost home, and she was out of practice. She heard Sarah's car before it reached the lot. She smoothed Mr. Langer's covers and gave him a squirt of water, parted his hair with her fingers. Outside, the Hudson's heavy doors thunked shut. She turned the radio on loud and with a rustle picked up the front page of the paper. " 'Yanks, Brits Slam Hamburg,' " she read, and hesitated as if he'd given her the okay. She kept going well after James and Sarah had come up the stairs, though she knew Mr. Langer could no longer hear her.

Jay was the only one who slept that night. James and Sarah sat beside their father, parting to let Anne look at him. She ran to the bathroom for water or a washcloth, to the kitchen for a new spoon for his medicine or more coffee. She knew how to be useful, how to stay out of the family's way. At first Sarah and James took turns holding his hand, but soon covered each other's.

"You were his favorite," Sarah admitted.

"He was yours."

"God knows why," she said, then added, "He wasn't that bad."

It didn't last long. Around two Anne was in the kitchen making James a sandwich when he came down. She had the bread knife out; he liked his cut diagonally, in triangles. He stopped her arm.

"Could you look at him?" he said.

She wiped her hands and followed him up.

James had turned the ceiling light off and put a lamp on dimly in the far corner. Sarah let go of her father's hand to let Anne through.

Her own father had finally gone, undramatically, in the middle of the afternoon. She'd checked everything herself, but still called the medical examiner. He came out from town with his bag and stayed for a cup of coffee, talking basketball with James. She knew that her father was dead, yet she needed someone else to tell her. It was the same with James now.

"Yes," Anne said. She removed the IV and slid his bruised-blue hand under the covers.

James held Sarah, then kissed Anne stiffly. When Sarah offered her arms, Anne realized she'd never hugged his sister before. It was the family, they didn't know how to show their feelings.

"What do we do now?" Sarah said.

"It's standard to wait until morning," Anne said, and they seemed relieved that someone knew what to do.

In bed, James couldn't sleep.

"Adrenaline," she said.

"It was so quick. Quicker than I expected."

"You can't expect it."

"I know," he said, not really agreeing. "I thought he'd say something or I'd say something. I suppose it doesn't make much difference."

"You were there. That's all you can do."

"I know," he said again. "Thank you."

"He was very good."

"He'd be glad," he said.

"And you're doing very well. That should help with Jay."

"I hope so."

For a while the room was quiet, and they could hear the sea, the trees, the sounds of the house.

"I can't sleep," James said.

"There's that sandwich. I'll come down with you."

"No," he said, "I don't need it."

Later she heard him get out of bed and fit his slippers on. He opened their door and closed it behind him and walked down the hall, but at the top of the stairs he stopped. She listened for the two steps he would take to his father's room, the solid wrench of the knob. They never came. He creaked down the stairs and across the living room. The latch of the icebox thunked. Anne wanted to go to him now, though she knew he had to do this himself, as she had last winter—all summer, really. Before, she'd thought it would be easier for him, if only because the two of them weren't close; now she thought the opposite was true. Like her with her mother, he'd spend the rest of his life trying to discover exactly what he'd lost. She didn't wait up for him.

The funeral service began at the old Presbyterian church and concluded at the New Burying Ground. Rennie had offered to drive down. James said it wasn't necessary. Sarah came alone. It was no surprise that their father had left James the house, but Anne could see she was hurt. Besides the hearse, a big Lincoln, theirs were the only two cars. James decided the oldest should go first, so they tacked through town, trailing the Hudson. On the sidewalk, a child stopped and took off his baseball cap. Jay sat between them on the front seat. He had a rose he was supposed to lay on the coffin—yellow, for remembrance. He hadn't seen his grandfather since the night he wouldn't touch his hand, and James thought this might be good for him. He was impressed when they went through a red light. As they passed the green, he said, "This is the way the parade went."

"Everything goes this way," James said. "It's a small town."

They turned through the gate and onto the dirt road, the Buick rocking in the ruts. At the crest of the hill, near where Rennie had given his speech, the procession stopped. She waited for James to get out. It was a hot day, the trees shedding seeds. Her black dress was a tent. The funeral home supplied four gray-haired pallbearers who carried the casket with grace and then stood off to the side patiently. Behind them, a tarp had been thrown over a mound of soil to keep it moist. There were stones for his father's parents, but none for his mother. She would be in some potter's field or a cemetery behind a boarded-up sanitarium. When her father died, Anne had such trouble finding a match for her mother's stone. She finally found where he'd bought it years before—a little Italian man below town. She described the marble to him, the floral border. "I know the one," he said, and took her into his backyard, a gravel patch filled with rows of blank memorials—flat plaques and polished obelisks, stones topped by interlocking hearts with room for two names. He led her down an aisle and pointed to an exact duplicate of her mother's. She asked him how much it was, then for an instant thought of what James would say. "Maybe too expensive," the man said. "Yes," Anne said, calling his bluff, but took it anyway.

Here the cemetery was older, more hallowed. The minister was her father's age, thin, his missal prickling with bookmarks. He read the standard service, pausing thoughtfully, as if waiting for them to catch up. Her father would have been appalled.

Anne stood beside James, both hands on her clutch purse, murmuring the responses by heart. James followed, a finger on the page. The forgiveness of sins, life everlasting. She could still believe in these, if desperately, unworthy. Her father had taught her well.

The minister nodded. James took Jay's hand and the two of them stepped forward. Jay placed the rose on top without James's help. After bowing their heads a second, they stepped back, re-forming the line. Sarah smiled her approval, her thanks. To Anne's surprise, Sarah was silently crying, dabbing at her cheeks with a tissue. James put his free arm around her. Jay offered Anne his hand. They stood together as the minister finished, Jay imitating his father's stately calm, and when it was over walked back to the car arm in arm. Anne thought anyone looking at them would think that, as a family, they were recovering nicely.

IT SEEMED TO JAMES THAT THEY WERE ALWAYS LEAVING—sweeping corners and closing windows. Anne had been ready to go the day after the funeral, but there was the business with the lawyer in town, Sarah, all his father's things. He'd offered Sarah the house; she didn't want it from him. They would put it on the market and split the profits. Until it sold, Sarah would be the caretaker. James thought it fitting. She belonged here more than he did.

Packing would take a day; the place needed a good cleaning. Before Sarah came over, he stowed the booze in the trunk of the Buick. While the two of them divided up the furniture on paper, Anne went through the rooms with a pail of bluish water and a scrub brush, her hair tucked up in a scarf. He couldn't resent her trying to be helpful, only her implication that he was stalling. Though he wanted to, it was impossible. Next week the school year began.

He and Sarah went through the effects together. His father's dresser was full of broken watches and old razors, nose plugs, boxes of orphaned buttons, new shoelaces, combs, Canadian coins, dried-out fountain pens, shoehorns. What were all the keys for? "Look at this," Sarah said, "he kept everything." It wasn't true; there were no old pictures of their mother, only a few posed shots of Sarah before the piano, James at his graduation, reaching to shake the dean's hand. Downstairs he had an entire album of Rennie and Jay, every shot selected by Anne. They dug through collar stays and darkened nubs of pencils, pins, nail clippers, a cigarette lighter from the Empire State Building, eyeglass screws, shoe polish, crumbling aspirins, peppermints oozing to a pink blur inside their wrappers, the blackened, mushroomed cork from a bottle of champagne, a button urging them to vote for Al Smith. They stirred it all like burglars, impatient and disinterested, until they came upon his pocket watch.

Sarah let him pick it up. "Does it run?"

The hinge was ruined, the gold plating worn through to the steel. The lid held no inscription; he'd given it to himself after closing the Inn. James wound it—yes, the visible works twirled—and passed it to Sarah.

"Do you want it?" she asked, but kept it in her hand.

"No," he said, "that's fine."

There was nothing he wanted; he didn't even want to see it. Their father hadn't kept these things, just hadn't had time to get rid of them. When they were done, he set the drawer on the bed and let Jay sort through it for pennies. Jay was more interested in the guts of an old music box, a cracked and caseless jeweler's loupe. After Jay had filled his cigar box, James emptied the rest into the trash and fit the drawer back into its slot. Sarah looked down into the wastebasket at the paper clips and half-used tubes of salve as if their father would scold them for throwing away his things, and James thought that it would be like this all day.

He was too big for his father's clothes, Rennie too thin. There was no sense trying things on. Out went the belts, the shirts and sweaters and jackets, the vests. A mound grew on the bed, reeking of mothballs. Thick cedar hangers clacked in the closet, bounced around his ankles. He remembered his father as a neat man, yet everything had a stain on it, or a hole. He'd been alone here so long.

"Remember this?" Sarah said, holding up a mustard cardigan their father loved. After supper he'd lead the guests on a promenade to the end of the breakwater, picking a lucky child to switch on the light. The beacon skimmed the cliff face, red every third turn. As the sky palled deeper and deeper blue and spray wet the granite, their father told them the old tale of the first citizens who set fires on the bluffs to lure ships onto the rocks. The sea worried them to split boards, casks, bales. Occasionally, he'd say (shouting above the waves), a sailor washed ashore, or rarer still, a maiden. In the happier cases, the town adopted these casuals of the sea. Upstairs, their mother lay in bed with one of her headaches. When James was little, Sarah said the reason their mother couldn't get up was because she was a mermaid, her green tail buried under the covers.

"I remember," James said.

"Look." He'd had two of the sweaters, identical. Sarah knew James knew this; it wasn't remarkable. Why did she have to remind him?

"I can't wear them," James said, and tossed them on the pile.

"Someone could use these shoes," she said.

"Start a box for the Salvation Army."

The ties were out of style, pure Japanese silk. In Montour Falls when the war started, the Chamber of Commerce staged a bonfire of products made in Japan. Tin toys and party favors warmed the mob. The shopkeepers weren't reimbursed. In spring the grass behind second base was smudged black. He tossed the snaky handful into the box and started on the hats.

He got rid of the pills on the night table and replaced the phone.

"What about the bedding?" Sarah asked.

"No one wants it," James said. "Throw it away." He was trying not to be cross with her.

He did the bathroom by himself. It was easier. He dumped the denture rinse and shaving soap and hair oil into the trash. Anne was right behind him with the bucket.

"What time do you want to get going tomorrow?" She asked so fast that her waiting for an answer seemed a demand. They'd moved so often that he was used to her sniping as they packed. The whole chaotic process set them both on edge. Anne found his little difficulties with doorways and suitcases hilarious. It was one of the few times she knew she could get a rise out of him, and, for him, one of the few times he could strike back with immunity. It was a ritual, a tradition. They'd fight in the car and arrive with headaches, only to make up later. Since the funeral she'd been hovering about him, paying him attention, and James wondered if this playful thrust was just a show of concern or a first attempt at reconciliation. He didn't even remember his own, only a period of mourning for Diane. Silences, drives. Anne wanted to know why, and what could he say? He didn't know himself. It was like waking up from a drunk, regretful yet amazed at having been gone so long. He thought he could see Anne beginning to figure out where she was, what she'd done. It was an undignified time of decisions, vows. He promised not to interfere, to wear his father's death lightly. He wanted her to think about herself, not him.

"I don't care," he parried.

"I'd like to get going no later than seven." She went off on a pointless explanation that he openly ignored, nodding his head yes as if everything had returned to normal.

Jay and Win helped him batten down the cottages for the winter.

They hooked the shutters from inside and padlocked the doors, and James shut off the breaker behind Fischer. The key ring jingled on his belt. He'd promised the boys could have a last afternoon together; he praised their painting, thanked them again for a job well done, and they raced up the cliff stairs. James stayed there looking at the sealed cottages, thinking he'd forgotten something. Fischer, Folger, Coffin, Gardner, Shelburne, Swain. This part seemed too easy, didn't assault him like his father's room, his closet. He wondered if, in his immediate grief, he was cheating his mother. All these years he'd thought of this as her place; now his father belonged here with her, forever separate, occupants of different rooms.

"Your mother loved you very much, both of you," was all their father would say. He gave no explanation, discouraged any further reminiscences. In a sense, by dying, he was still defending her. Was that what James resented? Was it possible to stop?

He checked the lighthouse to see if they'd left anything. Inside the door Rennie had lined up his empty beer bottles against the wall; he'd made it once and halfway around again. A mildewed towel left a wet spot on the floor. James draped it on the banister and tapped up the steel stairs. On the sill facing the sea sat Jay's spotter cards and binoculars, beneath them on the floor a single spent match. He imagined him sitting here smoking illicit cigarettes as he had, at the sound of the door flicking the still-lit butt into the sea and fanning the air with his hands. He worried about Jay's timidity, how he seemed younger than his classmates, and friendless. The match he took as a good sign.

He left the bottles, locked the door. The banked sides of the breakwater were slippery with sea grass, crusted with barnacles. Walking back, James took a last look at the stairs and the ranked cottages and the house, the trees rising green above everything. Gulls hung; the flag snapped. He seemed to notice everything, but none of it registered, like the sights you pass traveling, continually bubbling up in the windshield only to be replaced. He felt as if he'd already started leaving.

In the yard Sarah was beating a rug. Upstairs Anne thundered through the rooms. He went around back for the Adirondack chair. In the grass he found a muddied tumbler—from July, the worst time—and, as if in rebuttal, Jennifer's pacifier. The garden, now that Rennie had finally gotten it to bloom, he'd let go to ground. He coiled the hose and removed the key from the spigot so no one could use it. He lowered the flag and folded it away. There was space for the wicker chairs in the basement. While he was there he located the storm windows, wondering who'd taken them down. He cleaned them with scalding water mixed with a half cup of vinegar and wiped them dry with today's newspaper. The Germans had taken Rome back, the Senators were making it a race. On the stepladder, installing the storms for the living room, he could see Anne and Sarah inside, taking pictures off the walls. He concentrated on his job, thinking there wasn't much left to do.

As he was hanging the last window, Anne came out and asked if he needed help.

"What else is there inside?" he asked.

"Nothing. I need to know what clothes you want to wear tomorrow."

"Pants," he said, "a shirt." It was part of the game.

"You go and lay them out, I'm not your valet. Sarah has some pictures she wants you to look at."

The window was heavy, and he couldn't answer until he had it in place. "I don't want any of them."

"You tell her that," Anne said. "I've got to pack. Did you remember to tell Jay we're eating early?"

"How can I remember something you never told me?"

"Right," she said, "that must have been my other husband."

"Must have been," James said.

Sarah had the pictures lined up along the baseboards in the living room. Those from the downstairs were mostly turn-of-the-century prints of whalers and clipper ships, seascapes, harbors at sunset; upstairs there were more still lifes—roses and conch shells, fruit overflowing bowls. His father had ordered the whole lot out of a catalog from Boston. James squatted and inspected the one that had hung over his bed, a copy of a Winslow Homer, a faceless, slickered man rowing through high seas. As a child, he identified with the man, at night felt the chill wind under his warm covers.

He stood. "No, I don't want any of these."

"I don't have room for all of them," Sarah protested.

"You don't have to take them."

"But you're not going to," she said, distraught, and knelt to touch an ugly Millet. "I don't know why this is so hard. I didn't know we'd have to do this. I thought the service would be it and the rest of it wouldn't be so bad." She looked up at him, old and red-faced, blinking back tears. "I haven't been drinking, not once."

"I know that."

"It's so stupid," she said. "I hate these goddamn things."

"Leave them," he said, helping her up. "They're cheap. We'll sell them with the house. They belong here anyway."

"I do want some of them. One, just to have one. Which one should I take?"

"Which one was above your bed?"

"Oh, good," she said, as if he'd delivered her, "that's a good idea."

By suppertime, she'd recovered, and after the dishes were done and they were all sitting around with nothing to do, James made Jay turn the radio off and asked Sarah to play something for them.

"Yes," Anne seconded, "you haven't played for us."

"I'm sure it's out of tune," Sarah said, sitting down to the keyboard. She flexed her fingers and arched her back, ran up the scales and down again. It wasn't off by much. Jay looked over her shoulder while she played "The Golliwog's Cakewalk" to warm up, and then some of Schumann's *Kinderszenen* and a waltz by Chopin and finally the first movement of the "Moonlight" sonata. As she played, Jay looked back at him and Anne, his mouth open, astonished at how good his aunt was. James resisted memories of her practicing in the winter, the endless repetition of incomplete phrases, the botched fingerings. She made a few slips now, human and easily overlooked for the pleasure she was giving them. When she was done, they were silent, letting the last chord resolve itself into the night, the crickets, the crack and then the lush pour of the surf.

"Bugs Bunny played that," Jay said.

"Better or worse than me?" Sarah said.

She'd be back in the morning to see them off. She thanked Anne for dinner, kissed Jay. James walked her to her car and said goodnight, then watched the dust rise through her taillights, grateful that she hadn't made a scene. In the west, a line of red still clung to the bottom of the sky. The night was chilly, a cold smell of clamshells in the wind. Mist was sneaking out of the trees and across the backyard, and grudgingly he admitted that in Galesburg he would miss this time of day. September meant thunderstorms banging down the valley, the river running muddy. The sky said the weather would be nice tomorrow, the drive up the Hudson green. Dorothy would have dinner for them; Rennie was sure to have beer. In a week he'd be teaching. Basketball season wasn't far off, the warmth of the gym in winter. He needed the noise and heat of students in his room to give his prep periods the desperate calm of sanctuary. He'd tell them the first day—summer was over, it was time to get back to work.

Anne wanted to know what kind of sandwich he wanted for the car. "Jay's having egg salad."

"That's what I'll have," he said.

"He had the last of it."

"What else do we have?"

"Chicken salad."

"Then I'll have chicken salad," he said.

As he was leaving the kitchen, she called after him, "And don't forget to lay out the clothes you want."

He went directly upstairs and laid what he wanted on his bed. "Okay," he yelled down, "it's all here, you can pack now."

"I can't," she yelled back, "I'm making your lunch."

They tried to get to bed early, but Anne didn't want him to help her pack. Their suitcases gaped on their beds, surrounded by neat piles of clothes. She caromed through the room purposefully, and to stay out of her way he went downstairs to lock up. He did the back door first, shouldering it closed and slipping the bolt across. He shut the window over the kitchen sink and the small square one at the end of the pantry and—briefly remembering the last time—wished he hadn't packed the booze so deep. He turned off the kitchen light, and before night could silver the floor (I see you, James), took off for the front of the house. He did the living room, and was about to click off the lamp over Anne's chair when he noticed the chess set. Jay had said he wanted it; he must have forgotten. James balanced it on the newel post. He took care of the dining room windows, and, lastly, checked the front door. Only the hall light was on, the rest of the downstairs dark and quiet around him. Upstairs, Anne darted from closet to bed to dresser. July he'd sat in the black of the living room with a glass of scotch, listening to the radio. He'd lain down in the cold grass of the backyard and watched the stars turning imperceptibly above. That bad time seemed as distant and ridiculous as his childhood now, a chasm he'd climbed out of and which—like this house, these rooms he knew—he couldn't safely inhabit even in memory. It was gone and he was here. Rennie was alive; Anne had given him another chance. James inspected the chess set and for the last time headed up to his room. He turned off the light from upstairs.

"Just in time," Anne greeted him, and had him sit on their suitcases so they'd close.

He came awake around three-thirty, according to the clock on the night table. He'd been up every hour, unable to get comfortable. Trains came through, hooting. The thump of the waves made it sound like someone was in the house. He was thinking about tomorrow, how they wanted to get going early, and on top of that he'd dreamed of his father's best black suit, which he'd given to the director of the funeral home. Now, though, he could hear someone crying in another room. Before he could conjure up a ghost, he realized it was Jay calling for him. He sighed, hoping Anne might volunteer. In the other twin, she stirred, then resettled, turning away.

"I'll get him," he said, and noisily flung the covers aside.

Jay was sitting up in bed. From the lines under his eyes, James could see he'd been crying but didn't want his father to know. Tomorrow they'd have to remember to bring his night-light.

"What's the trouble?" James asked from the door. He wanted to avoid a long talk, for Jay's sake. The worse the dream was, the farther into the room he went. Jay's silence meant he'd have to come closer. He stopped at the foot of the bed, quickly losing patience with him. "Was it one you've had before?"

"No," Jay said, but didn't explain, and James had to sit down.

"Was Rennie in it?"

"No."

"Then what?" James said, too hard, and was immediately sorry. To soothe himself, James thought that this would be the last time he'd have to do this. Home, in his own bed, Jay would sleep dreamlessly. James patted his leg through the covers to reassure him. "What is it, champ?"

"When is the war going to be over?" Jay asked.

"Soon."

"Before six years?"

The arithmetic was automatic for James. "It'll all be over before you can get into the action, if that's what you're worried about. Now no more dreams."

"It wasn't a dream," Jay explained. "I just couldn't sleep."

"Stop worrying about it, because it's not going to happen. Now go to sleep; we have to get up in two hours."

Jay lay down and let James tuck him in. "I'm sorry," he said.

"For what?"

"For being a baby."

"You're not," James said, and stood and went to the door. He took a last look in to make sure everything was okay. Jay's nose poked over the covers like Kilroy's. At work they chalked him on bombs. *Special Delivery,* jokesters wrote, *c/o Mr. Jap*. James wanted to tell Jay there was nothing to be afraid of, but instead said, "Sleep."

Anne was done with her shower before he got out of bed. He dressed to the criminal smell of bacon and eggs—a surprise she'd been keeping. She flitted around the kitchen, taking their plates while they were still chewing. "It's six-twenty," she announced, as if someone had asked. She seemed happy to be leaving; James figured it was her right.

Sarah appeared on time. Win showed up to say goodbye before doing his paper route. Anne had mustered their bags at the head of the stairs. James carried them down while Jay entertained Win and

Anne had coffee with Sarah. His Buick was a good-sized car, but the trunk was full of food and trip by trip the backseat was slowly taken up with clothes. It was a beautiful day, and the lifting and the stairs made him sweat. They'd forgotten to box Rennie's blender. Anne was still packing bags. Cursing her, he tried to fit it all in but finally gave up and crowned the pile lashed to the roof with the tangle of their bikes.

The little crap was the worst—loose toys and pillows and shoes, the toothbrush glass. As James was stuffing their jackets into a crack beneath the front seat, Win came over to shake his hand goodbye. Jay held his bike. James said maybe next summer Win could come upstate; they'd go camping in the Adirondacks. Win said he'd ask his mother. He was sorry about Jay's grandfather; he'd liked him. James thanked him and watched him and Jay saunter off across the lot, lingering, trying to say goodbye. Though they never touched, it seemed to James a kind of love. When Win climbed the hill, Jay didn't watch him but stalked inside, crushed.

James went in for another bag, only to find Anne and Sarah hunting through the downstairs, unplugging everything. That was it; Sarah would defrost the icebox and lock up.

"Seven-thirty," Anne said, as if they were late.

"The car's all ready," he said.

In the kitchen, running a glass of water, he saw the japanned tray. He held it with one hand, appraising it as he gulped the water. Had he really thought he could leave without saying goodbye to her? He debated taking it with him, smashing it against the center wall of the sink, dropping it symbolically on the floor. He leaned it back against the wall under the cupboards where it belonged.

Anne and Sarah were on the porch. Jay was missing.

"I think I know where he is," James said.

"I've already peed," Anne announced. "I'll meet you in the car."

He thought he'd find him in his room, at his window, but he wasn't there. His night-light still stuck from the outlet; James carried it through the other rooms—his father's with its stripped bed, the now windowless maids' chambers. In his mother's room he thought he heard something and stopped just inside the door, a hand on the wallpaper, the great blown roses. The hair on the back of his hand had gone gray long ago, but the fact surprised him now. The room had barely changed; all he had to do was put on a different bedspread, draw the curtains, perfume the air with that dizzying mix of medicinal alcohol and unwashed skin. *I see you. You're running, James, don't run from your mother.* He had meant to end up here, he thought, he could only postpone it so long.

From the parking lot came the deep bleat of the Buick's horn, insistent, and upstairs in the attic something moved. James went into the hallway and, on tiptoe, pulled down the staircase.

Jay stood at his father's desk, looking out over the cottages, the breakwater, the sea. He had his cigar box and the chess set. Rennie's Ruptured Duck was pinned to his shirt pocket. The horn sounded again, and he turned to James as if he were surrendering. James surprised him by looking past him out the window. They stood there a minute, silent, separate, and James wondered if what they were seeing was at all the same. It couldn't be, and today at least, he was grateful. The summer had been hard enough on him, on all of them.

"Okay," he said. "Ready, champ?"

"Ready," Jay said, and James followed him down the stairs.

JAY SAT BETWEEN THEM IN THE FRONT SEAT, on the hump, his knees almost touching the radio. His mother and father had been fighting all morning. When they knew he was watching they tried to make it seem funny. They were hiding something from him, and Jay thought it couldn't be good. It was harder to pretend it didn't bother him in the car; there was nowhere to look, no place to go.

His mother's feet straddled a hamper filled with sandwiches and Pepsis. The Buick was so heavily loaded that Jay didn't think it would make the hill. They idled while Aunt Sarah leaned in his father's window, and then she kissed him and his father said, "And they're off!" and, still in neutral, revved the engine just to annoy his mother. Jay gazed straight through the windshield at the sky, gray and undecided, while his father wrestled the gearshift. They bumped across the lot toward the foot of the drive, but suddenly his father stopped and got out.

They watched him walk to the edge of the gravel and bend down to pick something up.

"Do *you* know what this is all about?" his mother asked Jay, not really looking for an answer.

He came back with it in his hand, an orange rag that Rennie had used when he was working on his Ford.

"For God's sake," his mother said, still trying to be funny.

His father tucked the rag under his seat and got back in the car. "Now then," he clowned. He slipped it in gear and, steering with one hand and waving blindly to Aunt Sarah with the other, started up the drive. The slope pushed Jay back into the seat like a pilot pulling out of a nosedive, but the Buick kept inching toward the top. Halfway up, his father dropped the car into low.

"Do you want me to walk up and meet you?" his mother said.

When with a final heave they'd safely gained the top, his father said, "There we go," and stopped to shift gears again.

"Seven-forty-five," his mother reported.

With all the bags piled in the backseat, Jay couldn't see the house behind them, only the line of water on both sides, the sky. He could picture it easily, but felt cheated of a last look, and wondered if already he wasn't forgetting little things like the old phones and brass gas fixtures, the way Dorothy walked across the lawn in the mornings. All he had left of Putney was the river, the way when the jam broke, the ice knocked the bottom of the bridges, but he'd only been a kid then. He'd remember everything that happened this summer, not just his dreams or fears or what he'd seen at the Regal or in his comic books or in Tarzan, but what had really happened—his parents fighting, Dorothy arriving with Jennifer, Rennie coming home, his grandfather dying. He'd remember the look Sylvia Jensen had given him, and Mr. Vogel coming to the door in the same clothes he'd had on the week before. The Roll of Honor. Playing catch after supper. How the light on the bluffs cut through the houses. He'd remember Attu and Dorothy's San Diego, the man who brought the telegrams and the broken window of the Shoals. His father's lost bike and his mother's walks on the beach. The way the rain sounded like the end of a record scratching all afternoon. He wished he could fit it all in his box, but his box was already full, the postcard from Hawaii on top. When they got home the first thing he'd do would be to go up to his room and write everything down so he wouldn't forget it.

On the town road they passed Win folding his papers outside Hickey's. His father honked, Jay waved, and he was gone. Victory Speed was thirty-five, but his mother asked if they were going to drive like this the entire way, and his father floored it. She ignored him and he settled in at fifty. They passed the boardwalk going so fast that Jay didn't get a peek at the Regal's marquee. In the desert, at the dried-up oasis, Humphrey Bogart was making a speech, trying to convince his handful of misfits to hold off the Germans one more time. The Ferris wheel loomed and then, moonlike, sank into the trees. His father began to hum something; his mother turned on the radio.

They made the light in town and went around the green and out the other side, past the graveyard. Respectfully, the car slowed to a crawl. His mother looked out and then back at his father, at Jay. He tried to think of Grampa Langer not in his box but, like the well-dressed corpses in *Amazing Stories*, at a party, drinking champagne and waving noisemakers. Though he knew it wasn't true (his grandfather was more likely to be by himself in a quiet room, secretly listening to a ball game), it was better than what was really happening to him, which made it all right for Jay to lie. At the end of the fallen stone wall they took off again.

Passing the sign for the town limits, his father honked. "Goodbye, Hampton Bays," he crowed. "Galesburg, here we come!" His mother reached over Jay to rub his shoulder. His father patted her hand, and, unexpectedly—as shocking as if she'd attacked him with her fists—she leaned across Jay, her body covering his, and kissed his father.

Jay sat there, afraid to move, to ruin it, smothered by her scent, her body hard against his. On the radio, the Americans were winning in Italy, the proof a crackly chatter of guns. His mother let go and smiled at him then, and it wasn't a lie. She really was that happy to be leaving, to be going home.

He'd remember this feeling, crushed between the two people he loved the most. All summer he'd been terrified of them; now they seemed the mother and father he knew, returned to him, like Rennie, from some distant country. He wanted to believe everything would be the way it was before, the way things always were, but it wasn't true. That was all gone, and yet, years later, he couldn't help but remember how safe it made him feel then, that hope he hadn't known he'd saved, how even that summer he'd clung to it, those rare blue days when the war seemed far away, and unable to touch them.